TWO FACED

TWO FACED

ROBIN MICHELE CARROLL

ISBN: 978-1-4834-8651-2 (sc)
ISBN: 978-1-4834-8652-9 (hc)
ISBN: 978-1-4834-8653-6 (e)

Library of Congress Control Number: 2018906593

Scripture taken from the King James Version of the Bible.

Lulu Publishing Services rev. date: 05/08/2019

CHAPTER 1

THE AIR WAS DAMP, HEAVY WITH HUMIDITY. The slight, muggy breeze caused the wind chimes to ring, the sound melodic in the still of the night. Despite the lateness of the hour, the temperature remained above eighty degrees. Like the man lurking in the shadows, summer had come with a vengeance.

Unaware of the violence that skulked in its perfect little community, the wealthy Connecticut neighborhood slept. Not a single light shone in the cul-de-sac of high-priced homes. The only illumination was the glow of streetlamps.

The dark figure climbed the stairs of the house on the end. His watchful actions were those of a man whose sole purpose was to remain unrecognized. Dressed in black, he knew he appeared more phantom than man—a ghost in the darkness.

He squatted to retrieve the house key from its hiding place under the stone planter box. The flowers flourished with vibrant, sweet-smelling blossoms, but in time winter would return, and the foliage would die, the stems and leaves curling and brown from the cold. Their time would come, like all living things, including the two unsuspecting targets inside. He smiled beneath the mask as he thought about the job ahead of him. Nothing and no one lived forever.

He slipped the key into the lock and eased the door open. Once inside, he paused for a few minutes to assimilate to his surroundings. From the living room to his right came the steady ticking of an antique clock on the mantel. To his left, a refrigerator hummed quietly in the kitchen. He couldn't discern any other sounds or movements, just stillness. Satisfied that everything was clear, he advanced up the stairs to the bedrooms.

The thick snore of a sleeping man echoed in the hallway. The intruder retrieved the weapon from its snug resting place—the waistband of his jeans—and followed the sound. The pistol, a .22-caliber semiautomatic, was lightweight and effective at close range. He'd purchased the gun from a drug dealer in Philadelphia, and once the job was complete, he planned to dump it in the nearest river.

He entered the bedroom and observed the couple who lay side by side—his latest victim and, next to him, his beautiful wife. The bed was rumpled, the sheets and blankets twisted around their hips and legs, half-covering them. In the sliver of moonlight that fell across the mattress, the woman's pale skin stood out, smooth and creamy.

He crossed to where she slept and pressed the barrel of the gun above the woman's breasts, right over her heart. He squeezed the trigger and smiled as the woman's eyes popped open. Her body convulsed at the bullet's impact. She gasped for air, the gurgling sound wet as fluid and oxygen met.

The man beside her opened his eyes and scrambled into a sitting position. Making small, squeaky sounds of terror, he inched backward until his spine pressed flat against the bed's headboard. His chest heaved as he looked frantically back and forth from the man dressed in black to his twitching, bloody companion.

"Hello, Robert." The predator circled the bed until he came face-to-face with his prey. "Someone has paid me a lot of money to rid the earth of you and your wife."

Robert moved his mouth, but no words escaped. He appeared to be a breath away from dissolving into complete, incoherent hysteria. He whimpered and wiped the errant tears that ran down his cheeks.

The killer whacked him across the face with the butt of his gun. "Pull yourself together, and quit acting like a little bitch."

Robert inhaled deeply to control his emotions and relieve the searing pain in his head. "You … you have the wrong person," he stammered.

"No. Unfortunately for you, I don't."

"You're making a huge mistake. I'm not …" He hesitated. "You don't understand."

"On the contrary, I understand it all, Robert. You should have just given him the files and photos from the list. Now I've been sent to retrieve them from you."

Robert shook his head. "I don't know what you're talking about."

"If you don't want to die, like your wife, then you'll tell me where they are."

"I don't have any files, and she's not my wife," Robert uttered.

"Who's not your wife?" he asked. For the first time, the killer examined the woman's features and realized that he'd made a mistake. He leaned toward Robert and pressed the barrel of his gun to the underside of the man's chin. "Where is she?" he hissed menacingly.

"I don't know. She disappeared without telling me. Maybe she left so fast because she has whatever you're looking for."

"You think I'm naive enough to believe that you trust your wife with your prized possession?" With his free hand, he grabbed a handful of Robert's hair and jerked him around to face his lifeless companion.

Robert watched the ever-growing pool of blood creep across the white satin coverlet toward him.

"I'm losing my patience, Robert. Now stop with the diversion tactics and tell me where Missy and the files are."

"She must have gone to see her friend Kayla in Miami, but I don't know her last name, so I don't think you'll find her."

"Finding people is what I do," he stated smugly. He squeezed the trigger. Brains and blood sprayed across the white headboard and onto the rose-patterned wallpaper.

He stared at the colorful mess, and like an artist with a freshly painted canvas, he beamed in appreciation of his creation. As he basked in the pungent smell of death, his excitement turned to desire. He unzipped his jeans and satisfied himself, leaving evidence of his arousal on the female corpse. Before he left the room, he placed the mistress's earrings and Robert's watch in his pocket as mementos.

After checking the rest of the house for the files and any information that would lead to Missy's whereabouts, the killer returned to Robert's room. He kneeled in front of the bed occupied by his victims and bowed his head. With eyes that glistened with tears, he prayed for absolution.

Missy couldn't sleep. She turned on the light and grabbed her phone from the nightstand. She was disappointed that there were still no texts or calls from Robert. She picked up a pen and her journal and began to write:

> I'm afraid of the dark. It exists merely to torment me as my unconscious mind becomes a barren wasteland inhabited by the lives of strangers. I want to silence the voices and obscure my view, but it's useless. I must bear witness to the nightmares that have taken up permanent residence in my innermost being. Every night I become intimate with my unwanted tenants, and each time I lose valuable pieces of myself.
>
> When I close my eyes, wordless images assault me, arbitrarily tossing me into the unknown. Demons swarm, chasing my thoughts around in the shadows until insanity reaches out for me. I struggle against its powerful tentacles, but it pricks my soul, gnawing at the emptiness of my existence. I'm sinking, in desperate need of a lifeline—something or someone that will spark life in me again.

A knock at the door interrupted her musings. She put down the pen and closed the book. "Come in."

Kayla entered the room and spied the book on the bed. "You're writing again. I would offer to read it, but your words are too deep for me. I need a dictionary to translate."

"It's for my eyes only, which is why my personal sentiments don't make sense to you."

"Sentiments? Is that what you call them? Your journal reads more like a Shakespearean play, complete with tragic characters."

Yes, the lives of the people in my dreams are tragic. Missy grinned. "Shakespearean? Really?"

"Really. You need to embrace your black-girl side more. At least then I'd understand what the hell you're saying."

Missy laughed. "I'll keep that in mind for the next chapter."

"That's right. Put some color in it is all I'm saying." Kayla sat on the edge of the bed. "So what brought on this writing frenzy at this time of night? Did you have another nightmare?"

"They're more than just nightmares, Kayla, and you know it."

Kayla shook her head. "I thought you'd stopped doing that."

"Doing what? Having visions? It's not like I have any alternative."

"You're not psychic, Missy, and that paranormal stuff is just creepy."

"I've never claimed to be psychic."

"At least we agree on that. What did you see this time?"

"What difference does it make? You won't believe me anyway."

"It's not that I don't believe you. It's—"

Missy didn't let her finish. "I think it's time for me to go home, Kayla. I've hidden away from my problems long enough."

"What? You're kidding me, right? You can't go back to Robert. He's a liar and a cheat!" she barked.

"He's my husband, and he needs me."

"Like his mistress needed him in *your* bed?"

Missy flinched at Kayla's scathing words. "I have to go. Someone important is about to enter my life, and I should be there."

Kayla sighed. "I know what you're doing. You're trying to use the possibility of a new guy to get your man-hungry friend to say it's okay to go home. Well, it won't work. I refuse to give you my blessing."

"I swear it's not like that, Kayla," she whispered.

"Then please explain to me what it's like—because I think you're making a huge mistake."

"I wish I could make you understand, but it's hard when I'm unsure myself," Missy said contritely.

Kayla tried to control her temper but failed miserably. "Why am I not surprised? This is the same psychic babble you've spouted over and over for the past twelve years. You never know what's going on, and that's always your excuse as to why you can't tell me."

"Kayla …"

"No. Don't say anything—because to be honest, I think it's all bullshit. Your 'gift' is a defense mechanism to shut people out of your life, including me. You've learned how to scare people away with your predictions. And it works since everyone just writes you off as a weirdo. But Missy, it's not real. You're great at guessing, but that doesn't mean you have clairvoyant abilities."

"You're wrong, Kayla. I would never purposely shut you out." *And I can never tell you the truth because you refuse to believe me*, she thought. "I realize that I haven't been the greatest friend with everything going on with Robert, but I promise to do better. I can't lose you."

The inevitability of losing her made Missy shudder with dread. An image of Kayla running down a dark highway with a "Roadside Motel" sign flickering in the background flashed in her mind. She heard her friend's labored intakes of breath and could feel her erratic heartbeat. Missy tried to hold on to the apparition, but it quickly faded into nothingness.

Shaken by the vision, Missy climbed out of bed and hugged Kayla. "I love you. No matter how angry you get with me, that will never change."

Kayla returned her embrace. "What's wrong? You're shivering."

"Promise me that you'll be careful on your dates. And please stay away from a place called the Roadside Motel."

Kayla backed away and stared at Missy. "Why in the hell would I be at such a shady-sounding motel? What type of woman do you think I am?" she asked indignantly.

"I swear I'm not questioning your character, Kayla. Just humor me, please," Missy implored.

"Fine. But for the record, I'm not a slut. Not since college, anyway," she said with a laugh. "And I still don't believe in your psychic mumbo jumbo."

"All I'm asking is that you believe in our friendship."

"I do. I love you like a sister."

Missy smiled. "I feel the same about you, Kayla. Now … can you help your sister pack? My flight leaves at midnight."

"What? That means it will still be dark by the time you get there. I don't think that's safe," Kayla said anxiously.

"Don't worry. I'll catch a cab home."

"I know how stubborn you are, so I won't argue. But I do believe you're making a mistake after the way Robert treated you."

"I'll learn to forgive him in time."

"That asshole doesn't deserve your forgiveness."

"Kayla, I—"

"Just forget it," Kayla muttered. "Will you at least tell me who this mystery man is? I think you owe me that."

"There's nothing to tell. Just some faceless person."

"Right. More secrets," Kayla said irritably.

"Not secrets … visions."

"Same thing. But don't worry. I won't push you. I'll go get dressed. Be ready in thirty minutes."

Missy didn't try to mollify her friend's obvious hurt. Instead, she watched her exit the room. *I'm sorry, Kayla, but the shock of discovering that the mysterious person is a woman will only cause you to doubt me more. How can I explain that I can sense her presence around me even now? The scent of her perfume whiffs through my nostrils like the sunlight that seeps through the blinds at dawn, bringing great possibility and long-forgotten hope. She seems like a phantom disappearing in and out of my psyche. Yet I know she's real. She is the individual that my grandmother warned me about many years ago, the one who will change my life.*

Missy was exhausted and planned to rest during the two-hour flight. She hadn't slept since her arrival in Miami and attributed her insomnia to her fight with Robert. Despite her efforts to subdue the memories, the images of him with another woman replayed in her head. A profound sadness washed over her, and Missy wondered what cruel imp of providence had led them to this hell. Tears rolled down her cheeks as she closed her eyes and drifted off to sleep.

Trapped in a room filled with mirrors, she spins around in a circle. Fascinated by all the distorted versions of her likeness, she inches closer to the glass. She stares at her reflection as it transforms into that of the faceless woman. She reaches her hand out to touch the apparition. Unexpectedly, the figure changes into Robert, his face bloody and maimed. A man in priestly garb stands directly behind him, holding a gun in one hand and a cross in the other. Robert calls her name in a high-pitched tone as the weapon is discharged. The bullet penetrates his head and exits through his eye, striking the mirror. The glass shatters into hundreds of pieces, and blood pours down the sharp, broken edges, filling the room with its crimson flow, rising higher and higher …

Missy awoke with a start. Her body was drenched in sweat as she glanced around. The sudden pain in her head and eye was excruciating.

"Ma'am, please bring your seat back to the upright position. We are beginning our descent into Bradbury International Airport," the flight attendant announced.

Missy adjusted her chair and prayed that the gory image of her husband was a nightmare and not a premonition.

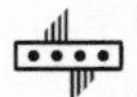

After the cab dropped her off, Missy walked the short distance from the curb to the front door. The house felt foreign with Robert's betrayal still fresh in her mind, but Missy ignored her doubts and entered the house. Upon seeing the living room in disarray, she dropped her luggage and rushed up the stairs. The smell of something burned combined with a strong metallic odor assaulted her senses as she got closer to the master bedroom. She walked in, and a scream flew to her throat. Blood was everywhere—spattered across the walls, soaked into the carpet, and drenched through the white satin sheets. The headboard was covered with blood and tissue drying in uneven patches like an awful red paint. Formless bits of tissue stuck to the wall, and below it were jagged shards of bone.

Missy's breath gushed out in one loud exhalation. The room tilted, and her stomach heaved. She struggled to sustain her equilibrium but was too weak to fight. A curtain of blackness descended over her, and she fainted.

Ten minutes later, a disoriented Missy stirred and looked around. The pool of blood on the floor was a stark reminder of what had happened, and she curled into a ball of agony. The tears flowed uncontrollably, and she let out a howl that was almost inhuman in its intensity. Once depleted, Missy rose to her feet and staggered into the adjoining bathroom. She turned on the faucet and splashed cold water on her face. She kept her head lowered to avoid the mirror, which would mock her with the truth of Robert's death. Missy tried to remain strong, but finally, she could no longer resist its taunting. With inflamed, bloodshot eyes, she gazed into the glass. Missy observed her own reflected image as it transformed into a mummified figure that grinned beneath the dressing.

The solitary light in the darkened room illuminated the white bandages, making the man look almost ethereal. He inhaled, relishing his final moments of anonymity. He was a man without a name and a face, but that was about to change. He took a deep breath and nodded his consent.

Robert stood behind the shorter man and unwrapped his face. Robert's smile widened as the face was exposed. Other than the swelling, Robert's latest creation was perfect. He'd successfully masked another monster. His pride was blatant, and the stench of his own self-worth filled the room. "Are you pleased?" Robert asked.

Greg glanced at himself in the glass. "Yes. I'm a different man."

"All you have to do is follow my instructions to the letter regarding your after-care, and no one will ever recognize you. You can resume your life as a criminal."

"The $150,000 we agreed upon has been wired into your account."

"What about the additional funds we discussed? I gave you a new face and identity. That should be priceless to a man like you."

"I'm not giving you extortion money, Melendez. You should know better than to try to blackmail a man like me. I don't need you anymore. It would be just as easy to kill you."

The scalpel shone brightly as Robert suddenly lifted his right hand and ran the blade from one side of the man's throat to the other. Blood spattered across the mirror and trickled down Greg's chest as he slumped to the floor.

Robert grabbed a can from the nearby table and poured the contents on Greg. The acrid smell of gasoline permeated his nostrils as he lit a match and tossed it on the body.

"See you in hell, Greg."

"Not if I see you first," Greg gasped.

Once the images faded, Missy walked into the bedroom and picked up the phone on the nightstand. She clutched the receiver in her pale hand, dreading the task. She dialed 911 and explained that her husband and his mistress had been murdered.

Minutes ticked by before Missy heard sirens in the distance. The police, coroner, and crime scene unit immediately took over, and before she knew it, her house was no longer her own. It was filled with strangers who didn't bother to conceal the suspicion in their eyes. *They all think I killed them, but if my vision was real, then it was Robert who was a killer.*

Detective Danielle "Dani" Cole received the call at 5:37 a.m.—a double homicide in an affluent section of Hartford County. In her twelve years as an officer with the Hartford Police Department, there had never been any violence in Bloomfield except for a few domestic disturbances. During those rare occasions, the neighbors had been uncooperative, and Cole knew the Melendez investigation would incite even more opposition. But she wouldn't allow their antagonism to prevent her from solving this case.

Cole was the lone female lead detective in the Hartford PD's homicide unit, and the spotlight shone mercilessly on her. Many of her peers didn't believe she merited the position, which was why she spent most of her time proving she could hold her own against the boys. Although she was small in stature, a mere five foot three, she commanded respect with her direct gaze and squared shoulders. Early on in her career, she'd learned the art of intimidation as a survival technique, and she was forced to use it on a regular basis. However, that skill didn't matter much when people thought she was inept at doing her job, so she needed a win.

Cole observed the hodgepodge of vehicles parked on the street as she pulled up in her unmarked car. She climbed out of the vehicle, and a brisk breeze seemed to capture her in an embrace. The wind aggressively twirled and tossed her around. Cole wrestled against the negative force until it bowed, defeated, and released her. Shaken, she took several deep breaths to calm herself. *What the hell was that?* she thought. *It felt like something was actually touching me. Am I in an episode of* The X-Files, *or is the stress getting to me?*

The patrolman posted in front of the residence didn't recognize Cole when she approached. He detained her at the perimeter of the police tape and spoke to her in an energetic tone. His name tag identified him as Adams. "Sorry, ma'am, but this is a crime scene. No civilians allowed."

"I'm Detective Cole, Hartford PD. I believe my partner, Detective Thomas, is already inside."

"Can I see some ID?"

Most officers in the city knew who she was, so the request was unexpected. Cole mumbled obscenities as she dug in her purse. Once she located her shield, she flashed it in his face.

He glanced at it and blushed. "I'm sorry, ma'am. I'm new to the job."

She ignored his apology. "Is Thomas inside?"

"Yes, ma'am."

He lifted the tape, and Cole walked into the front yard. She breathed in the smell of fresh-cut grass as she proceeded up the brick walkway.

"Nice house, huh?" Patrolman Adams called out.

"What did the guy do for a living?" Cole shouted in response.

"I hear he was a plastic surgeon."

"Figures," she murmured as she ascended the stairs to the front door. Cole donned her gloves and entered. She nodded at one of the CSU guys while she surveyed her surroundings. Cole noted the expensive decor and wondered if this case was about money. She made a mental note to check the victim's insurance policy.

Before she could go in search of the bodies, someone grasped Cole's arm from behind. Instinctively, she reached for her gun.

"Whoa, don't shoot," the person exclaimed, clearly amused. "Are you Cole?"

Cole turned to face the handsome stranger. "Yes. Do I know you?"

"I'm Sergeant Jason Merck. I was told by your partner that you were coming, and I wanted to introduce myself."

"Right. You're the new guy. Rumor has it that you were a bigwig in the NYPD, so what brings you to Connecticut?"

"I have a new baby on the way, and I thought that coming here would be a lot less … uh …"

"Dangerous?"

"Yeah. At least that's what the wife believes."

Cole was tickled by his wife's naïveté. "You may not want to tell her about this double homicide then."

Merck smiled. "I've heard a lot about you, Cole."

"Don't believe everything you hear," she said derisively. *I'm sure the gossips couldn't wait to tell him how I compromised a case and almost got my partner killed.*

"I just heard that you shoot straight from the hip."

Cole tried to mask her surprise. "Is that all?"

"Yes. Why? Is there more?" Merck inquired eagerly.

"Nope." Cole promptly changed the subject. "So what do we have?"

"Two vics in the bedroom—the owner of the house, Dr. Robert Melendez, and his mistress. No ID on her yet. Both were shot at close range. Shell casings suggest a .22. The woman has a single GSW to the chest. The man has one GSW to the head. Looks like the bullet entered through his chin."

Cole frowned. "Sounds gruesome."

"It is. You might lose your breakfast."

"Good thing I haven't eaten yet. So where's the wife?"

"Melissa Melendez, age thirty-two, is in the den, being questioned by your partner. She claims to be innocent. And get this—she said she saw her husband shot by a priest in a vision."

"So basically, Melissa is nuts."

"I hope not. It would be a shame for someone that beautiful to be crazy. Honestly, I think she's just setting things up to plead not guilty by reason of insanity. I'll let your partner tell you more about her. Do you want to join him, or would you like to check out the crime scene?"

"I want to see the bodies. Thomas can fill me in on what I missed later."

Merck headed toward the bedroom with Cole trailing close behind. Her first view was of the high cathedral ceiling and skylights. The area felt spacious, despite the number of techs in the room taking pictures and gathering evidence. With its white sheets, the king-size bed stood out starkly against the teal wallpaper. And there was blood. Lots of blood. No matter how many crime scenes Cole worked, the first sight of the blood always stunned her. A comet's tail of arterial splatter zigzagged across the wall and trickled down in streams. The source of that blood, Robert Melendez, was hanging off the edge of the bed. His face, or what was left of it, was a grisly mess.

Cole watched as Dr. Kenneth Stevens, medical examiner and chief crime scene investigator, collected some of the matter with tweezers and placed it into a plastic bag. It never ceased to amaze Cole how much the man loved his job. She'd known Stevens for eight years, and he'd helped her win several cases with his forensic knowledge and medical expertise.

"Who found the bodies?" Cole asked.

"The wife," Merck stated.

"Was the weapon found?"

"No. Searched the whole house, but there's nothing here."

"Do we have a time of death?"

"Between 9:00 and 11:00 p.m. according to the ME."

"Anyone talk to the neighbors?"

Merck chuckled at her rapid-fire style of questioning. "Yes, but they aren't being cooperative."

"They don't appreciate us disrupting their ritzy little community."

"The killer upset their tight-ass community, not us."

"Try telling them that." She moved closer to the bed to inspect the bodies. "Any suspects besides the wife?"

"No, but in my opinion, it's a professional hit. No sign of forced entry. Six sets of prints, but I doubt any belong to the killer. The hairs and fibers collected are probably our vics' too, but we might get lucky."

"You thinking the wife put out the hit?"

"That's usually the scenario. Let me know what you think once you speak with her since you're taking the lead on this one."

Cole spotted something on the dead woman. "Stevens, you may want to check the vic's abdominal area. It looks like she might have dried semen on her stomach."

"I noticed that too," Merck affirmed. "But Stevens and I agreed that it probably belongs to Melendez."

"Yes, Cole. You're late to the party," Stevens replied.

"I'll bet a month's salary that it belongs to our killer." Her voice was boastful.

"Why are you so sure?" Merck retorted.

"Because the killer sketched a *t* in the sperm."

"Wait … what? There's no way I missed that," Merck said dubiously.

Cole smiled and pointed out the pattern. "Do you see it?"

Merck leaned in closer. "Son of a bitch! That is a *t*. I wonder if he's trying to tell us something."

"Yeah, that he's a sick pervert. Stevens, can you check to see if she was raped? Or maybe our guy is into necrophilia."

Stevens shook his head. "The idea that someone can get sexual pleasure from a cadaver is disturbing."

"This from the guy who examines dead bodies all day."

"That's different, and you know it, Cole." Stevens leaned in close to the female corpse. "I don't think that's a *t* on her stomach. It looks more like a cross to me."

Cole glanced at it again. "You're right. It could be a cross."

"Maybe the perp is some kind of religious nut."

"That's possible. Make sure we get some good shots of it. I'll have Thomas look at the pictures and get his opinion."

"I'll have my guys take care of it."

"Great. Let me know when the files are ready." She glanced at Merck. "I need to go find my partner, but it was nice meeting you. I'm sure I'll see you around the station."

"The pleasure was all mine, Detective Cole. I hope we get to work together soon."

"I look forward to it."

After exploring the remainder of the house, Cole joined her partner in the den. She could hear small sobs as she greeted Thomas with a nod and sat in the chair diagonal from him. *Thomas is obviously being sucked in by the tears of a beautiful woman*, she thought. Cole focused her attention on the woman, who had her head down. Cole wanted to see her face, but for some inexplicable reason, she was uneasy about peering into the woman's eyes.

Thomas handed her a tissue. "I'm sorry this is so hard on you, Melissa."

Cole shook her head. *They're already on a first-name basis. I got here just in time.* She knew that despite Thomas's rugged, pale features, he had a certain charm when it came to women. He often used his best feature, his sparkling blue eyes, to his advantage. She'd witnessed his flirtatious techniques firsthand with the other female officers. But thus far, she'd been exempt, which was exactly how she wanted it.

Missy lifted her head and reached for the tissue. Her right hand trembled slightly as she wiped away her tears.

"Mrs. Melendez, I'm Detective Danielle Cole. I'll be joining Detective Thomas in the investigation of your husband's death."

Missy looked at Cole and gasped aloud. *It's her—the woman from my vision.*

"Is something wrong, Mrs. Melendez?" Cole asked.

"No. I'm fine." *I'm simply not emotionally equipped to meet you right now. But the energy you exude is forcing me to acknowledge your presence, whether I want to or not.* "I would say it's a pleasure, Detective Cole, but under the circumstances …" Missy paused and stood up as the reality of her situation finally hit her. She paced back and forth, her arms crossed and held firmly against her body. *I'm alone. For the first time in my life, I don't have someone to take care of me. And this woman, for whatever reason, is making matters worse. Who is she, and what role will she play in my life?*

Cole studied the woman, logging every detail of her appearance. Missy was medium height, about five foot six, with a delicate build. Her hair was jet-black with auburn highlights. Cole watched the long mane wrap around her shoulders like a silk cape each time Missy reached the end of the room and spun back. Missy's hazel eyes were accentuated by her caramel skin and full lips. Cole couldn't determine whether she was Hispanic or of mixed heritage. Not that it mattered, Cole mused dispassionately. She was merely doing her job and being observant.

Cole found it difficult to ignore Missy's exhaustion. She was on edge, and Cole was afraid she'd collapse at any moment. "Mrs. Melendez, please have a seat. I just have a few questions."

Missy turned her gaze toward the woman with the disheveled blondish-brown hair and violet eyes. *With eyes that extraordinary, a woman can get away with having unkempt hair*, she thought. *With eyes like that, she can get away with barking orders. With eyes like that, she could get away with almost anything, including haunting someone's dreams.*

Missy was transfixed by Cole's movie-star features, specifically her high cheekbones and cleft chin. She wished she could capture the innocence and undiscovered nuances of Cole's makeup-free beauty with her camera. *I really should be jealous of this fascinating woman with the unassuming clothing and police-issued shoes, but instead I'm curious. Why is such an attractive woman a cop?*

The idea of taking Cole's picture caused Missy to momentarily forget her situation. Photography was her passion, but it was the idea of what she could possibly learn about Cole through the lens of her camera that energized Missy. Last year while in her darkroom, Missy had discovered the ability to immortalize her prophecies on film. Reflections of unfamiliar people and places had appeared in the developer, and the result was images of monsters that refused to stay hidden. Shadows of the grim reaper and other terrifying beings had emerged, revealing death, evil, and a person's true character. Over time, Missy had come to realize what the disturbing silhouettes represented yet she decided to remain neutral instead of using her gift to help others. Sometimes the guilt attempted to swallow her whole, particularly when a life was lost, but it was the only way to preserve her peace of mind.

"Hey, are you all right?" Cole inquired, her voice laced with concern.

For a second, all the grief and desperation Missy felt nearly escaped. But rather than burst into tears and hurl herself into this stranger's arms, she remembered that Cole undoubtedly thought she had killed her husband. That reminder was enough to calm her. "I'm okay," Missy whispered.

"I'm sorry about your husband, Mrs. Melendez. It must have been hard to find him like that ... with another woman."

Missy shuddered from the memory. "I didn't kill them, Detective Cole, if that's what you're implying."

"I'm not implying anything, Mrs. Melendez, but I'm glad to hear it. Do you have any idea who would have wanted your husband dead?"

"I'll give you the same answer I gave your partner. I have no idea."

Cole watched her closely. "Any enemies?"

"I'm sure we all have enemies, Detective."

"Not all of us, Mrs. Melendez. At least not the kind that would want us dead." Cole paused. "What about his friends?"

"He didn't have any."

"What do you mean? Everyone has friends."

"Not Robert. All he had were acquaintances."

"He must have been an interesting man to live with," Cole commented idly.

You have no idea, Detective. From the first day she'd walked into Robert's office as a temp, Missy had known there was something charismatic about the older gentleman. She had been drawn to him immediately because he displayed enigmatic characteristics that she found intriguing. And although Missy had tried, she had been unable to use her foresight with him. Robert was unreadable, which was a new and welcome experience for her. It had taken months of dating for Missy to finally gain enough information to uncover the truth. Despite his money, good looks, and notoriety as one of the leading plastic surgeons in Connecticut, Robert was lonely. He tried to mask his vulnerabilities, but this didn't work with Missy because she recognized those same traits within herself. They were twin flames in solitude.

Robert sought a woman who could provide him with the type of affection he'd missed growing up without parents, and Missy longed to be that person. In the beginning, others had regarded their relationship as unconventional because of the fifteen-year age difference. But for Missy, the disparity was inconsequential. She yearned to fill the hole her mother had left when she died of cancer, and Robert was the ideal plaster for her fractured heart. Yes, he reminded Missy of her father, but that only made her adore him more.

With Robert's help, Missy had been able to heal the damage from her previous relationship. The unpleasant circumstances surrounding her first marriage and subsequent divorce had triggered further abandonment issues for the then twenty-six-year-old. Like Robert, Missy had needed to be emotionally salvaged, and his love was her balm.

During their six-year marriage, Missy had tried to prove to Robert that he was deserving of her adoration, but he made it impossible. She wanted to soothe his past wounds, but each time she asked about his childhood, Robert became angry. Missy assumed he was unwilling to discuss his biological parents or his years in foster care because the topics were too painful. Consequently, she had allowed Robert to dictate her friendships so that he wouldn't endure any additional heartache. That decision had backfired, however, and she had ended up the one hurt. Robert had demanded that Missy socialize only with his colleagues and their wives. She was not allowed to have any close friends except for Kayla. But even that relationship had restrictions. Missy was permitted to speak to her for ten minutes a day, but that wasn't enough. Thus, she had called and texted Kayla in secret. When Robert found out, he had forced Missy to distance herself from her best friend.

"Hello? Mrs. Melendez?"

Missy's reverie was interrupted by the agitation she heard in Cole's voice. "I'm sorry," Missy said quietly. "Can you repeat that?"

"Had you noticed anything unusual about his behavior lately? Anything out of character?"

"Yes. He'd been acting strange for months, but I assumed it was because of work. He was spending a lot of late hours at the office."

"I bet he was," Cole mumbled.

Missy felt deflated as the veracity of Cole's insinuation struck her. She knew it had been months since they'd made love, but until just recently, she had never thought Robert was cheating. He had become moody and short-tempered, and the few times she had attempted to get close to him, he had pulled away. Robert had always had a healthy sexual appetite, so his sudden disinterest had been surprising. What was even more disconcerting was Missy's naïveté in thinking things would return to normal. She choked back tears at the realization that the opportunity was gone. A moan of despair rose from deep in her throat. *What good is this so-called gift if I can't save the people I love?*

"Are you okay, Mrs. Melendez?"

"I'm fine." Missy closed her eyes and took several deep breaths. "You must be tired of asking me that."

Cole shook her head. "It's to be expected. You just lost someone dear to you. If you want, we can take a break."

"No. Let's get this over with."

"Okay, as long as you're sure," Cole answered evenly. "Would you say you were happy in your marriage, Mrs. Melendez?"

"Yes," she lied. *I wanted to be a good wife, but I felt suffocated by Robert's reclusive lifestyle and domineering attitude.*

"So what else can you tell us about Robert's behavior?"

"Nothing, except my dad noticed a change in him also. He thought he was involved in something illegal."

"And he was a plastic surgeon, right?" Cole's voice was full of contempt. *So that makes you the typical socialite who married an older man for his money. Only this one had a bonus, a surgeon's scalpel. That way you could get free facelifts and Botox injections.*

Missy replied without looking at Cole. "Yes, he was. And no, I've never had any work done, nor did I ever intend to."

So she's a mind reader too, or maybe this is part of her ploy to have us believe she's psychic. "Of course not, Mrs. Melendez. You're all natural."

Missy stared at her, trying to gauge her thoughts. "Is that some kind of backhanded compliment, or are you being facetious?"

"A little of both," Cole admitted. "Now you said your father thought your husband was doing something illegal. Why would he think that? And what was your father's relationship to your husband?"

"Well, at least you're honest."

"Your father?" Cole queried impatiently.

"My father is … was Robert's lawyer."

"And what did your father think Mr. Melendez was doing?"

"He wasn't sure, so I went through Robert's paperwork to see if there was anything unusual."

"Did your husband know you were doing that?"

"No. I worked on my photography three days a week. And the other days, I worked in the office. It was customary for me to be in the files."

"Was this done on your father's behalf?" Thomas questioned.

"No. I decided to snoop on my own. The last thing I wanted was a dishonest husband."

"He was dishonest, Mrs. Melendez. He was cheating on you. Unless, of course, you knew about that," Cole said matter-of-factly.

"I didn't," Missy snapped. "I thought my husband was happy." *Until I saw him with another woman in a vision.*

"So what did you do when you found out he wasn't? Kill him?"

Missy leaped from the chair and stood in front of Cole. She looked down at her with flames in her eyes. "Listen to me, Detective, because I'm not going to repeat myself again. I did not kill my husband or his mistress."

Cole stood and returned her pointed gaze. "If you didn't, then who did, Mrs. Melendez? Or didn't the murderer appear in your vision?"

Missy was taken aback by her last question. "I guess someone told you about my dream, Detective. However, I never said I was clairvoyant. I merely had a bad feeling." *I wish I could share my vision about Robert and the patient he killed, but I'm not sure if any of it was real. After all, it wouldn't be the first time I've been wrong. And even if I did tell the detectives, they wouldn't believe me. They'll simply humor me by asking where the body is or who Greg was, and I don't have the answers to those questions. I do wonder if Greg was the only person that Robert gave a new face to then tried to blackmail. Until I know for sure, I'm going to feign ignorance. No need to open Pandora's box for nothing.*

"That's not what I was told."

"I don't care what you were told. You're not going to label me as some nutjob that killed two people in a jealous fit of rage."

That's precisely what I think you are. "I never said you were a nutjob."

"But that's what you were thinking," Missy asserted. "Not that I can read your mind."

Thomas interjected, trying to defuse the situation. "You ladies should both have a seat and calm down."

Missy continued talking as if she hadn't heard Thomas. "Finding the killer is your job, right? I mean that *is* what you get paid for. So even if I did 'see' who my husband's executioner was, I wouldn't tell you. And if you're looking for someone to pin this on, you've got the wrong girl."

Cole thought the widow's use of the word "executioner" was significant. "I will find out if you killed your husband, princess, or if you hired someone to do it for you. And if you're guilty, you will spend the rest of your life in prison. I wouldn't worry, though, because you'll have plenty of women willing to be your companion, women with delicate names like Big Bertha and Shotgun Sheila," Cole spat.

Missy was suddenly besieged by Cole's overpowering presence and swayed a little. Cole grabbed the other woman and held her steady. Something passed between them—an undeniable current that both acknowledged by hastily stepping away. There was a poignant silence as they averted their eyes.

For the first time in her life, Missy had a comprehensive vision of a stranger while awake, and it rattled her. She saw Dani tied to a chair surrounded by men with guns. Missy could sense her fear as she glanced around in search of a way to escape. She wanted to help Dani, but Missy wasn't sure if it was a past or future occurrence. Typically, she only saw random glimpses of unknown people and places, not distinct images that raced through her mind like a movie. *Who is this woman? I can see so clearly inside of her, and she is like a mirror of me. The same darkness that she harbors deep within her soul breathes profoundly in me. That must be our connection.*

Thomas watched the exchange with avid curiosity. "Ladies, let's not make this situation any harder than it needs to be."

Cole nodded. "You're right, Thomas. I don't know what happened." For several seconds, this woman had held complete control over Cole's mental faculties. Somehow she had been able to delve into the inner recesses of Cole's mind, and the pieces that Cole had kept firmly hidden from the world were unveiled to the other woman like a freshly painted portrait. Somehow, through Melissa Melendez's psyche Cole had been able to witness her own pain and despair in its physical form. The episode scared the hell out of Cole. *Still, I can't let her perceive how unnerved I am*, she thought. "I apologize for my outburst, Mrs. Melendez. Are you okay? You seem a bit light-headed."

"I'm just physically and emotionally drained, Detective." *And how can I possibly explain that your life is in danger without appearing crazy? Despite the intimate moment we just shared, you would never trust my vision.*

"Please, call me Dani."

"Okay, Dani. And you can call me Missy."

Thomas glanced from one to the other, baffled by the rapid swing in attitude. "Melissa, is there someone you can call to come and get you? The guys will be here for a few more hours, but you should try to get some rest," he stated.

"My father, Ted Delaney."

"Good. Let him know we'd like to speak to him too. He can come down to the station, or we can come to him, whichever is more convenient."

"Thank you, Detective. You've been kind."

"Well, since we're all on a first-name basis, my name is Charles."

"Thanks, Charles."

"You're welcome. We're going to have more questions, but I can see that you're worn out. It's Sunday, so how about you come down to the station on Tuesday at 9:00 a.m.? That gives you a day to rest."

"I can do that. I'll go call my dad now." She headed toward the door, but before she could walk out, Cole offered parting words that hit Missy like a blow to the stomach.

"Hopefully, your dad is a criminal lawyer because you're going to need one."

CHAPTER 2

KAYLA STARED BLINDLY INTO THE GLOOM, acutely aware of where she was and the stranger at her side. Her thoughts sped up as she tried to retrace the last few hours, but nothing lucid came to mind. Everything was a blur—moments of disjointed figures and voices. Her last memory was of sitting at the bar, nursing a martini, when someone approached and offered to buy her another one. Now she glanced at the man next to her and acknowledged that it was him. *That bastard must have slipped something into my glass. There is no way I could have forgotten an entire night after a few drinks.*

Kayla vaguely recalled a conversation about them both being in the army and how impressed he had seemed to be with her stories. He had talked about his eight years of service and his duties as a clergyman for the Chaplain Corps of the US Army. He had seemed incensed by Kayla's question about why he had been discharged, which had prompted her to decline another drink. She had risen from the stool but immediately sat back down because she felt woozy. From that point on, her memory was blank. Kayla guessed what had happened next. Tears welled up in her eyes, but she knew there was no time to feel sorry for herself. She needed to get out of there.

Kayla checked to make sure he was still asleep and climbed out of the bed. As silently as she could, she got dressed.

"Going somewhere?"

She remembered that voice from last night. It had seemed sexy then. Now it sounded brash and menacing. Kayla turned toward him. He was resting on one elbow, watching her. She laughed softly and then meandered over to his side. She leaned down on the mattress and kissed his forehead. "Thank you for a fantastic night. I have the weirdest craving for ice cream, though."

"I'll call the front desk and get you some."

Kayla skimmed the room. "No offense, but this doesn't look like the kind of place that has room service."

"For the right amount of money, they'll do whatever I say," he proclaimed.

"That's great, but I don't want plain vanilla or chocolate. I need rocky road."

As Kayla started to move away, he seized her arm. "I'm sure they can send someone out to get rocky road."

Kayla tried to pull her arm away. "You're hurting me," she cried.

He removed his hand. "I'm sorry. I didn't mean to grab you so hard."

She gently rubbed the spot. "No, I'm sorry. I'm just feeling a little strange about last night. I don't even remember your name."

"It's Peter. And I would love for you to stay and get to know me."

Kayla stepped away. "We'll have plenty of time for that when I get back, Peter." She put on her shoes and grabbed her purse.

"I'm sorry, but you're not going anywhere," he asserted coldly. In the darkness he ascended from the bed like some dark mystical creature.

Kayla could see what kind of extraordinary shape he was in and abandoned the idea to try to outrun him. "I just want ice cream," she bemoaned.

He closed the distance between them. There was no malice evident in his face, just regret. "I don't believe you. And it's a shame too because I have a thing for Halle Berry, and you look like her—same complexion and haircut."

"What do you want from me? I don't have any money."

"I just want to know where Mrs. Melendez is."

Fear clogged her throat. "Missy? What do you want with her?"

He extended his hand and nonchalantly touched her hair. "I wish I didn't have to hurt you. We could have had so much fun together."

Kayla forcefully swung her bag and hit him in the head. She then slammed her knee into his groin. She heard his ragged intake of breath as she unlocked the door and escaped the room.

Kayla tried to remain calm as she sprinted through the parking lot of the motel. She had no idea where she was, but she noticed the check-in area. She dashed to the door, and once inside, she released a bloodcurdling scream.

Propped up in the chair was an older man with a bullet hole in the center of his forehead. Kayla moved closer, trying to ignore the dead man's stare, and picked up the phone. No dial tone. Hysteria threatened to overwhelm her. She leaned over as despair rigidly enfolded her, restricting her oxygen. Kayla took several deep breaths and reined in her emotions.

Seconds later, Kayla was racing down the driveway to the street. She spotted the motel's sign a few yards away, and the words "Roadside Motel" glimmered in the darkness. The realization that Missy had been right made her ill. Kayla wanted to dissolve into a puddle of hopelessness, but she knew she couldn't afford that moment of frailty.

She darted onto the main road and ran, spurred on by terror, pure instinct, and the desire to live. She became aware of a rasping sound and realized it was the ragged inhalation and exhalation of her own lungs. The motel was no longer in view, a small victory. Her only hope was to cover enough distance to find help before he caught up with her. And she somehow knew that he would, despite her efforts.

Kayla swallowed hard, discounting the agony that seared through her body and weighed down her limbs. Her insides were burning, yet the pain didn't matter. She had to keep going, regardless of the long road that stretched ahead.

Without warning, Kayla's legs buckled. She fought hard to stay on her feet as panic struck and coiled around her like a snake. She forced it down, begging for mercy. She had to save herself. More importantly, she had to warn Missy. It dawned on her then that she hadn't checked for her cell. She reached inside her purse and rejoiced as her fingers grazed the top of her phone. Kayla pulled it out to dial 911, but it wouldn't turn on. He'd removed the battery.

Lights flared in front of Kayla, abrupt and blinding. She stumbled to the car, dizzy over the miracle, and stood at the driver's door. "Thank goodness. Some nut is after me, and I ..." She saw the moonlight gleam off the metal.

"Need a lift?" he said.

Kayla went still. Her heart sank as she gazed at the driver and observed his slow smile.

"You're a great runner. I was almost afraid you'd get away. Now take a few steps. And if you try to run, I'll shoot you in the back." With the gun aimed at her, he opened the door and climbed out.

"You might as well shoot me because I'm not going to tell you where Missy is."

He placed the barrel of the weapon between her eyebrows. "Are you sure your friend's life is worth it?"

"You're going to shoot me either way."

"True, but I promise I'll make it less painful if you tell me what I want to know." He twisted the gun.

Kayla cried in anguish as the metal dug into her skin. "Please," she whimpered.

"I like it when my women beg." He cocked the gun. "So what's it going to be, Kayla?"

"She went back to Connecticut, back to her husband," she sobbed hysterically. *Please forgive me, Missy, but I'm just not as strong as you.*

He squeezed the trigger and then laid her lifeless body on the ground. Careful not to touch what was left of her face, he removed the silver chain from around her neck. He unzipped his pants and slowly aroused himself. Once satiated, he closed his eyes and prayed for both of their souls.

Missy struggled to breathe. She opened her eyes and gasped aloud. She gazed around the moonlit room as eerie shadows danced in front of her. The ominous silhouettes glided toward her, frightening in their intensity. Startled, Missy scrambled out of bed and turned on the lights.

The unexpected creak of a floorboard made her heart thump with fear. She imagined her husband's killer walking up the hallway toward her bedroom. Missy grabbed a nail file from the nightstand and crouched into a fighting position. She waited, poised for the person to break down the door, but when nothing happened, she put the makeshift weapon away.

Missy slowly looked around the room and wondered again why her father had kept it the same for the past twelve years. The walls were decorated with posters of the Backstreet Boys and NSYNC, her favorite groups when she was a teenager. The bookshelves were lined with dolls her mother had given her, but the books her father had purchased were now gone—probably sold. Many of the hardbacks had been rare copies written by renowned authors, but Missy had shown no interest in reading them. She didn't have the attention span needed to revel in the classic works of Shakespeare and Dickens, much to her father's chagrin.

Ted had formed lofty goals for his only daughter, especially after her mother died, when it was just the two of them. But even at thirteen, Missy had understood that she could never follow in his footsteps. If she had become a lawyer, like he wanted, she wouldn't have been able to control her visions. And Missy realized that she couldn't represent someone she knew was guilty. She had wanted to explain that to her father, but she didn't think he'd believe her. Instead, she had allowed his disappointment to burgeon, which had affected their relationship. Missy had tried to mend it by attending Penn State University, but she dropped out after her second year to be with Shawn, her high school sweetheart. Missy had hated college, but she was grateful for the time she'd spent there because of her friendship with Kayla.

The ringing of her cell phone snatched Missy away from her memories. Normally, her room would provide comfort, but not today. Instead, she was reminded of the circumstances behind her strained relationship with her father.

"Hello?"

"Melissa."

Missy was struck by a sudden sense of longing.

"Melissa, are you there?"

"Daddy, where are you?"

"Sorry. I'm running late. My plane is delayed," Ted explained. "I'll be home in a couple of hours. Are you okay? Is Mrs. Murphy taking good care of you?"

Missy smiled at the mention of the woman who had taken care of her since she was five. "She clucked over me like a mother hen all day. I finally got her to go home."

"She missed you. I'm sure she was ecstatic to have you there so that she could pamper you like old times."

"I missed her too. Why isn't she working full-time for you anymore?"

"That wasn't my choice. She wanted to retire and spend more time with her grandkids."

"I know. It's just … well … being here has made me realize how much things have changed. I've wasted a lot of valuable time wallowing in my own bitterness and guilt." Missy hesitated. "I'm sorry about everything that happened. I never meant ..."

"Let's not discuss it now, Missy. We'll talk when I get home."

"Okay. We have a lot to talk about."

"Yes, we do. Try to get some sleep. It's late."

"I will. Goodnight, Daddy."

"Goodnight, Pumpkin."

Missy beamed as she touched the screen to disconnect. She hadn't been called Pumpkin since ... Her smile disappeared as she slowly recalled the last time she'd heard that term of endearment. It was a crisp February morning in 2004. Her father Ted was on his way to the office and whispered to her, "Happy Valentine's Day, Pumpkin." She had responded with a disjointed "thank you" as she choked back tears. The moment her father's car pulled out of the driveway, she had allowed the waterworks to flow. Missy was openly distraught about leaving that night to elope with Shawn and never seeing her father again. Ted was against their marriage, so Missy felt she had no other choice. She loved Shawn and refused to let her father's disdain keep them apart. So on February 14, Melissa Nicole Delaney married Shawn Michael Colson before a justice of the peace in Nevada. The couple spent three blissful days honeymooning in Vegas before putting down roots in Philadelphia.

For several months the newlyweds were happy, until Missy noticed a shift in Shawn's attitude. He was no longer her handsome, blonde-haired, blue-eyed boy wonder. Instead, he'd become a stranger. The change had started when Ted canceled her credit cards and froze the funds in her bank account. With no income, both Missy and Shawn had to seek employment, but they encountered stumbling blocks because of their lack of experience. Ultimately, their financial troubles created an insurmountable rift between the pair, especially once Missy discovered that she was pregnant. Even without confirmation from a test, Missy knew instinctively that she was carrying their child. However, they couldn't afford a baby with their fast-food jobs, so she opted to leave. Shawn tried to convince her to stay, but Missy concluded that a trial separation was the best solution.

Missy returned to Hartford and pleaded for her father's forgiveness. Ted promised to overlook Missy's indiscretions if she agreed to his stipulations. First, she had to annul her marriage and never see Shawn again. Second, she needed to abort their six-week-old fetus. Ted believed that Missy couldn't finish her degree and determine a career path if she had a husband and child constantly demanding her time.

Despite his deft argument of his case, Missy refused to listen. No matter how much she respected her father, she wouldn't get rid of her child. That's why Missy walked away from him again and went back to her husband.

Once their marriage resumed, it took Missy several months to acknowledge that she'd made a mistake. Shawn was acting strangely, even more so than before. He was out smoking and drinking with his buddies every night and would often come home drunk. Missy tried to incite visions to determine Shawn's actions and whereabouts but was unsuccessful. When she tried to discuss her concerns with him, he denied that anything was wrong. Frustrated with his volatile behavior, Missy decided to return home. She would consent to the annulment, but she still wanted to keep the baby. Surely her father wouldn't be able to resist the prospect of a grandchild to spoil, Missy thought. She just needed to exercise her arbitration skills and present a strong defense to get him to concede. Then the only remaining obstacle would be her soon-to-be ex-husband.

When Shawn got home from work, she told him of her intentions to file for divorce. He didn't get angry and yell as expected. He simply nodded and left the apartment. Missy was worried that he'd do something reckless, so she elected to wait until morning to leave. Shawn returned several hours later, but Missy was so engrossed in a dream that she didn't hear him enter the room.

It was a blustery fall day. Leaves crunched loudly under Missy's feet while she pushed an empty baby carriage through the park. The wind carried a baby's cries through the atmosphere, the whimpers vibrating off the trees. Missy searched frantically for the source and tracked the sound to a sign that read "Dead End." Missy realized it was a warning, but before she could escape, her surroundings morphed into darkness. She tried to move forward, but something blocked her way. Although not religious, Missy uttered a quick prayer as the cold air ravaged her body. Once light was restored, she observed that her barricade was two males. She begged them to help her locate the infant. One of the men laughed while the other promised to take good care of her daughter.

Missy's world began to spin off its axis as she realized that the child was hers.

"Please don't harm my baby!" she shrieked. But it was too late as the images faded into oblivion.

Missy became aware of Shawn's presence and opened her eyes. She recalled the events from her vision and instinctively touched her belly. A wave of relief washed over her the moment she sensed the baby's heartbeat. Missy's reprieve was short-lived, however. When she sat up, she spotted two men in Halloween masks standing behind her husband. She screamed as they rushed toward her and placed a washcloth with chloroform over her face. Once Missy was unconscious, they used the back stairs to carry her out of the apartment building and placed her limp body into the rear of a black SUV truck.

An hour later, dressed in nothing but a sheer nightgown, Missy opened her eyes and surveyed her surroundings. The room's decor consisted of broken furniture and piles of trash. A rat scuttled across her bare foot, and Missy squealed in fear. She attempted to move but was bound to a chair by tape.

Missy heard someone enter the room. She knew, without seeing his face, that he was one of the guys from her earlier premonition.

"Why am I here?" she murmured.

"Don't worry. Your husband is taking care of everything."

"What does Shawn have to do with this?"

"He's going to give us our big payday. Your father should be delivering a million dollars right now to the designated spot."

"What?" she screeched. "You kidnapped me for ransom?"

"Yup. That was the plan from the beginning. Why else do you think Shawn put up with you?"

Missy shook her head. "We've been together for years. There's no way this was about money."

"Not at first. But when you left, something in him snapped. Grief turned to revenge. And when you begged him to take you back, he saw a chance to make good on his four-year investment."

"How could I be so stupid?" Missy moaned. "That's what he's been hiding."

Shawn and another disguised man walked in and threw several canvas bags on the floor. "There are three bags, one for each of us," Shawn announced. "The cops are on their way, so we have about ten minutes to get out of here."

"Bastard! I can't believe you used me like this. What about our baby?" Missy's voice was shrill.

"Just put it up for adoption. Your father wanted you to get rid of it, so now you can do it without a guilty conscience," he said coldly.

"Hey, Shawny-boy, why don't you let us have a taste of her before her daddy comes?" one of the men mumbled behind his clown mask.

Shawn's anger was glacial. "She's eight months pregnant, you sick bastard."

"So?" he chuckled. "I had sex with my girlfriend at nine months, and it was the best fifteen minutes of my life."

"Don't you dare touch her," he yelled. "You got what you wanted, and Missy wasn't a part of the prize."

Sirens echoed in the distance, which galvanized the two men. They grabbed their portions of the money and sprinted for the door.

Shawn walked over to Missy. He leaned down next to her ear and whispered, "I'm sorry."

"I hope you rot in hell," she hissed.

With his head bent, Shawn picked up his bag and exited the room.

Once alone, Missy sobbed hysterically. Betrayal lodged deep in her throat like a bitter pill she couldn't swallow. By the time the police arrived and freed her, Missy was doubled over in pain. She knew then what her dream had been about, without any confirmation from the doctor: she was going to lose the baby.

A few hours later, she opened her eyes and glimpsed her father's grim face. "No, Daddy," she whimpered as she touched her belly.

"I'm sorry, Melissa, but the doctors couldn't save your little girl."

Dr. George McCain stared at the television in stunned silence. According to the evening news, Robert was dead. The facts were sketchy, but the cops were labeling it a homicide. He reached for his cell and dialed a number.

"I know it's late, but did you hear about Robert?"

"Yes," the voice on the other end responded.

"You think someone knows, Bill?" he asked apprehensively.

"Don't panic. The last thing we need is to draw attention to ourselves. No one knows."

"You can't be sure of that."

"I'm sure. Meet me at the office at ten tomorrow. We need to do damage control."

"I have appointments starting at eight."

"Cancel them," Bill demanded. "If anyone asks, the office is in mourning."

"I'll have my secretary take care of it."

"Good. I'll see you in the morning. And George, keep your mouth shut because if you don't, you could easily end up like Robert."

The line went dead.

Shit, I'm in big trouble, George thought.

The criminal investigative division of the Hartford Police Station, the CID, was a breeding ground for fast-track, brownnose types. Many officers used the department as a stepping-stone to improve their opportunities for advancement, but there were a few detectives who enjoyed the work. Dani Cole was one of those people. She took pleasure in the morning roll calls in a dirty, beat-up room filled with dirty, beat-up desks, with beat-up cops getting migraines under harsh fluorescent lights. Due to renovations, homicide was crammed in one room, robbery was down the hall, and sex crimes was wedged into a large utility closet. Most of the guys complained about the accommodations, but Cole believed it was an atmosphere conducive to high-quality police work. She thought cops should follow the same protocol of the old TV shows she'd watched as a child. Back then, there wasn't time to lounge around and waste taxpayers' money. The detectives didn't care about newly painted walls, espresso machines, and fancy desks. Instead, their primary concern was obtaining justice. Cole too thrived in that kind of environment. But like everything else in her life, that would soon change. Cole was all for progress but wasn't fond of the upheaval that often came along with it.

A fraction of Cole's uneasiness stemmed from her inability to adjust to her new partner. It had been nine months since she'd been introduced to Charles Thomas. Cole didn't dislike him, but adjusting to his temperament and style of investigating had been tough. She was used to working with Joshua Blake, who she felt complemented her methods well. Thomas, on the other hand, was more of a rogue cop. Cole understood that on the mean streets of North

Philly, where he was from, some roughness was needed. In Connecticut, though, they had to go by the book.

Cole missed Blake but was happy that he had been promoted to lieutenant. His first undertaking had been to have his detectives resume riding with partners again. Their last boss had incorporated a high-concept team approach with rotating sleep-deprivation schedules that created division within the department. Cole hoped that Blake's decision to forgo the supposedly groundbreaking model would repair the damage. She had nothing personal against teams, but it slowed down a case when there were too many roosters in the hen house.

Cole noted the perfect example of a rooster as Blake strutted back and forth in front of her cubicle. "Why is Thomas always late?" Blake asked, visibly annoyed.

Cole laughed. "Is that a rhetorical question?"

"It's not funny. I've been waiting for over ten minutes."

"You should be used to his tardiness by now."

Thomas chose that moment to appear. "Sorry I'm late. I was, uh … stuck in traffic."

"Again?" Cole asked.

Blake shook his head. "I have a meeting with the captain in less than fifteen minutes, Thomas. I don't have time to deal with your crummy excuses. Give me everything you have on the Melendez case so far. The mayor is friends with Melissa Melendez's father, so there can't be any mistakes with this one." Blake looked directly at Cole as he stressed the last few words.

She knew what he was referring to, but Cole refused to address it in front of Thomas.

"There is nothing to tell until we get the forensic results, Lieutenant," Thomas proclaimed. He popped a stick of gum in his mouth and then spit it back out. "That is the worst shit I've ever tasted. I'd rather chew on rat droppings."

Cole smirked. "And that would taste different from a cigarette how?"

Thomas scowled at her. "You know I'm trying to quit. A little support would be nice."

"I'll support you as soon as you get serious about it."

"Why do you think I'm chewing this crap?"

Blake interrupted their banter. "I didn't know you smoked, Thomas. When did that start?"

"You mean he picked up this nasty habit when he became my partner, Lieutenant?"

"I've never seen him pick up a cigarette, not once since he transferred here from Philadelphia."

"I smoked for years. Bad habit I got from my ex-partner. We had to do something, working around drug dealers and murderers all day. It's not like we could drink on the job. I started back up when Doris left."

Silence prevailed. No one ever discussed Thomas's wife, even if he was the one who brought her name into the conversation. He was touchy and occasionally belligerent about Doris, so all the detectives respected his privacy—everyone except Cole.

"Wasn't that months ago? Get over it, Thomas. None of us have even met the woman. We probably wouldn't have liked her anyway. People leave all the time, but life goes on," she said.

"Fuck you, Cole. If you weren't a woman, I'd—"

"You'd what?

"I'd kick your ass."

"I'd like to see you try."

"Okay, enough, you two," Blake declared. "You're behaving like children."

"She started it," Thomas whined.

"And I'm finishing it," Blake stated adamantly. "I'll expect those forensic reports on my desk the minute you receive them. Good day, Thomas. You too, Tinker Bell."

Cole placed her hand on her gun, which triggered a burst of laughter from Blake. He'd given her the moniker because of her tiny stature. However, he'd learned over their five-year partnership that despite her height and build, she was tough. Blake had never seen a more passionate, committed officer.

"I'm going to get you," Cole whispered.

Blake nodded. "I look forward to it." He wanted to say more, but the timing wasn't right. He was just thankful that they seemed to be bridging the distance between them. He understood why Cole had been disappointed when he moved up in rank. They'd made a formidable team—well respected throughout the city and the department. It had been a daunting task to leave the streets behind, but at thirty-eight years old, Blake was tired of witnessing death on a regular basis. Criminals seemed to be falling from the sky like acid rain, and the drops had been slowly eating away at his flesh. Blake was broken, and after seventeen years on the force, he felt incapable of healing those wounds. He needed to shield himself from the downpours, and a cushy office was the ideal shelter. If that made him a sellout, then so be it. At least he'd be alive.

Officer Vincent Adams peeked his head into the cubicle. "Sorry to interrupt, Lieutenant, but there's a Mrs. Melendez and Mr. Delaney here to see Cole and Thomas."

"Have them wait in interrogation room one, Adams."

"Sure, sir." Adams turned and left.

"Showtime," Thomas affirmed.

"Wish I could sit in with you guys," said Blake.

"Why? Are you bored in that comfortable office, Lieutenant?"

"Not at all, Detective Cole. I'm sure you and your partner have everything under control."

"Yes, we'll be sure to report back once we're done."

"I'll wait to hear from you."

As the two detectives headed toward interrogation, Thomas blurted out, "You two should just screw each other's brains out and get it over with."

Cole shot daggers at him. "You should go fuck yourself."

Thomas laughed. He was growing accustomed to her outspoken nature. He'd argued against working with a female partner, especially one as beautiful as Cole, but over the past few months, she'd earned his respect. That wasn't easy to do, given what a hard, cynical, and chauvinistic man he was.

Thomas opened the door, and Cole preceded him inside. The room was small, or what some considered "intimate." In keeping with the latest theories on how best to interview suspects, the table was tiny and round, with no dominant side. Everyone was equal—buddies, pals, confidants.

Ted Delaney's southern genteel breeding oozed from his posture as he stood in the corner. He was tall and slender with smooth coffee-colored skin that belied his fifty-five years. His hair was reddish-brown with gray sprinkled along the temples. He wore a black pinstripe suit accompanied by a gold tie and cufflinks to match. He tapped his pricey black leather shoes on the tiled floor while he warily observed Cole and Thomas with his hazel eyes.

Missy was positioned beneath the wall-mounted video camera, a few feet away from her father. She was dressed in a cream-colored two-piece pantsuit, with coordinating cream high heels and purse. She wasn't wearing any jewelry except for a pair of diamond stud earrings and her four-karat wedding ring.

Cole observed how Missy twisted the silver band on her finger, a common ploy used to gain sympathy. She completed her "I'm innocent" look with little to no makeup and her hair pulled back into a neat ponytail. In Cole's opinion, she resembled a small girl playing dress-up, not a killer.

"Can I ask why Missy is here when she had absolutely nothing to do with her husband's death?" Ted queried brusquely.

"Murder, Mr. Delaney. Your son-in-law was murdered. He didn't just die."

"I know that. I'm not stupid, Detective ...?"

"Didn't say you were, sir. And my name is Cole."

"I've been a member of the bar for over thirty years, Detective Cole, and I'm not going to let you pin this on my daughter."

"Mr. Delaney, I'm Detective Thomas. We just have a few more questions for Mrs. Melendez. No one is trying to pin anything on her."

"I'm fine with answering their questions, Daddy. I have nothing to hide."

"Great. Let's all have a seat then," said Cole.

They moved to the table and sat down.

"Can you tell us again what happened on the night of June 17, Mrs. Melendez?" Cole asked.

"Robert and I had a fight that Thursday the fourteenth because I found out he was cheating on me."

"How?"

Missy sighed. "I walked in on the two of them together."

"Was it the same woman we found dead in your bedroom?"

"Yes," she murmured.

"We identified the victim as Connie Gordon. Does that name sound familiar to you?"

"No, it doesn't, Detective Cole. I'd never seen her until that day."

"Okay, so you and Mr. Melendez argued about his mistress, and then what happened?"

"I left."

"Where did you go?"

"I went to Miami to visit a friend."

Thomas skimmed his notepad. "Kayla Bell, your friend from college, right?"

"That's right."

"How long were you there?"

"Two days."

"Why did you come back?" Cole asked, her tone cynical.

Because of you, Missy thought. "I wanted to work things out with Robert."

"You wanted to work things out with the man who was cheating on you?"

"He was my husband. We took vows ..."

"Which he broke," Cole interjected. "Look, if you don't start being honest with us, Mrs. Melendez, you'll have to trade those designer clothes in for an orange jumpsuit."

Ted rose from his chair and glowered at Cole. "Your ignorance and contempt are unappreciated, Detective Cole." He turned his attention to Thomas. "Are we done here?"

"Please sit back down, Mr. Delaney. We would like to get this case solved as soon as possible, and we need your cooperation to do it."

"And while you're wasting your time interrogating my daughter, the real killer is still on the loose."

"It's fine, Daddy." Missy made direct eye contact with Cole. "I have nothing to hide."

Ted nodded and reclaimed his seat. "I'll defer to Missy's wishes, this time."

Cole immediately swooped in with the next question. "Do you own a gun, Mrs. Melendez?"

"No," Missy declared emphatically.

"Did Robert?"

"Absolutely not. I wouldn't allow one in the house."

Thomas jotted down some notes before asking the next question. "Do you know of anyone who would want your husband dead, Mrs. Melendez?"

"I can think of a few," Ted interjected.

"Do you have names, Mr. Delaney?" Cole inquired.

"No, but Robert was into something."

"Something like what?" Thomas asked.

"I have no idea."

Cole shook her head. "You were his lawyer, correct?"

"Yes. Until a few weeks ago."

Missy was noticeably shocked. "What? You didn't tell me that."

"I never got the chance. I was out of town on business for a week, and when I came back, you were in Miami. Then I had to fly back out again."

"But I don't understand," Missy stated blankly. "Why didn't Robert tell me?"

"I'm sure he planned to, Missy."

Cole rolled her eyes. *Or perhaps he just planned to continue lying. He wasn't exactly the epitome of honesty.* "Mr. Delaney, why weren't you working for your son-in-law any longer?"

"He fired me, Detective."

Max Peterson drove along the empty highway, sipping the coffee he'd purchased from a local bakery. He grabbed a glazed doughnut from the box perched on his passenger seat and took a bite. Unlike his health-conscious wife, Max wasn't concerned about high cholesterol. The doctor had warned him about his weight, but Max preferred to eat what he wanted. That way, he'd at least die a happy man.

The sun vibrantly rose over the horizon, reminding Max of why he loved mornings. It was his favorite time of the day because he didn't have to deal with the bustle of rush-hour traffic. What's more, he could avoid the hazards of nighttime drivers who either were intoxicated or ignored the dangers of traveling too close to a two-ton rig.

Max needed to empty his full bladder but hated to leave his truck unattended even for a few minutes. He'd driven this route for years, so he knew there was a motel about a mile up the interstate. Nevertheless, he doubted the manager would appreciate him stopping in simply to use the restroom.

Max put on his flashers and climbed out of the truck. He trekked several yards through the trees and brush to avoid being seen. Before he unzipped his pants, Max scanned the area and spied a woman's shoe. The skin on the back of his neck prickled, and the feeling of impending doom threatened to paralyze him. Max moved forward a few feet and spotted a woman's body half hidden beneath a pile of shrubs. The stench of rotting flesh assaulted his senses, and he lost his breakfast. Once his stomach settled, he hurried to his truck and dialed 911.

"911. What's your emergency?"

"I need help out on Interstate 84. I found a woman's body," Max squealed.

"Do you know the deceased woman, sir?"

"I'm not sure."

"What do you mean you're not sure?"

"Her face is missing."

George sat in his car and stared at the building that housed Hartford Plastic Surgeons. When he started at HPS, over five years ago, he had been excited to work with some of the best cosmetic specialists in the country. HPS had been George's springboard into greatness. It had boosted his reputation as a surgeon and helped build his clientele. But now that his mentor was dead, he was no longer certain that he should stay. George knew exactly what Robert had been doing, so he was worried that the killer would soon come after him.

The clock in his car read 9:52 a.m. George reached for the door handle and climbed out of his Mercedes S600. After checking his prized possession for scratches, George walked toward the entrance. Without warning, a searing pain assaulted his body, and he crumbled to his knees. He gazed at his shoulder and saw a red stain on his white Armani shirt. Shock overcame him as he realized it was blood. Before darkness overwhelmed him, George heard someone whisper, "Get the files from Missy, or the next time I'll kill you."

Cole wore leggings, a tank top, a baseball cap, and sneakers. She hoped that if the neighbors saw her, they would assume she was a jogger. Cole's true identity needed to be concealed since she was about to defy protocol and enter a crime scene without her partner. She had tried calling Thomas's cell to have him meet her at the Melendez house, but he hadn't answered. Cole realized now how little she knew her partner. She always had been aware of Blake's whereabouts, even when they were off-duty. However, she wasn't familiar with Thomas's hangouts, his family, or his vices. And what information she did have, she had discovered through the rumor mill. Despite her curiosity, Cole didn't ask questions. She wanted to keep her distance with Thomas. That way, if he deserted her like Blake had, she wouldn't be disappointed.

To make her runner facade believable, Cole sprinted several laps around the block, away from Missy Melendez's house. By the time she climbed the back fence, she had worked up a sweat. She ascended the back stairs and unzipped the fanny pack she had strapped to her waist. She took out a pair of gloves and slid them on her hands. She removed her burglary kit, and in less than a minute, she had the back door unlocked.

Once inside, she paused to listen, but there was no sound—just the hollow silence of an empty house. *Except it's not empty,* she thought. *Missy's essence is here. I can feel it loitering in every corner like some dynamic apparition. Her heartache beckons to me and conjures up images of my own personal demons. Still, I have to ignore their cries because I'm not equipped to face them.*

Cole proceeded to the dining area and gazed at the prints on the wall. A young Missy, around age six, was perched on the lap of a woman who looked to be in her midtwenties. Cole guessed she was Missy's mother. With the exception of skin color and hair, Missy closely resembled the woman. The portrait showed a beautiful brunette with the same high cheekbones, full lips, and hazel eyes as Missy. However, her lineage appeared to be European, maybe Italian or Spanish.

Wedding pictures of Missy and her husband adorned the opposite wall. Upon review of the photos, Cole understood why Missy had been attracted to Robert. He was over six feet tall and had an aura that exuded wealth and self-confidence. His black hair was curly and peppered with gray. His sky-blue eyes, which were accentuated by fine lines around the edges, seemed out of place against his bronzed skin. The delicate lines on his forehead gave him an air of distinction and strengthened his appeal. Most women would consider him handsome, but not Cole. She recognized the arrogance in his smirk and the coolness in his stare. It reminded Cole of her father, and she suspected that Robert had been cruel like him.

Cole turned her attention to Missy and was captivated by her smile. One photo in particular illustrated her carefree nature as she did a ballerina pose in her wedding gown. Cole was surprised that Missy was capable of such joy. The person she'd met on two separate occasions seemed unhappy, but Cole acknowledged that the bereavement process could transform anyone. Still, Cole's instincts were telling her that Missy had changed long before she found those dead bodies.

After staring at one particular image for what must have been several minutes, Cole shook off her reverie and moved into the foyer. She noticed a room the size of a walk-in closet and assumed it was Missy's darkroom. She knew the area had been thoroughly checked like the rest of the house, but she felt it would still be a treasure trove of information. A burning feeling in her gut warned Cole that there was something incriminating within those four walls. The notion gave her pause. Ordinarily, she would be excited about the prospect of cornering a suspect with corroboration of guilt, but not this time. *You're getting too involved, Dani. This assignment can't be like the Cavanaugh case, when you neglected your duties to foolishly entertain the devil.*

Cole opened the door and turned on the light. She gasped aloud as images of children, animals, and sunsets bombarded her. Cole loved the beauty of nature, and Missy had captured its essence in every shot. *This woman is extremely talented*, Cole thought. *There's no way these pictures were taken with a camera phone.*

Cole wanted to see through Missy's eyes and experience each specific moment, so she studied each photo. After a few minutes, her phone rang, and she retrieved it from the pack.

"Cole."

"Detective, this is Missy Melendez. I hope you don't mind, but the station gave me your cell number."

The idea of talking to Missy while trespassing in her house made Cole uneasy, but she kept her tone professional. "What can I do for you, Mrs. Melendez?"

"My friend is missing," Missy declared anxiously.

Cole instantly became alert. "What do you mean, 'missing'? When did you speak to her last?"

"The night I left Florida."

"Then it's only been a few days. I'm sure everything is fine. You're probably just paranoid because of what happened to your husband."

"You don't get it, Detective. I speak to Kayla every day, whether it's a call, text, or direct message on Twitter. I know she's heard about Robert by now since it's all over my Facebook page, and she hasn't called. Something is definitely wrong."

"Okay, but your friend doesn't live in Connecticut, so how can I help you?"

"You can ask the Miami police to do a welfare check. They will listen to you. I would fly there myself, but I'm not permitted to leave town," she asserted scornfully.

Cole ignored her sarcasm. "Kayla is over eighteen. A missing person's report from out of state won't take precedence over the precinct's other cases."

"Please. Can you do this for me?" Missy pleaded.

Her supplications momentarily imprisoned Cole's heart, and the detective couldn't refuse. "Give me the information. I'll see if I can get someone to visit her place. I'm not guaranteeing anything, though."

"Great. I'll text you her address. Please call me if you find out anything."

"Sure."

"Oh, and Dani?"

"Yes?"

"I hope you're enjoying the pictures in my darkroom."

Cole couldn't mask the disbelief in her voice. "What?"

"I can feel your presence there," Missy stated matter-of-factly.

"I'm not," Cole denied. "How …" She faltered.

"You don't have to deny it. I won't tell anyone that you're there … alone." Missy emphasized the last word. "I'll just wait to hear from you. Thanks again for your assistance." She disconnected the call.

Cole glanced around but couldn't detect anything that would alert Missy that she was there. *I'll get forensics back out here to look for listening devices and hidden cameras.*

After Googling the number for the Miami PD on her phone, Cole called and spoke to a patrolman. He promised to call her back once he had verified her badge number and checked on Kayla.

A half hour later, her phone rang. "This is Cole."

"Detective Cole, I'm Detective Bolton from the Miami PD. I heard you were looking for Kayla Bell."

"That's correct. You have something for me?"

"Yes. A body was brought in this morning, and we got a positive ID from the vic's personal belongings."

Cole's heartbeat accelerated as she anticipated his next words.

"Ms. Bell is dead. A trucker found her body off of Interstate 84."

"Cause of death?"

"She was murdered—single gunshot wound, close-range, to the face."

"That's horrible." *Sounds like the same MO as the person who shot Melendez.*

"Bell's purse was found a few feet away from the body. It contained her driver's license and credit cards, so we ruled out robbery. I would like to talk to the woman who asked about the vic. We need next-of-kin information."

"Her name is Melissa Melendez. Let me get your direct number, and I'll have her call you."

Cole took down his number with the agreement that if the two crimes were related, the departments would exchange information. Next, she dialed Missy's number, rifling through the remaining photographs as she waited.

"Hello," Missy replied groggily.

"Missy, it's Detective Cole. Did I wake you?"

"No. I'm up."

"I have bad news for you." A picture caught Cole's attention, but she continued to speak. "I hate to be the one to have to tell you this, but Kayla was found murdered."

"Oh my God, I'd hoped my premonition was wrong."

Cole paused. "Your premonition?"

"Uh … I mean I had a bad feeling."

Cole's heart dropped as she studied the remaining photos in the pile. "I'm sorry, Mrs. Melendez, but there's more."

"More? What do you mean?"

"Please just stay where you are. A patrol car will be there soon."

"What? Why?" she asked, bewildered.

"To arrest you for the murders of Robert Melendez and Connie Gordon."

CHAPTER 3

HE TROD BACK AND FORTH LIKE A CAGED animal. "What the hell happened?" he roared. "Melissa Melendez shouldn't be alive. She's seen the list and can expose everyone."

"I don't need you to remind me. I know what's at stake," the man in the black robe declared.

"Then what kind of shit show are you running? Instead of killing her, you take out Robert's side piece? I thought you didn't make mistakes."

"I don't."

He stood still. "So you meant to kill her?"

"No witnesses. That's my rule."

"And what about Kayla Bell? She wasn't a part of the deal."

"I don't expect compensation. Consider her a freebie," he scoffed.

"There's enough attention around these murders without your gun-happy freebies. You've got twenty-four hours to finish the job, or I'll find someone else who will. And he won't leave any witnesses either, including you."

Cole returned to the station with the pictures from the Melendez house in her fanny pack. Desperate to relieve the pressure in her head, she rushed to her cubicle and grabbed her medication from the drawer. As she always did, Cole swallowed the pills without water and sat down. While she waited for the pain to subside, she recalled the doctor's words of caution about the dangers of stress. Although she had verbally acquiesced, there were limited opportunities to relax in her profession. If she let down her guard, a killer could go free.

"You're in big trouble," Ulrich announced.

Leave it to the nosiest cop in the CID to state the obvious, she thought. Whoever said women gossip too much had never met Richard Ulrich. "What are you talking about?"

"Like you don't know. It's all over the precinct that you arrested the Melendez woman without authorization."

"I don't need permission to do my job," she scoffed. "Anything else?"

"Blake is looking for you. He told me to let him know if I see you."

"And let me guess—you're about to run to his office right now and snitch."

He chuckled. "Snitch? Nah, I'm just doing my civic duty as a concerned coworker."

"How conscientious of you." *You egotistical, arrogant piece of*… "For your information, I planned to check in with Blake once I confirmed some things regarding the Melendezes' finances."

"Anything I can help you with?"

"No. I have everything under control."

"Okay. I'll just poke my head in the lieutenant's office and tell him I saw you."

What you need to do is unpoke your head from his ass. "Thanks," she said mockingly as he walked away.

Hartford General Hospital was humming with activity when Thomas ambled through the doors to the emergency department. He hated the smell of hospitals. To him, the stench of death permeated the walls no matter how hard the janitors tried to camouflage it with the equally pungent odors of bleach and disinfectant. Despite his revulsion, Thomas whistled as he strolled to the nurses' station. He leaned against the counter and stared at the woman whose white uniform made her pale skin appear lucent. Her name tag read Patsy, but Thomas had dubbed her Scarlet. He'd asked the beautiful redhead out numerous times, but she'd repeatedly spurned his offers.

"What can I do for you, Detective Thomas?" Her tone was professional.

"Hey, Scarlet. I'm here to see George McCain."

"My name is Patsy," she stated doggedly. "And Dr. McCain just got out of surgery. I doubt he'll be up for questioning."

"It'll only take a few minutes. Then what do you say we grab a cup of coffee?"

"I'm not interested. I told you I'm seeing someone."

Thomas frowned. "I don't remember you mentioning it. But hey, if he doesn't treat you right, I'm available. A woman can never be wined and dined too much." He winked at her.

"You are definitely a charmer. Maybe if things don't work out with my boyfriend, I'll reconsider."

"That's all I ask. What room is McCain in? I'll try to concentrate on my job, but it'll be tough with a beautiful woman around."

Patsy blushed. "He's at the end on the left—room 221."

"Great. I'll stop by here on my way out to see if you still have that boyfriend."

She laughed. "You're incorrigible."

"You're right," Thomas declared self-assuredly.

A minute later, a queasy Thomas entered the victim's room. The man lying in bed appeared peaceful despite the tubes in his nose and arm.

As Thomas moved closer, George McCain opened his eyes and stared blankly at him. The surgeon tried to speak, but all that came out was an inaudible moan.

"Hi, Dr. McCain. I'm Detective Thomas. I'm here to ask you some questions."

George attempted to reposition himself but was too weak to sit up.

"Please, don't try to move. I just want to ask if you saw the person who did this to you."

He slowly shook his head.

"Do you know of anyone who would want to hurt you?"

He whispered something indiscernible.

"Can you say that again?" Thomas asked.

"Mi … miss … sy," George mumbled.

The dark figure headed toward the church's altar. He observed the hundreds of candles that adorned the platforms and illuminated his surroundings. He noted how the flickering shadows resembled spirits, and that terrified him. He feared

that the silhouettes embodied all the people he'd executed, so he uttered an absolution prayer before they could exact their revenge.

He dipped a chalice into the holy water and kneeled on the carpet. He put the goblet, along with a small chest, in front of him. He opened the container and carefully emptied the contents. He spread the items on the floor and immersed his fingers in the water. He sprinkled what he called God's tears on each of his kill toys while reciting the Lord's Prayer. By the time he reached the last line of the invocation, tears were streaming down his face. His cries echoed through the empty pews as he looked up at the cross and begged for forgiveness.

He was so engrossed in his own pain that he didn't hear the gentleman come up beside him. The other man gently laid his hand on his shoulder. The dark figure instinctively reached inside his jacket for his gun and shot the pastor in the stomach. Blood splattered all over him and his trinkets. Furious that his prized possessions had been tainted, he let off a few more rounds. Once his anger cooled, he stood and turned around.

"Mrs. Melendez, wake up. We're at the station."

Missy glanced at the officer. "What?"

He held the car door open. "I need you to get out of the car," he stated impatiently.

Missy tried to resurrect her vision, but the images were lost. *Fuck, I just lost the opportunity to come face-to-face with my husband's killer.*

Cole checked Missy's financials and her history on social media as she waited for her migraine to abate. She'd hoped to gain insight into Missy's personality, but Missy's online presence was even more mysterious than the woman herself. There weren't many updates on her Facebook, Instagram, or Twitter pages. And the few tweets and status updates that she had posted didn't disclose anything of a personal nature. Cole wanted to dig deeper but realized that she had waited long enough to face Blake. If she didn't appear soon, Blake would come looking for her, and that would cause even more friction between them.

With her stomach in knots, Cole stood and made her way down the hall. His door was open, so Cole entered Blake's office and took a seat. Blake sensed her presence, but he didn't budge from his spot at the window. He peered out, seemingly immersed in the beauty of the landscape. Cole glanced at his reflection in the glass and silently admitted that Blake was handsome. His athletic build and chiseled features reminded her of a Ken doll. It was hard to believe that some lucky woman hadn't persuaded him to renounce his bachelorhood yet. With his sandy-brown hair and green eyes, Blake was the type of man who could melt an icy heart with just his dimpled smile. Throughout their years together, Cole had witnessed countless women's endeavors to win his love, but each one had failed. Cole wouldn't categorize him as a playboy, but she doubted he would ever settle down.

Blake finally turned and gazed at Cole. His disappointment was palpable, and Cole found it difficult to identify the man in front of her as her former partner and friend. At that moment, he was nothing more than her boss. And Blake looked the part in his crisp, navy blue suit, white shirt, and gold tie with matching cufflinks. His office was decorated in leather and mahogany, oozing the same sense of wealthy, genteel breeding his wardrobe tried to convey. Cole recognized it for what it was: a charade. Blake had grown up poor on the south side of Chicago. His mother, a schoolteacher, had raised Blake alone after his father abandoned them. Thanks to her, he had been able to attend school on an academic scholarship and graduate with a degree in criminal justice. Blake had aspired to have a career in law enforcement like his grandfather, and through hard work and perseverance, he had achieved his goal. Cole admired him, even though she never voiced that to Blake. And she knew that if his mother were alive, she'd be proud of him too.

"So how long are you going to make me sweat, Lieutenant?" Cole's tone was wary.

Blake shook his head. "I'm sure your intentions were good, but as of now, you're off this investigation."

Cole hopped out of the chair. "What? Without even hearing what kind of evidence I have?"

"Whatever you found, turn it over to Thomas. He'll work solo until I pair him with someone else."

"That's not fair, Blake. At least let me explain before you kick me off this case. With our history, I think you owe me that."

"Guilt won't work, Detective, especially when you know how adamant I am about not working a crime scene alone."

"I wasn't in any danger."

"That's not the point."

"I didn't corrupt the crime scene either."

"Again, not the point."

"Come on, Blake. You know I'm always careful. And please remind me of a time when guilt hasn't worked on you," she said with a laugh.

He smiled. "True, but you're not getting off that easily."

Cole unfastened her pack and removed the Ziploc bag with the pictures. Donning gloves, she removed the photos and placed them on Blake's desk in a horizontal row. "I think these will make you change your mind."

Blake scrutinized each image. "According to the dates on these, Mrs. Melendez knew about her husband's infidelity weeks before she said she caught him. The ones with Robert Melendez kissing Connie Gordon show they were more than friends."

"That's right. And the shot on the far left shows Robert buying a gun from someone in an alley. It's a bit blurry, but I'm certain that's him."

"Did we find a gun in the house?"

"No, but this proves that Mrs. Melendez also lied about Robert owning a gun."

"So she's dishonest. That doesn't make her a killer."

"There's more. Robert had three life insurance policies, each worth a million dollars."

Blake whistled. "That's definitely a motive."

"Yeah, I thought so too, which is why I decided to recheck Mrs. Melendez's financials. She has a separate bank account from her husband under her maiden name. There was a large withdrawal for $10,000 made right around the time the pictures were taken."

"You think she hired someone?"

"Yup. And because she was out of town when the murders happened, she has the perfect alibi."

"It's all circumstantial. Still not enough to hold her."

"I know, but it's a start."

"Did you verify her alibi?"

"I didn't get the chance. Kayla Bell is dead."

"What?" he said, his tone incredulous. "Isn't that the friend she visited in Florida?"

"Yes. The Miami PD identified her body using her driver's license."

"Cause of death?"

"She was murdered—shot at close range. Sound familiar?"

"Shit. This is unbelievable. Do they have any suspects?"

"No. I just found out a few hours ago. I spoke with a Detective Bolton, who's going to keep me aware of any new developments, including the ME's findings."

"It's not a coincidence that Mrs. Melendez's only alibi witness has been murdered. Has to be our guy."

"I agree. But that would mean he jumped on a plane the same day of the murders to get to Miami in time to kill Bell."

"Check all flights from here to Miami that would have taken off from the first two victims' time of death until this morning."

She smirked. "Already working on getting the passenger list."

"Does Mrs. Melendez know about her friend's death?"

"I had the unfortunate task of telling her."

"Was that before or after the arrest?"

"Does it matter?"

"I guess not." He warily gazed at her. "You need to play this straight, Tinks. No screwups."

Reflexively, Cole's spine straightened. Blake's subtle reference to her past mistakes hurt. The Cavanaugh case had been over a year ago, but it continued to haunt her. It had been her first case as a lead detective in the CID, and she'd compromised everything and everyone for a suspect. Her incompetence had almost cost Blake his life, so she couldn't fault him for questioning her ability to follow procedure. But Cole's acceptance of his feelings didn't change her feelings of inadequacy.

She inched her chin up and replied icily, "I will strictly adhere to protocol. You and the department have nothing to worry about."

"That's all I needed to hear. You can stay on this, but the first sign I see that it's too much—"

"I'll take myself off the case," she interrupted.

"That's good enough for me, Tinks. Please make sure Thomas is present when you interrogate Mrs. Melendez."

"I know the rules, Lieutenant," she asserted. "Unfortunately, I have no idea where he is."

"I'll locate him. Just stay put until then."

"I'll wait diligently in my cubicle like an obedient employee should," Cole stated derisively.

"Always the smart ass."

"You wouldn't have me any other way."

After receiving a call that the silent alarm had been activated, Bill hurried into HPS. Once he arrived, he punched in his code but didn't turn on the lights. He retrieved the .38 special from his jacket pocket and inched along the darkened hall. He noticed the soft glow coming from under Robert's door and raised his gun as he approached.

"Come in, Bill."

He recognized the voice and slowly entered the office. Once he was certain they were alone, he put his weapon away. He fixed his brown eyes on the documents scattered on the desk before turning his attention to the person seated in Robert's chair.

"What are you doing here?" Bill asked angrily. At six foot three, Bill was a formidable presence, but the intruder was undaunted.

"Protecting my interest. I didn't find anything in his records that identify me or any of us, but we both know those files are out there somewhere."

"I doubt they will ever turn up."

"Sounds like you know something, or you have them. Which one is it?"

"Neither."

"Why don't I believe you, Bill? You plan to finish what Robert started?"

"I know better than to double-cross you."

"I want to believe that, but I can't shake the feeling that you're going to fuck this up. And I will not go back to prison."

"That won't happen. I have everything under control," Bill proclaimed.

"What about Melissa? Does she know anything? Is she the one with the list and the photos?"

"Don't worry about Mrs. Melendez. It's handled." Bill glanced at the briefcase. "You have Robert's patients' files in there? Those documents can't leave this office."

"I don't have anything that doesn't belong to me," he affirmed malevolently.

Bill sighed and ran his hand through his dark hair. "You can't come here again."

"Don't get your designer boxers in a bunch. No one saw me. I came through the back."

"But if someone recognizes you ..."

"I paid you a lot of money to make sure no one does. Remember?"

"Yes, you did, but it's still not a good idea."

He stood. "As long as you deal with Robert's unfinished business, I won't be back. And Bill, you need a more serious weapon. My nephew carries a .38, and he's thirteen." His laughter echoed as he disappeared down the corridor.

Blake entered Cole's cubicle and sat on the corner of her desk. "I finally caught up with Thomas. He's at Hartford General. One of Robert Melendez's partners, George McCain, was shot this afternoon."

"You're kidding?"

"I wish I was."

"Who in the hell is doing this? There's no way it's the same guy."

"I doubt it. We got lucky on this one, though. He's alive, and Thomas went to speak to him."

"Hopefully, he'll give us some answers."

Blake couldn't mask his apprehension. "This investigation is going to be a tough one, Tinks. It's going to take a lot of time and effort. Are you sure you can manage it?"

"Yes. I have nothing but time for my job."

"No one knows that better than I do," Blake said solemnly.

Something in his voice made Cole uncomfortable. Seconds ticked by as the silence became awkward. "I should get back to work," she uttered self-consciously. "I have the digital forensics team checking the Melendezes' computer. I'm hoping there's something incriminating on the hard drive."

"What about phone records?"

"Nothing so far."

"Maybe she used a burner phone, and that's why you're coming up empty-handed."

"That's a definite possibility. I'll check into it after I get the cell phone tower records. If there are any pings that put Mrs. Melendez in Connecticut during the time of the murders, we'll know she lied about her whereabouts."

"What about Robert? Any luck with his past?"

"No. I still can't find anything in the database. It's like the man didn't exist before 1997."

"You'll figure it out, Tinks. You always do."

Cole blushed. "Thank you, Blake."

"Make sure you keep me updated on any changes in the case. And please be careful."

Her smile was forced. "I always am."

Blake struggled to calm his wayward thoughts. But he couldn't curtail the fear that churned in the pit of his stomach.

While she waited for Thomas to return, Cole searched passenger lists for flights to Miami on the night of the murders and the following morning. Only two of the passengers had criminal records, but neither gentleman had been arrested for violent crimes. That put Cole back to square one. She knew one of the 321 travelers was her killer; she just needed more than speculation to prove it. Cole dialed Thomas's number again and immediately heard it ringing nearby.

He walked into her cubicle with his phone raised in the air. "Can you hear me now?"

"You're an ass, Thomas. You know that, right? And please get a new ringtone. That one is obnoxious as hell."

"But I picked it just for you. Women love Beyoncé's 'Single Ladies.'"

"I don't."

"That's because you're a killjoy."

"I'd like to kill—"

"Please keep your murderous thoughts to yourself," he interjected. "Blake told me that you went to the Melendez house without me. I'm surprised. That's not like you."

"I didn't intend to. I wanted you to meet me there, but your phone went straight to voice mail."

Thomas's smile disappeared. "You keeping tabs on me, Cole? My wife left, remember? I don't owe any woman a play-by-play of my whereabouts."

"Aren't we touchy?" she derided. "You on your period, Thomas?"

He ignored her dig. "Just fill me in on what you found at the Melendez house."

"I'll share the incriminating pictures on our way to interview Mrs. Melendez. Did anything useful come out of your visit with McCain?"

"Sure did. When I asked him if he knew anyone who wanted him dead, guess who he named."

"You're kidding, right?"

"Nope. He fingered our girl."

"Let's go get her then."

Missy sat paralyzed in the interrogation room. Tiny beads of sweat formed on her brow as the walls started to close in around her. Missy had seen enough movies to recognize that the two-hour delay was a police tactic to try to secure a confession. The objective was to isolate her until she felt defenseless. Missy was claustrophobic, so she was concerned that their strategy might work. She took several deep breaths to calm her nerves and silently prayed that her dishonesty would be pardoned. Missy had opted not to disclose her dreams about Robert and the unknown woman to the detectives for fear of ridicule. She had known they wouldn't believe that she'd taken photos of just Robert but that when she developed the roll, he and his mistress had appeared together in the pictures. A place and time when they had met secretly in the past had manifested in the present on film. Each photo was time-stamped, so Missy had been able to identify the exact date of the encounter and corroborate their affair.

The door swung open. Cole and Thomas entered and sat in the chairs opposite Missy.

Cole glanced at her watch. "Is your father coming, Mrs. Melendez?"

"I called his office. He should be here soon."

"Do you want to call him again for an ETA?"

Before Missy could respond, Ted breezed into the room, followed by Detective Ulrich.

"I showed Mr. Delaney here so that he wouldn't get lost," Ulrich announced.

Thomas and Cole exchanged looks. "Thank you, Ulrich. I'm sure he wouldn't have found it by himself," Thomas stated disdainfully. "You can leave now."

Ted glowered at Cole as Ulrich exited the room. "Why in the hell is my daughter here again, Detective? What kind of circus are you running?" he bellowed.

"We have some important questions to ask Mrs. Melendez since we now have proof that she lied. Turns out she knew Robert was cheating long before he was killed," Cole said.

"And what's your alleged proof?"

"We found pictures of Robert and his mistress, Connie, in Mrs. Melendez's darkroom. According to the date stamped on the prints, they were taken thirteen days before his death."

"That's not enough to detain her, and you know it."

"Mrs. Melendez was also dishonest about Robert owning a gun. He bought a .22 a few weeks prior to his death."

"Melissa wasn't the one who purchased the gun; therefore, it's irrelevant."

"It's not irrelevant because she lied about it," Thomas declared.

Ted shook his head. "You're wasting our time, Detectives."

"That's not all, Mr. Delaney. Two days before the murder, there was a large withdrawal from Mrs. Melendez's bank account, enough to pay someone to—"

"I didn't hire someone to kill my husband!" Missy shrieked.

"Don't say another word, Melissa. The gun and money don't substantiate the allegation."

Cole smirked. "What about the almost five million dollars that Missy will inherit from Robert's life insurance policies?"

Missy gasped in shock. "What?"

"Are we supposed to believe that you didn't know about the insurance?" Cole's tone was incredulous.

"No, I knew he had insurance—we both did. I just didn't realize it was that much since Robert took care of everything." Missy paused, her confusion visible. "Why would he do that?"

"Your husband wanted to make sure you were well taken care of, Melissa," said her father. "There's nothing nefarious about that, despite what they're insinuating."

"Mrs. Melendez, do you know George McCain?" Thomas interjected.

"Of course, I do. He's one of Robert's partners."

"He was shot today."

"George was shot? When? Was it the same person who murdered my husband? Is he alive? Can I talk to him?"

"Whoa ... slow down, Mrs. Melendez," Thomas said. "This is an open investigation, so we can't answer that. What I can tell you is that when I talked to him, Mr. McCain admitted that he felt threatened by you."

"Why would George say that?" Missy asked incredulously. "I've never threatened anyone in my life."

"He specifically said your name. How do you explain that?"

Ted stood up. "She doesn't have to, Detective Thomas," he spouted angrily. "Let's go, Missy. This interview is over."

Missy glanced at Cole. "Are you sure, Daddy?"

Thomas nodded. "He's right, Mrs. Melendez. You're free to go."

"I will be talking to the mayor about your incompetence when he and I play golf this Sunday. You'll be lucky if you still have jobs after this fiasco," Ted avowed.

"We're just doing our jobs, Mr. Delaney. We will continue to do so until justice is served. It doesn't matter who you know."

Ted stormed out the room with Missy trailing behind him.

Thomas clapped. "Gotta hand it to you, Cole. You may be a woman, but you have the biggest balls I've ever seen. Now let's just hope we are both still employed by Monday morning."

Dani was drowning. She struggled to breathe while the liquid tentacles gripped her forcefully like a violent lover. As her will to live waned, she recalled the countless

times she had been thrust into the deep end of the pool as a child. Her cries had fallen on deaf ears each time, which had triggered the three-year-old's survival instincts. Still, there were occasions when Dani couldn't stay afloat. On those days, she was rescued by her father and then later punished. Over time, David Cole Sr.'s harsh instruction had transformed her into a practiced swimmer. However, the resentment Dani continued to harbor toward him made her want to surrender to her watery oppressor.

Seconds passed, and Dani sank lower onto the ocean floor. The waves reverberated in her waterlogged ears, but she could still perceive sound. Dani heard a female voice and directed her eyes to shore. She observed a woman's outstretched hand and sought to grab it, but her attempt was futile. Her arms and legs were paralyzed. She wanted to scream, but silence obliterated her. Dani's saturated lungs throbbed mercilessly as the tide engulfed her, and her savior's image faded into obscurity.

Cole gasped and sat up in bed. She knew the nightmare wasn't real, but that didn't lessen its effects. She'd had the same images intrude upon her subconscious before, but this occurrence had newly featured Missy. She could still hear the other woman's pleas for Cole to grab her hand. Missy's energy beckoned to Cole, her dynamism so powerful that even now it loomed around her. It calmed her terror and dissipated the cloud of loneliness that blanketed her. Cole was perplexed by a murder suspect's sudden incursion in her life, yet she inherently knew that Missy would play a significant role in her mental recovery.

Cole frowned at her musings. She'd finally acknowledged her desire to be rehabilitated, which signaled progress. However, she knew there was someone else who needed it more. Cole thought about her younger brother, David, whom she hadn't spoken to in years. They had been inseparable as children until a traumatizing event had caused a rift between them. Neither sibling discussed the incident, but it had transformed their family dynamic. Their environment had turned hostile, and that hostility was frequently directed at Cole. She had wrapped herself in denial to survive her journey into adulthood, whereas David had used manipulation to cope. His exploitation of others had advanced him in the business world, but Cole saw beyond his facade. She knew that he was an insecure man who drank too much and beat his wife. Cole found his behavior to be objectionable, but their parents had extolled his inadequacies and covered up his violence. Consequently, she blamed them for his disreputable actions.

The doorbell rang, and Cole glanced at her phone for the time. She climbed out of bed, donned her slippers and robe, and then made her way down the stairs to the living room. Cole turned on a lamp and peered out the window to see Lieutenant Blake on her doorstep. She became flustered as she thought about her messy hair and the bags under her eyes.

Cole opened the door. "To what do I owe the pleasure of your company, Lieutenant?"

Blake gawked at her. Cole's diminutive figure stood out like a beautiful silhouette in the moonlight that spilled into the room. Blake noted the pink robe with the matching fluffy slippers and thought that Cole was the sexiest woman he'd ever seen. His body tightened as he resisted the urge to run his fingers through her unruly hair.

Cole waved her hand in his face. "Earth to Blake."

Blake cleared his throat. "Sorry, my mind was someplace else."

"Clearly." She stepped aside. "Come on in."

Blake entered and perused the living room. It was painted a soft eggshell color, and there were no pictures or decorations adorning the walls. The setting was utilitarian, with nothing more than a sofa, a chaise longue, and a coffee table filling the space. He spotted the boxes lined up in the corner and shook his head. "Tinks, it's been five years since you moved in here. When are you going to unpack the rest of your boxes and make this place a home?"

"I'm working on it, but it's hard because I'm never here." She closed the door. "Can I get you something to drink?"

"When we were partners, you never offered me food or beverages."

"I've turned over a new leaf."

His grin was wide. "Hmm, I like this new you. So what do you have to offer?"

"Excuse me?" She hesitated. "Oh … you mean beverages?"

"Yes. What did you think I meant?"

"Nothing. It must be this headache."

His eyes glimmered with concern. "You're still getting those? Are they as bad as before?"

"Yes, but I'm on different medication now. If I take a pill at the onset of my symptoms, I'm back to normal in about twenty minutes."

"That's great, Tinks. I remember all the times you were in pain, and there wasn't a damn thing I could do about it. It's hard taking an oath to protect and serve when you can't even protect the person you care about the most," he said earnestly.

Cole stared at Blake and glimpsed the yearning in his eyes. She attempted to look away but couldn't muster the strength. The atmosphere in the room shifted as an electric current passed between them. They both found it difficult to breathe as the tension increased.

Cole finally broke the spell. "Um … there wasn't anything you could do, Blake," she stammered. "Don't beat yourself up about it. Uh … I'm going to run and get you that drink."

Cole scurried into the kitchen, where she trod back and forth across the floor. *There's no way the butterflies in my stomach are real. Blake simply caught me at a vulnerable time, that's all.* She stopped and opened the refrigerator door. The Styrofoam village inside mocked her, reminding Cole of her unhealthy eating habits and schedule. *There's no place in my life for love.* She removed a bottle of water and headed back into the living room.

He gazed at the bottle and then at her. "So all this fuss was about water?"

She refused to look at him. "Yup. Either take it or leave it."

He took the bottle from her and sat down. "I guess I should be happy you didn't bring me faucet water."

"I thought about it." Cole took a seat in the chaise across from him. She pretended to organize the periodicals on the table to avoid the sexual energy that continued to linger in the room. She had bought the magazines to help her find ways to beautify her house, but they had merely ended up as decoration for the redwood.

"I bet you haven't read any of those," he taunted.

"That's none of your business."

He laughed. "That means I'm right."

She ignored him. "So when are you going to tell me why you're here, Blake?"

"Just cut to the chase, huh?"

"You know I like to keep it professional."

"How could I forget?"

She heard the dejection in his voice. "Blake ..."

"It's not important. I dropped by to tell you that I got a call from the mayor's office this evening. As I mentioned before, Mr. Delaney and the mayor are old golfing buddies. He requested that I allow Mrs. Melendez to attend her best friend's funeral in Miami."

"Are you freaking serious? Daddy's money buys her a one-way ticket out of town and to freedom? That's not fair, Blake, and you know it."

"I know it's not, Tinks, but you understand how politics work. You're my best detective, and I need your full cooperation on this."

"A compliment? You must want something."

"You know me well. I agreed to let Mrs. Melendez go to the funeral with one stipulation: an officer accompanies her." He waited for an outburst and was stunned by Cole's initial silence instead.

"And I'm that officer?"

"Yes."

"So because I'm a woman, I get the babysitting gig."

"That's not true, Tinks. If you go to Miami, you can talk to the detective working on Kayla Bell's case and determine if there's a connection."

"Fortunately for you, I've already considered that possibility."

"Well, that explains why I didn't get the anticipated outburst."

"Exactly. When do I leave?"

"Sometime next week. Mrs. Melendez wants to have her husband's funeral this week even though the ME hasn't released the body yet."

"A memorial service?"

"Yes. It could be a while before she can bury the body."

"Maybe we should have extra guys there."

"Already done. I thought it would be a good idea with two, potentially three, deaths that may involve Missy Melendez, plus our GSW vic."

"It'll be interesting to see who shows up."

"I'm just hoping that it doesn't turn into a media circus."

"That's a pretty unrealistic hope given the amount of coverage this case has already received. What will Thomas do without me?"

"He's going to continue working the McCain angle and checking out some of the practice's patients."

"That's good. I know someone botching up my boob job or giving me a nose where my lips should be would make me want to kill them."

He nodded in agreement. "I'm glad you're okay with this, Tinks. I thought I was going to have to pull rank to get you to do it."

"You can use your authority anytime you want, Blake."

"What?"

She blushed. "Not like that. Get your mind out of the gutter."

"That would be a lot easier if you weren't walking around here in a robe and pink fluffy slippers. It's so girly. Not to mention your hair being down. I've never seen you like this before."

"Pink slippers turn you on, Blake?"

"They can be sexy on some women." He emphasized each word, his eyes never leaving hers.

Awareness flickered between them and intensified like kindling added to an already burning flame. Cole's mouth went dry. She quickly stood, breaking the trance. "Thanks for coming by and letting me know what's going on." She moved toward the door and opened it.

He rose and followed her. "I guess we're through here," he stated dejectedly.

"I'll see you in the morning," she said, a little too enthusiastically.

"Goodnight, Tinks. Sleep tight," he whispered.

She averted her gaze. "I will. Goodnight, Lieutenant."

Blake hesitated for a few seconds and then strolled wordlessly through the entranceway.

Cole closed the door and muttered, "I'm in deep trouble."

Dr. Bill Roman tried to remain calm as he sat in the small, dimly lit room, but with each passing second, his anger escalated. He blamed Robert for his current predicament and silently berated himself for ever having approached him about becoming partners. At the time, he had felt he had no other choice. He and Robert were rivals, and Bill had lost several of his loyal clients to the younger doctor. Bill wasn't surprised since Robert was more skilled with a scalpel than anyone he'd seen in his thirty-year career. Robert promised to give his patients a new identity and consistently delivered, which was why he had been deemed "the miracle worker." Bill realized that he couldn't compete with Robert's talent, so he asked him to join HPS as lead surgeon. Robert declined Bill's initial proposal but changed his mind once he was offered 55 percent of the company's profits. From then on, even though Bill was the owner on paper, Robert had been in charge, which had created tension within the practice. The other partners had felt they had to pick sides, and most had chosen Robert.

Bill tried to tamp down his resentment as Cole and Thomas entered the room and introduced themselves. "I would like to get this over with quickly, Detectives. I have a business to run, and with one partner dead and another in the hospital, it's chaotic right now."

Cole nodded. "We understand, Dr. Roman, and we won't take up much of your time. Before we get started, would you like something to drink? Coffee? Water?"

"No, thanks. Your questions please?"

Thomas sat across from Bill, and Cole took the seat next to him.

"Do you think any of Robert's patients could have killed him?" Thomas asked pointedly. "Like someone who wasn't satisfied with the results of their surgery?"

"No. Robert's reputation was spotless. He had an eight-month waiting list. Clients even flew in from other countries for a consultation, so I doubt anyone was unhappy."

Cole detected an edge in his voice. "Were you jealous of his recognition, Dr. Roman?"

Bill chuckled. "Yes, I was a bit envious of him. But not enough to kill him, if that's what you're getting at. Robert was an arrogant ass, but he had that right because he was an excellent surgeon."

"So because he was good at nose jobs, he had a right to be a complete douche?"

"Yes, he earned it," Bill insisted. "Let me show you something." He pulled out his phone and went to Robert's Facebook page. "This is the result of the last surgery Robert did before he died. The client posted it on Facebook Live and tagged him in the video. He shows a picture of what he used to look like before he unveils his new face." He laid his phone on the table so that Cole and Thomas could watch. When the video ended, Bill went to Robert's Instagram page and showed them all the before and after photos posted by former patients. "See? You have it all wrong, Detective Cole. Being a plastic surgeon is about more than rhinoplasty. It's about improving the self-esteem for a burn victim and—"

Cole interrupted. "I get it, Dr. Roman. And thanks for the show, but you're trying to sell the wrong person. I live on a cop's salary and can't afford your services."

Bill studied her face. "Personally speaking, you don't need it."

Taken aback by his unsolicited adulation, Cole lowered her head to mask her embarrassment.

"I apologize, Detective. I didn't mean to make you self-conscious. Just stating the truth. You're a beautiful woman who doesn't require cosmetic work." His scrutiny intensified. "Do you know how much my clients would pay for those cheekbones?"

This is a creepy moment, thought Cole. "No, but thank you for the compliment, Dr. Roman," she said. "Now can we get back to our discussion?"

"Despite how you feel about plastic surgery, Detective Cole, others don't share your viewpoint. Robert made his clients look and feel their best, which you saw in the video. That's why many treated him like a god. I honestly don't think he cared if a few detested him. It was a small price to pay for being wealthy and successful."

Cole couldn't hide her annoyance. "And soulless."

Before Bill could retort, Thomas redirected the conversation. "Do you know of anyone in Robert's personal life who would have wanted him dead, Dr. Roman?"

"You would have to ask George or Robert's wife that question. We didn't socialize outside of the office. He had his circle of friends, and I had mine."

"I would have thought that the two of you traveled in the same circles," said Cole. *The rich, pompous snobs' club.*

"Not at all, Detective Cole. Robert wasn't our type."

And racist too. "Why? Because he was Hispanic?"

"I'm not a bigot, Detective. I didn't care what nationality Robert was. It's just that, well, he was different. He was a loner who kept to himself. My wife and I invited him out several times, but he always refused. Eventually, we stopped asking. It was evident that he wanted it to be just him and Melissa. No outsiders."

"What about his relationship with George?" Thomas asked. "You said we should ask him about Robert, so they must have been closer."

"He and George were friendly but not friends in the true sense of the word. Robert tolerated, for lack of a better word, George—or more like exploited him. He was Robert's lap dog. He did whatever Robert wanted, no questions asked. If Robert couldn't control you, then you weren't of any use to him. He made that apparent in his dealings in and outside the practice."

"A real charmer," Thomas mumbled.

"You have no idea."

"Did you notice any changes in Robert's behavior over the last few months, Mr. Roman?"

"I have to admit, he was acting a bit strange. He postponed all of his surgeries just weeks before his death. If it was an emergency procedure, he gave it to either George or myself. In my opinion, he was sick and didn't want to tell anyone. He seemed a bit pale and forgetful at times. I had the feeling that he was afraid to perform an operation for fear he'd make a mistake and ruin his reputation."

"What do you think was wrong with him?"

"I'm not sure, Detective Thomas. It could have been something as simple as carpal tunnel or even arthritis. I saw him take pills one night when he thought he was alone."

"Did his wife know?"

"I doubt it. Robert was excellent at keeping secrets."

"I see." Cole glanced at Thomas, who nodded. "I think that's all for now, Mr. Roman," she proclaimed. "We'll be in touch."

CHAPTER 4

SERGEANT JASON MERCK SAT IN THE shadows, with his gun strategically placed on his lap. His car was sweltering from the heat, but because he was in the worst neighborhood in Hartford, he couldn't risk rolling down the windows. It wasn't the corners piled with rubble or the dilapidated houses that whispered of the residents' impoverished suffering to Merck, but more the hopelessness that hovered over the community like a thunderous storm cloud. After working some of the meanest boroughs in New York, he had grown accustomed to depravity and misfortune. However, in his fifteen-year career, Merck had never witnessed such impudence. Even at 2:05 a.m., the streets were booming with criminal activity. It was obvious the police had abandoned the residents, which made it the ideal location to meet an informant. Merck didn't know the guy personally, but he felt this informant was vital to his investigation. Typically, he would use less sanctioned methods to obtain information from such a disreputable character, but Merck was determined to follow the rules this time. He didn't want to repeat the mistakes he'd made a few months ago. If his wife discovered the real reason he'd transferred to Hartford, she'd leave him. Merck couldn't afford to lose his family, particularly now that his wife Marie was in the last trimester of her pregnancy. Thus far, he'd been able to keep his suspension a secret, but Merck knew it was only a matter of time before she and everyone else discovered the truth. He was determined to solve this case before that happened.

The tap on the window surprised Merck. He recognized his late-night visitor from the picture that had been texted to him earlier. "You're late," he reprimanded as the other man climbed into the passenger seat.

"I almost didn't come. Nice alley, by the way," he said.

"I picked a spot where you'd fit right in," Merck said derisively. "Now let's get down to business."

The man handed him a piece of paper. "You were right. Melendez changed the faces of the fifteen guys on that list and gave them new identities. There are others, but those are the only ones I could get."

Merck extracted a penlight from his shirt pocket and clicked it on. He was familiar with the names and their various offenses, but he hadn't realized that Melendez had performed surgery on so many felons. That fact made his job more difficult.

"My source says Melendez was blackmailing them. He had files on each person with their birth name, a copy of their fake ID, before and after photos, and known addresses."

"Everything needed to find a ghost."

"Exactly."

"So his patients were paying him to keep their real identities a secret?"

"Yeah, the ones who had something to hide. I bet it was a sweet deal until Melendez got greedy and blackmailed the wrong person."

"If that's true, then it was probably a professional hit."

"I've heard a few things that back up that theory, but if you want more info, it'll cost you."

Merck shook his head. "That wasn't our agreement."

He smirked. "I changed my mind."

Merck reached for his gun, but the visitor was faster.

The informant seized Merck's weapon and aimed it at his chest. "It would be a shame to get killed with your own weapon, Detective. And if they found your body in this neighborhood, they'd think you were dirty." He opened the door and tossed the gun out.

While the other man was preoccupied with the disposal of his weapon, Merck stealthily removed a knife from his jacket and unfolded it. "You're wasting your time threatening me. I'm not going to pay you."

"Too bad, Merck. I'd hate for something to happen to your wife and baby."

"Don't you dare bring my family into this," Merck uttered through clenched teeth.

He chortled. "Why? What are you going to do? Shoot me?"

Merck extended his arm and stabbed the other man in the neck. He gasped, and his eyes bulged as he clutched Merck's shirt. Merck swatted his hand away and climbed out of the car. He scanned his surroundings before walking around to the passenger side in search of his gun. Once he found it, he tucked it in his waistband. Merck opened the door, withdrew the body, and laid the man none-too-gently on the ground. He bent down and glared into the other man's eyes, where his agony was clear. Merck extracted his knife and watched as the blood spurted from the wound like a broken faucet. The man tried to cover his wound, but his hand rapidly turned crimson.

"You got blood all over my favorite knife, jackass." Merck grabbed a tissue from his pocket, cleaned and folded the blade, then placed both back into his jacket. "If you're lucky, someone will find you before you bleed out. But be warned, if anything happens to even a hair on my wife's head, I will hunt you down. And death will not be swift. I will torture you until you beg me to spare your life."

Merck frowned as the man's eyes rolled back in his head and he passed out. "Shit. Another corpse on my watch. So much for protocol," he mumbled.

Missy heard voices as she lay beneath the covers in the pitch-black room. She glanced at the clock on the nightstand and wondered whom her father could be talking to at 3:15 a.m. She turned over in an attempt to ignore the heated exchange, but the volume increased. Missy had forgotten how easily sound carried through the vent in her bedroom. As a child, she had thought it was a magical box because it allowed Missy to listen to conversations her parents deemed too mature for her. Missy always felt closer to them after eavesdropping on their discussions. The love and devotion they displayed through their words and actions reflected the type of relationship she desired as an adult. However, on the night of her tenth birthday, she had realized that their happiness was nothing more than a fabrication. And suddenly, those small slits on the floor had become oppressive with burdens too heavy for her tiny shoulders to bear.

Exhausted from her birthday party that afternoon, Missy had gone to bed early, but a howl of pain in the wee hours of the morning forced her awake. Concerned, she leaped out of bed and placed her ear to the vent. Missy listened intently as her father tried to calm her mother. "I'm so sorry you lost the baby, Maggie. I honestly thought having another child would give you the courage to forgive me. But instead, I've imposed more hurt on you. I was wrong in thinking that Samuel could fix us. Now I'm not sure if we'll ever be able to restore our marriage to what it once was before my indiscretions."

Her father's words triggered something in Missy, and flashes of him kissing another woman intermingled with visions of her mother lying in a pool of blood. A baby's incessant cries accompanied the image, followed by her mother's ear-piercing screams. Missy saw the boy's features and knew instinctively that he was her brother. A part of her wanted desperately to hold him, but the other part was relieved that he'd passed away. She sensed that something horrific was coming, and she didn't want Samuel to suffer.

Missy didn't understand how she was able to glimpse her parents' private moments, but she knew the visions weren't isolated incidents. Frightened of her new abilities, Missy hopped back into bed and covered her head with a pillow. But hiding didn't ease the anguish that tormented her mind. With her face drenched in silent tears, she mourned her brother, the marriage she had thought was faultless, and the loss of her innocence.

The intensity of the voices below snapped Missy out of her reverie. They weren't raised in anger, but the tone worried Missy. She sat up and turned on the nearby lamp. She threw her legs over the side of the bed and quietly exited the room. As she descended the steps, an ominous feeling came over her. *I will not lose my father too.* She picked up the pace, and within seconds, she stood before the sliding doors that separated the kitchen from the living room. *Should I walk in? If I do, and he's not in trouble, he'll be livid that I interrupted his meeting. Do I want to take that chance?* Missy was about to knock when a familiar voice gave her pause.

"I don't care what Robert did. He's dead now, so it doesn't matter."

"Lower your voice. I do not want you to wake my daughter."

"God forbid that your precious Melissa discover what a liar and cheat you are."

"It's time for you to leave."

"Not until you tell me when I can expect my money."

"I have nothing to do with that. I didn't hire you, so it is not my responsibility to pay you."

"Fuck that. You didn't hire me, but you're involved. And if I don't get my $100,000 soon, I'll make sure everybody knows how you helped get your son-in-law murdered."

Ted's tone turned hostile. "I had nothing to do with what happened to Robert. And please refrain from cursing in my home. I deplore gutter talk."

He chuckled. "The famous attorney hates gutter talk but hangs with people straight out of the gutter. Go figure."

"I'll show you out."

"I'll go, but we're not done."

"Yes, we are. And if I were you, I'd keep that in mind the next time you decide to show up at my house. I'm sure you don't want to end up like Robert."

The doors opened, and Missy hastily ran deeper into the darkened kitchen. She slumped against the wall and took a deep breath. She could hear her heart beating feverishly in her ears as she prayed that she wouldn't be spotted.

Once they were at the front door, Missy tried to catch a glimpse of the other man. She couldn't see his face, but he was short, stocky, and bald. *I'm pretty sure he was one of Robert's patients. That's why he seems so familiar.* Missy watched him exit and waited for her father to go upstairs. Ted didn't immediately comply. Instead, he headed back to the living room and glanced around. *Is he making sure there's no evidence of his late-night visitor?* Satisfied, he turned out the light and left the room.

When Missy was sure he was gone, she stepped out from her hiding place and positioned herself in the spot her father had just vacated. She attempted to pick up on Ted's energy in hopes that it would reveal what his involvement was in Robert's death, but her efforts were ineffective. Missy tried again but was blocked by a mental force so powerful that it caused her physical pain.

It was too dark for Missy to see Ted leaning over the banister, watching her. "Sorry about the headache, Melissa, but I can't let you access my subconscious. I learned to control what my mother saw, and I can control you too," he whispered into the shadows.

As Cole predicted, the memorial service was a media circus. She hovered in the back of the church and surveyed the reporters, photographers, and mourners wandering around in search of a seat. In her opinion, there wasn't enough manpower present to handle things if a situation became too unruly. And with so many people's lives possibly at stake, she needed the funeral to run smoothly.

Cole looked around for Blake and spotted him a few feet away, speaking with an officer. She waved him over, and as he slowly approached, her pulse began to race. Cole yearned for Blake to hold her and to feel the warmth of his body against hers. But her head quickly overruled the sentiment of her heart. She couldn't allow herself to fall in love, not again.

Blake sighed. "This is going to be a long day."

Cole took several deep breaths to calm her rapid heartbeat. "Yeah, for both of us."

"Are you okay? You look a little flustered."

"I'm fine. It's hot with everyone crammed in here. And the extra people are why I called you over. Do you think we should get more officers to cover this spectacle, just in case? We can post them outside."

"Adams and another rookie are already on their way."

Cole smiled. "Did you forget the other kid's name?"

"Of course, but that's because I'm old. What's your excuse?"

"You're assuming I don't remember it."

"It's not an assumption. We both know how terrible you are with names. It took you three days to memorize mine."

"That's not true. It was only two."

Laughter filled the small space between them but soon shifted to an awkward silence. The air crackled with electricity as they gazed at each other. Cole was mesmerized by the longing she saw in Blake's eyes and inched closer. She opened her mouth to speak, but someone brushed against her and ruined the moment. Cole was frustrated by the interruption but thankful for the reminder that they were still on duty.

"I, uh, should go check on Mrs. Melendez," Cole mumbled.

Blake shook his head. "How long are we going to do this, Tinks?"

Cole feigned innocence. "Do what?"

"Pretend that there's nothing between us. I miss my …"

"Your what?"

He hesitated. "My … partner. But I know we'll never have that again. It's just—"

Cole interrupted him. "This is not the time or the place to talk about this. I have a job to do, so please let me do it."

Blake moved aside to let her pass. "Go to it, Detective."

"I'll be back in a few minutes," she whispered.

Cole tried not to bump into anyone as she rushed down the aisle. She hated what was happening with Blake, but she wasn't sure how to fix it. Since that night at her house, Cole had been avoiding him. A part of her wanted to maintain her distance to keep her feelings at bay, but that meant she'd lose her only friend.

Cole silently admitted that she'd been behaving childishly. On the days she couldn't escape Blake, she had refused to look him in the eye. Blake's reaction had been to simply refer to her as Detective Cole, instead of using her nickname. Cole had grown so accustomed to "Tinks" that whenever he addressed her formally, it hurt. That unfamiliar emotion was forcing Cole to reevaluate her relationship with him, and what her heart was revealing deeply troubled her.

"Detective Cole?"

The voice startled her. Cole turned to face its owner, and her shock immediately turned to anger. "What are you doing here, David?"

"Is that any way to speak to your long-lost brother?"

"Don't be coy. Why are you here?"

"Susan insisted on coming."

"What? How does she know the victim?"

"The doc did a little work on her."

Cole was taken aback. "Why would your wife need a plastic surgeon?"

"If you must know, she had a small mishap, and Dr. Melendez took care of her."

"Why didn't anyone call me?"

"I assumed Mom would tell you."

Cole shook her head. "She didn't."

"Maybe she thought you wouldn't be interested since you never call or come by the house."

"I call Mom," Cole insisted. "She never returns my messages or texts."

"Whose fault is that, Danielle? You've been MIA for so long that even my boys have forgotten what you look like."

Cole cringed at his words. She knew he was trying to press her buttons like he had when they were children, but she refused to take the bait. "Just tell me what happened to Susan."

"She fell down the stairs and broke some bones in her nose and jaw. You know how clumsy she can be."

"Her clumsiness is from you using her like a punching bag."

David remained calm in the face of her accusation. "Now what reason could I possibly have to harm my wife? You really have a vivid imagination, Danielle."

"You know I hate that name." *Especially when you and Dad say it.*

"Would you prefer to be called The Executioner?"

With eyes ablaze with hatred, Cole lunged at him. "You vile son of a bitch!" she shrieked.

Blake emerged from the corner and inserted himself between them. "Cole, you can't do this," he whispered.

"You better listen to your knight in shining armor, or you could easily end up like Susan."

Cole pushed against him to get to her brother, but Blake was too strong.

"Get the hell away from me, David."

"Your anger just proves why you shouldn't be allowed to carry a weapon, Danielle. You're clearly unstable." He gazed at Blake. "I thought you would have left her by now, Detective, especially after she almost got you killed."

Blake balled his hands into fists. "It's Lieutenant now. And you should go find a seat. The funeral is about to start."

"Oh, you're her boss now? Interesting. I guess my sister nearly getting you killed paid off," he stated snidely. "Next time, you may not be so lucky." He glanced over Blake's shoulder. "Nice seeing you, Danielle. I'll give everyone your regards."

Blake waited until he was out of earshot before he spoke. "That man is pure evil."

"He wasn't always that way. My father did that to him."

"I'm sorry. I know how much your family gets to you. I'm just glad that I recognized David and was able to intervene before you did something you'd regret."

"Thank you, Blake. I …"

"No need, Tinks. I'm always here for you. That's what knights in shining armor are for, right?"

She smiled. "Right." *But I can never be your damsel in distress.*

"Now go talk to Mrs. Melendez and make sure everything is okay. I'll meet you in the back."

Missy was transfixed by the exchange between Cole and the man who had to be her brother. Based on their striking resemblance, Missy guessed they must be siblings. She couldn't hear the conversation, but Missy was subjected to every second of Cole's pain and anger through her connection to that fragile piece of the detective. Missy wished that she could sever her bond with Cole. She'd never experienced such a powerful connection with anyone, and it frightened her.

Missy watched Cole as she approached the pew. She wanted to hug her, but Missy knew that would be awkward, especially with her father seated next to her. "Are you okay, Detective Cole?"

"I'm fine. Guess you didn't know that I moonlight as a boxer," she teased. "Anyway, I should be asking you that."

"Why am I not surprised that my daughter's grief is a joke to you, Detective? After all, you've shown us repeatedly how incompetent you are. You're supposed to be breaking up fights, not participating in one. You're not a real cop; you're just playing dress-up."

Ted's words crushed Cole as he unknowingly exposed one of her deepest fears. After what had transpired with the Cavanaugh case, Cole believed she was no longer a good cop. Every day when she donned her gun and badge, she felt like a fraud. She wanted to quit, but her career was the only viable thing in her life. Without it, she would perish.

Missy was so overwhelmed by Cole's vulnerability that she felt suffocated. She watched the emotions race across her face and knew that the other woman was about to crumble. She had to somehow prevent Cole's disintegration, or

Missy would go spiraling with her. Missy hoped she could keep her father from making things worse.

"Daddy, you can't do this here. It's not right."

"Tell that to Detective Cole. She shouldn't be airing her dirty laundry at your husband's funeral."

"I'm . . ." Cole's voice was temporarily debilitated as she choked back tears. "I'm sorry. My conduct was unprofessional, and it won't happen again."

"That's not good enough, Detective Cole. I will be calling your superior in the morning and reporting this farce. I want you off this investigation immediately."

Embarrassed, Cole attempted to slink away, but Missy grabbed her hand. Cole glanced into the other woman's eyes, and what she saw glistening in their depths shattered her. Cole wanted to scream, but her lips were sealed. The room spun, and the lone sound was a buzzing in Cole's ears. Tears streamed unchecked, and she could no longer breathe. She sensed the darkness, but just as she was about to descend into its pits, Missy tightened her grip. A powerful current passed between them, and it seemed to revitalize Cole.

Once Cole's strength was restored, Missy abruptly released her. Cole thought she might fall but through sheer willpower remained upright. Confused by what had transpired, she gawked at Missy, who quickly averted her gaze.

"I hope you're feeling better, Detective Cole. I will see you in the morning," Missy murmured dismissively.

"Wait. How did you do that?"

Just then, the reverend appeared at the podium and asked everyone to be seated. Cole ignored him and kneeled at the end of the pew where Missy was seated. Cole laid her hand on top of Missy's, but Missy quickly yanked hers away.

"Will you please talk to me?" Cole pleaded. *I must understand what just happened.*

"You need to leave so that my daughter can grieve in peace," said Missy's father. "You will have the opportunity to speak with her tomorrow on your way to Miami—that is, if you're still lead on this case."

Still shaken, Cole stood. She opened her mouth to speak but sensed Missy's sorrow. The single tear that ran down the widow's cheek reminded

Cole of her insensitivity. She whispered, "I'm sorry," and departed without another word.

The service began, and Missy wept for Cole. She had given the broken detective everything she had, and she was exhausted from their encounter. She hated ignoring Cole, but she couldn't explain something that she didn't fully comprehend. Besides, she just didn't have the energy.

She cried for Robert and the life they would never have together. But the real grief came from guilt. She hadn't wanted Robert to die. But if it not for his death, Missy never would have met Danielle Cole. And for that, she was eternally grateful.

"Did you take care of it?"

"Yes. I mixed the poison in with her migraine medication. The substance is tasteless and odorless, so she won't realize what's hit her until it's too late."

"How soon?"

"She's only getting it in small doses, so it could take weeks."

"We don't have that kind of time."

"There's time. She doesn't know anything."

"You better hope so. We don't want this whole thing to blow up in our faces."

"It won't. The poison will eradicate Detective Cole before she figures it out." He paused. "You know, if he finds out what you're doing, he'll kill you."

"He won't realize that we had anything to do with it if you tie up loose ends."

"I have it under control."

"Good. Our lives depend on it."

Susan Cole sat on the sofa and waited for David to return from his business trip. With every second that ticked by, she agonized over the person she'd become during their eight-year marriage. She restlessly stood up and walked over to the mirror that hung above the fireplace. Susan didn't recognize the woman with stringy blonde hair and pale complexion who screamed obscenities back at her. She traced the scar on her left cheek, a constant reminder of David's cruelty, and let the tears flow. Gone was the vibrant, curvaceous woman with sparkling green eyes that she once had been; she now was a shell of her former self—unwanted and unloved.

Susan sadly acknowledged that it was the transformation in her appearance that had compelled David to cheat. For months, she'd suspected that he was lying about his whereabouts, but now she had proof. She turned and glanced at the evidence scattered on the living room table. She'd found David's stash of DVDs, as well as a gun, while cleaning the garage. Each disc showed David doing unspeakable things to other women, which sickened her. However, Susan was more repulsed by the presence of a gun with two small children in the house.

Susan was terrified to confront her husband, but the cold steel in her hand gave her courage. She wanted her kids to live in a safe environment devoid of the violence she'd undergone throughout her years with David. She had allowed him to make her subservient, but Susan knew that it was time to take a stand. She couldn't continue to be David's physical and emotional punching bag.

Susan heard David's car pull into the driveway and wiped the tears from her face. She was relieved that her oldest son was at school, and her three-year-old was asleep upstairs. Typically, David waited until the boys were in bed before he beat her. But this time, she wasn't sure he'd be able to control himself.

David noticed the clutter the moment he walked into the living room. He hated for things to be out of place and considered Susan's untidiness a betrayal. He briefly closed his eyes and contemplated the different ways he would punish her. "What the hell is wrong with you, Susan? Why do you have this mess lying around?"

Susan remained silent as she walked over to where he stood, the gun hidden behind her back.

"Do you hear me talking to you?"

"Why, David?" she uttered.

"Why what?" He glanced at the items on the table again and finally realized what they were. "You nosy bitch," he spat.

"How could you do this to me, David?" she asked, her voice full of disappointment.

"Do what? Have sex? Try new things that might interfere with your prim and proper Catholic upbringing? I'm a man with needs, Susan, or has it been so long that you've forgotten that?"

"How could I ever forget about your needs, David, when you've forced me time and time again to remember?"

"I've never made you do anything except perform your wifely duties. Now if you have a problem with that, you can always leave. But wait … where would you go? What would you do? You have no money, no skills, and no family. You're officially screwed," he stated maliciously. He picked up a DVD. "Or should I say I'm the one who's been screwed … and well. Maybe I'll get the young lady on here to come over and show you a few tricks. You could use some lessons."

Susan's hands shook uncontrollably as she pointed the gun at him. "You've ridiculed me for the last time, David. I'm not going to take it anymore."

David laughed raucously. "Put the gun down, Susan. You don't have the guts to kill me."

"You don't know me, David."

"I know you're a weak woman who will only shoot me if I tell you to. So go ahead and pull the trigger, Susan," he goaded.

The sound of the baby crying wrenched Susan out of her angry stupor. A single tear rolled down her cheek as she realized that David was right—she wasn't brave enough to pull the trigger and leave her children without a father. Suddenly, the 9 mm felt like hot coals in her hands, and she dropped it. The gun tumbled to the floor and went off, the blast echoing in the room. Susan watched in slow motion as blood stained David's shirt, and he collapsed on the carpet. Overwhelmed by what she'd done, a wave of dizziness assailed Susan. The room started to spin, and before she lost consciousness, Susan thought *Who will take care of my babies?*

Cole strode down the aisle of the airplane in search of Mrs. Melendez. She sensed the indignant stares of the other passengers, but Cole ignored their disdain. She'd inconvenienced most of them by having the airline hold the flight for her, but she'd had to stop at the drugstore to get her migraine medication before boarding. She couldn't go to Miami for several days without her pills.

Cole spotted Missy in a center seat, with a gentleman sitting next to her on the aisle. She excused herself, and they moved into the aisle to accommodate her. Cole slid into the window seat, placed her small carry-on bag under the chair in front of her, and buckled her safety belt.

Missy sat beside her. "Running a little late, aren't you, Detective?"

Cole shrugged. "I had something important to do."

"Police business, I assume."

"Of course. Why else would they hold the plane for me?" *I wonder if she can tell that I'm lying. After yesterday, I'm not so sure that she can't.* "How are you holding up, Mrs. Melendez?"

"It's Missy. And I've been better. I never imagined that I'd be burying my husband and best friend one right after the other."

"This has to be hard for you. I'm surprised your dad didn't come along for support."

"He had an important business meeting in New York. He's going to try to fly out in time for the funeral."

"I hope he can make it. You need your family during this difficult time."

"Thank you. But as much as you dislike my dad, why would you want him there?"

"My opinion of him doesn't matter, Missy. He's just trying to protect you."

"That's true. And with Robert and Kayla gone, he's all I have left."

"You don't have other friends?"

"No. I was too busy trying to be a good wife. There was never time to make new friends."

"I understand completely."

They both fell silent as the flight attendant pointed out the emergency exits. Cole surreptitiously glanced at Missy while the woman detailed how to use their seat cushions as flotation devices. Cole wanted to ask her about what had happened at the funeral, but she was terrified to hear the truth.

"I know you're dying to ask me about yesterday, so what are you waiting for?" Missy inquired.

So she can read minds too? "I couldn't sleep because of what transpired between us. How were you able to do that?"

"What exactly was I able to do, Detective?"

"You somehow transferred your energy to me. It was like I had a low battery, and you were able to recharge it when you grabbed my hand."

"I prayed for you, so it was God who gave you that strength, not me."

Cole glared at her in disbelief. "So you're saying it had nothing to do with you?"

"Do you have another logical explanation?" *Maybe I should be honest with her. She may be open to hearing it now.*

"I don't believe in some magical being who dictates what happens in my life."

"Wow. I never would have pegged you as a nonbeliever."

"I rely on what I can see."

"If you don't think that God exists, then you certainly don't believe that I have special powers that were able to revitalize you."

Cole hesitated. "I guess not, but—"

"Then it's settled," Missy interjected. *You're still not ready to accept me.*

One of the flight attendants announced that they were number two for takeoff and told the passengers how long they would be airborne. As he discussed the current weather in Miami, Cole closed the window shade and pulled her seat-belt strap tighter.

"Are you scared to fly, Detective?" Missy's tone was gentle.

"No. I dislike takeoffs and landings. I'm fine once we're in the sky."

"But flying is safer than driving."

"I know that." Her tone was mulish.

"Then what's the problem?"

"Most crashes happen while on the ground," she spouted.

Missy smiled. "You're just full of surprises, Dani. You seem tough, but you hide your true nature to avoid being taken advantage of and to keep anyone from getting too close. Am I right?"

Cole nodded her head. "I have to."

"Why? Would it be so bad to let someone get to know the real you?"

Cole didn't immediately respond. But after a few seconds, she lowered her head and spoke softly. "I did once, but I learned the hard way not to become emotionally involved when you do what I do. If I remain unattached, there's less chance of some scumbag trying to get to me through the people I love."

"So you never intend to get married or have children?"

"It's unlikely. My career is the most important thing in my life." Cole's tone indicated a mixture of regret and acceptance.

"Sounds like a pretty lonely existence," Missy asserted compassionately.

Cole gazed at her, powerless to conceal the sadness in her eyes. "I survive."

"You need to do more than just survive, Dani. You have to live." Missy paused. "Perhaps if circumstances were different, we could have been friends. Sounds like we could both use one."

"Maybe. But things aren't different," Cole declared. "I'm here to do my job, nothing more."

"For the record, I think you would make a great wife and mother," Missy whispered.

Cole disregarded her remark as she listened to the wheels roll down the runway. She closed her eyes when the plane ascended and waited patiently for the butterflies in her stomach to dissipate. She thought about what Missy had said and imagined her life with friends and a family of her own. She cherished the idea, but her past had proven that she couldn't be entrusted with either. *It's better not to delude myself with dreams of participating in the game of happiness when I can only afford to watch the plays from the sidelines.*

The dark figure sat behind Mrs. Melendez on the airplane. He knew he would be in close proximity to his target so he drastically changed his appearance. His new look included a salt and pepper wig as well as a fake beard and moustache. The hazel color contacts he wore started to itch, but he resisted the urge to remove them because he didn't want to ruin his disguise. He was dressed in priestly garb, which helped to soothe his overwrought emotions. However, that didn't prevent his mind from wandering to the woman he almost killed in the terminal. She said her name was Lynn, and before the dark figure boarded the plane, she made him listen to her confession of infidelity. She wanted absolution, but as she spoke, all he could think about was choking her. The desire was so strong that his fingers tingled with need. He'd reached out his hands to exact God's vengeance for her transgression but was forced to stop when a man arrived with two small children. The dark figured concluded that the intrusion was divine intervention and silently moved from his chair. If he was meant to kill Lynn, they'd meet again, he thought.

The dark figure pushed aside his fantasy of murdering Lynn to concentrate on the conversation between Mrs. Melendez and Detective Cole. When his informant told him about the flight, he'd never imagined that he'd be seated near the target. He'd been prepared to lie or bribe one of the passengers to switch seats with him, but that hadn't been necessary. To him, that was a sign that God was pleased, and that Missy Melendez's days were numbered.

Thomas rushed into Lieutenant Blake's office and closed the door. "We have a problem," he proclaimed.

Blake flipped over the file he was reading. "What's so urgent?"

"I just got word that Cole's sister-in-law was arrested for shooting her husband."

Shock registered on his face. "What? When? Is he alive? Has Susan been booked?"

Thomas held up his hand. "One question at a time."

"Just tell me what you know."

"She said it was an accident. David hasn't given his side of the story yet. He's at the hospital now. The bullet only grazed his shoulder, so he should be released in a few hours.

"What about Susan?"

"Mrs. Cole is in booking. They found her unconscious when they arrived at the house. She fainted."

"If it was an accident, why is she being booked? I'll have to make a call and get the details before I speak with Cole. Knowing her, she'll jump on the next thing smoking back here, and I need her in Miami."

"Maybe we shouldn't tell her until she returns," Thomas suggested.

"And be on Cole's shit list? No, thank you. You probably haven't experienced the full brunt of her temper, but I have. Trust me—you don't want to make her angry."

"Oh, I believe you. I've already seen bits and pieces of it."

"Those are the calm before the storm," Blake said with a laugh. "I will call Cole later today."

Thomas chuckled. "Great. Better you than me."

"Actually, Thomas, while I have you here, I need to ask you again about your transfer records and files from Philadelphia. I still haven't received them. You said you would talk to Lieutenant Jamison last week and find out what the holdup was since HR couldn't reach him. Any word on that?"

"Yes. He promised me that the missing paperwork was on its way. There was a fire at the precinct, which is why HR was having such a hard time reaching him. They temporarily moved into a different building while the repairs are being completed. He said some files were destroyed, and the ones that weren't are stored in boxes. According to him, it has been chaotic, and he apologized for taking so long. If you want, I can give you his cell number, and he can explain what happened."

"I have his cell number, Thomas. I've just been too busy to call him with everything else going on lately. But if I don't receive the documents this week, I'll contact him. The captain has been asking me about your review, and I can't finish it without looking at your past evaluations."

"I came highly recommended through Lieutenant Jamison," Thomas affirmed.

"I'm not questioning your right to be here, Thomas. I've spoken with Jamison several times, and he's only had great things to say about you. Plus, you've done an admirable job since you've been here. You're one of my most reliable detectives."

"But?"

"No buts. I just hate having incomplete files. I'm sure Tinks … I mean Cole has told you how anal I am about paperwork."

"It's been mentioned. So, uh, what's the deal with you and Cole anyway?"

"There's no deal, Thomas. We were partners for many years. We're familiar with one another."

"That's what they call it nowadays, huh … familiar?" he said dubiously.

Blake averted his eyes for fear of what Thomas might glimpse in them. His heart was alight with the newness of his emotions for Cole, and he wasn't sure he could mask those feelings while in the hot seat. "Yes. Cole and I have a long history together," Blake countered.

Thomas didn't miss his boss's dodging tactics. He could tell Blake had it bad for Cole and wondered how many other people in the department knew.

"If you don't need anything else, Thomas, I'd like to get back to work."

Thomas realized he was being dismissed. "Sorry, Lieutenant. I didn't mean to make you uncomfortable. But I do have something else." His voice was bleak as he sat down in the chair.

"I don't like the sound of that."

"They picked up a guy in an alley on Martin Street. I saw him being wheeled into emergency at Hartford General while I was there following up on McCain."

"Crime in that neighborhood is nothing new," Blake asserted. "Let the beat cops handle it."

"I would, but the man I saw was Carlos Sanchez."

"Sanchez?" Blake began to tap his fingers on the desk. "You're kidding me, right? We've been after him for almost two years."

Thomas gazed at Blake's hands and smirked at his nervous habit. "That's what Cole told me when we were going over some of your old cases. I recognized him from his mug shot. Charming guy."

"A real pillar of the community," Blake said sarcastically. "Do you think he has something to do with this case?"

"Yes. Sanchez is an informant and a hired killer. What if he was given the Melendez contract? I checked his file, and these murders follow his MO. The killer used a .22-caliber, and that is Sanchez's gun of choice. Melendez was murdered close-range with no visible sign of forced entry and no prints, the same as Sanchez's other victims. The only time he seems to deviate from his pattern is when he's backed into a corner. It just makes sense to suspect him."

"We haven't heard anything from Sanchez since the Cavanaugh case. He's been lying low for almost a year now. I doubt he would resurface again this soon, particularly when we were so close to capturing him the last time."

"Money talks. And enough of it will bring anyone out of retirement."

"That's true." He hesitated. "Did Cole tell you about Cavanaugh?"

"No. She hasn't been talkative. I got the impression that it was too personal."

"Yeah, it was personal for both of us."

Thomas made a mental note to read the Cavanaugh file and to ask Ulrich some questions regarding the case. Thomas loved a good mystery, and there was something intriguing about this one. He'd always been curious about what had caused Blake and Cole to end their partnership. He knew that Cavanaugh had been their last bust together, but the details were limited. He had learned through subtle inquiries that much of the record was sealed. Only the higher-ups and internal affairs could access it, but Thomas was determined to get his hands on all the documents.

"Care to share any more details?" Thomas queried.

"Not really. All you need to know is that several people got hurt, and several bad guys got away."

Thomas's interest was piqued. "Was one of those people you or Cole?"

"I'd rather not talk about this now," Blake replied ruefully. "You have access to certain parts of the file, but the rest is confidential."

"I'll take a look. What about Sanchez?"

"Do you know the extent of his injuries?"

"He was unconscious when they brought him in. One of the nurses informed me that he'd lost a lot of blood and was on his way to surgery."

"Send someone to the hospital to keep an eye on Sanchez. We can't allow him to escape again. And make sure he's not permitted any visitors. Once he's out of surgery, have the patrolman report back to me immediately. I need to know what we're up against."

"I'll handle it. Do you want me to tell Cole about Sanchez?"

"I'll take care of that. And please don't discuss this or the Cavanaugh case with any of the other detectives. Also, make sure that whoever you send over to babysit Sanchez doesn't talk. I don't want it to get out that we're close to nailing this creep."

"Why? Do you think there's a leak in the department?"

"I'd like to believe that we simply have a few officers with big mouths who talk to their spouses about police business. However, I can't take that chance. I want this guy, Thomas. It will help bring closure to a painful chapter of my career. Cole's too."

"Was this case the reason you took a desk job and got off the streets?"

"It was certainly a part of it. But what's more important is putting Sanchez in prison where he belongs. Get someone over to Hartford General ASAP. No one goes in or out of that room except doctors and nurses. Sanchez has a habit of disappearing."

"I doubt he's going anywhere in his condition."

"We have no idea what his condition is, which makes our timing even more crucial."

"You're right. I'll send Adams over there right away." He stood and left the office.

Blake turned the file back over and stared at the stamp: "CONFIDENTIAL." What was inside had ruined lives and would destroy countless others if he made the wrong decision.

CHAPTER 5

MERCK TOTTERED THROUGH THE FRONT door of his newly rented condo and breathed a sigh of relief. It had been a long day, and he was drained. He walked to the downstairs bathroom and shut the door. He didn't want to disturb Marie, who he assumed was asleep upstairs. Her due date was drawing closer, and for the last few weeks of her pregnancy, she'd been placed on bed rest. They'd had a brief scare a few days ago with labor pains, but those had been diagnosed as Braxton Hicks contractions. Both Jason and Marie had been relieved. They couldn't survive losing another child. After two miscarriages, they were extremely nervous about the health of the baby and desperately wanted this child.

Merck turned on the faucet, bent his head toward the sink, and splashed water on his face. He lifted his head and stared at his reflection. The guilt that darkened his character was overpowering and visible in his brown eyes. Self-reproach was a profound burden that had disfigured him. He was a contemptible, unrecognizable creature. In Merck's perverse mind, he'd slaughtered his children. Each time Marie had miscarried, he had been on assignment and couldn't be there until it was too late. He blamed himself for both losses. With each baby, he had lost a part of his soul and become more inhumane.

Marie hated his job, and whenever he was on an assignment, she obsessed over his safety. She wouldn't eat or sleep, which was unhealthy for any expectant mother. Merck contemplated ways to ease her anxiety, but the only viable solution was to quit. However, he loved being a cop. He'd done some things he wasn't proud of, but he had done them in the name of justice and decency.

He grabbed a towel off the rack and dried his face. The newly formed lines on his forehead and the wrinkles around his mouth told the story of his life as an undercover detective. He resembled a man in his fifties instead of his late thirties. His dark hair was mixed with gray, and he had permanent dark circles under his eyes. Merck had defective knees and a chronic back injury from years of pursuing suspects. His body was directing him to resign, but his meeting had confirmed that it wasn't the right time. He had to finish what he'd started.

Merck hated that Sanchez was still alive. He hadn't set out to hurt the man, but he had to defend his family against Sanchez's threats. He'd hoped the man would die alone in that alley and do the world a favor. But according to the nurse Merck had spoken to, he was in surgery with a good chance of a full recovery.

He closed the toilet lid and sat down. He retrieved the piece of paper from his pocket and glanced at the fifteen names listed. He recognized eight of them, and each one was capable of murdering Melendez. But he knew it would be nearly impossible to find them with their faces altered.

An abrupt knock on the door startled him, and he dropped the paper. "Just a second, babe," he called. He leaned down to reclaim the document and placed it in his inside jacket pocket. Merck opened the door and smiled. The sight of his beautiful wife always made him happy.

Marie Merck was dressed in a blue nightshirt with the words "Bahama Mama" written across the chest. The shirt was too small to fit over her protruding belly, but it was her favorite. Despite her husband's urging, she refused to wear maternity clothes. In her opinion, it was bad luck. With the last two pregnancies, Marie had spent hundreds of dollars on baby items, but she had never made it past her second trimester. This time, she hadn't purchased anything and was in her thirty-third week, which to her was a huge accomplishment.

Merck attempted to hug his wife, which made her giggle.

"You know my stomach is too big for you to get your arms all the way around," she said.

Marie's laughter reminded him of the day they met at NYU over fifteen years ago. He was a senior studying criminal justice, and she was a freshman pursuing a degree in journalism. They dated for four years and tied the knot after Marie graduated from college and Merck graduated from the police academy. They didn't always have the best marriage, with all the complications surrounding Merck's job and the miscarriages, but neither had contemplated separation.

Unlike Merck, Marie looked younger than her thirty-five years. She had no visible white strands in her reddish-brown hair, and her green eyes sparkled against her beige complexion. As a fitness enthusiast, Marie loved to exercise, and it showed in her muscular build. However, she'd been forced to slow down per the doctor's orders and because it was more difficult with the additional twenty pounds she was carrying in baby weight.

"You look tired, Jay. Did you have a long day? I texted you, but I didn't get a response." Marie's voice hummed with concern.

"Every day is a long day when I'm away from you and Junior," Merck replied.

Marie swatted his hand away. "That's sweet, but you can't say that around the baby. What if it's a girl? She doesn't need to know that her daddy wanted her to be a boy. She'll be born with self-esteem issues."

"I just want a healthy baby, whether it's a boy or girl. I would love to have a miniature you running around." He kissed her on the cheek. "Since you're awake, how about I take you out to breakfast? It's been a while since I've been on a date with my wife."

Her face lit up. "Are you serious? I haven't been out of this house in weeks except for doctor's appointments. I would love it."

"Go get dressed then. We'll leave in an hour."

Marie's excitement rapidly dissipated. "Wait, I'm not supposed to be out of bed. What if this affects the baby?"

Merck pulled out his phone and made a call. "Can I speak to Dr. Abbott? This is Jay Merck, and I'm calling for my wife, Marie Merck." He listened to the voice on the other end. "Can you just ask the doctor if it would be okay to take my gorgeous wife out to eat for a few hours?"

Marie mouthed the words "Thank you" before she turned and exited the bathroom. As Merck waited for the doctor's answer, he again thought about Sanchez. He would die before he allowed anything to happen to Marie and his unborn child.

Cole tried to close her eyes, but she was unable to sleep. Her heart and mind were heavy, but she couldn't pinpoint why. Exhaustion burned beneath her eyelids like red-hot coals, and the moisture from her unshed tears evaporated under the heat of the embers.

"What's wrong?"

Cole was taken aback by the question. "I thought you were asleep."

"I can't. I'm too restless."

"Why are you restless?"

Missy was ambivalent about disclosing her feelings, but she couldn't control her emotions. "I never got the opportunity to say goodbye or tell Kayla that I love her." Missy took a deep breath to stop the cries that begged for release.

"If it's any consolation, I'm sure your friend knew how much you loved her. You have to try to find comfort in that."

"It's just too much," she cried.

Cole wasn't sure how to comfort Missy. She'd never been an affectionate person, and dramatic outbursts were foreign to her. Cole was considered cold and aloof by others, and she willingly embraced those labels. The wall she had built around her heart had helped her endure childhood trauma and abstain from personal relationships, particularly with men. Someone had found a way to penetrate those barriers once, and it had nearly caused her professional suicide. She had sworn that she would never allow anyone else to get that close to her again. But new complications were making it difficult to uphold her word.

Cole was hesitant to touch Missy, but she pushed down her anxiety and laid her hand on the other woman's. "It'll be okay. Just give it time. And remember, you do still have your dad."

Missy was surprised by the contact and clasped her hand. "Thank you."

"Um … you're welcome," Cole muttered as she pulled her hand away. She grabbed a magazine from the seat pocket in front of her and pretended to read.

Missy started to speak but changed her mind once she glimpsed the terror in Cole's eyes. The detective's panic was identical to what Missy had witnessed when Cole was talking to the handsome gentleman at Robert's funeral. There was something going on between them, but Missy suspected that Cole was afraid of it. *Just like I'm afraid of her. But my wariness doesn't matter since I'm inexplicably drawn to her vulnerability. It shines like a beacon of light and illuminates her spirit. I'm fascinated by its truth and its radiance.*

"We are now about to make our final descent into Miami International Airport. Our flight attendants will be coming through the aisles to pick up any final trash you may have. Please take this time to look around your area and put your seats in the upright position."

He ignored the message as he watched the two women interact. He detected that there was more going on than merely a police officer escorting a suspect. The thought made him smile. Their blossoming friendship could be beneficial if Detective Cole became negligent in her duties like she had with the Cavanaugh case. He'd heard the rumors, so he was aware of her weaknesses.

He took a final sip of his beer and handed the empty can to the flight attendant as she came down the aisle. She beamed at him as he thanked her.

"Like taking candy from a baby," he murmured.

The doctor ambled to room 312 and nodded at the officer standing at the door. He entered and moved steadily to the bed. He placed his hand on the patient's arm and waited for him to open his one good eye. "What do you want me to do?" he asked.

"Kill … his … wife. Don't care how. Just … do it," Sanchez stammered.

"What about you?"

"You get … me … out later."

"I'll take care of it. Will you be okay to leave the hospital?"

"Yes. I just need … pain pills."

"I'll get those to you right away. Anything else?"

Sanchez didn't respond as he drifted off to sleep.

His vehicle idled by the curb. Once he saw Merck and Marie get into their car and drive away, he discreetly followed. He knew it was only a matter of time before Merck realized that he was being tailed, and that's exactly what he wanted. He wanted to have the man's complete attention when he killed his wife.

Merck noticed the truck behind them and sped up to determine whether his suspicions were correct. The SUV accelerated and then rammed into the back of them. Merck's car swerved, and he clutched the steering wheel to maintain control. "Son of a bitch!" he roared.

The vehicle slammed into them again.

"Jay, do something!" Marie screamed, her voice full of terror.

"I'm going to try to outrun him. Hold on, Marie."

Merck pumped the gas and recklessly maneuvered through the busy streets. He tried to avoid running red lights, but it was impossible. Their hunter was relentless in his pursuit.

"Marie, I know you're scared, but I need you to dial 911."

"I can't. I left my phone at home."

"Mine's in my back pocket. Use that."

"Is it connected to the Bluetooth?"

"Shit. No. And I can't risk you trying to get it with the way I'm driving. Press the emergency button for OnStar. They'll call the police for us."

When the customer service representative answered, Merck gave her his badge number and location and asked her to send help. He continued to speed through downtown Hartford until sirens were heard in the distance.

The other man turned off the road, and Merck slowed down. He glanced at Marie, who grasped her belly in pain. "Honey, are you okay?"

She took a few deep breaths before glancing at him. "I think I'm all right," she said slowly. "I felt a few sharp pains, but they've subsided. Perhaps it was just the baby's way of complaining about all the excitement." She attempted to giggle, but it was forced.

"I'm taking you to the hospital right now."

"Maybe you should hurry," she mumbled.

The ride to the hotel was silent. The tension between Cole and Missy was thick as they grappled with the ramifications of their burgeoning relationship.

Cole wasn't accustomed to gratis compassion. Typically, a person expected reciprocation, but not Missy. And that made Cole uncomfortable, so much so that she contemplated giving the Melendez case to another detective until she remembered how crucial it was to her career.

If Cole thought that Missy was being kind only to try to beat a murder charge, she would annihilate her without regrets. But Cole knew that Missy was sincere, which made her job more difficult. *That doesn't mean she's not a killer, Dani. You cannot let this woman get under your skin.*

Cole's phone rang, and she answered it. "Perfect timing, Blake. I was just about to call you. We arrived in Miami about twenty minutes ago." She listened as he recounted what had happened between her brother and sister-in-law. "Is he hurt badly?" she asked anxiously.

Her tone caught the attention of Missy, who paused in the middle of the text she was typing. "Is everything okay?"

"Just family stuff," Cole whispered.

"Oh." *In other words, mind your business, Missy.* She quickly finished the text to her father so that she could eavesdrop on the remainder of Cole's conversation.

"Is Susan in jail?" Cole asked. She shook her head as Blake explained the challenges of procuring her release. "Thank God she's getting out. I appreciate you taking care of her in my absence, Blake. I wouldn't be able to sleep knowing she was in there because of my brother." She listened for a few more seconds before hanging up.

"Is there anything I can do to help?"

"No. But thank you. Even though it's my family, it's still a police issue, which means I can't share the details."

"I understand. But if you need to talk, I'm here."

"Why?"

Missy was confused by the question. "Why what?"

"I'm the enemy—the cop who arrested you, the person who accused you of killing your husband, your unwanted escort on this trip to bury your best friend. Why are you being so damn considerate?" Cole demanded suspiciously.

Missy chuckled. "You have no clue how to accept kindness, do you?"

"Not when it's undeserved."

"Everyone deserves empathy, Dani, even a cynical cop. You wear an intimidating mask, but I've seen the cracks in your veneer. It's time to rid yourself of those broken pieces that transmit misconceptions of who you really are. Yes, you've been burned, but those flames have been extinguished. And now you have to allow your inner beauty to rise from the ashes."

Cole lowered her head to shroud her bewilderment. *Who is this woman? And how does she know me so well?*

"And I know of at least one man who would like to assist you in clearing off the dust and debris from the fire."

Cole's eyes widened. *How does she know about Blake?* "I have no idea what you're talking about."

"That was him on the phone, right? The one you thanked for helping your family?"

"We shouldn't be talking about this. It's not right, Missy. You're a suspect in a murder case that I'm investigating—nothing more," Cole asserted.

Missy turned away, clearly wounded by Cole's words. "I'm not trying to jeopardize your job, Detective Cole."

Cole wasn't certain whether she should apologize for hurting Missy's feelings. She disliked the notion of spending the next few days in an environment steeped in friction. But an apology could expose her to other, analogous conversations. Cole wasn't emotionally equipped for that type of intimacy with another person. She understood that most women talked about everything, but that wasn't her personality.

"I'm sorry, Missy. I didn't mean to sound heartless, but I need our relationship to remain strictly professional. I can't have the lines blurred or my judgment clouded. I need to stay focused on the facts and not allow my feelings to compromise my job. Another mishap could end my career."

Cole's eyes belied her words. She needed a friend—they both did. However, Missy decided to respect her wishes. She wasn't certain what mishap had caused Cole's insecurity regarding her competence as a detective, but she swore to uncover the details. "I promise not to do anything that will negatively affect your position, Dani."

"I hope you mean that because there's a long, hard road ahead for both of us." Cole reached into her purse and retrieved her medication. "Excuse me. I need to take this." She opened the bottle and swallowed a pill.

"Don't you need water?"

"No. I'm used to taking them without it."

Missy was about to ask what the pills were for when the cab driver announced their arrival at the hotel. *Probably better that I don't pry since that's a question for a friend. Dani has made it abundantly clear that she doesn't want that from me. And that hurts almost as much as losing Robert and Kayla.*

"Now that we're here, I should tell you that we have adjoining rooms," said Cole. "You're free to come and go as you please, but I would appreciate it if you'd let me know."

"The only place I'm going is to a funeral."

Cole wasn't sure how to respond, so she opened the door and exited the car. Missy followed her lead, and they grabbed their luggage from the trunk. Cole observed another cab a few feet away, but she didn't pay attention to the occupants. If she had, she would have spotted in the back seat the man who had sat next to them on the plane.

Susan stood on the steps outside of the police station and glanced around. She was a free woman, but she couldn't go home; David was there. She wouldn't dare darken his parents' doorstep since she was certain they now hated her for shooting their son.

A hand gently clasped her shoulder, startling her. "Are you okay?" a soothing voice asked.

She turned to face the man who had secured her release. "Yes. Thank you for what you did. I don't know how I can ever repay you."

"Don't worry about it. I'm confident you'll be cleared of all charges."

"I wish I could believe you," she replied despondently. "You don't know David. It's his word against mine, and he'll say it wasn't an accident."

Although Susan was trying to appear strong, Blake knew she'd had more than her fair share of pain. He wanted to hug her, but he recognized that the police station wasn't the place to embrace an attempted-murder suspect. "Can I drop you off somewhere?" he quietly offered.

"I don't have anywhere to go."

"What?"

"I'm alone. I don't have any friends or family, just my boys. And because of David, I can never go home again," she whimpered.

"I'm sorry, Susan. I'll help you in whatever way I can. Let's start by getting you a place to sleep. There's a hotel right down the road."

"I can't let you do that. You don't even know me."

"If Cole were here, she'd let you stay with her, but since she's not, I'm going to check you into a hotel. Once she gives me permission, I'll let you into her place."

"You have a key to her house?"

"Yeah, but it's not what you think. It's just a spare key."

"Sure," Susan said skeptically. "Still not a good idea, though."

"It's what Cole would want. And just so you know, you're not alone. You have Cole, and now you can add me to the list."

His words were so earnest that Susan couldn't stop the tears from flowing. "Thank you, Detective Blake. Cole is a lucky woman to have you."

"I wish she knew that," he laughed. "Now let's go get you settled in."

"Can you please do me a favor first?"

"Sure. What do you need?"

"I need to know where my boys are."

Ted drank a few glasses of scotch as he watched the waitstaff sprint back and forth with trays of food. The patrons were distracted by fine cuisine and conversation, which was why he'd chosen this restaurant. It was an excellent place to meet and avoid recognition, although discretion wasn't Ted's top priority. His guest had a new face courtesy of Hartford Plastic Surgeons, so he could hide in plain sight. Still, Ted wanted to be cautious in his dealings with him. He hadn't been vigilant with Robert, and he wasn't going to make that mistake again.

Ted had almost lost everything because he'd gotten caught up in his son-in-law's schemes. He'd made a few bad investments with the turn in the economy, and he hadn't been able to recoup his losses. An innocent conversation with Robert about needing clients had transformed into a business venture that proved lucrative for both parties. Ted had recommended his disreputable clients who needed facial alterations to HPS in exchange for a fee. And in return, Robert had sent his patients who required legal counsel or a new identity to his father-in-law. Ted hadn't thought a few dubious clients would hurt anything, but he was wrong. He hadn't counted on the danger. He hadn't counted on the threats. He hadn't counted on murder.

"So hell must have frozen over," the man stated as he sat down at the table.

"No, Samuel. Hell continues to burn hot for people like you."

"You're a sweet-talker, Teddy, but I'm not the only one at this table going to hell."

"I took the liberty of ordering you a beer. I assume you still drink Budweiser."

"I do. Now tell me why I'm here."

"I need something fixed, and I know you can take care of it … discreetly."

"Are you asking me to kill someone, Counselor?" Sam questioned coolly. "You know I don't do that kind of work anymore. I'm a new man with a new face. I have you and Robert to thank for that."

"Cut the bullshit, Samuel. I know you're still in the business."

He laughed. "Okay, fine. How much are you willing to pay to make your problem disappear?"

"I'll double your normal asking amount."

Sam whistled. "Wow, you must be desperate."

"I am. Now what did you find out about Robert's murder?"

"He blackmailed some folks and was killed for it. End of story," Sam asserted.

"Do you know who did it?"

"If I did, I wouldn't tell you. Wouldn't want your hands any more dirty," he retorted derisively.

"Fair enough," Ted acquiesced. "All the information you need to complete the job will be sent to you tomorrow afternoon. I need this done as soon as possible."

"Works for me."

The waiter approached and set Samuel's drink on the table along with another scotch for Ted. "Can I take your orders, gentlemen?"

"We haven't decided yet. Can you come back in a few minutes?" Ted asked.

"Not a problem. Take your time." He walked over to the next table.

"As always, it's good doing business with you, Teddy." Samuel picked up his mug. "Now let's make a toast to you making me even richer." Their glasses kissed.

"Cheers."

Thomas spent the day speaking with Robert's neighbors, who all agreed that Missy and Robert had been the perfect couple who never caused any trouble. The consensus was that his death was merely a domestic dispute gone awry, which meant their perfect rich utopia was still intact. Thomas couldn't prove otherwise, but he was frustrated by their apparent agreement to stick together and not provide him with any useful information.

He ambled through the front door and threw his briefcase on the sofa. Despite how drained he was, his adrenaline was high. Tonight, he was going to learn what had happened in the Cavanaugh investigation. He'd "borrowed" the files and needed to return them before someone discovered they were missing.

He entered the kitchen and retrieved leftovers and a beer from the refrigerator. He placed the container in the microwave and opened the can while he waited for his dinner to warm. Once the microwave beeped, he grabbed everything and headed to the living room. He placed his beer and day-old Chinese on the table before sitting down. He opened the briefcase, took out the massive folder, and started reading.

Two hours later, the food was cold, and the beer was tepid. He'd forgotten about both as he pored over and interpreted the ambiguous notes from internal affairs and the police therapist.

Roy Cavanaugh was the biggest drug supplier in the tristate area, and he had made Connecticut his home base. He had been responsible for the deaths of countless people, including several police officers, but there had never been any evidence to prove his involvement. He covered his tracks by using his large construction company, Cavanaugh Builders, as a front for his illegal ventures. The mayor and chief of police wanted Cavanaugh out of business, so they sent Blake and Cole, the department's dynamic duo, undercover to attain enough evidence to bring about his demise.

Cole's job was to get close to Cavanaugh. She applied for a job as a temporary assistant at his company, and she was hired because of her looks. Per reports, Cavanaugh couldn't resist a pretty face, and despite Cole's propensity to downplay it, she was a beautiful woman.

Blake's task was to gain enough trust on the streets to be brought into the inner circle of Cavanaugh's top dealers. He wasn't readily accepted, which left Cole as the only one in Cavanaugh's privileged world. She was alone for months with no contact with anyone—not even Blake. Thus, the burden of the case fell squarely on her shoulders.

Cavanaugh became enamored with Cole, and after a few months of dating, he proposed. Cole knew she couldn't get too close to him and rejected the ring. Cavanaugh refused to take no for an answer, and eventually, Cole fell for him. She knew her feelings were inappropriate, and she requested that the undercover operation be aborted. But her appeal was denied. She was the only one close enough to bring Cavanaugh down, and the higher-ups knew it.

Blake attempted to minimize the pressure on Cole by performing a stunning act to get noticed by Sanchez, who was Cavanaugh's right-hand man. He killed a major drug rival to prove his loyalty and gain trust. His plan was successful, and Blake was received by the other men. However, that didn't let Cole off the hook. She was still the only one who could obtain the information needed to prove Cavanaugh's guilt. However, her feelings for him made her vacillate until she heard about the new guy and his reckless behavior. Cole realized then that she had no choice; it was either Cavanaugh or Blake. Her partner was trying to protect her, and it was Cole's responsibility to do the same for him.

After an anonymous tip, Sanchez became suspicious of Cole. He had her followed and installed hidden cameras in his boss's home and office. Cole was caught on camera going through Cavanaugh's private documents. Sanchez had his men kidnap her and bring her to a deserted warehouse outside of Hartford. There Sanchez ordered Blake to execute Cole, warning that if he didn't, Sanchez would kill him too.

Blake tried to maintain an impassive expression as he aimed the gun at his partner. Sanchez stood behind Cole, gun ready, waiting for him to pull the trigger. Blake wondered if he could save both of them with Sanchez's other goons and Cavanaugh positioned in the rear of the building.

The details of what happened next were vague because Blake's and Cole's stories differed. Blake shot Cole. The bullet skimmed her shoulder and hit

Sanchez in the stomach. When Sanchez went down, Cole grabbed his gun and started shooting Cavanaugh's other men. Simultaneously, Blake turned and started firing.

Sanchez escaped despite the gunshot wound. Cavanaugh was captured a few blocks away. After being convicted of drug trafficking and attempted murder, he was sentenced to fifteen years in a federal prison.

Thomas now found himself even more intrigued by the Cavanaugh case. In his opinion, both detectives should have been killed in that shootout. Things didn't add up, and he was determined to find out the truth.

He grabbed his cell phone and dialed a number. "I need to talk to you about the Cavanaugh case. Can you meet me at Louie's in about an hour?"

Louie's Bar was an infamous hangout for law enforcement. It wasn't upscale, nor did it serve the best food and drinks in town, but everyone loved Louie, a former police lieutenant, and they enjoyed the ambiance of the place. It was the perfect spot to relax and talk shop.

Thomas saw Ulrich and took the seat opposite him in the booth. "Have you been waiting long?"

"No, I just got here," Ulrich replied. "I ordered you a beer. Wasn't sure what you drink."

"If it has alcohol, I drink it."

"Something we have in common." Ulrich took a sip and set his mug on the table. "So what do you want to know about the Cavanaugh case?"

"I heard that Blake shot Sanchez and Cole at the same time—and that he was somehow able to take out the rest of the bad guys. How is that even possible?"

Ulrich laughed. "It's not, unless he's a superhero. It was all over social media that Cavanaugh shot Sanchez and several of his own men to keep them from talking."

"But that doesn't make any sense. Cole and Blake would have been killed, so there wouldn't have been anyone left to betray him—unless Cavanaugh thought there was a leak in his own organization and used that as an excuse to execute them."

"Allegedly, there were a few, but I think Cavanaugh really loved Cole. That's why she escaped with the scars you can't see."

"You're saying he shot his own men and got arrested to save Cole?" Thomas's tone was incredulous.

"Yup. That was the story the other detectives in the department believed."

"That's unbelievable."

"Not really. Cole is a beautiful woman, and some men will do anything for a pretty face. I think by giving up his freedom, Cavanaugh became proof of that. And Blake is another example since he almost lost his life for her."

"That confirms their relationship is more than professional."

"There's been talk, but personally, I don't think they've done anything about it yet."

Thomas snickered. "I thought I was the only one who picked up on that."

"Nope." Ulrich downed the last of his beer. "I don't even think Cole knows that Blake has feelings for her."

"If she didn't know before, I think she's starting to."

"If that's true, things could get interesting with that rule about dating inside the department."

"And I have a front-row seat," Thomas bragged. "So why didn't they remain partners after the Cavanaugh fiasco?"

"Internal affairs was brought in, and they were put on desk duty during the investigation. Blake was mad at Cole for getting personally involved with a suspect. Plus, I think he was disappointed in himself because it was Cavanaugh who saved Cole's life and not him. He was supposed to protect his partner at all costs, and he failed. And from what I hear, some of the things he had to do to be accepted by Sanchez were grisly. A lot of details were left out of the official report—that's how bad it was."

"I can imagine," Thomas said thoughtfully.

"Whatever he did, it changed him. Blake was different after that. And not in a good way."

"Did he blame Cole?"

"Blake said he didn't, but no one believed him. Then things got really awkward."

"That's probably when their partnership ended?"

"Blake made the decision to walk away. It was announced that our lieutenant was being transferred to another precinct, and Blake applied for the position. That was right around the time he was cleared of any wrongdoing."

"Was Blake looking to move up the chain before the case?"

"Nah, I think he was just burned out."

Thomas nodded. "That makes sense. But if I had to guess, I'd say the higher-ups set up the transfer to separate them. It sounds like they handed the position to Blake on a silver platter. From my experience, no one goes from detective to lieutenant without going through the ranks and political BS."

"I see you're a conspiracy theorist too," Ulrich chuckled. "A few of the other guys thought it was a good way to keep Blake quiet."

This piqued Thomas's interest. "Quiet about what?"

"Corruption in the department. Blake supposedly discovered some shady dealings in homicide and narcotics while undercover."

"That's surprising in a small city. Do you think any of it is true?"

"Hell if I know. They've kept the allegations a secret. I have no idea what happened or who's involved."

"Maybe Cole knows and will share the details with her new partner," Thomas stated buoyantly.

"You'd have better luck finding a four-leaf clover or the Loch Ness monster. Cole never discusses the case, especially since she lost Blake and the man she loved."

"I still can't believe straitlaced, by-the-book Cole fell for a suspect."

"Yeah, that surprised all of us. But between Cavanaugh's money and good looks, I can understand how Cole got sucked in. Undercover work can make the most hardened cop shaky. And for a woman, maybe it's even more difficult."

"Don't let Cole hear you say that."

Ulrich shook his head. "Oh, believe me, I know better."

"Prosecuting Cavanaugh must have been hard for Cole. How did she handle the trial?"

"Not well. Cavanaugh was stalking her. He'd send text messages, call her from blocked numbers, and leave gifts at her house. Cops patrolled the area, but he was never caught in the act. Cole had cameras and a security system installed, but Cavanaugh still avoided detection."

"Hard to believe a judge granted him bail. I'm surprised he didn't skip the country."

"And leave Cole behind? No way."

"What happened to the rest of Cavanaugh's men?"

"Most of them were never captured, and Sanchez just vanished."

"From what I've read, Sanchez is a pretty bad dude."

Ulrich's phone vibrated. "Yes, he is. That's why Cavanaugh chose him." He read the text message and quickly typed a response. "I'm sorry, but I have to go. Did I answer all of your questions?"

"Yes. The conversation was very interesting. Look, I'll take care of the bill. Thanks again for meeting me."

Ulrich stood. "You're welcome. And if you ever want to talk shop again, I'm available." He drank the remainder of his beer and left.

CHAPTER 6

MERCK PROWLED THE ER LOUNGE AS HE waited for news of his wife and baby's condition. It had been hours since Marie was wheeled into an operating room, and with each passing minute, he grew more anxious. Merck had tried to speak with the head nurse several times, but she couldn't answer his questions.

Growing increasingly restless, Merck pulled out his phone and called the station. "This is Sergeant Jason Merck. I'm still at the hospital, and the officer that's supposed to guard my wife's room hasn't arrived yet."

"The officer we were going to send had an emergency," the desk detective said.

Merck nodded. "Just send Adams then."

"His mother is sick so he's unavailable," the other man responded.

"Oh, I didn't know his mother was ill. When will he return to duty?" Merck asked.

"I'm not sure."

"Well, send whoever is free. Captain Kessler has already approved it."

Merck disconnected the call and then headed to the cafeteria for coffee. When he returned, the doctor was inquiring about him at the nurses' station.

Merck walked up behind him and introduced himself. "I'm Jason Merck."

The doctor turned to greet him. "I'm Doctor Gordy."

"How's my wife and baby, Dr. Gordy?"

"Your daughter is in an incubator in the NICU. I had to deliver her prematurely to save both their lives. She's only four pounds, five ounces, and her lungs are too weak for her to breathe on her own. I'm not sure if she's strong enough to make it."

"Oh my God," Merck whispered. "What about Marie?"

"She's stable for now. She began hemorrhaging postpartum and lost a lot of blood. We had to give her a transfusion."

"Will she be okay?"

"I can't answer that, Mr. Merck. But I believe your two girls have the strength needed to live. Many times that fortitude is more effective than any medicine I could ever prescribe."

"When can I see them?"

"Your wife is heavily sedated, but you can visit her. The nurse will let you know when it's okay to see your daughter."

Merck paused. "I guess I'll have to come up with a name for her."

"Let's just hope we can call her a miracle."

Cole is strapped to the wall with her arms and legs spread apart. Her nude frame glistens with sweat, and blood drips from the lacerations on her body. The man standing in front of her is laughing wildly at her agony as she pleads for release. He takes perverse pleasure in cutting her again and again with his blade. Each scream causes his body to shudder with desire. He unzips his pants and touches himself. He closes his eyes and quotes his favorite Bible verse—1 John 2:16. "For everything in the world, the lust of the flesh, the lust of the eyes, and the pride of life, comes not from the Father but from the world."

Missy approaches him from behind. She gazes into Cole's anguished eyes and tries to reassure her without words. The gun in her hand feels foreign, but she's prepared to use it. Missy can hear his groans as she eases closer. She raises the gun.

Suddenly, the man turns and stabs Missy in the abdomen. She touches her stomach and feels the warm stickiness seeping from the wound. She glimpses the hazy image of the perpetrator as she tumbles to the floor. Missy hears Cole call her name right before she takes her final breath.

Unnerved by the vision, Missy rushed to Cole's hotel room. "Dani, are you in there?" she yelled as she banged on the door. Once Cole opened it, she breathed a sigh of relief.

"Why are you banging on my door like you're the cop?"

"Thank God you're okay." Missy stared at Cole's messy hair and bloodshot eyes. "You look like shit, though."

Cole stepped aside to let her in. "Gee, thanks. I feel like shit too."

"What's wrong? Do you still have a migraine?"

"Yes, in addition to nausea and dizziness."

"I'm sorry, Dani. You're probably just stressed because of me and this case. I wish there were something I could do." *I should tell her about my dream. Both of our lives are in danger. But if I say something, she'll think I'm nuts.*

"I appreciate your kindness, Missy, but there's nothing you can do. I've had migraines since I was a little girl. And as much as I would like to blame someone, you're not the culprit." She glanced at her watch. "Give me a few minutes to throw some water on my face, and we'll head over to the police station to talk to Detective Bolton."

"Are you sure you're up for that?"

"I don't have a choice in the matter. It's my job." Cole headed to the bathroom and closed the door.

Cole and Missy entered the police station and stopped at the front desk. "I'm Detective Cole from the Hartford PD." She flashed her badge. "We're here to see Detective Bolton. I believe he's expecting us."

"Perfect timing, Detective Cole. I was just about to head back to my office. I'm Brett Bolton." He held out his hand, and she shook it.

Cole studied the tall man with the brown hair and blue eyes. "This is Melissa Melendez. She's the victim's friend."

"It's nice to meet you both. I'm sorry about Kayla, Mrs. Melendez."

"Thank you, and please call me Missy."

"If you two would like to follow me, we can get started."

Bolton's office was the size of a large walk-in closet, with barely enough space for a desk and three chairs. The laptop and phone were partially hidden by paperwork. Files were scattered over the floor and piled in the corners. There were no windows, which made the room appear dark and gloomy. It was functional but a bit too constricted for a claustrophobic like Missy.

"Excuse the mess, but until I can squeeze a file cabinet in here, there's not much I can do," Bolton explained. "Please have a seat."

"No need to explain," Cole stated as she sat down. "Before they renovated our building, there were four of us crowded into an office like this. I enjoyed it because I got more work done."

"I guess I should be grateful then." He lowered his large body into the chair behind the desk. "I couldn't imagine sharing such a small space with anyone, especially since I'm six-six." He grabbed a folder from the pile perched on the edge of his desk and passed it to Cole. "You may want to view that in the hall so that Mrs. Melendez doesn't have to see the pictures of the deceased."

Cole glanced at Missy to gauge her reaction. "I can step out if you want."

Missy took a deep breath. "It's okay. I can handle it." *I've already seen them in my nightmares.*

The first photo made Cole gasp. She'd seen thousands of grisly pictures in her career, but these seemed more personal. She quickly flipped through the rest and closed the file.

"Dani?" Missy's voice sounded hollow.

"I'm sorry, but I can't let you see these. I don't want you to remember your friend like this," Cole said sincerely.

Tears welled up in her eyes. "Is it that bad?"

"Yes." One simple word spoke volumes.

Missy glanced at Bolton. "Was she in a lot of pain?"

"No. She died instantly," Bolton affirmed. "Do you need some water or something?"

"I'm fine. I just miss her," Missy whimpered.

Cole could feel Missy's pain as if it were her own. "I wish there were something …" She sensed Bolton watching her and hesitated. *I can't become emotionally involved. Her compassion begets forgetfulness, comforting me, imploring me to disregard my reservations. And how do I fight against that when it feels like she can read my mind and understands my inner struggles? It's fucking scary.* "I know this is painful, but we need to move forward," Cole stated coolly. "We have three murders to solve."

Missy shut down, effectively cutting off Cole's connection to her. "I know your concern is strictly professional, Detective. I haven't forgotten that I'm just a murder suspect to you."

Cole felt Missy free her, as if she once again had been holding her hand.

Cole was relieved. *I'm an ass for hurting her, but that's exactly what I needed to do to keep some distance between us. She must know that I have nothing to offer. I barely have anything for myself. The only thing I can possibly give her is freedom once I prove her innocence.*

"Good," Cole said. "Then let's not take up too much of Detective Bolton's time. He has some questions for you."

Bolton nodded. "Only if you're up for it, Mrs. Melendez."

"That is the only reason I could come, so please ask your questions, Detective."

Bolton noted the derision in her tone. "Per eyewitnesses, Kayla was at a bar downtown called Brownie's on the night of her death. Ever heard of it?"

"That was her favorite spot. We would go there every time I came to visit. Everyone knew her." Missy's voice was raw as she held back tears.

"Several of the patrons reported that they saw her leave with someone and that she seemed out of it. But when we talked to the bartender, he stated that she only had two drinks."

"Sounds like she might have been drugged," Cole contended.

"We're still waiting for the autopsy, but I agree."

Cole nodded. "Please let me know what you find out."

"I will." Bolton glanced at his notes. "The descriptions of this gentleman have varied and are extremely vague, so we have no idea who we're looking for. The only things we do know are he's about five-ten, Caucasian, late twenties, possibly early thirties. He was wearing a hat, but we're told he has dark hair. Does that sound like anyone you might know?"

"Honestly, that could be any number of people."

"I know, but I figured I'd take a chance. Do you know if she was seeing anyone?"

"No. She hasn't dated since she broke up with Aaron, over six months ago."

"What's his last name?"

"Lowell. He lives in Pennsylvania. He moved there for a job. That's why they broke up. Kayla wasn't ready to move."

"We'll get in contact with him." He looked from Missy to Cole. "Uh … I have some other things to discuss about the case that I don't think Mrs. Melendez should be here for."

Missy abruptly rose from her chair. "I'll wait outside."

"Tell Officer Boyd at the front desk to get you some coffee," Bolton said. He waited for Missy to leave before he spoke again. "I believe this was a professional hit."

"That possibility crossed my mind too, but I'd like to hear your thoughts."

"There's a motel about a mile down the road from where the body was found. The night manager was executed—a bullet right between the eyes—a few hours before Ms. Bell's estimated time of death. We identified the location as the place where the killer took our victim. Forensics checked—no blood in the room, so she wasn't murdered there. Her fingerprints were on the phone at the motel's check-in counter. We doubt she tried to make a call when they first arrived, particularly if she was under the influence of drugs and alcohol."

"So she escaped and ran for help, only to find the guy at the front desk with a bullet in his head."

"And tried to dial 911."

"Seems feasible. Did you find her cell phone?"

"No. We assume he destroyed it."

"We couldn't locate Robert's or his mistress's phone either. Luckily, we were able to get their phone records, but so far, that's been a dead end."

"Sounds like it could be the same killer. Do you think Mrs. Melendez hired someone, or did she commit the murders herself?"

He's trying to bait me. He realizes I'm too close to Missy after our earlier exchange. "I don't think she did it. Still, I can't rule her out."

"Any evidence leaning toward another suspect?"

"No. Right now, we have nothing. We're waiting for fingerprint analysis, but I'm sure the killer wore gloves. I do think he may have slipped up, though."

Bolton gave her a look of surprise. She had his complete attention now. "How?" he asked.

"He left semen on the dead woman's body. Apparently, he's into necrophilia. Do you know if Kayla had any discharge on her body?"

"I don't know, but I'll have the ME check."

"If so, see if there's a *t* drawn in it."

"What does the *t* mean?"

"We think it's a cross, which means this guy could be some type of religious freak."

"Wow. This could be a huge break for both of our cases."

"That's what I'm hoping."

"I hate to get too personal, Detective Cole, but are you sure you're not too close to Mrs. Melendez to be objective? Because after what I witnessed—"

She interrupted him. "My opinion of Mrs. Melendez will not stop me from doing my job, Detective Bolton." *I knew this was coming. No one will ever let me live down Cavanaugh.*

"If she's guilty, then what?"

"Then she will spend the rest of her life in prison." Cole reopened the file and began reading the notes. Her head was lowered, so she missed the uncertainty on Bolton's face.

Cole had no idea what to say to Missy on the ride back to the hotel, but she refused to apologize for doing her job. The idea of a genuine friendship was appealing, but she couldn't risk her livelihood. Her past mistakes haunted her and served as constant reminders of her ineptitude. If she allowed Missy to get too close, her impartiality would once again be questioned, and those ghosts would never be exorcised.

Cole sighed. "I am looking forward to this case being over."

Missy looked hurt by her dismissal. "Yeah, I'm sure you'll be glad to have me out of your hair. I was a fool to think we could ever be friends."

Shit, I didn't mean to say that out loud. "Wait … I didn't mean it like that."

"Of course, you did. But don't worry, I get the message."

"Missy, you don't understand. It's just …" Cole's emotional floodgates opened, and a small piece of her wall crumbled from the pressure of the surge. "I've never actually had a real friend. Every relationship I've ever had, I've ruined. I'm not good with affection. I'm not good with feelings. I'm not good with anything except being a cop. That's all I have. That's all I know." She took a deep breath. "Not long ago, I got personally involved with a suspect. It almost cost my partner and me our lives. I can't let that happen again. I won't."

In those few moments, Missy glimpsed the real Cole—probably for the first time. She saw her vulnerability, sympathized with her pain, and embraced her frailty. She yearned to ask questions but knew Cole wouldn't respond.

She sensed the other woman's embarrassment over having permitted Missy to witness those tiny fractures in her facade.

"Dani, what ..." Missy wavered, unsure of what to say.

"I can't talk about it." *I can't disclose the details of the Cavanaugh case and let her know how much of a screwup I am.*

"I respect that. But if you want to talk, I'm here."

"Thank you, but I simply can't. It's not professional."

"Dani, please don't let other people's opinion be the thing that breaks you, even if that opinion is the same as your own."

Missy's poignant words stirred something indefinable within Cole. She wanted to seize the emotion, but it was too elusive. *The sooner I solve this case, the sooner Missy will be out of my life. Then I won't crave things I know I can't have. And I can go back to not feeling.*

Cole's and Missy's eyes spoke silently as the cab pulled in front of the hotel. Neither wanted to say the words out loud, but they understood the truth of their situation. Despite their mutual need for friendship, they could never be any more than suspect and cop.

The nurse walked into the room and opened the curtains. The sun flickered on Merck's face, stirring him from a mostly sleepless night. He stood and stretched to knock the kinks out of his neck and back. "That chair is pure evil," he said in frustration.

"You're not the first person to say that," said the nurse as she checked Marie's IV and vital signs.

"Any change?"

"No, but she's stable, which is a good sign. Give it time. She'll open her eyes soon."

"I pray you're right. Do you know how my baby girl is doing?"

"I don't, but I can check for you. What's her name?"

"Her name is Miracle Taylor Merck."

"Oh ... that's pretty. I'll let you know what I find out."

After she had left the room, Merck reached into his pocket and retrieved the list. He knew what he needed to do, but he was concerned about his wife and daughter getting hurt.

"Jay?"

At the sound of his wife's quiet voice, he dropped the paper and sprinted to her side. "Hi, sweetheart. I've been worried about you."

Marie inched her hand downward and touched her belly. "Where's the baby?" she screamed as she frantically tried to sit up.

"Honey, calm down." He grabbed her hand. "The baby is alive. She's in the NICU."

"But it's too early!" she cried.

"She's four pounds but holding her own. We just have to pray that she'll make it."

Marie laid her head back on the pillow. "I can't believe we have a baby girl," she whispered.

"I hope you don't mind, but I already named her. I know we discussed Taylor if it was a girl, but I used that for her middle name. I decided to call her Miracle because she's our little miracle."

She repeated the name. "Miracle. Miracle Taylor Merck. I like it."

"I'm glad. I was worried you wouldn't like it."

"It's beautiful." She squeezed his hand. "When can I see her?"

He straightened and grabbed a nearby chair. "She's in an incubator. The doctor said it might be a while before we get to hold her."

"Is she healthy?"

"They're still running tests, but so far, no abnormalities."

Marie sighed in relief. "Thank God."

Merck's cell rang, and he glanced at the number. "I need to get this. It could be about the bastard that tried to run us off the road. I'll be right back." He went into the corridor and answered his phone.

"Hello."

"Time is running out for you and your family, Merck," the menacing voice whispered.

"I said I would take care of it, and I will!" Merck roared before ending the call.

When he returned to the room, Marie looked at him with concern. "Is everything okay, Jay?"

"Yes, but I have to go. There's something I need to take care of immediately."

"I know that tone. Please don't do this, Jay," she pleaded.

He kissed her on the forehead. "Everything will be fine, Marie. I'll be back. I promise."

"Maybe this time, but one day, you won't."

He ignored her words and whispered, "I love you," before walking out the door.

The incessant knocking on the door forced Susan awake. She skimmed the room and remembered that she wasn't at home, but in a hotel. "No housekeeping service right now. Come back later!" she yelled.

When the banging continued, she scrambled out of bed and tottered to the door. She looked through the peephole, but the person was blocking the opening. "Who is it?"

"Let me in, Susan, or I'll rip the wood off the hinges!" he shouted.

Her heart accelerated. "How did you find me, David?"

"It doesn't matter. Open the door, or you won't see your kids again."

Susan reluctantly obliged. "Why are you here? Who's taking care of the boys?"

"You weren't concerned about the kids when your dumb ass shot me. You tried to make sure they lost both their parents."

"I didn't mean to shoot you," she asserted.

"Well, you can tell that to a judge, but I don't think that will keep him from granting me full custody of Brady and Hayden."

"You can't do that."

"I can, and I will. Unless …"

"Unless what? I'll do whatever you say," Susan pleaded.

"Get your stuff. We'll talk about it on the way home."

Cole felt helpless as she listened to Missy cry on the way to her best friend's funeral. Each sob resonated in the back of the taxi, etching tiny, poignant footprints on her heart. Cole wanted to console Missy, but instead she pretended to be engrossed in the rolling scenery outside of her window. Still, the gnawing in Cole's stomach would not dissipate, even with the distraction. She assumed it was because of her connection to Missy. When they arrived at the church, Cole realized that the issue was more than sympathy pains. She exited the car but couldn't ascertain what had her on edge. She gazed over the hood of the car at the woman with the red, puffy eyes and wondered if her anxiety stemmed from her desire to prove Missy's innocence.

After spotting some of Kayla's friends, Missy asked if she could walk with them. Cole ignored her instincts and agreed. As she trailed behind the quartet, something kept niggling at her. Cole abruptly stopped and noticed a glint in the sunlight. Once she recognized the source, she retrieved her gun from her waistband and sprinted toward Missy. "Get down!" she yelled.

The bullets whizzed past her as she tackled Missy. They hit the ground hard, and neither woman moved until Cole heard sirens in the distance. She stood up and deposited her gun back in its resting place. "Are you hurt?" Cole asked, her voice full of concern. "Do you need me to help you up?"

"I'm okay. But are you sure it's safe?"

"Yes. The sirens should have scared away whoever it was."

Missy got to her feet and nervously assessed her surroundings. "Can we go in the church, Dani? I feel like I have a bull's-eye on my back."

Cole nodded. "Of course. I'm glad everyone else made it indoors."

"Yeah. I guess I was the only one distracted by your voice."

The glib statement made Cole uncomfortable. "Um … I need to make a phone call, so give me a few minutes."

"Can't you do that in the vestibule, where you'll be out of harm's way? The shooter might return."

"This place will be swimming with police in a few seconds. He'd be a fool to come back. Besides, I need to survey the area to see if the person left any evidence behind."

Missy sighed heavily. "I can't believe someone tried to kill me."

Cole opened the door. "It certainly looks that way."

"You could at least lie to me," Missy declared as she walked inside.

"Now where's the fun in that?"

"You can be such a bitch," she joked.

Cole smirked. "I know. It's a part of my charm."

The wheels squeaked as the nurse rolled the chair into Sanchez's room. She positioned his getaway vehicle near the bed and gently helped him climb into it. She handed him two pills and the glass of water that had been resting on the table. The nurse waited for him to swallow them before pushing him out of the room.

"I'm taking Mr. Sanchez for tests. He'll be back in about an hour or so," she said to the guard at the door. She quickly headed to the elevator before the guard could respond.

Sanchez's rage surged as soon as the doors closed. "I've been waiting for you for an hour. What took you so damn long?"

"There were provisions that needed to be made," she explained. "I needed to—"

"I don't care about your provisions. I have shit to do, and I can't do any of it from a hospital bed!" he bellowed.

"I'm sorry."

"Was the job completed?"

"Not exactly," she admitted tenuously.

"What do you fucking mean, not exactly? Is the cop's wife dead or not?"

"Marie and her baby are both alive and here in the hospital."

"Good. That should make it easier to kill them. I want it done tonight."

The elevator stopped on the parking-garage floor.

"I'll let him know."

"Tonight or else."

She wheeled Sanchez out and waited for her contact in the designated spot. The car pulled up a few minutes later, and she assisted Sanchez as he climbed into the back seat. They sped off, and she proceeded to where her vehicle was parked, shedding her disguise along the way.

Despite the earlier disturbance, Kayla's funeral was set to begin on time. Detective Bolton, who had appeared a few minutes after the commotion, had helped Cole secure the church by placing officers throughout the building. Cole had planned to stay with Missy during the service, but she was relieved when Ted unexpectedly arrived. His presence meant she didn't have to console Missy, and she could perform her job without babysitting the other woman.

"Since your dad is here, Missy, I'm going to head outside with Detective Bolton and check the perimeter."

"Why? Is there something wrong, Detective Cole?" Ted asked warily. "There seems to be a lot of security here for an unknown like Kayla."

Missy took a deep breath. "Someone tried to..."

Cole interrupted Missy's words, "Kayla was murdered so we like to study the mourners because sometimes the killer attends the funeral to admire his dirty work."

Bolton glanced at Cole curiously before chiming in, "Yes, and that's why we're here. We wanted to give Detective Cole some assistance."

"Who are you?"

"Mr. Delaney, this is Detective Bolton from the Miami PD. He's investigating Kayla's murder."

"I'd like to chat, Mr. Delaney, but this thing is about to begin. Maybe we can talk afterward?"

Ted nodded. "Yes. I would love to see where you are with the case, Detective Bolton." He pointedly looked at Cole. "Hopefully further along than the investigation into my son-in-law's homicide."

Cole didn't miss the jab at her. "We'll be outside if you need us."

Cole and Bolton canvassed the area as she described in detail what happened. She believed that the gunman's fire came from the park across the street so they headed in that direction. Once there, they combed through the large shrubs and spotted shell casings on the ground. Bolton waved a member of his team over to bag them while he and Cole continued to look around.

"So are you going to tell me why you didn't want Mrs. Melendez's father to know about the shooting?" Bolton inquired.

"Because he would have verbally attacked me, which would have ruined the funeral for his daughter."

"I see. You do plan to tell him when the funeral is over though, right?"

"Of course."

"Good. Next question. Did you happen to see this guy's face?"

"No. He was too far away."

"And you think it was the same guy who murdered Bell and Melendez?"

"Yes. My theory is that Robert and Missy were the original targets, but the mistress was killed instead."

"That means he needs to finish the job."

"If I'm right, then yes," Cole affirmed. "I can't believe the idea didn't cross my mind until now. It was a case of mistaken identity. That's why Mrs. Melendez is in danger."

"If your guess is correct, then this guy is definitely a professional. I'm surprised Mrs. Melendez isn't dead."

"Yelling my head off and running at her like a bull in Pamplona probably helped, not to mention wrestling her to the ground."

Bolton chuckled. "Hey, it worked. She's still alive."

"Hopefully, I can keep her that way."

"I'm certain that you have it all under control, which is good because I need to head to the station for a bit. I'll be back in about an hour. Should we meet in front of the church then?" Bolton asked.

"Sure. I'll just go inside and keep an eye on everything."

"Great. I'll text you when I return."

After he left, Cole walked back to the church and entered quietly. She didn't want to draw attention to herself so she sat on the last pew. Cole watched the mourners cry and share stories of Kayla for forty-five minutes until she received the text from Bolton announcing that he was outside. Cole stood and glanced at the crowd one final time, before she exited through the double doors. She immediately spotted Bolton standing next to his car in the parking lot and strolled towards him.

"Did you find out anything about our shooter?"

"Nothing yet. Is the funeral over?"

"No. But it will be soon. They seemed to be wrapping things up."

"Well, there are people headed in this direction so I think it's over."

Cole saw the doors to the church being propped open and nodded in agreement. "Looks like you're right." *Which means Missy's father will be coming my way in five, four, three, two ...*

Ted stormed out of the building and came barreling toward Cole, with Missy trailing behind him. He halted directly in front of the duo. "Detective Cole, Missy just informed me that someone tried to kill her. What kind of sideshow are you running here? Your lieutenant reassured me that you were one of his finest, but I personally think you got your badge from a Cracker Jack box."

Missy stood several inches away from her father, out of the line of fire. "Daddy, if not for Detective Cole, I wouldn't be alive."

Cole tried to restrain her anger. "I had no idea that someone would try to kill Mrs. Melendez," she said between gritted teeth.

"It's your job to know," Ted stated harshly.

"Mr. Delaney, Detective Cole did her job by shielding your daughter from bullets. There was nothing else she could have done."

Cole was moved by Bolton's defense of her. "I apologize for not realizing sooner that Mrs. Melendez's life was in danger, Mr. Delaney. But now that I know, I'll have the department step up security."

His chocolate-brown eyes bore into hers. "Good. My daughter's life is first and foremost, Detective. Don't you ever forget that."

"We have a few promising leads, and we'll catch this son of a bitch soon," Bolton insisted.

"Don't blow smoke up my ass, Bolton. If this is the same person who murdered my son-in-law, then you have no idea who the guy is. If you did, he'd be in custody."

"I can assure you that we're doing everything we can." Bolton turned to Cole. "I'll give you a call if I find out anything. You have my number, right?"

"Yes, I do," Cole replied. "We'll talk before my flight in the morning."

"Definitely. I'm headed back to the station. I'll let the uniforms finish securing the scene."

Ted waited until Bolton was gone before turning to his daughter. "I know food is probably the last thing on your mind, Missy, but I think we should grab dinner in about an hour or so. What do you think?"

"Dinner for three sounds great," Cole declared. "From now on, Mrs. Melendez doesn't go anywhere without a police escort."

"Is that really necessary?" Missy asked. "I just want some time alone with my father and a chance to grieve in private." Her eyes shimmered with tears.

"Until we catch this guy, you're stuck with me. I can't protect you if I'm not there."

"You can barely keep her safe when you are there," Ted said mockingly.

"Would you like for me to leave, and you can protect her on your own with no gun and no training?"

"You've made your point, Detective. All I want is for my daughter to be safe."

"I understand, Mr. Delaney. I don't want anything to happen to Missy either. I've grown pretty fond of her."

Missy's heart felt lighter after Cole's remark. "There's this great Italian restaurant nearby that Kayla loved. It seems fitting to go there today. And Detective Cole loves lasagna."

"How could you possibly know that?"

Missy smiled. "I know a lot of things."

Yeah, that's part of the problem. "I bet."

Ted wasn't certain what was going on between the two women, but he didn't like it. "I guess it's settled then. I'll come by the hotel to pick you up."

CHAPTER 7

THE SMALL TAVERN IN THE AIRPORT WAS crowded with patrons enjoying food and drinks before their flights. Cole was noticeably preoccupied, too restless to respond to Missy's attempt at small talk. She tried to concentrate on the other woman's words, but the throbbing in her head made focusing unbearable. Cole had taken her migraine medicine earlier, but it had been ineffective. Now she was concerned that the pain would slow her reflexes if something transpired before they reached Connecticut.

"After this mess is over, I'm going to enter the space shuttle program and fly to the moon," Missy declared.

Puzzled, Cole stared at her. "What?"

"Ah … so I finally have your attention. What's going on? Are you still feeling sick?"

"No. I'm much better," Cole lied.

"Good. Daddy was worried about you last night when you didn't finish your dinner. He said you looked pale."

Cole's expression was skeptical. "I find that hard to believe."

Missy nodded. "I don't blame you. His interest surprised me too. But he asked about you when we were saying our goodbyes this morning."

"I appreciate his concern, but I'm okay." *I can't tell her that I spent most of the night on the bathroom floor. These hangover-type symptoms make no sense since I haven't had any alcohol.*

Missy frowned. "Are you sure? Because you still seem ill to me."

Cole rolled her eyes. "Is that your polite way of saying I look terrible?"

"No, Dani. That's not what I meant."

"Don't worry about it. I know I'm not my best today. I didn't get much sleep last night, so I probably look like death warmed over."

Missy tried to curtail her giggle, but she couldn't stop it from bubbling out. "What exactly does death warmed over look like?"

"Hell if I know. My mom used to say it all the time, especially when I refused to get my hair done or wear makeup."

"You don't need either. Maybe a little eyeliner to accentuate your eyes, but you are gorgeous without the customary female embellishments."

Cole lowered her head, embarrassed by the compliment. "Thank you," she mumbled.

"I'm a photographer, so beauty, in all its forms, catches my eye. I'm sure you've been told how stunning you are. And if you haven't, the people in your life have done you a great disservice." She paused. "It wasn't my intention to make you uncomfortable, but I won't apologize for telling the truth."

"I've heard it. I just have a hard time believing it," she whispered.

"If I had my camera, I'd take your picture so that you could see what I see."

"I don't need a photo. The mirror is enough for me."

Missy shook her head. "Someone did a serious job on you. Was it your parents? An ex? The suspect you fell in love with? Who was it?"

"I don't want to talk about it." She glanced at her watch. "Our flight will be leaving soon. We should pay the bill and get to our gate." She stood and reached for her purse.

"Eventually, you should let someone in, Dani. There are people that care about you. Surely, you can see that."

"You don't know anything about me or my life, Mrs. Melendez, so can we please just drop it?" she snapped.

Missy observed Cole as she marched to the cashier. *I wish I could, Dani, but I can't. I won't.*

Cole and Missy loitered in front of the sliding doors at Bradley International Airport while they waited for their car to arrive. Cole had made the reservation that morning, but the Uber driver was late. Cole thought that taking Uber would be quicker than catching a cab, but apparently, she'd been wrong.

She checked the app on her phone again to gauge his location and saw that he was still five minutes away. After the turbulence from the flight, Cole was feeling worse, and she was desperate to get home.

Once the driver arrived, he loaded their luggage into the trunk as they climbed into the back seat. Cole looked at her phone and then glanced at the person behind the wheel. She couldn't see his face clearly because of his hat, but he didn't resemble the photo Uber had sent her.

"Excuse me, but is your name Evan?"

"No, ma'am. Evan had to drop off a passenger across town, so they forwarded me the fare."

"Then what's your name?"

"I'm Noah. My information should show up on your phone before I drop you at your destination. That's what typically happens when there's a change in drivers."

"Good to know. I'm new to Uber, so I'm not exactly sure how it works."

"No problem, Ms. Cole. I hope you enjoy the ride."

Something about the way he said the last sentence made Cole uneasy. "How long before we get there?"

"About twenty-five minutes, ma'am."

Missy sensed the other woman's tension. "What's going on, Dani?"

"Everything is fine. I'm obligated to distrust everyone. It's an occupational hazard."

Missy glowered at the back of the driver's head and then looked at Cole. "You're not wrong," she whispered. "He's not a nice person. And his name is not Noah."

"And you know this how?"

"I just do," Missy asserted.

Cole chuckled. "You mean like how you knew that I liked lasagna? Lucky guess."

"I'm serious, Dani. I can see things, and we're in danger."

Cole didn't register Missy's caveat as she suddenly realized where they were. "Excuse me, but why are we still in Windsor Locks? I put in the app that I wanted to go to 145 Terry Road. We should be on I-91 by now, heading south."

"I'm sorry, Ms. Cole. They have the address in here incorrectly. Can you please reenter it so that I can bring it up on my GPS?"

Missy quietly interrupted. "Dani, don't you think we're moving a little slow?"

"Maybe he's lost. He did say there's a problem with the data in his phone," Cole whispered. She furtively tugged on the door handle, and just as she suspected, it was locked.

"No, it's because we're in trouble. We need to get out of this car!" Missy shrieked.

Without warning, the car took a sharp turn and careened off the road. The driver steered the vehicle rapidly along an embankment, heading straight toward the river. Before either woman comprehended what was happening, Noah abandoned the car. Cole tried to climb into the front, but she got tossed around as the vehicle accelerated downhill. Cole's second endeavor landed her upright in the driver seat, but she couldn't stop the car in time. It plunged into the water and rapidly began to fill. Cole swam out of the open driver's window as the vehicle sank into the murky depths. She pulled on the back door's lever to help Missy, but the door was still locked. Cole tried to use her hands to direct Missy to the front, but Missy was immobilized by fear.

Water filled Missy's lungs, and she couldn't breathe. Her body felt lighter as the car descended into the pits of darkness. *This is Dani's nightmare, not mine. Why am I here? Perhaps this is my chance to forget the pain and sorrow of the last few weeks. Maybe this is how I will find my peace.*

Cole reentered the vehicle and grabbed Missy by the shoulders. She hauled her out, and although Cole's body threatened to collapse, she found the strength to pull the other woman to the surface. She laid Missy on the grass and checked her pulse. Nothing. Cole immediately began CPR, and after a few seconds, Missy started to cough and sputter water. Grateful, Cole exhaled, but her respite was short-lived. A loud boom forced her to duck for cover. She shielded Missy with her body as the vehicle exploded in the water. The sound was deafening at such close proximity. Wreckage and water flew everywhere, raining violently on Cole's back. She screamed in agony as debris assailed her.

Minutes later, Missy slowly regained consciousness. She couldn't recall what had happened, but she knew from their positions on the ground that Cole had protected her. Missy wanted to move, but Cole still had her pinned down.

"I think it's over," Missy uttered to the detective. But she was met with a frightening silence. She tried to lift Cole's body from her own, and after several attempts, she succeeded. She crawled to her knees and gazed at her rescuer. Panic set in when she saw the red stains on Cole's clothing. Missy looked around for her phone but remembered it was underwater with her purse.

Missy sat numb and motionless until the sound of sirens stirred her into action. She lightly touched Cole's face and whispered, "I know we don't know each other well, but I can't lose you." *I need to find out why you're so different, why you make me different.* "Please don't give up. Help is on the way."

Missy scrambled up the embankment and beckoned the police and ambulance over to her location. While the cop asked her questions, the paramedics grabbed their equipment and went to retrieve Cole from the muddy terrain. Missy silently prayed as they worked on her for several minutes and then ascended the hill, almost capsizing the stretcher twice. She clutched Cole's lifeless hand as the paramedics loaded her into the van.

"Can I ride with her?" Missy implored.

"You're sure you don't need any medical attention, lady?"

"No. I'm fine."

"You should probably still get yourself checked out," the paramedic stated.

The officer nodded. "He's right. Go to the hospital with your friend. I'll be there in about an hour or so to follow up with you."

Missy contemplated whether to divulge the truth about Cole's identity and their relationship to the officer. *If I tell him, he'll probably take me to the station, and I won't be there for Dani. I'll just tell him everything when he comes to the hospital.*

She held out her hand, and the paramedic helped her climb into the vehicle. As the doors closed, Missy wondered if her vision had been wrong and this was how Cole would die. *Please let the answer be no. I need more time.*

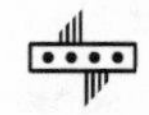

"Dani, help me!" David screams.

"David, where are you?"

The six-year-old's voice quivers. "I'm in the closet. Please open the door. I'm afraid of the dark."

"I'm coming, Davie. Be brave!" Cole yells.

He starts to weep. "Hurry! He's going to come back and hurt me again. Please don't let him."

Cole circles the room in search of David, but her efforts are futile. There are no windows or doors—just walls saturated with her brother's suffering. She occupies a corner and pounds frantically on the plaster. She doesn't realize her hands are bleeding until tiny droplets strike the floor.

"David, I'm so sorry. I don't know how to reach you."

"You have to find me. I'm scared," he whines.

"Give it up, Danielle. You'll never find him," her father taunts. "You're weak and a failure, just like your mother. You can't protect him. He's mine."

Cole crouches down on the carpet and covers her ears, something she hasn't done since she was a child. "I won't let you have him, Daddy," she cries.

His laughter is cruel. "You're too late."

"You promised, Dani. You broke your promise." David's sobs echo in the barren space until there is nothing left but an eerie quiet.

The smell of antiseptic and the beeping of the monitor alerted Cole that she was in the hospital. She wanted to analyze her nightmare, but the aching in her body caused her to discount it. Cole opened her eyes and whimpered in pain. The sound notified the others in the room that she was conscious.

Missy rose from the chair and dashed to the bed. "Thank God you're awake. We were worried."

Blake moved beside Missy. "How are you feeling?"

"Don't ask." Cole stared at them and frowned. "Why are the two of you here?"

"You don't remember what happened?"

"Not really, but the IV in my arm tells me I'm in the hospital. And if my pain is any indication, whatever put me here was bad."

"It was. But I'll let Missy explain everything while I go get the doctor," Blake declared.

"Hurry back, Lieutenant Blake," said Missy. "Sounds like she's really hurting."

"That's an understatement. Now tell me how I got here," Cole grumbled as Blake exited the room.

Missy did not relish the idea of recounting her second near-death experience in a matter of days. She took a deep breath and spoke softly. "We were heading from the airport, and you became suspicious of our Uber driver, so you started asking him questions."

"Why?"

"He wasn't the person in the picture the company sent to your phone. You knew something wasn't right. We both did. I guess he got spooked and veered off the road. We went down an embankment, and he jumped out right before the vehicle nosedived into the water. You climbed into the front seat and tried to keep us from going into the river, but it was too late."

"And what were you doing while I was risking my life?" Despite her subdued tone, Cole's words were accusatory.

Although the detective's censure was justifiable, Missy still resented it. "Someone is trying to kill me, not you."

"Yes, and I'm collateral damage."

"I'm sorry that my presence puts your life in danger."

"I'm the one who signed up for this job, Missy. And thus far, I've kept both of us alive, so there's no need to apologize," she stated coolly. "What happened after that?"

Missy sighed. "I was frozen with terror in the back seat. You pulled me out, and a few moments later, the car exploded. Your head and back were pummeled with fragments from the car when you shielded me with your body. Dr. Thurman said you have a concussion and a sprained back. At least that's what I overheard him tell Lieutenant Blake."

"Did you also happen to overhear when I will be able to leave?"

Missy shook her head. "You were unconscious for more than twenty-four hours, and you're already talking about leaving? Perhaps the bump on your head is worse than originally thought."

"A couple of pain pills, and I'll be fine."

"That's not funny," Missy asserted.

"Who's joking? I—"

The doctor entered the room before Cole could finish. "Glad to see you're awake, Ms. Cole. How do you feel?"

"Like I've been run over by a tractor trailer."

"Pain is a promising sign with your type of injuries. But I still need to check you for paralysis."

"She could be paralyzed?" Missy's fear was tangible.

"There's some likelihood that there was damage to the spinal cord, which could cause loss of muscle function, accompanied by a loss of feeling in the affected area," Dr. Thurman explained. "There may be some sensory damage as well as motor, but I need to completely rule out both possibilities."

"If there is, it's my fault," Missy whispered.

"Missy, please. I'm the one who's injured," Cole admonished. "Besides, it's my job."

"I wish you would stop saying that. I know it's your job, but that doesn't mean I can't care."

"Um … maybe you should wait outside with Lieutenant Blake until I'm done with the examination, Mrs. Melendez."

"Okay. I'll be in the hall." She scurried out of the room and leaned against the wall. She struggled to control her emotions but ultimately released the stream of tears.

A few minutes later, Blake stumbled upon Missy curled up in a ball on the floor. He bent down and touched her arm. "What's wrong, Melissa? Did something happen with Cole?"

Startled by the contact, Missy gaped at him. "The doctor is checking her for paralysis. He asked me to wait out here."

"Does he think she's paralyzed?" Blake's voice trembled with fear.

"No. I think it's merely a precaution."

"Thank God," he breathed.

"I'm sorry. I probably should have said that in the beginning. I'm a bit emotional lately."

"You lost your husband, your best friend, and almost your own life. I think that more than justifies your feelings." He offered Missy his hand. "Let me help you up."

Missy stood and wiped away her tears. "You should probably go in and check on her."

Blake nodded. "Yeah. That will make me feel better."

Missy sensed his anxiety, and that made her smile. She knew, after seeing them interact at Robert's funeral, that Blake was in love with Cole. "I know you're not supposed to tell me, but …"

"I'll let you know what the doctor says."

"Thank you. Do you mind if I go get a cup of coffee?"

"You really shouldn't go anywhere alone. Your life is still in jeopardy."

"I promise not to go far. And if I'm not back in five minutes, you can send out an APB."

He laughed. "Okay, but don't be long."

Missy watched him enter the room. She envied what could be the beginning of something beautiful between Blake and Cole. Although things hadn't always been great with Robert, Missy longed for his companionship, his strength, his all-encompassing love. She yearned for the tiny beads of desire that seeped in through the night's gentle caress, pleading with her body to come alive. For the dawn that brought sweet memories as her heart flooded with aching pleasure. Her heart now searched for an imprint, a remembrance of those warm sensations that had once set her soul ablaze.

A single tear ran down her cheek, then another, and then another. *I wonder if I will ever feel like that again or if I am doomed to live a life with nothing but my dreams to keep me warm.*

Dr. Thurman's tone was drab as he spoke with Blake in the hallway. "I wanted to speak to you alone, Lieutenant Blake. I'm concerned that Ms. Cole will try to leave the hospital before she's fully recovered."

Blake exhaled deeply. "Shit, Dr. Thurman. I thought you were going to tell me that she was paralyzed."

"No. Everything looks okay. I still want to keep an eye on her, though. The problem is, she's demanding to be released today."

"Yeah, that sounds like Cole."

"I advised her that it could be at least a week, or more, before she's discharged. I don't think she was happy with that news. If she had her weapon, I think she would have shot me."

"You're right. She would have," Blake affirmed matter-of-factly.

Dr. Thurman chuckled nervously. "Lucky for me then that she doesn't have it."

"So you need me to try to convince her to stay put until she's fully healed."

"Exactly. Do you think you can?"

"I'll try, Doctor. But I can tell you now that no one can make Cole do something she doesn't want to do."

"Maybe the possibility of permanent paralysis will help convince her."

"Wow. Did you tell her that?"

"Of course, I did," he proclaimed. "Now if you'll excuse me, I have other patients to see. Have a great day." He unceremoniously strolled away.

"No wonder Cole wants to shoot him. He's an ass," Blake said out loud.

Missy stood at the sink and washed her hands. She saw a mother walk into the ladies' room with her young son, and she smiled. Although the little boy seemed familiar, Missy knew that she had never seen him before that day.

The boy entered one of the stalls, and the woman stood outside to wait for him. "Are you sure you don't want me to come in there with you, Jordan?"

"No, Mommy. I'm a big boy. I can do it by myself. And as a reward, can I watch cartoons when we got home?"

The child's voice unexpectedly propelled Missy into a vision. She tried to fight the images by splashing cold water on her face, but she couldn't control the vision. Her last coherent thought before the dream fully consumed her was that the child in the dream resembled the one in the bathroom.

Luke quickly turns off the television when he hears his father enter the house, but he is too late. The man rushes toward the little boy and smacks him hard across the face. "I told you that you're not allowed to watch Satan's box." He snatches the remote from Luke's hand and throws it against the wall.

"But Mommy said I could watch cartoons," he whines.

"That's because your mother is a sinner like the people on TV." Bob glances around the trailer. "Where is she?"

"She's asleep."

"You mean she's drunk."

"Don't hurt her again, Daddy. She's just sad."

"You're going to be the sad one, Luke, when I return with my paddle."

Luke watches him walk down the hall to their bedroom. He rocks back and forth and covers his ears to block out his mother's screams. Tears flow down his cheeks as he listens to his father hit her repeatedly.

"Leave her alone!" the voice in his head yells. "Someone should hurt him instead of him always hurting us."

Suddenly, Luke stops swaying and climbs off the sofa. He goes into the kitchen, gets a knife from the drawer, and heads to his parents' room. The boy quietly moves toward the mattress on the floor, where Bob is on top of his mother, having sex. He lifts the knife high in the air and brings it down on his father's back over and over. Harriet begs him to stop as the blood sprays on her face and arms. But Luke doesn't drop the knife until Bob is completely motionless.

"It is finished," Luke whispers.

Harriet shoves Bob's body off her and grabs Luke's bloody hand. "Oh my God, Luke. What have you done?"

"I've given us absolution," he utters. "Now close your eyes, and let's pray that Daddy's soul is at rest."

Missy wasn't sure how long she was out of it, but when she opened her eyes, the woman and her son were gone. She dried her face and hands and then exited the bathroom. When Missy turned the corner, she collided with a man whose hostile energy instantly put her on alert.

"Excuse me," she whispered as she attempted to escape.

"Melissa? Melissa Melendez?" His voice transformed into baleful tentacles that gripped her legs, forcing her to halt.

"Do I know you?" she asked.

"I'm Dale Markham. I was one of your husband's patients."

She stared at him. *Short and stocky.* "Right, I remember you." *You're the man that was arguing with my father that night at the house. I'll never forget your voice.*

"I heard about what happened to Robert. My condolences."

"Thank you." She paused. "Aren't you also friends with my father?"

His look of shock was fleeting. "Yeah. I was one of Ted's clients. He's great at his job, and he gets paid pretty good for it." His latter words were dripping with contempt.

"The price of justice is high," she replied.

"Sometimes too high."

She attempted to keep her tone casual. "It's quite a coincidence that you know both my dad and my husband."

"Not really. Bobby recommended me to your father when I needed legal help."

"My husband told you to call him Bobby?"

"He didn't tell me to do anything. I called him whatever I wanted … period."

"Oh. I'm a little surprised, that's all."

The quiet that ensued was charged with tension. Missy had a lot of questions, and she recognized instinctively that this man would answer them with the unadulterated truth. She just wasn't sure she was emotionally equipped to hear it.

"Well, it was nice meeting you," Missy lied.

"Make sure you tell Ted that you saw me and I'm still waiting."

Missy struggled to speak as the tentacles wrapped themselves around her neck, strangling her. "I'll tell him."

"It was great seeing your pretty face. I'm sure this won't be the last time." His departing words sounded more like a threat than a farewell.

Once her airways were open again, Missy took several deep breaths. She closed her eyes and was trying to conjure up his face in hopes that it would trigger a vision when a sudden thought occurred to her. Dale's name had been on the list of about thirty names that she'd found in Robert's office. Robert had been enraged when he caught sight of the document in her hand. That was the first time she'd ever glimpsed his inner character, and it had terrified her.

"Don't ever touch my personal files again, Melissa. Those documents are off-limits."

Missy had watched as his features transformed into something inhumane. "I'm sorry," she had said. "They were just sitting on your desk, out in the open."

He had turned his back and moved the painting on the wall to reveal his safe. He twisted the dial a few times left and then right before opening the door. He put the piece of paper inside and closed it with a resounding "stay the hell out" slam.

An unexpected surge of vulnerability caused Blake to hesitate in the doorway of Cole's room. The burden of unrequited feelings weighed profoundly on his shoulders. Blake cared for Cole, but he knew she wasn't ready for a relationship. That's why he had to exorcise the gnawing in his chest. If he didn't, desolation would darken his doorstep. He could feel it, see it, taste it. Cole possessed the power to hurt him, unlike any other woman. Thus, he needed to liberate his heart from love's uncompromising grip.

He approached the bed and gazed at her. Her eyes were closed, but she wasn't asleep.

"Stop staring at me like some demented stalker," Cole muttered. "It's weird."

"Is there any other kind of stalker besides a demented one?"

"Well, since you're the culprit, you tell me."

"I see that even a slight derailment doesn't keep your sarcasm train from chugging along."

"Of course not. It's one of the reasons you love me."

The truth of Cole's words hung awkwardly in the air until she disrupted the silence. "Where's Missy?"

Blake was grateful for the respite. "She went to get coffee."

"Alone?"

"The hospital is safe, Tinks."

She sat up and tried to climb out of bed. "I need to check on her."

Blake grabbed her by the shoulders. "Please lie back down, Tinks, before you make your injuries worse."

Cole placed her palm on his chest. "She could be in danger."

Electricity flickered between them. Blake wanted desperately to kiss her, but instead he removed his hands. "Uh …" He cleared his throat. "I'll go."

Cole watched him leave the room. She took a deep breath to calm her rapid heartbeat. *I can't fall in love with Blake because he'll hurt me more than Cavanaugh ever could.*

Susan gazed at herself in the bathroom mirror. Despite the throbbing pain, she was fascinated by the colorful shades adorning her swollen eye. The hues stood out in stark contrast to her ethereal pale skin, making her injuries appear more severe.

Susan touched her face and traced the almost imperceptible mark on her left cheek. It had been two years, and she was still in awe of Dr. Melendez's work. When she had first visited him, she thought the damage from the so-called accident was permanent. After the surgery, Susan had acknowledged that Dr. Melendez was a miracle worker. He had reconstructed the bones in her face and made her pretty again, but Susan wasn't pleased. She had realized that her disfigurement could be the catalyst needed for David to leave her. But once the bandages came off, and she viewed the results, her optimism had faded.

Susan glanced at the scissors perched on the edge of the sink. She picked up the shears and began to cut her hair. With indifference, she watched the thin brown tendrils fall to the floor. She knew David would punish her, yet she didn't care. When he pounded on the door fifteen minutes later, she simply smiled and let him in.

David reeked of alcohol. It radiated from his pores. "What the fuck did you do to your hair?" he bellowed.

"I cut it. Do you like it?" Her tone was goading.

"You look like a damn boy. I didn't give you permission to do that."

"It's my hair, David. I thought it would look sexier short."

Without warning, David lunged for her. He wrapped his right hand around her neck and thrust her toward the mirror. The back of her head was planted firmly against the glass while the remainder of her body dangled against the sink.

"Bitch, I don't pay you to think."

Susan gasped for breath. "You don't pay me at all. You must have me confused with one of your whores."

David yanked her head forward and then smashed it forcefully against the mirror. "You dare talk to me like that! Have you forgotten what I will do if you don't obey me? Do I need to blacken your other eye? You have no mouth unless I tell you to talk. You have no legs until I tell you to move. And you have no brain … ever. Got it?"

Susan tried to nod, but she couldn't move. "Yes," she mumbled.

"Good." He removed his hand. "You need to call the salon and have them fix that mess today, Susan. And when you get back, watch DVD number 5. I have them all marked. That one features Mandy, with the pixie haircut. Tonight, you will do everything she did to me on that recording. Take notes because if you make a mistake … well, you know what will happen." He snickered as he departed the bathroom.

"Ms. Cole, there's something I need to discuss with you," Dr. Thurman announced as he entered the room.

"What's wrong?" Cole asked anxiously.

"When you were brought in, there was a prescription bottle in your pocket with the label missing. You were unconscious, so we asked the young lady with you if she knew what the pills were. Because she didn't, I had one analyzed."

"Sorry you wasted your time, Doctor. Those pills are for my migraines."

"Actually, it wasn't a waste of time. Have you been feeling more fatigued and nauseous lately?"

She nodded. "Yes. I planned to call my doctor when I got home. I don't think the medicine is working for me anymore."

"It's not," he stated bluntly. "Did your pills look different this time?"

Cole was taken aback by his abrasiveness. "Yes, but the pharmacist explained that I was getting Imitrex in capsule form because they were out of tablets. What is this about, anyway?"

"The capsules are filled with arsenic."

"Shit. Someone's trying to kill me too?"

"It certainly looks that way."

"But only a few people know about my migraines," she groused.

"Sounds like your first priority when you get back on your feet, Detective." He scribbled something in her chart and placed it back in front of her bed. "And just so you know, I'm still obligated to inform the police department of your poisoning, even though you're a cop. Now get some rest because the sooner you leave here, the sooner you can catch the bad guy."

Cole tried to tamp down the desire to throw something at him as he left. *How does he expect me to rest after telling me that someone wants me dead?*

Missy hovered next to Cole's bed, momentarily putting off the inevitable. She wanted to rush out of the room, but she knew that would only cause further problems. After the run-in with Robert's former patient, she had to warn Cole.

"Are you asleep?" Missy whispered.

"How could I be when this room is a revolving door?" Cole said sarcastically.

"I'm sorry. Would you like me to go back out into the hall and knock?"

Cole sat up. "Why bother? You're already here."

Missy shook her head. "I'm going to ignore your attitude since I know it's the pain talking."

"If telling yourself that makes you feel better, then so be it." She glanced at the door. "Where's Blake? He was supposed to find you."

"He did. But he stayed behind to take a call."

"I wonder if it has something to do with the guy who did this."

"You shouldn't be worrying about that right now. I guess being hurt doesn't turn off your cop instincts, huh?"

"Nope. I'm always on guard."

"How long have you been a cop, Dani?"

"Twelve years. I started young because I needed something—anything—to take me away from my dysfunctional surroundings. I needed ..." Cole vacillated.

"You needed what?"

I needed to be loved. "Doesn't matter," she mumbled. *What is it about this woman that makes me want to bare my soul?* "You were gone awhile. Where did you go?"

"Why? Were you worried that I skipped town?" she joked.

"There's nothing funny about almost being killed, Missy. You need to take the threat on your life seriously. That means a police escort at all times."

"I'm sorry. I was just trying to lighten the mood. To answer your question, I went to get coffee but stopped in the ladies' room first. As I was leaving, I ran into one of Robert's former patients. My conversation with him reminded me of something that might help the case." She sat in the chair next to the bed. "Robert kept a list of names locked in his office safe. I came across it on his desk one day, and once he realized I'd seen it, he fired me. The man I saw—his name was on the list."

"You didn't mention before that he fired you. What could be so important about a bunch of names that would compel him to terminate his own wife?"

It probably has something to do with that vision I had of him killing a patient, but I can't tell you that. Missy shook her head. "I don't know."

"What was the name of the guy you saw today?"

"Dale Markham, I think."

Shock registered on Cole's face. "Are you sure his last name wasn't Mecham?"

"He introduced himself as Markham today, but now that you mention it, yeah, the name Dale Mecham was on the list too, in the first column. Dale Markham's name was in the second column right next to Mecham."

"Shit. This is unbelievable," Cole groused.

"Who is he?"

"Murderer, arsonist, thief … the scum of the earth."

"Why would Robert have someone like that as a client?" *And why would my father be involved with him too?*

"I don't know. You were married to him. Maybe it was his choice of patients that got him killed."

Her words stung. "You really can be cruel sometimes."

"It comes with the job," she said rigidly. "Can you remember any other names from that list?"

"Yeah. Carter Garrison … uh … Trevor Mason. Wait, no, it was Moore, not Mason. And there was a woman … Daphne Todd. That's all I can remember for now."

Cole was speechless. It was like Missy was reading off a who's who of the country's criminals. "Do you recall the names in the second column for the people you mentioned? I believe those could be their aliases."

"No, Robert interrupted me before I could finish reading. Mecham and Markham were easy to remember because that was only place on the list where the first name was the same in both columns."

"Do you have the combination to your husband's safe? Do you know if he kept patient files in there as well?"

"I saw some binders in there, but I don't have the combination."

"What about Robert's partners? Would they have the combo or know what was in his safe?"

"I doubt it since he wouldn't even share it with me."

"You mean like how he shared the fact that he had a mistress with you?"

Missy stood and turned to leave.

"I'm sorry, Missy," Cole called out.

Missy stopped and looked back at her.

"Every day on this job seems to chip away at my humanity. I've let all the ugliness that I see on a regular basis erode my compassion. It's not fair to take that out on you."

Missy sighed. "You can't keep pushing yourself. No matter how many criminals you catch, that won't atone for your childhood. You can't save the world."

"What are you talking about?"

"It wasn't your fault, Dani. You did your best to protect him, but you were too young to defeat the giant."

"Giants only exist in fairy tales. And who couldn't I protect in this make-believe world of yours?"

"Your brother," Missy whispered.

Cole gaped at her. "How …" Her voice trailed off.

"I've seen your dreams. I've felt your pain. In many ways, it's become a part of me."

Cole shook her head. "Um, did the doctors check you out? I think you may have been hit in the head with some debris. You might have a concussion."

"I'm not crazy," Missy asserted.

"Then what are you? Psychic?"

"No. I can sense things. And occasionally, I have visions that come true."

"Isn't that what psychics do?"

"Look, I know you don't believe me, but our lives are in danger."

"I realize that, not because of some Magic 8-Ball or tarot cards but because of good old-fashioned police work. I remember when I was a rookie, I spent a lot of time tracking down leads from so-called psychics. I wanted to prove myself and was willing to try anything at the time. But all it did was make me look like a fool. That's why I don't believe in telepathy, ESP, or any of that other supernatural crap. I follow my gut."

Missy was visibly disappointed. "So do I. And right now, mine is telling me to go get Blake. We're clearly done here." She sprinted to the door but hesitated before leaving. "By the way, the next time you're drowning, Detective, I won't extend my hand to help since you don't need me." She walked out.

Cole wanted to stop her but was immobilized by fear. The only way Missy could have known about Cole's watery death in her dream was if her professed ability to see Cole's most intimate thoughts was authentic. And to Cole, that possibility was scarier than any would-be assassin hell-bent on killing them both.

Dale drove into the garage and discarded his lit cigarette in the ashtray. He pressed the opener to close the door and then climbed out of the truck. He entered the house through the kitchen and flipped the light switch. Instantaneously, the house exploded, the sound thunderous and deafening. Fire entangled Dale in flaming vines, and after a few seconds, his agonizing screams faded in the glow of the moonlit night.

CHAPTER 8

MERCK KNOCKED SOFTLY ON BLAKE'S door. "Is now a good time?"

Blake waved him inside. "Yes. I'm just finishing up some paperwork for Cole. Have a seat."

"I'm sorry for calling you away from the hospital, but this is important." He sat down in one of the empty chairs. "How is Cole?"

"She's doing okay. She just needs to take it easy for a few days."

"I don't know Cole that well, but I have a feeling that's going to be hard for her to do."

Blake smiled. "You're right, but I'm not giving her any choice."

"I know you two used to be partners. It's good that you're still looking out for her."

"Of course. That will never change."

"Even in death, the bond between partners is unbreakable."

Blake detected the sadness in his voice. "Did something happen to your partner?"

"Yes. He's the reason I'm here in Connecticut. I need your help finding his killer, but first, I need to know whether I can trust you."

"You can. You have my word."

"I was hoping you'd say that because in New York it was hard to trust anyone. The corruption within my department was widespread. And the person responsible for my partner's murder had not only cops but even city officials on his payroll. His boss's influence stretched far and wide, so I wasn't exactly sure what I was walking into when I came here. But once I heard the details of what happened between you and Cole in the Cavanaugh case, I realized that I had to come to you."

Blake leaned forward in his chair. "So this is about Cavanaugh?"

"Yes. For the last few years, I've been investigating a large narcotics ring that spans several states, including New Jersey and Pennsylvania—Philadelphia being one of the biggest drug-trafficking areas. It was believed that the head of this drug cartel was headquartered here in Connecticut, but he had one person in command in each region. Since New York is such a huge place, his guy there, Trevor Moore, was well-known. There were rumors that Moore and his partner Mitchell Conrad were plotting to take over the whole tristate operation and dispose of Cavanaugh. Moore was wreaking havoc in my jurisdiction by killing anyone who wasn't on board with his agenda. We were finding the bodies of drug dealers every week. These were guys who were afraid to go against Cavanaugh because they knew he'd kill their families. The man is ruthless."

"Yes, I'm aware of this. But Cavanaugh is in jail. Why come here?"

"When Cavanaugh was arrested, Moore abandoned his idea of getting rid of him since he felt it was no longer necessary. But Cavanaugh continued running his business from prison, with Sanchez as his go-to guy. Once Cavanaugh discovered the truth, he put a hit out on Moore and Conrad, and both men disappeared for years. I wasn't sure if they'd left town or been killed."

"Probably the latter."

"That's what I thought too. And several months ago, my suspicions seemed to be confirmed, but the timing was all wrong. A body was found in the Delaware River inside of a car—one shot to the head, execution-style. Per the medical examiner's report, the body had been in the water for three months. That meant it couldn't have been either of my suspects unless they had been in hiding and finally gotten caught. We ran the picture and name found on the driver's license on news stations and social media sites for weeks, but no one claimed the body."

"Was it Moore or Conrad?"

"Neither, according to the name and picture on the ID. But after we checked our faux John Doe's DNA, he was identified as Mitchell Conrad. He'd apparently had extensive facial reconstruction."

"Which led you to Hartford because his plastic surgeon was Robert Melendez."

"Bingo. Seems Mr. Melendez was changing bad guys' faces and then blackmailing them to keep their aliases a secret. Some of the names mentioned by my informant besides Moore were Dale Mecham, Michael Tucker, and Lucas Burns. He gave me a partial list that he received from a man that wanted him to get rid of Melendez. He, of course, wouldn't tell me who ordered the kill or if he was the one who carried out the hit. I assume the guy who wanted Melendez dead is on that list too, but without Melendez's records, we have no idea who else we're dealing with, especially if they have a new face."

"There are records?"

"Yes. My informant also told me that Melendez kept files on each one of his criminal patients, including names, addresses, IDs, and photos. I searched Robert's house and office, but I didn't find anything."

"You're not primary on this case, Merck. You shouldn't be investigating Melendez behind my detectives' backs," Blake admonished. "This isn't New York. We go by the book here."

"I realize that, and I apologize, Blake. I was a bit anxious once I heard that Mrs. Melendez's life was in danger. She's seen the list, so she's a threat to them," he asserted. "I just don't want anyone else to get hurt."

Blake shook his head. "It's Cole and Thomas's job to protect her, Sergeant Merck, not yours."

"All I want to do is help, Lieutenant Blake. And after the information I just disclosed about my history in New York, you know I can be an asset."

"I'll let Thomas and Cole make that decision. You already know where Cole is. And Thomas is interviewing the Melendezes' neighbors who just returned from Italy, but he should be done soon."

"I've heard great things about Cole, but I don't know much about Thomas. How long has he been with the department?"

"Not long. Thomas is a decorated officer who was an integral part of the security detail for Philadelphia's Mayor Nutter. He transferred once the city's new administration took over."

"Oh. I'd heard that he came here because of his wife."

"Yeah, that's true, but I hate the idea of my precinct gossiping about another officer's personal life. What exactly did you hear?"

"His wife left him and moved to Connecticut. He followed her here and tried to talk her into coming back to Philly. She refused and gave him an ultimatum—Hartford or nothing. To make a long story short, he decided to stay. But after he sold his house, switched jobs, and moved here, she left him again. He hasn't seen or heard from her in months. Supposedly, she ran away with her boss. He came home one day, and she was gone. Wrote him the old 'Dear John' letter saying she still cared about him but was in love with this other guy."

"A tough blow for a guy who gave up everything. So that's why he's so reserved."

"Yeah, I can't imagine how hard that was for him."

Blake's phone rang. "Excuse me for a second." He answered and listened to the voice on the other end. He hung up and looked directly at Merck. "We may have just found Dale Mecham."

"Not to brag, but it's clear you shouldn't go anywhere without your other half," Thomas declared as he walked into the room.

Cole rolled her eyes. "Fuck you, Thomas. I don't need you to protect me. I'm not some helpless damsel in distress."

He laughed. "Lying in a hospital bed kind of takes away from your argument."

"I may be sick, but I can still kick your ass." She propped herself up on the pillows. "What are you doing here?"

"Can't I come check on my partner?" He laid some files on the table and then sat in the chair next to the bed. "Don't tell Blake that I brought you these case files, or both of our asses will be in a sling."

"I won't say a word. And thank you. I'm going stir-crazy, not knowing what's going on with the case. Is there anything new?"

"I just came from McCain's room. He's not cooperating. He's afraid he'll end up like Robert."

"I know how he feels. I found out today that someone is trying to kill me."

"What? You mean because of the Melendez woman?"

"I'm not sure why, but someone put poison in my migraine medication."

"That's unbelievable, Cole. Do you have any idea who it could be? I'm assuming not many people know about your migraines."

"No. Just a few cops and my family." *Plus Cavanaugh.*

"Have you told Blake?"

"Not yet, but I will. Listen, I have things to tell you before Missy returns."

"I'm surprised you let her out of your sight."

"Blake put a uni on her."

"Good. So what's going on?"

"Missy told me that her husband kept a list of patients' names in a safe in his office. I think he gave them new faces."

"But that's what plastic surgeons do. Why hide it?"

"Because they're all criminals."

Thomas was taken aback. "Are you serious?"

"Yes. Dale Mecham is on that list. And get this … Trevor Moore."

"Moore? No way. I always thought he was a ghost haunting his victims."

"And that's exactly what Melendez turned those criminals into, which is why we've been unable to catch them."

"It makes sense," said Thomas. "Plus, it gives someone the perfect motive for murder. Kill off all the people who know the truth about the killer's real identity—Robert, George, Missy."

"And what about Bill Roman?" said Cole. "Do you think he's next?"

"It's possible, unless he's involved."

"Either way, we need to keep an eye on him."

Thomas nodded. "You're right. Did Mrs. Melendez mention any other names?"

"Yes. I had her write down what she could remember." Cole handed him a piece of paper.

"Okay, I'll check into these names and follow up on Roman. In the meantime, try to take it easy. I need you 100 percent and back at work. There's no one else to bust my balls."

Cole laughed. "Is that your way of saying you miss me?"

Thomas smiled. "Maybe. But I'll deny it if you tell anyone." He stood and laid his hand on her arm. "Seriously, I'm glad you're okay, partner. Now get some rest, and I'll let you know if I come up with anything new."

The envelope taunted Merck with its clandestine contents. He fingered the edge, knowing that once he opened it, his life would irrevocably change. He'd done a lot of unscrupulous things in the name of lady justice, and she was determined to seek revenge.

Merck gasped aloud as he shuffled through the contents. He dropped the pictures on the desk and hastily made a call. "This is Merck. Is my wife okay?"

There was a pause as the officer presumably peeked into Marie's room. "Yes, Sergeant. She's resting right now."

"Have someone check on Miracle and confirm that she's safe too," he stated anxiously.

"The baby is fine. Mrs. Merck just came back from seeing her a half hour ago. Is something wrong?"

Merck exhaled deeply. He hadn't realized he'd been holding his breath. "No. I'm just happy my wife is feeling better. Hopefully, I will be able to bring her home soon."

He disconnected and made another call. "This is Merck. If anything happens to my wife or daughter, I'll make sure the entire world knows your true identity."

Missy lounged on the sofa in Ted's study and glanced at her watch. Her father's car service from the airport was due to arrive at any moment. She hadn't seen him since Kayla's funeral, but she had called to tell him what happened to her on the way from the airport. He had been livid at the news that there had been a second attempt on her life and had insisted that she be at the house when he returned home.

Missy heard the door open, and her heart fell to her stomach. She wasn't sure she was ready to confront her father about Dale, but it had to be done. *If he's involved in something illegal, can I turn him in? Can I do that to the one person I have left?*

Ted entered the room and held his arms open for Missy. She stood and readily walked into them. "I'm glad you're home, Daddy," she whispered.

He stroked her hair in a comforting gesture. "I can't believe someone tried to kill you again. What in the hell are the police doing?"

Missy stepped back and looked up at him. "Don't start. There's a police escort outside, and I'm still alive. Isn't that what's important?"

"Yes. You're absolutely right, sweetheart." He headed to the minibar and poured himself a glass of vodka. After a few sips, he walked over to his favorite chair and sat down. "I know this probably isn't the best time, but we need to discuss Robert's will."

"Not now," she asserted. "I need to ask you a question."

"Fine, but afterward we are going to talk about the will. We've been putting it off long enough."

"Okay." She momentarily wavered. "Daddy, who is Dale Markham?"

Ted was shocked. "Where in the hell did you hear that name?"

"He was one of Robert's patients. I can tell by your reaction that you know exactly who he is."

"Unfortunately, I do." His voice was laced with derision.

"Please tell me that you and Robert didn't have anything illegal going on with him—because he mentioned that he was one of your clients too."

"You saw him?"

"Yes. I ran into him at the hospital."

"Did that bastard threaten you?" he asked tautly.

"No. But the way he looked at me, his words … I was frightened."

"I'm sorry, Missy. What did he say to you?"

"He said he's still waiting to hear from you and that it wouldn't be the last time he would see me."

"Don't worry. I'll take care of it. I'm sorry you had to endure that."

"Daddy, you didn't answer my question. Were you and Robert caught up in something illegal? You can be honest with me."

"I said I would handle it, Melissa. There's nothing for you to be concerned about."

"Well, I am concerned. He was my husband, and you're my father. I have a right to know."

His inner struggle was reflected in his dark eyes. "All right. I'll explain what I can." He faltered for a few seconds, unsure of how much he should share with her. "Robert and I had a simple gentleman's agreement. Several of my clients were victims of violent crimes who needed surgery to repair their scars, so I recommended them to Robert. And he did the same for me."

"Meaning what? If one of his patients needed legal advice, he'd send them to you?"

He nodded. "Yes. That's the general idea."

Missy gazed at him in confusion. "But you're a corporate lawyer."

"I've been practicing criminal law for several years now. That's why I'm able to represent you."

"I didn't realize … I'm sorry," she murmured.

"You and I haven't talked much since you became Mrs. Robert Melendez. How could you know?"

Missy sighed. "Don't do that, Daddy. I feel bad enough as it is. I don't need a guilt trip."

"Believe me, that wasn't my intention."

"Yes, it was. You use disparagement as an evasion tactic. You did it with Mom, and you've done it to me. But it's not going to work this time," she stated adamantly. "I want to know why Robert fired you. What happened?"

"Nothing happened. I just wasn't comfortable representing lowlifes who wanted me to break the law for them. When I told Robert that, he said he'd find another lawyer who would."

"So that's it? There's nothing else?"

"That's all there was for me. I have no idea what was going on with Robert beyond that."

"Are you telling me the truth, Daddy? Because whatever Robert was involved in got him killed. And whoever murdered my husband now wants me dead too."

"Don't you think if I knew why someone was after you, I'd put an end to it? I would never let anything happen to you, Missy."

"Then why did this Dale character make it seem like you know what's going on? He said he's waiting like you owe him something."

Ted shook his head. "I blame Robert for that. Mr. Markham claims that Robert owed him money, and since I used to represent your husband's business, he thinks I should pay him. I told him that I wouldn't."

"I'm worried about you, Daddy. I hear he's a bad person."

"Everything will be fine. I deal with scum like Markham all the time."

"I'm sure Robert thought that too." She hastily stood up. "I'm going to head back to the hospital and check on Cole."

"I don't understand why you care so much about the woman who's trying to send you to prison," he said irritably.

"She's my ..." There was an awkward pause. "She risked her life to save mine ... again."

"That's her job," he snapped.

"She could have died," Missy whispered.

"I hope you're not being delusional about this woman, Melissa. She's not going to invite you out to shop or over for tea. You're a murder suspect to her. I'm sorry if that hurts you, but we both know it's true. I know you miss Kayla, but Detective Cole won't replace her. You two will never be friends."

Silent tears rolled down Missy's face as she realized that her father's lecture was true. She turned and left without another word.

The smell of smoke and charred debris permeated the air. Ash fell from the sky like snowflakes and accumulated on the ground in small heaps. Blake and Merck, along with men from federal departments, treaded carefully through the rubble. The flames were so recent that some sections continued to smolder from the blaze. The one known casualty had been zipped into a body bag and loaded into the coroner's van.

"Are you sure that's Mecham?" Merck's tone didn't mask his skepticism.

"The person who left the tip claimed that he used one of his best explosives to incinerate the legendary Dale Mecham," Blake stated.

"Well, if that's true, the only way to identify Mecham will be through dental records. That body was burned beyond recognition."

"You're right. Do you know if anyone on Melendez's list was a bomb expert?"

"I believe there's an arsonist, but I'll have to confirm when I get back to the station."

"Great. I called Thomas. He's on his way here. I told him there's a chance this could be related to the Melendez case."

"Maybe I can meet with him once he's done here, or I could go to the hospital and meet with both of them."

"The latter would probably be best."

"Okay. Tell Thomas that I'd like to set something up." Merck's phone vibrated, and he quickly glanced at it. "I've got to run, but let me know if they find anything here. I'm anxious to learn whether our guy in the van is in fact Mecham."

"I'll keep you posted. I'm going to wash all this dirt off, then head to the hospital to speak with Cole." Blake offered Merck his hand. "We'll talk later."

Merck shook it. "Deal."

As David pounded on the door, Susan stood behind him, hoping his associates weren't home. She didn't want to be entangled in her husband's disreputable dealings, but David had left her with no other choice. It was either obey his orders, or go to prison for attempted murder. Susan couldn't bear to leave her children, so the decision was clear-cut. Plus, she knew that if she double-crossed him or discussed his illicit activities, he'd kill her.

The door swung open, and Susan gaped at the man standing in the entranceway. He was tall and slender with features that would frighten small children. His face looked as if it had been mauled by a wild animal.

"That's Tucker," David mumbled. "Don't talk to or gawk at him. It'll only make him angry."

"I have no intention of speaking to anyone, David. I shouldn't even be here."

"You're just as much a part of this now as I am. If I go down, we both do."

"You forced me to help you."

"Are you two going to come in or stand out there and bicker?" Tucker asked gruffly.

"Ladies first." David grabbed Susan's arm and shoved her inside.

Susan entered the dilapidated house, and her nostrils were immediately assailed by the repulsive odor of decay and feces. She walked into the living room and quietly observed the man lounging on the tattered, filthy recliner. She moved toward the stranger and waited for him to speak.

He lifted his head and gazed at her with his one good eye. "We finally get the chance to formally meet. I'm Carlos." He held out his hand.

She tried to ignore the patch over his eye as she offered her hand in return. "I'm Susan. I wish I could say I'm pleased to meet you, but …"

David yanked Susan by her arm and forced her behind him. "She didn't mean that," he declared apologetically.

Carlos chuckled. "I like a woman with spunk, David. When she helped me escape from the hospital, I thought she was weak."

Susan closed her eyes to try to block out the memories of her subterfuge. She was ashamed that David had used her to pose as a nurse and sneak Carlos past the police guard. She had been terrified of getting caught, and those feelings hadn't dissipated until she'd driven out of the parking lot. "Not weak, just an unwilling participant," she whispered.

"What did she say?" Carlos inquired.

"Nothing," David stated. "Susan does as she's told."

Carlos nodded. "My kind of woman."

"What's the deal with this place, Carlos? You're a rich man. Why are you slumming?"

"It's called laying low. In case you haven't noticed, I'm a wanted man."

"I've noticed. That's why I'm here. I have some information for you."

Carlos glanced at Susan. "I'm not sure we should discuss this now."

"She won't say anything. You have my word on that."

"Right, because we both know how much you can be trusted," Carlos said sarcastically.

"I have never given you any reason not to trust me. With everything I've done for Cavanaugh over the years, my loyalty should never be questioned. I've even stabbed my own family in the back to prove my allegiance."

"Yeah, we appreciate you telling us your sister's secrets. But your betrayal happened way before you came to work for us."

Susan's gasp was audible. "David, that's horrible. Why would you do that to Dani?"

"Don't pretend like you care about her, Susan. You two don't even talk. She stopped being your friend and a part of our family a long time ago. All she cares about is being a cop, and you know it."

Although some of his words rang true, Susan was stunned by David's callousness. "It's still wrong. She's—"

"I don't think your wife should be here since she's still loyal to your sister," Carlos asserted. "That could mean trouble for us."

"He's right, Susan. Go wait in the car."

"I never should have been here in the first place," she mumbled on her way out of the room.

Once Susan was gone, David provided Carlos with the details surrounding his sister's car plunging into the river. "The accident should keep Danielle out of our hair for at least a week," David stated.

"I'm not worried about your sister, jackass. Is Mrs. Melendez still alive?"

"Yes. She's at the hospital right now with my sister. If your guy hurries, he can get to her while Danielle is incapacitated."

"I'm sure the cops have a protective detail on her."

"They do. But none of them are like my sister."

"Is that pride in your voice?"

"I may have problems with her, but she's a good detective."

Carlos chuckled. "Except for when it comes to you. She still doesn't know that you're involved in Cavanaugh's organization and the one who set her up. Hell, even her former partner knows. We may be able to use that to our advantage. If your sister were to find out that Blake knew and still put her life in danger, their relationship would be over. And anyone can see he has feelings for her."

"Yes, so he'll want to keep it a secret."

"Having a police lieutenant owe us a favor will come in handy."

"Blake is a by-the-book cop. He'd never do anything dirty, even for my sister."

"We'll see," Carlos said arrogantly. "I'll send someone over to Hartford General to finish off the Melendez woman. And maybe you should go talk to your wife. You need her on a tighter leash."

"There's no need for concern. I have her under control."

"You better, or she could end up like Robert."

David nodded and silently left the house.

A few minutes later, Carlos bellowed, "Tucker, get in here!"

"Yes, sir."

"It may be time to do something about David. He's been nothing but a pain in the ass from the beginning, and now we have his wife to worry about too. No matter what he says, I don't think he can handle her. She's a loose cannon that could destroy this entire operation. With the plans we have coming up in the next few weeks, we can't allow anyone or anything to get in the way."

"I will take care of them," Tucker vowed.

Carlos paused, his face convulsing in pain. "Not yet. First, I need you to make sure that Melissa Melendez is dead. That's top priority. She's more of a danger to us than anyone else. There will be plenty of time to get rid of the other two problems."

"Are you okay, Boss? Do you think you'll be ready in time?"

"If I'm not, then you or one of the other guys will have to pick up the slack. Everything is already in place."

"Don't worry. We got your back. Do you want me to take care of Mrs. Melendez?"

"No. Let our guy finish the job he started. And if he's unsuccessful again, she's all yours. Then you'll get two for one because he'll need to be eliminated too."

Tucker's grin was wide. "I'll go check on him right now."

Cole located her clothes and struggled to get dressed. The pain in her back was unbearable, but she wasn't going to allow the discomfort to stop her. She was tired of lying around, and despite doctor's orders, she was checking out of the hospital. She was going stir-crazy and needed to return to what she was most familiar with: police work.

Cole's mind was working nonstop regarding the list. All the different players and possibilities had her practically salivating. She instinctively knew that Robert's files were the key to finding the killer and saving Missy, but she couldn't locate them from a hospital bed.

She opened the door, and her legs buckled. Before she could collapse to the floor, Blake rushed in and caught her. Cole looked up and smiled shyly at him as he lifted her by the shoulders and held her steady.

"Are you okay?" Blake breathed as he closed the door with his foot. He stared at Cole's tousled blondish-brown hair and flushed face. His heart raced at the striking picture before him. Cole had never looked more beautiful.

Cole glanced at him and nodded. She forgot the ache in her back as her body throbbed in anticipation. Unfamiliar sensations, frightening yet equally thrilling, staggered her. The tension between them heightened; their chemistry was palpable.

Blake recognized the vulnerability in Cole's eyes as he stared into their violet depths. He tried to fight the emotions ravaging his body, but her earlier smile had twisted his stomach into knots, making him helpless. He reached out and tenderly caressed her face. He inched his hand along her cheek and ran his fingers through her hair.

Cole severed eye contact to try to block their powerful connection, but it was too late. The warmth of his body beckoned to her, inviting her, drawing her in. Her desire was mirrored in Blake's eyes and in his touch. Cole wanted to defy her urges, but she wasn't resilient enough to combat her wayward heart.

"Look at me," Blake quietly implored. He tilted her head up, forcing Cole to look at him. He gradually leaned in, and his mouth covered hers, slowly, deliberately.

Passion sparked, and the flicker rapidly ignited into a flame. The kiss took on a life of its own as they became submerged in each other. They gave into a yearning that neither had wanted to admit to or accept. Their bodies strained to get closer, wanting, needing, begging for more.

Cole abruptly broke off the kiss. She put her fingers on her wet, tingling lips, and warily backed away from him. "We can't do this," she cried.

"Why not?" he asked bleakly. "You want me as much as I want you. I can see it in your eyes. I could feel it in that kiss. I know you've been hurt, but whatever this thing is between us is not going to go away, no matter how much you try to deny it, Tinks."

She shook her head. "You're wrong, Blake. What we're feeling is lust, and we both know that's fleeting. I understand that better than anyone else." She stumbled over to the bed and sat on the edge. "As far as I'm concerned, this never happened."

"When did you become such a liar?" His words were laced with anger.

"I'm not," she said stubbornly.

"Then why are you lying to yourself and to me? Come on, Tinks. We've both denied our attraction for years, but it has always been there, lingering just beneath the surface."

"We can't risk our friendship, Blake. It's not worth it."

He closed the distance between them. "I'm not Cavanaugh, Tinks. I won't hurt you." He kneeled in front of her and grabbed her hand. "At least give us a chance. I promise you that love is worth the risk."

"Please don't talk to me about love," she murmured.

"Why? Because of Cavanaugh?"

"I don't want to talk about this, Blake."

"He didn't truly love you, Tinks. Not the way you deserved to be loved, not like—"

The door suddenly swung open, and Missy walked in. She looked from one to the other. "I'm sorry. Did I interrupt something?" *Is he asking Cole to marry him? If so, she doesn't look happy about it.*

Blake rose and gazed contritely at Cole. "No, it's okay. We were just talking."

"Yeah, it was nothing," Cole declared.

Missy noticed Blake's disillusionment at Cole's remark. "I still should have knocked," she said.

Blake strolled in her direction and opened the door. "Don't worry about it, Melissa. It wasn't important." He looked at Cole. "I'll be back in a half hour to discuss the case, Detective."

Cole tried to hide her feelings once Blake left, but Missy noticed the slump of her shoulders and the shimmering of unshed tears.

"Are you okay?" Missy asked sincerely.

"I'm fine," Cole replied with forced conviction.

Missy sat beside her. "Do you want to talk about it?"

"No, we were just talking about a difficult case that brought up bad memories."

Missy hesitated, unsure whether she was crossing an undefined boundary. "I'm not trying to pry, Dani, but whatever was going on here seemed like a lot more than just shoptalk."

"It wasn't."

"Look, I know it's none of my business, but you obviously have feelings for Lieutenant Blake. And for whatever reason, you're determined to sabotage it."

"How dare you?" Cole uttered through clenched teeth.

Missy stood and turned away from her. "I'm sorry … I didn't mean …"

"My life is none of your business, Mrs. Melendez. Our relationship is strictly professional. Why don't you get that?" Cole barked.

"I do get it. I'm nothing more than a murder suspect to you."

Cole ignored the hurt in her voice. "Exactly. Which reminds me that I need to ask you another question regarding the case."

"Do I have a choice?"

"Not really." Cole shifted her position to minimize the pain in her back. "Was Robert ever abusive?"

"What? No. Robert wasn't perfect, but he never raised a hand to me."

"Thomas interviewed his mistress's sister, and she claims that Robert hit Connie."

"I don't believe that."

"Why is this so shocking? It's consistent with what you've shared. Robert was possessive, moody, and often controlling, and those are classic signs of an abuser."

"That's true, but—"

Cole interrupted. "But because he didn't beat you, that makes it impossible to believe? Some men view women as property, Mrs. Melendez. They want their investment to maintain its value. They cherish and nurture that investment but take their frustrations out on other things and people."

"Is that your way of saying Robert didn't hurt me because it would have ruined the way I look?"

"Yes. You were his trophy wife, and he couldn't have his prize damaged."

"Is that how you see me? As a trophy? You probably think I married Robert for his money too, don't you?"

"Your reasons for marrying your husband are of no concern to me—unless, of course, they're the reason he was killed."

"Wow. You just answered my question."

"I did no such thing," Cole countered.

"Your evasion said it all." Missy rubbed her forehead in frustration. "Do you have any other questions, Detective? If not, I'd like to go."

Why do I always put my foot in my mouth with this woman? "If your escort is outside, then that's fine. We're done here."

"Clearly. And yes, Officer Tate is out there, so I'm no longer your responsibility. I'm sure he'll be able to keep me safe."

It was Cole's turn to feel wounded. "Unlike me?"

"Don't put words in my mouth. I didn't say that."

"That's what you meant, though. See, you're not the only one who can figure out unspoken thoughts."

"You're completely wrong. I've spent hours defending you to my father because if it weren't for you, I wouldn't be here. You risked your life for me, twice."

"I was just doing—"

"Your job. Yes, you've said that. I know I mean nothing to you, so there's no need to keep repeating it," Missy said firmly. "I think it's time I go before one of us says something we'll both regret. Have a good evening."

The dark figure lingered in the hospital parking garage and awaited the appearance of Mrs. Melendez and her police escort. He realized that after several failed attempts, this might be his last opportunity to complete the job. His boss was getting anxious and had warned that if he didn't kill her now, he'd lose the remainder of his fee and see his reputation destroyed.

After thirty minutes of waiting, he observed them getting out of the elevator. The cop looked visibly disgruntled, which generated a smile on the dark figure's face. He knew that an irritated cop would be irresponsible in his babysitting duties, unlike Detective Cole, who cared about Mrs. Melendez. Officer Tate wouldn't protect the target the way she had, and that cleared the way for a successful hit.

He pushed the button, and the window eased down slowly. He halted it a quarter of the way and pointed his gun through the opening. Once he had them in his line of vision, he fired off four quick rounds. The dark figure watched as Officer Tate and Missy crumpled to the ground. He remained in position for several minutes to ensure that neither person stirred and then departed the scene.

Merck answered his cell after one ring, tension evident in his voice. "What's going on?"

"I still have the forensics results. What do you want me to do with them?"

"How much longer can you stall Cole and Thomas?" Merck asked tautly.

"I don't know. Cole has been calling every day. Even Blake has been inquiring about the files."

Merck shuffled through the pictures of his daughter again. "Can you hold them off for a few more days? A lot is at stake."

"I may be able to buy you another forty-eight hours, but it'll cost you."

"How much?"

"Another five thousand should cover it."

"Fine. You just make sure they don't get those results, and you'll have your money."

"We have a deal. I'll see you in two days at our normal place. You can text me the time."

"Got it." Merck ended the call.

Missy closed her eyes and unwillingly floated above the scene. She heard voices calling her name and acknowledged that they were the voices of the faceless inhabitants of her visions, entreating her to join them. They tugged at her, mercilessly draining her energy. She wanted to succumb and escape the world in which she had no control over her thoughts. But something forced her to wage war against her demons. She fought them until her spirit thrust its way back into its rightful space.

Once her spirit was restored, Missy had a déjà vu moment as the dead weight of the officer pressed down on her. She attempted to move, but the left side of her body was numb. Hysteria threatened to overwhelm her, but she subdued it. Missy couldn't afford to panic like she had in the water-filled car with Cole because no one was around to save her this time.

Missy could feel the officer's blood seeping through her clothing. The pain that riddled her extremities reminded Missy that some of the red fluid encircling her on the ground was probably her own. The thought made her nauseous.

"Help!" she screamed. "Somebody help!"

Missy was unsure of how long she laid there—seconds, minutes, or hours—but her consciousness was waning. By the time Officer Tate's body was lifted from hers, she could barely perceive sound and movement. She heard someone say Tate was dead, and her heart sank. Silent tears rolled down her cheeks, and her eyelids grew heavier. Prior to closing them, she whispered Cole's name.

Cole experienced a rush of uneasiness, but before she could ascertain why, Blake entered the room. Several awkward minutes ticked by as she ignored him and examined the paperwork spread out on the bed.

Blake sat down in the chair. "Did Thomas bring you those files? You know taking classified documents out of the precinct is prohibited, right? You could both get suspended or worse."

Cole decided to keep her answers evasive. "I don't know what you're talking about. I haven't seen Thomas."

"I guess those official police records just miraculously appeared in your hospital room?"

"Yup. God works in mysterious ways."

"Damn it, Cole. You're going to get me in trouble if the captain finds out about this."

"He won't. Thomas will be back soon to pick them up."

He shook his head. "I will take them with me when I leave. That way, I can ensure that no one will discover that the files were missing."

"Works for me." Her tone was flippant.

"Tinks, I … never mind." After a pause, he continued, keeping his tone professional. "Listen, I came here to discuss Sergeant Merck. I need you and Thomas to meet with him. He has information from a case he was working back in New York that may be connected to Melendez. Seems the good doctor altered the faces of some pretty infamous criminals and kept a list of their real names and aliases."

Cole glanced at him. "You're kidding."

"Nope. I'll tell you what I know so far."

Cole listened intently as Blake recounted what Merck had told him. She had a few questions but chose to wait until he was done. By the time Blake finished speaking, he'd unknowingly provided all the information Cole needed to put the missing pieces together.

"I shared some of this story with Thomas earlier. I already knew Melendez was changing faces," Cole declared.

"How did you know?"

"Mrs. Melendez told me about a man she saw here in the hospital—a former patient of her husband. Seeing him triggered a memory of a list that Robert kept in his safe. She viewed the names on the paper, and the ones that she remembered all belonged to felons."

"Right. Her knowledge of Robert's extra dealings is probably why someone wants her dead."

"But how would they know that she knows? I doubt that's something Robert advertised."

"Maybe he did publicize it. He was blackmailing these guys, so he probably informed them that he had proof of their real identities. He might have even suggested that if something happened to him, his wife would take the list to the police."

"That's possible. He could have implicated Missy without her knowledge. But although Missy saw the list, she had no idea how important it was until now."

"What about McCain and Roman? Do you think they know?"

She gestured to the papers spread across her bed. "These files are phone records, financials, and background checks on both. I haven't found anything yet that would incriminate either of them."

"What about Robert? Did we uncover any more information on him?"

"No. He's practically a phantom. We don't know what his name was prior to Robert Melendez, so that's making things a little more challenging."

"What about fingerprints?"

"Still waiting, but I'm assuming he didn't have a criminal background, so that will probably be a bust too."

"Let me know if you need anything from me."

"Will do."

"One other thing. Before I came here, I was at a crime scene—house fire, arson, conceivably explosives. One victim. Male. Got a tip that it could be Dale Mecham."

"What? He's the person that approached Missy here at the hospital."

"I doubt that's a coincidence. Makes me wonder if whoever killed Melendez is responsible for Mecham's death too."

The sense of foreboding Cole had felt earlier returned with vigor. "I need your phone," she said urgently.

"Why?"

"Call Officer Tate because something is wrong."

Just as Blake reached into his pocket, his phone started to ring. "This is Blake." He listened for several seconds then disconnected the call. He stood and glanced at Cole. "Shots were fired in the parking lot. Officer down."

"And Missy?"

"I'm not sure, but Tate is dead." He headed toward the door. "I'll tell you what happened the moment I find out."

She crawled out of bed. "The hell you will. I'm coming with you."

Blake was about to argue but realized that it would be a losing battle. "I guess it's a good thing you're already dressed. Can't show up to a crime scene in a hospital robe."

"You're wasting time, Blake. Let's go."

"Fine. But for the record, I'm against you being out of bed."

"Duly noted."

He watched as she sprinted in front of him, sheer determination propelling her forward.

"Mrs. Melendez is extremely lucky. The bullet only grazed her side," the doctor explained.

"So she's going to be okay?" Blake inquired.

"She'll be fine."

Cole exhaled in relief. "Can we see her?"

"Yes, but only for a few minutes. She needs to rest."

"We won't stay long. Thank you, Doctor," Cole replied.

When Cole and Blake entered Missy's room, they were surprised to see her sitting up in the bed. Other than her pasty skin and untidy hair, she appeared normal. Once they moved closer, they noticed the bruises on her arm and face.

"Shouldn't you be lying down?" said Cole.

"I could ask you the same thing, Dani," she whispered. "But I understand how you feel now. I can't be stuck in this bed, especially with someone trying to kill me."

"Did you see the person who shot you?" asked Blake.

"No. It all happened so fast. I heard loud popping sounds then I felt the piercing in my side, so I knew I'd been hit. I tried to get up, but I couldn't."

"Staying put might have saved your life, Missy," Cole stated. "The killer probably waited around for a few seconds to see if either of you moved. If you had, he would have finished the job."

Missy was visibly fighting back tears. "I can't believe Officer Tate is dead, and I'm to blame. I know you're going to tell me it isn't my fault, but that still doesn't make it right. He had two little boys, and now they don't have a father because of me," she said, choking on the tears. "How am I supposed to live with that?"

"It's difficult, but you'll get through this, Mrs. Melendez," said Blake. "It'll just take time. You've had a lot of death in your life in the past few weeks—more than any one person should. Cole and I have come up with a way to keep you out of harm's way and hopefully prevent anyone else from getting hurt."

"What else can you do, other than catch the person responsible?"

"The plan may seem extreme to you, but we think it will work. We're going to announce the death of Officer Tate to the media but also include you as a fatality."

"What? You want to fake my death?" she asked incredulously.

"Yes. So far, we've been able to keep the media away from the scene in the parking garage, and believe me, it's been a daunting task. No one knows about the shooting except a few officers and hospital staff. If you agree, we'll make sure they keep silent."

Missy stared at Cole, mouth agape. "This is crazy. Where would I go? What would I do?"

Cole responded in a reassuring tone. "We have several safe houses we could hide you in. Typically, we reserve these sites for witnesses whose lives are in danger."

"Right, not murder suspects."

Cole hesitated. "Right. But we think in your situation, it's necessary."

"Your solution to my situation is witness relocation? Whoever this person is, they went all the way to Miami to murder my best friend and tried to kill me there too. I seriously doubt you can keep him from finding me," she argued. "Plus, I've been shot. I don't know if it's such a great idea for me to leave the hospital so soon."

"We're going to have a nurse meet us at the secure location," Blake asserted. "I've already spoken to one who can do the job."

"For Dani or me? Because she's in no condition to go anywhere either."

"Detective Cole won't be going with you. Detective Thomas will."

Cole's sharp intake of breath was audible. "Are you serious? I will not let you bench me, Blake!" she screeched.

He ignored Cole's outburst and directed his attention to Missy. "The place we have in mind for you is outside the city. We've only used it twice, and it's isolated. You'll be safe there."

"'Outside of the city' and 'isolated' is your way of saying the woods—or as my mother liked to call them, the boonies, the place where Jason Voorhees lives."

Blake chuckled. "I see you're a fan of the *Friday the 13th* movie. I love horror films too."

Their trivial exchange provoked Cole's anger even more. Her eyes shot daggers at her former partner. "Blake, you can't disregard what I said and pretend like I approve of your decision."

"Fighting me on this is pointless, Cole. I've already made up my mind. And if you go against my orders, I'll take your shield and gun," he stated authoritatively.

"That's bullshit, Blake, and you know it. You owe me this."

The color drained from Blake's face as the truth of her words struck him. "You're right, Detective Cole. You are lead on this investigation. You should be there," he said grimly. "We can discuss it further in your room. Let's leave Mrs. Melendez alone to rest."

Missy glanced from one to the other as the tension in the room intensified. She intuited Cole's remorse in addition to Blake's anxiety, and she quietly wished that she could lighten the mood. Their emotions were draining what little energy Missy had left. However, she sensed that whatever was going on between them was too raw and deep for her to subvert. Instead, she changed the subject. "Has my dad arrived yet?"

"We didn't call him, Mrs. Melendez. I'm sorry, but he has to think you're dead for this plan to succeed."

"No, I can't put him through that!" Missy exclaimed. "Not after losing my mom."

"Missy, we can't leave this entire investigation in your father's hands and hope he can be convincing. Lives are at stake. One little slip could destroy everything."

"I won't do it."

"Then Ted's tears will be shed at your actual funeral. And the way things are going, that will be sooner rather than later," Cole declared harshly.

Missy gasped out loud. Her disappointment saturated the atmosphere like humidity on a hot summer's day. "Wow, Detective Cole. You really are heartless."

"All I'm trying to do here is protect you, Missy. I need you alive and not just because it's my job, but because it's what you deserve."

Cole's unexpected, sincere words left Missy bewildered. She longed to feel safe again, but not at her father's expense. "I understand why you don't want to tell my father, but I still don't know if I can do it." *If I say yes, I will need to figure out a way to block him so he doesn't sense that I'm alive. Despite his reticence, I'm certain that he inherited my grandmother's clairvoyance. I've personally seen small glimpses of his abilities. And with my luck, his gift will fully manifest itself now and expose this entire charade.*

"Believe me, Mrs. Melendez," said Blake. "Once this is all over, your dad will appreciate the fact that he still has his daughter, even if we had to lie to him for a few weeks."

Despite the ominous sensations that disturbed her spirit, Missy wavered. "Fine, I'll do it." *I just hope this doesn't sign the death certificate of everyone I care about, as well as my own.*

CHAPTER 9

COLE AND THOMAS STOOD SILENTLY BY Blake's side as he fielded questions from reporters. Cole scanned the crowd and looked for anything out of the ordinary, but nothing seemed amiss. The journalists appeared to be buying into the ruse, allowing the press conference to end sooner than expected. Once it was over, Thomas left for the safe house while Cole and Blake headed to Missy's room. The duo quickly hustled her into the elevator and out the hospital's side entrance.

Blake spotted the truck idling at the curb and dismissed the officer who was driving. After Cole and Missy climbed into the back seat, Blake quickly sped off. He spent the first five minutes taking side streets to make certain they weren't being followed, before finally getting on the highway.

The plan was to meet Thomas in two hours, which meant they could take only a few breaks during their hundred-mile trip. Blake wanted one of their stops to be a clinic located at the midway point. He'd already made an appointment for a doctor to check both ladies' injuries. He didn't share that news with Cole until they were already a half hour into the trip, and she was displeased with the oversight.

While Blake and Cole quietly argued, Missy stared out the window. The fleeting scenery coupled with her pain medication made her drowsy. She closed her eyes, and within minutes she was in the throes of a vision.

The young man hovers in the doorway. "My sergeant signed me up for a session, sir."

"Yes, Private Boyd. I've been waiting for you. Come in and have a seat."

Boyd closes the door and sits down in the nearby chair. "Did Sergeant Butler tell you why he wanted me to come here?"

"Yes, he did. He stated that you'd given him permission to share your dilemma with me. And don't worry. Whatever we discuss here today is completely confidential." He opens his Bible to the book of Leviticus and lays it in front of Boyd. "Now tell me how long you've been having inappropriate feelings for men, Private."

Boyd hesitates. "For as long as I can remember. And those urges have only gotten stronger with age. You have to help me, sir, or my family will disown me."

"I promise you that no one will ever find out that you're gay, Private. Now tell me, what does Leviticus 18:22 say in the good book?"

Boyd picks up the Bible and reads the verse. "You shall not lie with a male as one lies with a female; it is an abomination."

"That's right. It's an abomination. And my job is to rid you of those demonic desires."

"But how, sir?" Boyd asked anxiously.

"Why don't you take a few sips of tea and then close your eyes? I want you to relax before we get started."

Once Boyd starts to drift off, Luke rises from his desk and moves behind him. "I'm going to lay my hand on top of your head and pray for you, Private, so don't be alarmed." He pulls his prayer scarf from his pocket and stretches it out. "The Lord is your Shepherd, you shall not want … men." Luke wraps the cloth around Boyd's neck and tightens it.

Boyd gasps and desperately clutches the material, but his reflexes are slow from the drug-laced tea.

"He made you to lie down in green pastures with women, not men. And with death, he will restore your soul." Luke pulls harder on the cloth until Boyd is motionless.

Luke places the scarf in his pocket and picks up the phone on his desk. "Hi, Sergeant Conway. I'm afraid I have some bad news. When I showed up to my office for my appointment with Private Boyd, I found him hanging from my ceiling fan." Luke looks up and smiles at the rope dangling a few feet above Boyd's head. "I pulled him down, but I need the paramedics here as soon as possible." He listens for a few seconds. "No, it's too late. I've already given him his last rites."

Cole gazed at Missy and detected her uneasiness. She scooted closer and touched her arm. "Are you okay, Missy?"

Missy slowly shook off the disturbing images. "Yes." *Except I think I just met my husband's killer.*

"Was it a vision?" Cole asked skeptically.

"You don't believe in those, remember? My wound is bothering me a bit, that's all. I probably just need to take another pill."

"We can have someone from the clinic examine you at the next stop."

"Okay," Missy said despondently.

"Is this about your father? I was honest with you—he took it hard, but I hope you'll be home before the shock of your death can even sink in. You should take comfort in knowing that you're saving lives, yours and his."

"And making your job easier."

"What's that supposed to mean?" Cole asked tightly.

"I didn't mean that the way it sounded. I simply meant that if everyone thinks I'm dead, you can do your job without interruption."

"So I can't do my job and protect you at the same time?"

"I'm not saying that. I'm—"

Cole interrupted. "I wasn't responsible for you getting shot, Missy. That didn't occur on my watch. I was laid up in a hospital bed from rescuing you the last time."

"I wasn't questioning your competency as a cop, Dani. I know you're good at what you do. And I know if it weren't for you, I wouldn't be here. For that reason, you'll always have my loyalty and my ..." Missy paused, unsure of the message she intended to convey.

"Your what, gratitude? It's not deserved or necessary."

"I swear, if you or any other cop says to me one more time that it's your job, I will shoot you with your own gun. It's getting old and trite," Missy said in exasperation. "You should learn how to accept kindness, Dani. I know it's not what you're used to, but not everyone's intentions are evil."

Cole sighed. "Despite what has taken place in the last few weeks, you're still a suspect. I can't afford to forget that."

"I know I'm still a suspect. But regardless of your continued doubts about my innocence and your borderline cruelty, I'm going to continue to treat you with a modicum of empathy, whether you deserve it or not."

"I don't," she murmured.

Missy shook her head. "We all do. And if you believe otherwise, then someone has truly done a number on you."

"Like I've said before, my personal life is not up for discussion."

"But mine is because I'm a murder suspect, right?" Missy said resentfully.

"I don't make the rules."

"You just enforce them, no matter who gets hurt in the process."

"I'm not the one who hurt you."

I wish that were true. "Maybe we should just end this conversation. We're both on edge, and I don't want either of us to say something we'll regret."

Cole put distance between them, physically and emotionally. "Agreed."

Blake, who had heard everything from the front seat, decided to try to dispel some of the friction. "I need to stop at the convenience store up ahead and get something to drink. Why don't you join me, Tinks?"

"Sure." Cole glanced at Missy. "Look, we need you to stay hidden, but I'll get you something if you'd like."

"I'm okay. Thanks."

"Please don't leave the truck under any circumstances," Cole admonished as Blake pulled into a parking spot.

"I'm not stupid, Detective. I won't get out of the car," Missy replied sharply.

"You sure you don't want anything?"

"What I want, you can't get me."

"What's that?" Cole inquired curiously.

"My life back."

Cole started to say something but changed her mind. She opened the door and silently climbed out of the vehicle.

George entered the HPS building and scanned his surroundings. Everything appeared the same, but he felt out of place. HPS was no longer his home, his place of refuge. He couldn't trust Bill and his newly acquired silent partner. He wasn't sure who had shot him, but his instincts told him that Bill was somehow involved, even if he hadn't pulled the trigger.

George opened Bill's door without knocking and walked in. He planted himself in the closest chair and asked indignantly, "So who did you tell?"

Bill peered up from his paperwork. "Hello, Georgie. Nice to see you up and about. When did you get released from the hospital?"

"Today, but let's dispense with the pleasantries, Bill. Who did you share my private business with? The only people who know are you and Robert, and he's dead."

"Telling your secret would completely destroy this business, George. If our patients, former or current, discovered that you were performing surgeries without a valid license, HPS would be inundated with malpractice suits. The cost would be so exorbitant that sooner or later, we'd have to shut down permanently. I've spent too many years building my reputation and this practice to let some hack obliterate it."

"Is that why you tried to have me killed? You knew someone would discover the truth, and you'd lose everything?"

"I wasn't responsible for what happened to you. However, once I discovered that your license was forged and that you were an overall phony, the thought did cross my mind."

"Well, someone is blackmailing me, and I have the sneaking suspicion that you're involved."

"What the hell are you talking about?"

"A note, along with a copy of my counterfeit license, was left for me at the nurses' station. It was given to me before I was discharged."

"You're mistaken, George. I would never allow your secret to become public, especially when the outcome would be detrimental to me and my business. I'd have to be a fool."

"So you're saying you have no idea who is behind this?"

"I wish I did because I stand to lose just as much as you do."

"Then you'll help me figure out who the culprit is?"

"I didn't say that."

"Like you said, you have just as much to lose as I do—more, in fact. Imagine the scandal if the truth was revealed, and your name was splattered all over the internet. As the founder of HPS, you'd have the negative publicity falling squarely on your shoulders."

Bill was silent for a few seconds. "I'll see what I can find out. Now if you'll excuse me, I have a patient arriving momentarily. You know the way out, George," he said dismissively.

George rose from his chair. "I'll be in touch."

After George exited, Bill made a call. "George needs to be taken care of once and for all."

Susan handed David a beer and sat beside him on the sofa. "I know this is none of my business, but how did you get involved with this Sanchez person? And why in God's name do you hate your sister so much?" Her voice was little more than a whisper.

David glanced at his wife. Minutes ticked by as he debated whether to disclose anything to her. After the meltdown at Sanchez's house, he wasn't sure he should trust her. Susan could destroy everything he'd worked so hard for over the years.

David was an accountant at a successful accounting firm, but his love of money had introduced him to a sordid world—one filled with weapons and drugs. His immoral deeds might seem a bit misguided to some because of his profession and the fact that his sister was a cop. But all David cared about was becoming rich, while wreaking havoc right under his sister's unsuspecting nose. He'd never been caught, which in his mind meant that he was smarter than his big sister. And David did want to boast about that to Susan.

"If you repeat any of this, I'll kill you," he warned.

"I know that, David. Now tell me."

"I got involved with Sanchez by accident. My friend Andy needed me to pick him up after his car broke down one night. He asked me to drop him off in an empty parking lot instead of taking him to his apartment. He told me that he had some business to take care of and would catch a cab home. I didn't feel comfortable leaving him alone in such a seedy part of town. We waited for about ten minutes before a BMW with tinted windows pulled up beside us. Andy handed the guy a package, and in return, the guy gave him a wad of hundred-dollar bills."

"What was in the package?"

"At first, he was hesitant to tell me because of Danielle. But after I reminded him that she and I were estranged, he decided to trust me and admitted that it was drugs."

"David, why would you get involved with drugs?"

"I figured we could use the extra money, especially with two kids."

"You make over six figures. We're doing just fine."

"We can never have too much money."

Susan shook her head. "This is about greed."

"Isn't everything?" he said arrogantly.

"No, but you don't want my opinion."

David took several sips of beer and placed the bottle back on the table. "You're right. I don't."

"Okay, well, you still haven't told me how Sanchez is connected to all of this. Does he run the drug ring that Andy works for?"

"Yes. We both work for Sanchez, but he's not the boss. Cavanaugh controls everything, and Sanchez is his right-hand man."

"Cavanaugh? Why does that name sound familiar?"

"Danielle arrested him in one of the largest drug busts ever on the East Coast. Cavanaugh's capture was big headlines for months. It catapulted my sister's career. She became famous," he proclaimed spitefully.

"Wait … I remember now. That was when Dani got shot. She was undercover, and somehow this Cavanaugh guy found out that she was a cop."

"Yes, and everyone thought my sister fell in love with Cavanaugh. But it wasn't just a rumor—it was true. I was on the inside. I saw the whole thing."

Susan stared intently at him as all the pieces of the puzzle started to fit together. "Oh my God, it was you. You were the one who exposed Dani," she said incredulously.

He smiled. "Yup. Imagine my surprise the day I went to Cavanaugh's main headquarters to meet up with Andy for lunch and saw a familiar face walk out of the building. I hid so that she wouldn't see me, but there was no denying it was Dani. Andy came out a few minutes later, and I asked him about her identity. He thought I was attracted to her and told me that she was Cavanaugh's new assistant—and off-limits. He'd never met Dani through me, so he had no idea what she looked like. And up until that point, I'd been struggling to prove myself to Sanchez. He wasn't sure about trusting some accountant with no criminal background, even though Andy vouched for me. What better way to prove myself than rat out my own sister? I texted her graduation picture from the academy to Sanchez."

"She could have been killed, David."

"You don't think I know that?"

"And that's exactly what you wanted, isn't it? I can see it in your eyes. You're disappointed that she survived. Why would you want your own flesh and blood dead? What happened between you two?"

David hesitated. "All right, I'll tell you, but that doesn't mean our relationship has changed."

"I'm your wife. I know what that means and what it doesn't."

As he began to speak again, his voice took on a disturbing quality that Susan didn't recognize. "Dani was Dad's favorite. She was athletic, a straight A student, a competent swimmer, great with a gun, and never got in trouble. She was all the things he wanted in a son, all the things I could never be." He sighed. "I was more of a mama's boy, and my father despised me for it. He wanted to do the usual father–son things, and when I refused, he'd punish me. And if I failed at a task he assigned me, he'd punch me in the face or stomach. That was his way of toughening me up. I was only two years younger than Danielle, but it was impossible for me to keep up with her. I was forever in her shadow, when all I ever wanted was my father's love."

"How your dad treated you was horrible, David, but your not having his love wasn't Dani's fault."

"You don't understand!" he shrieked. "She was supposed to protect me. She promised that she would keep him from hurting me."

"She was just a little girl."

He ignored her and continued to speak. "I just wanted to make cookies with my mom, but he said boys don't bake. Instead, he would drag me outside for target practice. I tried to shoot the can off the fence. I was only six. My fingers weren't strong enough to aim and pull the trigger, so I usually missed. I would be reminded, in the face of his disappointment, how Dani could hit the mark at five. So he'd reload and force me to do it again and again, until I'd start to cry. Then he would get so angry at me for crying that he'd lock me in a closet. I'd yell for someone to let me out, but no one ever came, not even Dani. It was dark in there, and I was afraid."

"But why blame Dani when your mother didn't let you out either?"

"Don't talk about my mom. She did the best she could."

"She didn't protect you," Susan insisted.

"I said be quiet," he said hostilely.

"Okay, I won't mention her again." Susan laid her hand on his. "Is there more to this than Dani leaving you alone in the dark?"

"Well, right before my seventh birthday, my dad threw me in the pool as a part of my swimming lesson. Dani was there, and I screamed for her to help me. She tried to jump in the water, but he grabbed her from behind. That bastard didn't let her go until I went underwater. Dani jumped in to save me. She was the one who begged my mom to call 911 while she gave me CPR. And she was the one who sat beside my bed in the hospital until I got better. It was always her."

"Dani saved your life. I don't know how at that age, but she did. So why do you hate her so much? If there's anyone you should hate, it's your father. He tortured you."

"He made me suffer because of her. She was perfect, and I was the screwup. My life was a living hell. I got beatings, black eyes, and broken bones because I wasn't good enough. Those evil and cruel times made me into the person I am."

"Your father was cruel to her too. Like you, she was battered and bruised. I know because she told me one night when she'd had too much to drink. That was one of the few times she's ever shared anything personal with me. She's damaged too. She didn't come away from your childhood without bad memories. It couldn't have been easy for her to live up to your father's high expectations either. You're close to him now, and she's not—she hasn't been for a long time. And you know why. She chose a different career than you, but she doesn't deserve this. She did all she could."

David stood up abruptly. "You don't know what you're talking about. You weren't there," he asserted. "Danielle wasn't abused. She was Daddy's little princess. I took the brunt of everything. I was the punching bag, the anger-management dummy."

Susan knew that David's perception was unmistakably clouded, but she wasn't going to try to change his mind. If she took on Dani's cause, there would be dire consequences. And she had already pressed her luck several times with the way she'd spoken to him. Despite his openness and vulnerability during the reciting of his past, Susan knew not to let her guard down. David was still cold-blooded, but now she understood that it was no one's fault but his own. Danielle had turned out fine, and if he truly had wanted to be a decent person, he could have been as well.

"Dani deserves her family's love, David."

"She deserves exactly what she got, especially after what she did to my dad."

"What did she do besides try to save you from your father's whippings and evil ways?"

"She shot him. Dani shot our father."

Once Missy spotted Blake and Cole coming out of the convenience store, she closed her eyes to feign sleep. She didn't want to go another round with the prickly detective, particularly since she was exhausted. She hoped that her subterfuge would eventually turn into the real thing, and she could get some rest.

Cole hung up her phone and climbed into the passenger seat of the truck while Blake walked around to the driver's side. She glanced in the back and was relieved to see that Missy was asleep. "Good, she's taking a nap. I have some important things to discuss with you, Blake."

Blake buckled his seat belt and started the truck. "Maybe you should try to get some sleep too."

"I'm fine. By the way, thanks for the new cell. I felt bare without one."

"You're welcome." He pulled out and checked the mirror to make certain they weren't being tailed. "Is your back hurting? The doctor at the clinic said you should limit your movement as much as possible."

"My back isn't bad right now. The pills he gave me are miracle workers and should last four to six hours."

"I'm happy to hear that the medication is giving you some relief. Now what did you want to talk about? Was that Thomas on the phone?"

"No. It was Detective Bolton in Miami. He said one of the witnesses who saw Kayla's killer in the bar that night remembered that the suspect had a tattoo. He must have been in the military because he had the American flag and the US Army star logo on his right arm. Bolton is going to have a sketch artist draw it and text it over to me."

"That's great, but it doesn't narrow down our suspects. Did he have anything else to say? Any more leads?"

"He's waiting for me to send him the forensics report, but I told him I still haven't received it, which is unusual. When you return to the station, can you find out what the holdup is? I've never waited this long ..." Cole hesitated as suspicion intervened. "Maybe someone is deliberately keeping those results from me."

Blake's expression was perplexed. "Are you saying there's a leak in the department?"

"Come on, Blake. It makes sense. The killer has been one step ahead of us from the beginning. And he always seems to know our whereabouts."

"The guy is obviously a professional. He wouldn't have any problem tracking you or Melissa. Your agenda hasn't exactly been a big secret."

"What about the fact that someone tried to poison me by putting arsenic in my migraine pills? No one knows about my headaches except cops."

Blake abruptly pulled the vehicle over to the side of the road and stared at Cole. "Why am I just now hearing about this? How long has this been going on?" His voice communicated both anger and concern.

"The ER doc told me a few days ago. I haven't had time to tell you with everything else going on."

"Damn it, Tinks! You should have told me immediately."

"Why? So you could use that as some crappy excuse to remove me from this case?"

"I would not have done that," he said emphatically.

"That's not true, Blake, and you know it. You would have allowed your personal feelings to distort your professional judgment."

"What personal feelings? I'm your boss and nothing more. You've made that perfectly clear."

"I have, but our hearts tend to not listen to our minds, no matter how much we tell them to," she stated glumly.

Blake understood her unspoken meaning and nodded his head in acquiescence. "We should probably get back on the road, or we'll be late. Don't think I'm letting you off the hook. We can finish talking on the way."

Cole rolled her eyes. "No one told you to stop. Of course, the conversation isn't over. You're still a nosy cop, aren't you?"

"Yup. And proud of it." He gradually eased the truck back onto the road. "How long has someone been poisoning you?"

"Since before Miami. I picked up a new prescription right before I got on the plane."

"Who knows about your migraines besides Thomas and me?"

"Ulrich knows, which translates to everyone."

"True," Blake sighed. "If there is a leak, Tinks, we're in trouble. The person will know that Missy is alive and come for her."

"Yeah, I thought about that too." She peeked over her shoulder to make sure Missy was still asleep. "Can we change locations?"

"No. I would need at least forty-eight hours to find another site and set things up."

"Then maybe we should go to a hotel instead," Cole suggested.

"That's a possibility. Let's talk to Thomas once we get to the safe house and figure things out from there. Also, there's something I need to tell you before we get there. I've been putting it off until you felt well, but after what you told me about the poisoned pills, it can't wait."

"This sounds ominous."

"It is. Sanchez is back."

Cole was flabbergasted. "What?"

"He was admitted to the hospital, but he somehow escaped."

"I can't believe this. Didn't you put a police guard on him? How long has it been since he escaped?"

"Is that important?"

"Son of a bitch!" she bellowed. "That long, huh? I can't believe you've been keeping this from me. And don't you dare say we're even."

"I wasn't going to. Look, I know I should have told you sooner, but you were in Miami. I wanted you to focus on the Melendez case."

"You didn't think I could handle my job and that too? Nice to know you have faith in me," she said irritably.

"It wasn't like that, and you know it."

"I know you haven't believed in me as a detective since Cavanaugh. It's always been the elephant in the room with us."

"No, you chose to turn the Cavanaugh case into this ginormous, inexcusable mistake, Tinks. Your guilt has nothing to do with me. I told you a long time ago that I forgave you, but the key is forgiving yourself. Until you do, you will never be happy, professionally or personally."

"We shouldn't be talking about this with Missy in the car," she admonished. "What information do you have on Sanchez?"

"Tinks, we both know that you're using Mrs. Melendez as an excuse not to explore your feelings about Cavanaugh. I'll play along this time, but we can't continue these evasion tactics. It's not healthy for either of us."

"Stop trying to psychoanalyze me, Blake. You're not my shrink. I'm fine," Cole said. "Now can we please change the subject?"

"Fine," Blake said impatiently. "But there's not much I can tell you about Sanchez. He was found in an alley on Martin Street. I don't know what he was doing there. He's not some low-level street dealer."

"Did CSU find anything?"

"No. Apparently, that's a popular location for murders and drug transactions, which makes their job more difficult."

Cole nodded. "Any word on that house fire yet?"

"Yes. Dental records confirmed that it was Dale Mecham."

"Damn. So your tip was correct. Are you going to tell me who gave you that information?"

"Merck."

"Does he know about Sanchez too?"

"Yes."

"I hate to say this, but maybe Merck's our leak. He came out of nowhere and knows a lot about Cavanaugh and this case. Maybe Cavanaugh is involved too and pulling strings from behind bars."

"You're right. Merck could be a part of it. I'll call his former lieutenant and see what I can find out about him. If you're uncomfortable about Cavanaugh's possible connection and want me to take you off this case, just let me know."

"No," she stated emphatically. "This is my assignment. I refuse to let him dictate my life ... not anymore."

"That's good to hear, Tinks. I need my best detective handling this investigation."

His sincerity triggered an unexpected moment of frailty in Cole. "I wish I could give you what you want, but I don't think that I ever can," she uttered hopelessly. "I'm too much of a mess. You deserve better."

Blake recognized how hard it was for Cole to share her feelings, particularly about their relationship. Thus, he chose his next words carefully. "I've worked with you for many years. I know exactly who you are, and I like it … a lot."

"But you don't really. I—"

Blake interrupted her. "How about when this is all over, you have dinner with me? Just two people enjoying one another's company over a meal."

"I think I might like that," she said, sounding a little lost.

He smiled brightly. "Good. Then it's a date."

Cole and Missy were asleep when Blake halted the truck in front of an old farmhouse in Bridgewater, Connecticut. The small cottage looked abandoned. Shutters dangled crookedly from the hinges, and the house's dull blue paint was peeling, revealing yellow as the primary color. The lawn hadn't been mowed in months, and the weeds were nearly knee-high. The exterior made the place appear unlivable, which to Blake translated into the perfect hideout.

Blake cut the ignition and surveyed the area. It was secluded, with the closest neighboring house located ten miles down the road. The thought equally terrified and comforted him. Blake wanted the two women to be safe, and he believed that housing them out in the middle of nowhere was the solution. Then again, if anything dangerous happened, it would take a while for assistance to arrive.

Cole opened her eyes and looked at Blake. "Are we here, or is this another stop?"

"We're here. It doesn't look like much, but with any luck, the inside will at least be habitable and critter-free. I know you hate them."

"I can't stay here if there are rodents, Blake," she said anxiously.

He chuckled. "It amazes me how you can chase down men ten times your size yet be frightened of a tiny mouse."

"It's not funny. My brother used to torture me when we were younger. He used to put dead mice in my bed while I slept."

"That's awful, Tinks. At least now I understand where your phobia comes from."

"Look, I'm not proud of my fear. I do need to face it one day." She gazed hesitantly at the house. "But today won't be that day."

"Don't worry, I'll thoroughly check the place out to make sure there are no signs of your little friends," he said playfully.

"Thank you."

"I don't think Thomas is here yet. I don't see his car."

"That's strange. He should be here by now, unless he went to get groceries."

"You're probably right. Thomas does like to eat. Why don't you wake up Sleeping Beauty while I go check out the place?"

Cole waited until Blake entered the house before she climbed out of the truck. She slowly canvassed the front and back of the residence and then returned to the vehicle. Cole opened the back door to rouse Missy and was surprised to see that she was already awake.

"I'm glad you're up. We're here at the safe house. Blake is waiting for us inside."

Missy struggled to extract herself from the effects of her dream. "I … uh … can you give me a few minutes please?" She could still visualize the woman chasing her, calling her name in a raspy voice. She knew the blonde was dangerous, despite her assertions to the contrary. Therefore, Missy had continued to run, searching for Cole. The woman had shouted that Cole was dead, which had frozen Missy in her tracks. The pain she had felt in that moment was overpowering, and Missy had fallen to her knees. Too stunned to move, Missy had watched as the blonde approached and shot her in the head.

"You look pale. Are you in pain?" Cole asked with concern.

Missy gazed at Cole and marveled at how the grief she felt at the thought of losing Cole for even a second was a hundred times greater than the heartache of Robert's death. "A little bit. I think the medicine is wearing off." Missy peered at the house and grimaced at its uninviting appearance. "This is the best the Hartford PD could do, huh?"

"I know you're used to places like the Ritz, but you'll just have to learn to slum it for a few days."

Missy shook her head. "I wasn't complaining."

Cole's phone rang. "Actually, you were." She turned her back on Missy and answered. "Cole." She listened to the person on the other end for a few minutes and then disconnected the call.

"Is everything okay?"

"Yeah. I just need to head back to Hartford for a few hours. You'll have to stay with Thomas until I return."

Missy's expression was uncertain. "But I don't know him."

"I won't be gone for long. Thomas is a good cop. He'll take good care of you."

"I know that, but it doesn't make me feel any better about being alone with him."

"You'll just have to get over it then, princess, since you have no other choice," Cole stated sharply.

"You don't have to be rude," Missy asserted irritably. "And please don't call me princess. I hate that."

"Is Thomas the reason you don't want to stay, or is it because this house is not good enough for you?"

Missy's expression was dubious. "Are you serious? I don't care about the house. You don't know me at all."

"You're a suspect. That's all I need to know."

"Hell, I give up!" Missy barked. "Why don't you just stay in Hartford and let Thomas protect me? Maybe with him in charge, I won't get shot at or almost drown."

Cole felt as if she'd been kicked in the stomach, and it showed on her face. "You're right. I have been lax in my duties. Thomas will babysit you going forward." She turned and headed toward the farm.

Missy leaped out of the truck and followed her. "Cole, wait. I'm sorry," she called.

Blake almost collided with Cole as he walked out the front door. "Hey, I thought you were going to wait until I gave the all clear before coming in."

"I got tired of waiting. Can I hitch a ride back with you to Hartford?" Cole asked restlessly.

Blake could sense the tension between Cole and Missy and assumed that was the reason she wanted to return home. "Why?"

Cole's voice was tense with frustration. "My CSU files have disappeared, which explains the runaround I've been getting for weeks. I need to speak to Stevens because someone is trying to sabotage my investigation. And that person is either a cop or someone on his team."

"It's not necessary to put yourself through another grueling two-hour car ride. I can talk to Stevens and find those missing reports."

"This is my case, Blake. I should be the one to take care of it—unless there's a reason you don't want me to go," she said guardedly.

"You're kidding me, right? After everything we've been through as partners, after caring about ..." He faltered. "So I can't be trusted, is that it?"

Cole shook her head. "Of course, I trust you. You're probably the only person in my life I can trust. I'm just on edge right now. I can't screw this case up, nor can I have you riding in on a white horse like you always do. I need to stand on my own and prove that I'm still worthy of my shield."

Blake moved closer to her, but she discreetly stepped back. "You're a great detective, Tinks. You don't have anything to prove."

"That's where you're wrong." Cole glanced over her shoulder at Missy. "I do, if not for anyone else, at least for myself."

"Dani, I'm sorry for what I said earlier," Missy stated. "I didn't mean—"

Cole interrupted her. "It doesn't matter, Mrs. Melendez. You were being honest."

Blake looked from Cole to Missy. "What's going on with you two?"

"Nothing," they answered simultaneously.

"Okay. If you don't want to tell me, that's fine. But if it has something to do with this case, I need to know."

"It doesn't," Cole asserted.

The roar of an engine caught their attention. "Good. Thomas is here," said Blake. "We'll leave once we get Missy settled in, Tinks. We need to be on the road in the next hour if we want to get to the station before everyone goes home for the day."

Thomas approached with multiple bags in his hands. "There are more groceries in the car, Blake. Can you grab them? We don't want our injured ladies doing any manual labor."

Blake headed to the car, and the remaining three entered the house. Both Cole and Missy were amazed that the inside was so modern. The plaid furniture was contemporary, with accent pillows and chairs that matched the teal colored walls. The paintings that hung over the sofa and love seat were of beautiful landscapes that enhanced the ambiance of the room. The hardwood floors were polished to perfection, and the area rug in the center was made of silk.

"I guess the old saying is true. You can't judge a book by its cover," Missy said softly.

Thomas nodded. "That's what I said when I first walked in too. Excuse me. I need to put the food away. Why don't you go upstairs and decide which bedrooms you want?"

"Missy can go pick out her room," said Cole. "I need to speak to you alone, Thomas. We can talk in the kitchen."

"Sounds serious," he joked.

"It's not." She turned toward Missy. "I'll meet you upstairs as soon as I'm done here."

Cole and Thomas proceeded to the kitchen while Missy headed up the stairs.

Thomas laid the bags on the table and started taking the food out with Cole's assistance. He grabbed a handful of grapes and popped one in his mouth. "What's up, partner?"

"I have to go back to Hartford tonight. I need you to stay here with Missy. Someone misplaced the forensic files for the Melendez case."

"What the hell!" Thomas roared. "How is that even possible?"

"That's what I plan to find out. Those files didn't just disappear. Someone either hid the results or destroyed them."

"What a shit storm. Our whole investigation is in jeopardy without that evidence."

"Exactly. We can't let whoever this person is get away with murder. That's why I'm going to see Stevens."

"I'll go with you. Blake can keep an eye on Mrs. Melendez until we get back."

"We can't ask our boss to babysit a suspect. Besides, I may need him in Hartford in case I have to get the captain involved."

"You're not fully recovered. Wouldn't it be easier for me to talk to Stevens?"

"Yes. But the truth is I forgot my new migraine prescription. And since I'll be back in Hartford, I can stop by the hospital and pick it up."

"I can take care of that for you too."

"Uh, I know you're my partner, Thomas, but my doctor isn't going to just hand over my scrip to you, especially after what happened with the arsenic. He's even less trusting than I am."

Thomas sighed in frustration. "I'm sure if you give the doc a call, he'll make an exception."

"Why do the extra work when I can pick it up myself? Look, it just makes more sense for me to go," she argued. "I won't be gone long. I'll let you know the minute I find out anything."

Blake walked in and placed the rest of the groceries on the counter. "Why does it sound like you two are about to start World War III in here?"

"Thomas has a problem staying with Missy for a few hours, which seems asinine to me. We've both conducted separate interviews and done individual work on this case. It's not about exclusion. At this point, it's about common sense."

"There's no need to get defensive and make this into more than it is, Cole. I'm not the enemy," said Thomas. "I was just trying to make things easier for you so you can heal from your injuries."

Blake kept his tone neutral as he tried to mediate. "It's natural for tempers to fly in high-pressure cases, particularly now with the loss of crucial files. But it's important that we remain calm and work together to catch this killer."

"You sound like a politician," said Cole. "When you officially decide to run for office, let me know, and I'll donate to your campaign."

"Yeah, me too." Thomas paused. "So what's it going to be, Boss? Who's heading back to Hartford with you?"

"Since Cole is the lead detective, she should work on getting those files."

Thomas glared at Cole. "The boss has spoken. I'm not surprised he took your side."

"I don't know what's gotten into you, Thomas, but you're being an ass right now. This is not the time or the place," Blake said.

Thomas took a deep breath. "I'm sorry. It's just ... well, I had a great lead that I wanted to follow up on back at the station. I thought that if I got this information on my own, it would show you that I'm good enough to be lead on the next big case."

Cole shook her head. "You're trying to prove yourself too? Seems there's a lot of that going around, right, Blake?" she said thoughtfully.

Blake nodded. "Yes. I apologize, Thomas. I didn't know."

"How could you? It's not like I ever said anything. But since you're both heading back, you can check on a man named Alan Christie, who I believe is Melendez's uncle."

Cole could barely contain her excitement. "Are you kidding me? This means we could finally learn something about Melendez's past."

Missy appeared in the doorway, and the conversation abruptly ended. "Is this a police convention or can anyone join?"

"We're just talking shop," Thomas replied. "Is your bedroom okay?"

"Yes, it's fine," Missy stated.

"Great," said Blake. "Cole can decide which bedroom she wants later. We need to head out now if we want to make it back to Hartford before dark."

"I guess that means Thomas is staying with me," Missy acknowledged dryly.

"Yes. I'll drop Cole back here this evening since she's not allowed to drive yet. Thomas, remember to keep an eye out for Patsy, the nurse. She should be arriving here in a few hours."

"And please take care of Missy," Cole stressed earnestly.

"Don't worry. She's in good hands."

As Cole and Blake departed, Missy avoided looking at the other woman for fear Cole would see the overwhelming sadness in her eyes. Something was terribly wrong, and she sensed that she might not ever see Cole again.

CHAPTER 10

MERCK RANSACKED THE APARTMENT, looking for information. After coming up empty-handed, he waited in the shadows for the apartment's occupant to arrive. The temperature in the room was oppressive, and Merck felt like he was drowning in his own perspiration. But he couldn't risk turning on the air conditioner because that would alert his target that something was amiss before he could ambush him.

Merck was relieved twenty minutes later when he heard a key turn in the lock. He promptly jumped to his feet and stood by the door. Once the man entered, Merck gripped him from behind and placed him in a light chokehold.

"Hey, Sammy. Long time no see," Merck declared.

"Merck? What the hell are you doing here? How did you find me?"

Merck hastily released him. "I'm a cop. It's my job to find people." He pulled out his gun and aimed it at Sam. "You may have a different face and identity now, but old habits die hard—for example, your propensity for blonde hookers, who you love to dress up like Marilyn Monroe. And your need for a certain bottle of wine that can only be found in France. You pulled a lot of strings and paid a lot of money to have that delicacy transported to the US. I just followed your breadcrumbs. Oh, and guess what, Sammy? I'm getting close to exposing the rest of your associates too."

The man guffawed. "I'll admit—you're smart, Merck. But I seriously doubt you'll find everyone."

"It wasn't that difficult to track you down, and let me just say how impressed I am that you still recognize me after all this time. I feel special," Merck taunted.

Sam ignored his jibe. "I have no idea why you're bothering an innocent citizen, Merck. I've been clean for months."

"Innocent, my ass. Criminals like you never go completely straight, Sam. All it takes is the right amount of money to bring you out of retirement."

"You're wrong."

"I'd bet my badge that I'm right. So why don't you tell me who hired you to kill Mecham?"

"Like I said before, Merck, I'm out of the business. End of story."

"Seems like your handiwork to me. Has your name written all over it."

"I don't know what you're talking about," he quickly denied.

"Sure, you do. I went through my files and said to myself, 'Who from the old gang handled explosives?' Lo and behold, your name popped up."

"The gang broke up years ago. I have no idea where half of the guys are now."

"You probably wouldn't recognize them anyway since I was told that you each have a new face."

"I have no idea what you're talking about. I was in a car accident. I didn't have a choice. It was either plastic surgery or look like the elephant man for the rest of my life."

"You're a lousy liar, Sammy. If you don't tell me who took out Mecham, I will pull the trigger. You personally know my reputation. You know I'll do it."

"Fine, Merck, but I don't know who killed Mecham. The man had dozens of enemies. He was so arrogant that he didn't even bother to change his real first name. He made it easy for people to find him."

"What about Trevor Moore? You two were close. I'm sure you know his whereabouts."

"Nope. For all I know, he's dead."

Merck smashed him in the face with the butt of his gun. "I'll put four rounds in you if you don't tell me what I want to know."

Sam spat blood on the floor. "I think you knocked my tooth out."

"You're lucky I didn't break your jaw."

"I thought you were going legit."

"I am legit. The old me would have already shot you. Now tell me where Moore is, before I have flashbacks to the day you tried to kill me, my wife, and our unborn child."

"That wasn't me."

"Bullshit," he countered heatedly. "I traced the car back to you. You could have at least changed the plates. You're slipping, Sammy. I guess retirement will do that to you." His tone was harsh. "Now where's Trevor?"

Sam chuckled. "It's kind of funny, but Trevor has been under your nose this whole time, promising to protect and serve."

Merck pointed the gun at Sam's chest. "Who is he?"

"I'm not sure, but he's a cop. He could be any one of you. Hell, he could even be your lieutenant." He took a few steps backward. "Now let me go."

"Why would I do that?" Merck sneered.

"Because you got what you wanted. You don't need me anymore."

Merck put his gun back into his jacket pocket. "You're absolutely right."

"Good. I'll see you out." Sam walked to the door and opened it.

Merck followed him and, without warning, forcefully grabbed Sam's head from behind with both hands. With one quick twist, he snapped Sam's neck. "That's for Marie and Miracle," he whispered.

Cole waited restlessly in the crime lab for Stevens to arrive. On the drive home, she'd called him to arrange a meeting to discuss the Melendez case. The ME had asked a lot of questions, but Cole had refused to be interrogated over the phone. Once Stevens realized that he couldn't change her mind, he had agreed to speak with her after-hours.

Cole tried to focus on what she would say to Stevens regarding the possible corruption in his department. Instead, her mind wandered to Blake. She had asked him to go run the background check on Alan Christie instead of coming along to the meeting so that Stevens wouldn't think she was pulling rank by bringing the lieutenant. Cole knew that Blake was disappointed with her plan to do it on her own. But she didn't want another reminder of how well they worked together. Cole desperately missed her partner and, more importantly, her friend. So when he had suggested they go to Felipe's after this, prior to heading back to the farmhouse, she had eagerly accepted. Still, Cole was apprehensive about the intimacy associated with dining alone in a romantic restaurant. All of their past meals had consisted of fast food eaten in the car or at a desk. And Cole wasn't certain she was prepared to take their relationship to the next level. She was already struggling with breaking her professional codependency on Blake. She wondered how much harder it would be if she became personally reliant on him too.

Stevens rushed into the room and interrupted Cole's thoughts. "What's up? You made it sound like it was an emergency."

"It is. Hello to you too, Stevens."

His chocolate-brown skin glistened with sweat. "It's not that I'm unhappy to see you, Cole, but shouldn't you be in the hospital?"

"I checked myself out. You'd know that if you'd come to see me."

He shook his head. "So to recap, you were your usual stubborn self and went against doctor's orders. And don't whine to me about not visiting when you were only there for two seconds."

"Actually, it was three seconds. Now where is my crime scene information for the Melendez case?"

He looked perplexed. "What are you talking about, Cole? I sent that data weeks ago."

"I never received anything. When I followed up with someone in your office, I was told that the files had been misplaced."

"Then you were misinformed. This office doesn't lose files."

"Well, no one seems to know where they are. Without that evidence, my suspect could walk. Now I have to ask, do you think someone on your team could be corrupt?"

"Absolutely not," he said adamantly. "What about your guys? Maybe someone saw the file and confiscated it."

"The thought did cross my mind."

"How do you know it wasn't me, Cole?" he asked curiously.

"I've known you a long time. This lab is your life. You wouldn't give it up for anyone or anything."

"Sad but true," he sighed. "I guess the only thing to do now is rerun those tests."

"Can you put a rush on it? Having that information could point me directly to my killer." *And further away from Missy.*

Stevens sighed deeply. "Sure, but there goes my vow to leave my office at a decent hour every night."

"I'm sorry. I know how much time you spend here."

"Yeah, almost as much time as you do upstairs."

"Yup. Just two workaholics with no life," she joked.

"Kindred spirits," he murmured fondly.

"Don't do it, Stevens. We share some similarities but not enough for you to ask me out. The answer will once again be no."

"It's because I'm overweight, isn't it? A fat guy can never win the beautiful woman, except in movies," he said lightheartedly.

"That's not true. I don't care about your weight, no matter how much I tease you about it."

"So why don't you want to date the Notorious K-E-N?" He laughed. "You probably have no idea who or what I'm talking about."

"For your information, I love Biggie."

"What? You listen to rap?"

"Yes. My favorites are Jay-Z, Eminem, and Drake."

"Why am I just now hearing about this?"

She smiled. "You never asked. Look, don't be offended. I don't have time to date. This case is keeping me busy."

"And the case before that and the case before that. The job has been your excuse for years, Cole. It's getting old. Why don't you tell me the real reason?"

"Being a devoted cop is the reason."

"You've told enough fat jokes at my expense over the years that I think I have the right to be completely honest with you: it's because you're in love with Blake."

"You're mistaken," she said vehemently. "Blake and I are friends and colleagues, that's all."

Stevens's voice softened. "Cole, do you remember that night I found you in the parking lot, crying in your car? It was your first day back from the leave the former lieutenant imposed on you."

"Yes, I remember. I'd finally gotten the green light to return to active duty. But I still felt like a cloud of suspicion was hovering over me."

"Right. I asked what was wrong. You told me that you were worried about Blake. After what had transpired in the Cavanaugh investigation, you thought he was hurt and angry. You were devastated because you thought you'd failed him. You two hadn't spoken in weeks, and you were mourning the loss of your relationship. Not once, during that entire conversation, did you mention

Cavanaugh, the man you'd supposedly fallen in love with. Everything was about Blake. He was—"

"He was my partner," she interjected. "Of course, I was concerned."

"Your eyes were vacant that night, Cole, totally devoid of purpose. You were lost without him, and that's when the truth hit me. Your feelings for Blake are much more than just that of a partner. I know denial is a practice you hold in high esteem, but maybe it's time to stop making it your priority."

Cole vigorously shook her head. "I can't believe this. I have one vulnerable moment, eons ago, and you use it to psychoanalyze me. Well, I don't need or want it, especially from someone who doesn't know how to interact with the living," she asserted flippantly. "Maybe you should mind your business and stick to dead bodies."

"Can't say that I'm surprised by your reaction. But if you're not careful, you're going to spend the rest of your life by yourself. This job can't hold you and keep you warm at night. Believe me, I know. I've led a solitary existence for much too long. You don't want to wake up on your fiftieth birthday like I did and feel nothing but regret. Don't you want kids someday? Don't you want someone to come home to every night? I know I do, and with any luck, it's not too late for either of us."

A single tear rolled down Cole's cheek, and her voice quivered. "I don't want kids, not after the upbringing I had. I refuse to screw up an innocent child's life the way my family messed up mine. I would never put anyone through that, especially my own flesh and blood."

"I don't know what type of demons you're battling, Cole, but I think it's time you exorcised them." Stevens grabbed a tissue from the box on his desk and handed it to her. "No matter what kind of hell your parents put you through, you're not them. You wouldn't be that way with your own children."

Cole wiped her face. "Listen, I know you're only trying to help, but I can't continue this conversation with you."

"I completely understand. I just hope that one day you'll feel safe enough with me that you will."

"Maybe one day." She tossed the tissue into the nearby trash can. "So when can I expect the new crime scene report? I have a murderer to catch."

"I'll work day and night to get it to you. And I'll keep my eyes and ears open for whoever lost the originals."

"Do you have all the evidence you took from the crime scene? Will redoing everything be a problem?"

"No one has access to what's taken from a crime scene except me and my second-in-command, Bobby, so there shouldn't be any issues."

"Great. I'll give you a call tomorrow."

"Pestering me every hour won't make the process move any quicker."

"I wouldn't dare call you every hour—maybe every two." She smiled. "I hope you find someone special, Kenny. You truly deserve it."

"You too, Cole," he muttered to himself as she left.

Missy tried to unpack her bag, but exhaustion and the ache in her side forced her to lie down instead. After a thirty-minute nap, she climbed out of bed and took two pain pills. Once the throbbing abated, Missy put her clothes away and then headed downstairs. As she approached the living room, she could hear Thomas speaking in hushed tones. Missy loudly cleared her throat, alerting him to her presence.

Thomas spun around in surprise. "I'll text you later," he muttered to the person on the other end and disconnected the call. "Sorry, Mrs. Melendez. I didn't realize you were there."

"I thought we agreed that you would call me Missy." She sat down on the love seat. "Were you talking to Detective Cole?"

"No. That was my angry girlfriend, Josie."

"Why is she angry, if you don't mind me asking?"

He sat across from Missy on the sofa. "I had to cancel our concert date for tonight because I won't be in Hartford."

"I'm sorry. I'm the reason you're evening is ruined. I feel terrible."

"It's not your fault. Shit happens. Things are going pretty well so far. There'll probably be other nights."

"Why do you sound surprised that things are going well?"

"My ex-wife really did a number on me when she left. I'm still a bit shell-shocked," he admitted glumly.

"Well, that was her loss. You're a good guy. You deserve to be happy."

"Thank you, Melissa." He glanced nervously at his watch.

"Is something wrong?"

"Looks like the officer I asked to stay with you until Cole returned is a no-show. I canceled with Josie because he was supposed to be here over a half hour ago. Maybe he got lost along with the nurse, who also should have been here by now."

"I didn't realize another officer was coming here," she said tensely. "I thought only a few people were supposed to know that I'm still alive."

"One more cop won't make a difference."

"But the more people who know, the more danger I'm in, correct?"

"Not in this situation. Trust me, I have everything under control," Thomas asserted calmly.

"You went over Blake's head and involved someone else. How is that being in control?"

"That's not what happened. I had to reach out to the captain when I couldn't get ahold of Blake, and he gave me permission. Blake must have been in a bad reception area when I called because I tried Cole too, and she didn't answer either. I sent them both a text, so they know what's going on."

Missy shook her head. "Why is it okay for the captain and this other officer to be told the truth about me, but not my dad?"

"Your father isn't a cop, Melissa. I don't mean to sound harsh, but we need his grief to be genuine to make your death believable."

Missy was about to respond when an alert on Thomas's phone interrupted her.

Thomas glanced at the screen and excused himself. "Sorry, but it's police business. I'm going to respond to this text, then head outside to smoke a cigarette. Will you be okay by yourself for a few minutes? I'll be right outside the sliding doors."

"Don't worry. I'll be fine."

"Great. I'll be right back after I get my nicotine fix, and we can talk more."

"Take your time. I think I'll get some ice cream as a pick-me-up."

"Hopefully, you like vanilla, chocolate, and strawberry. Those are the ones I bought."

She grinned. "I like them all."

"Good. Just leave some for me."

Cole knocked on Blake's door and entered his office. "You ready to go?"

"Not quite." He typed for a few minutes on the keyboard. "Alan Christie is currently in Africa on a religious mission, according to his website." He turned his monitor around so that Cole could see the website. "He's a traveling evangelist. And after everything I've read about him, I'm certain he's not Melendez's uncle."

Missy took a seat in one of the chairs. "Who is he then?"

"He and his wife used to be foster parents. They mostly took in teenage boys, even though they weren't much older than the kids themselves. They had a teenager named Robert Costa stay with them from age sixteen to seventeen. I'm thinking that was Melendez."

"Did you run Robert Costa's name?"

"Yes. There's a trail until age twenty-two, so it's not inconceivable that Robert had a few identities before he became Melendez."

Cole yawned noisily. "You're right. That is a possibility."

Blake stood and stretched. "You must be beat, Tinks, especially after those long drives with your back injury. How about we go to your place and order takeout? We can eat and talk about everything we discovered. And that will give you the opportunity to take a quick nap before we head back to Bridgewater."

Cole vacillated, unsure of what to do. Lying down in her own bed sounded like heaven, but she was scared to be alone with Blake. "I guess we can do that, but you can't let me sleep for long."

"I won't. Now let's get out of here." He headed to the door. "You want Mr. Wong's sesame shrimp?"

"Of course, I do," she replied animatedly. "I haven't had Mr. Wong's in weeks."

"Well then, we're both long overdue." He smiled. "For a lot of things."

Cole's stomach fluttered with butterflies at his evocative words. She was terrified of getting hurt, but the inevitability of her and Blake was too formidable to fight.

"My boss called me. He knows that someone has been holding up those files. This better not come back to bite me in the ass, Merck!" he shouted.

Merck turned down the volume on his cell phone. "There's no need to yell, Bobby. What did you tell Stevens?"

"I didn't tell him anything. I blamed it on one of the techs."

"Good. I know you can't hold this investigation off anymore. Let Stevens know that you're willing to help in any way you can to redo the tests. I appreciate your help, Bobby. You'll be well compensated."

"You could lose your job if anyone ever found out, Merck."

"So could you. Look, no one will find out. I made sure of it. As long as you keep your mouth shut …"

"I will, but I still don't understand why you had me do it."

"It's personal. I need to get to the suspect before Cole. I had to make sure she wouldn't discover who it is."

"Are you going to kill the person?"

Merck's answer was immediate. "Yes. And I'm going to enjoy every minute of it."

A knock on the door triggered a burst of nervous energy in Missy. She trod lightly toward the foyer and peered out the window. The man standing in the doorway seemed vaguely familiar, but Missy was unsure whether she should answer the door or get Thomas.

The visitor sensed her gaze and reached into his pocket. He flashed a badge in her direction, and Missy visibly relaxed. She moved to the door and opened it. "Can I help you?" Missy asked politely.

"Are you Mrs. Melendez?"

"Yes. Who are you?"

"I'm Officer Vincent Adams. Detective Thomas is expecting me."

"So you're the new babysitter," Missy said irritably.

"I'm just here to do a job, ma'am."

"Yes, but that doesn't mean I have to be happy about it." Missy stepped aside to let him in. "I think I've seen you at the police station."

"You have a great memory." Adams surveyed his surroundings. "I wish we were meeting under different circumstances, though."

"Me too. If you're looking for Thomas, he's outside taking a cigarette break. I'll let him know you're here."

Adams trailed Missy into the living room. "That's okay. I'm sure he'll be right back."

Missy assessed his appearance while he spoke. With his dark hair, pointed nose, and brown eyes, Adams wasn't handsome in the classic sense of the word. But he did exude a cockiness that Missy found slightly attractive. "Do you smoke, Officer Adams?"

He frowned at her. "No. I would never do anything to destroy the temple that God gave me."

Something about his voice was recognizable, and warning bells sounded within her. "Can I ask you a question, Officer Adams?"

"Sure."

"Why aren't you in uniform?"

"I'm off-duty, ma'am. Even though I'm being paid, I'm only here as a favor to Thomas." He winked at her. "Maybe I should take off my jacket? It's warm in here."

"It is a bit stuffy." Missy walked over to the thermostat. "According to this, it's eighty degrees."

"That's why it feels hotter in here than outside. Does this place have air conditioning?"

"I don't know," she said, shrugging. "But please, take your jacket off and relax."

"Thank you." He slowly removed his jacket. "Can you tell me where the bathroom is? I've been driving nonstop for hours."

Missy was markedly silent for several seconds, after she noticed his tattoo. "Uh," she sputtered, "it's down the hall to the left."

Adams noticed that she was pale as a ghost. "Are you okay, Mrs. Melendez? You look ill."

"I'm okay. I just felt a sharp pain in my side. I should probably take another pain pill."

"If you tell me where your medicine is, I'll bring it to you with some water."

"Thank you. The bottle is on my dresser, in the third bedroom on the right, next to the bathroom."

"Great. I'll be back in a few minutes."

Missy waited until Adams disappeared at the top of the stairs and then sprinted to the back of the house. She opened the sliding door and glanced around, but there was no sign of Thomas. Missy poked her head out and whispered his name several times. She was greeted with silence.

Adams wandered up behind Missy, startling her. "Is everything okay?"

She spun around to face him. "Yes," she replied anxiously. "I was looking for Thomas. He's been outside for a long time. I was getting worried."

"He's probably taking a walk. When I texted him earlier, he said he wanted to check out the neighborhood."

"But he seemed eager to get out of here and meet his date," Melissa said.

"This is Thomas's case. It's his job to secure the perimeter." he retorted warily. "Now I think you should sit down because you still seem a little wobbly to me. I put your pills and water on the table."

Missy took one last look outside and then pulled the door closed. She followed Adams into the other room and sat across from him on the sofa. Missy was unsure what to do next since she didn't have a cell phone. She gazed at Adams's arm and determined that the direct route might improve her chances of survival or at least buy her some time.

"Were you in the army, Officer Adams?" Missy inquired.

"Yes. I was an army chaplain, in fact. Why do you ask?" He noticed her staring at his arm and found the answer to his own question. "I've had this tattoo since I was nineteen. I added 'Only God can judge me' on my other arm after I was discharged. I've never wanted to get rid of them, even though they do stick out like name tags," he asserted grimly.

Pieces of the puzzle began to fit together. And it finally dawned on Missy why she felt like she knew him. "You're Luke," she breathed. "Your features are different, but you're him."

Adams was noticeably stunned. "How do you know that?"

"Listen, Luke, what your father did to you and your mother was wrong," Missy said softly. "He used violence and religion as a method of control, and it transformed you into a monster."

Adams reached behind his back and drew his gun. He positioned it on his lap and observed her intently. "My father is the reason I'm a skillful assassin. I'll always be grateful to him for that."

"I don't understand. He hurt you and your mother. Isn't that why you killed him?"

He gaped at her. "Why do you know so much about me and my family? Are you psychic or something?"

"Or something," Missy uttered.

"I was only joking, but I guess that explains why you've been suspicious of me since the moment I arrived." Adams laid his gun beside him and grabbed the glass of water from the table. He drank half of it and offered Missy the rest.

She shook her head, declining the water. "What happened to your mother, Luke?"

"My mother was an alcoholic who did nothing to protect me from my father. She deserved God's wrath."

"God's wrath? Does that mean you killed her too?'

"No, she's alive. Did you miss that part of the show when you were snooping around in my file?" he asked mockingly. "She went to prison for butchering my father."

"But she didn't do it."

"You're wrong. She slaughtered him during a drunken stupor. I saw the whole thing."

"You're disgusting," Missy spat. "I can't believe you let your own mother take the blame for something you did."

"I freed her from his abuse at seven years old. Don't you think she owed me the chance at a life?"

"Why? So that you could grow up and use religion as your motive to execute innocent people like my husband and best friend?" she cried.

"They were sinners, Melissa. God chose me to grant them absolution through death."

Her voice shook. "You're not godly, Luke. You're a maniacal phony cop."

"The name is Vince now, Melissa. Luke passed away when those bandages came off. I graduated from the police academy over two years ago, so I believe that makes me a real officer. Having a badge allows me to get around effortlessly and opens doors that would otherwise be closed. It's the perfect alibi."

"You're not going to get away with this."

"I already have. I've been under Cole's nose this entire time, and she's never suspected me," he asserted smugly. "I was even at the house when she arrived that morning to investigate your husband's murder because I wanted to see the effects of my handiwork. I left there and went straight to the airport for my flight to Miami. I killed your friend that night and immediately flew back. I didn't even miss a shift."

"You're a narcissistic psychopath," Missy proclaimed as she glanced in the direction of the backyard.

He smiled. "I love when you call me names. And just so you know, you're wasting your time looking for Thomas. He's on the side of the house, bleeding to death. He won't be coming to your rescue."

Missy's heart sank. "Who hired you? I at least deserve to know the truth before you kill me."

"I have no idea. I deal with the middlemen. But this thing is way bigger than just your husband. These guys are like the mob, with lots of players and high stakes. Robert got out of line, so he had to die, and you are collateral damage."

"I know nothing about whatever Robert was doing, I swear."

Adams stood and closed the small distance between them. "It doesn't matter. The damage has already been done. Nothing can save you now." He placed his gun against her temple. Adams was about to squeeze the trigger when someone tackled him from behind. The two men fell to the floor together and wrestled for the gun.

The struggle was intense, with the advantage shifting constantly. Missy was thankful that Thomas was still alive. However, judging by the blood on his shirt, he was badly hurt. Despite his valiant efforts, Missy didn't have confidence that he would prevail, so she decided to run. She rose quickly from the sofa and rushed toward the front door, which was now wide open. She darted outside and headed blindly into the darkness.

Ted grabbed a photo album from one of the bookcases in the study and sat on the sofa. He opened it and forced back tears as he stared at the pictures of a buck-toothed, smiling Missy. He turned the pages, which gradually carried him through her preteen years to her rebellious teenage stage. Photos of her adorned with various hair colors and styles of clothing danced in front of his water-logged eyes. He vividly recalled the days that she struggled to discover her identity like most young people her age. She was a handful during that time, but he wouldn't change a moment of it.

"I just want my daughter back," he cried to the empty room.

Ted took a few deep breaths to calm his emotions then flipped to the next page. He gasped aloud at Missy's graduation photo. He'd forgotten how much she resembled his mom, particularly around the eyes. But what really captured Ted's attention was the aura of loneliness that seemed to embody his daughter. He knew from experience that a portion of Missy's isolation stemmed from the burden of being forcibly thrust into someone else's mind and thoughts. He understood it because, like Missy, he'd inherited his mother's sixth sense. The only difference was he refused to acknowledge or discuss his extrasensory abilities with anyone, including his wife when she was alive. Missy had never admitted to Ted that she was clairvoyant, but he was raised by a gypsy fortuneteller so he recognized all the signs.

At the age of seven, Ted started going to work with his mom, Gloria, and watched as she predicted people's futures. Ted had an analytical mind so he never believed any of her prophesies. Instead, he'd argue the details of each revelation to prove that she wasn't psychic. Disheartened by his attitude and the uncertainty he caused in her customers, Gloria eventually sent her twelve-year-old son to live with family members. She attempted to call and visit, but Ted wanted nothing to do with her. Over time, Gloria's efforts to stay in contact with her son ceased, but occasionally she'd pull Ted into one of her visions. That connection forced Ted to accept that his mother's gift was real, and that he'd been cursed with it too.

As Ted grew older, his resentment towards his mother turned to hatred. He wanted Gloria to regret abandoning him, so he accomplished the one thing she had been unable to—he became a lawyer. Gloria had dropped out of law school in her first year because she'd gotten pregnant with him. Ted had never known his father, but he understood how much he'd hurt his mother. Gloria was a nomad, a dreamer, and she blamed Ted Sr. for the desertion of her dreams.

For years, Ted pushed himself academically. He graduated summa cum laude from college and was ranked first at Harvard Law School. Still, success didn't come without challenges. After opening his own practice, Ted had a difficult time attracting business. Some people felt he wouldn't be as competent in court as his Caucasian counterparts so they declined his representation. However, once Ted established an undefeated record, people began to look beyond his skin color, which helped Delaney Law became the fastest-growing legal firm in Connecticut.

Ted was proud of his accomplishments since that meant he could give his family anything they desired. Missy reaped the benefits of having a famous attorney as her father, but that didn't seem to satiate the void in her life. Ted knew that she missed her mother, who died a few months after Missy's eleventh birthday, and that his attempt to be both parents was a complete failure. Missy needed friends to help fill that emptiness, but she often complained to Ted about how the other kids thought she was either too pretty, too ethnic-looking, too rich, too weird, or too something else for anyone to get close to her. They called her a snob since she didn't invite them over for sleepovers. And Missy wasn't permitted at their houses either. Ted blamed himself for the other kids disliking her because he only wanted her to associate with the children of his affluent friends. He thought that would help people forget that she was half black, but all it did was force people to judge her solely by his money and not by her character.

Frustrated by his own shortcomings as a father, Ted slammed the book shut and allowed the tears to flow unfettered. He wanted to make it up to Missy but realized that he would never get the chance now. Rage boiled up inside of him and threatened to spill over. He glanced at the gun on the table and decided that someone needed to pay for the death of his only child. He retrieved the weapon and headed for the door. This time, instead of being a lawyer, Ted planned on being judge, jury, and executioner.

Blake stood and gathered the containers from the table. "I'm going to dispose of what's left of the Chinese food, Tinks. How about you take your pain medication and rest for an hour? That will put us back in Bridgewater around eleven, okay?"

Cole nodded. "Yes, but I doubt Thomas will be happy about it."

"You let me worry about him." Blake placed the cartons into a brown paper bag. "If you don't mind, I'm going to take a quick shower while you sleep."

"No, I don't mind." *Except I'll probably dream of your wet, naked body now.* "There are towels in the hallway closet. Help yourself."

"Thanks. If you need anything, just yell."

She smiled. "I will."

Cole popped two pills and closed her eyes. She instantly drifted off to sleep, but a few minutes later, the incessant, loud ringing of the doorbell forced her awake. She felt inebriated as she rose from the couch and walked to the front of the house. She glanced out the peephole and sighed heavily when she saw her unkempt visitor.

Cole opened the door. "What are you doing here, Mr. Delaney?"

"I need to talk to you, Detective Cole."

"You have no right to just show up at my house like this," she said irritably. "Can't this wait until I'm back at the station?"

"No. I'm sorry for the intrusion, but it's important."

Cole let him in, and Ted warily examined his surroundings.

"Are you alone?" he asked.

His nervous energy made her uneasy. "I should be the one asking questions, Mr. Delaney. I assume you're here to talk about Missy's murder, but I can't discuss an ongoing investigation with you."

"I need you to tell me who killed my daughter, Detective," he replied sharply.

"I have no idea. I understand that you're grieving, but coming here was a mistake."

"I wanted to believe that her death was a mistake, that the police were wrong. But I can no longer feel her," he murmured.

"What are you talking about, Mr. Delaney?"

"It doesn't matter. You wouldn't understand, anyway." He suddenly pulled a .45-caliber gun from inside his disheveled suit and pointed it at her. "Just tell me who did this, Detective. I need a name."

"Mr. Delaney, please put your weapon away," Cole said calmly. "I don't know who killed her. Believe me, I want to find the person as much as you do."

"Don't pretend like you cared about my daughter. Missy was all I had. I want the son of a bitch who took her from me!" he shrieked.

"This is not the way to do it. You have to let law enforcement to do its job and prosecute the person responsible. You're an attorney, not a vigilante. Please put your firearm away before this stunt causes you to lose everything."

The gun wobbled in his unsteady grip. "I already have," Ted cried.

Cole tried to gauge the distance between her and the coat rack behind Ted. Her gun was in her jacket pocket, but she realized it was too far away to get to without possibly getting injured. "If you shoot me, you'll never get the answers you're looking for. I don't think Missy would want her father to spend the rest of his life in prison, trying to avenge her death."

Ted's rage was palpable. "You have no idea what Missy would have wanted. She was just a scapegoat for you. I know all about your past, Cole. You tried to pin a murder on my daughter to redeem your tarnished reputation."

Cole wanted to dispute Ted's statement, but she wasn't confident in her own denial. Her original goal had been to solve the Melendez case to compensate for the damage she'd done in the past. And she wasn't certain that plan had changed. "Mr. Delaney, I'll admit that I've made some bad decisions in my career, but this is about you, not me. I don't believe you're the kind of man who could shoot anyone in cold blood. You're a man of integrity."

"Integrity," he snickered. "Are you kidding me? I'm a lawyer, for God's sake. I send innocent men to prison and get the guilty ones off with a slap on the wrist. There's no respect or distinction in that. You should know firsthand what a person will do when they are desperate. We both see it every day in our professions. The simplest thing can cause someone to become reckless. And my daughter's murder was anything but simple."

"Mr. Delaney, please be rational ..." Cole paused as she noticed Blake on the stairs in her peripheral vision. She swiftly devised a plan to divert Ted's attention long enough for Blake to disarm him. She inched her way to the window and opened the curtains wide enough to see what Blake was doing in the reflection off the glass.

Ted's breathing quickened, showing his agitation. "What the hell are you doing, Detective? Don't take another step."

"Are you going to shoot an unarmed woman in the back, Mr. Delaney? I know you're angry, but you're not a coward."

"I don't trust you," Ted spat. He pivoted away from the staircase and rapidly approached her.

"Well, that makes two of us," she said.

Cole watched Blake's reflection as he quietly advanced from behind and positioned his gun at Ted's back. "Drop it, Delaney," Blake ordered.

Ted kept his gun raised. “I could still shoot her.”

“And I will kill you. Now put your weapon down slowly.”

Ted let his arms fall to his side, and Blake removed the gun from his limp hand.

Blake looked over at Cole. “Are you okay?” he asked softly.

“I’m fine. I don’t think I was in any actual danger. Mr. Delaney clearly wasn’t thinking straight because of his grief.”

Blake nodded. “I agree. Go call this in, and I’ll keep an eye on Mr. Delaney.”

“Sure.” Cole grabbed her cell from the table and dialed the station. She hung up a few minutes later. “The cavalry is on the way.”

The road stretched endlessly ahead of Missy—unforgiving, cruel, mocking her fear. Still, she ran. Missy heard Kayla’s voice in her head, encouraging her to endure, willing her to survive. Pain and exhaustion coursed through her body like molten lava, scorching her lungs and rapidly spreading to her legs and feet. Missy’s breathing was labored, and her heart threatened to explode out of her chest. Her clothes were pasted to her skin from the sweat and blood that oozed from her pores and reopened wound. Missy stumbled once the ache became too excruciating, and she realized that she couldn’t go any farther. She stopped and prayed that someone would come along to help her.

A few minutes later, her prayers were answered as a car pulled up beside her. Missy tried to see inside, but it was too dark. She did, however, recognize the owner as a woman.

The woman rolled down the window. “Hey, are you okay?”

“Can you … I need to … to … I need the police,” Missy stammered. Her head began to whirl, and she collapsed to the ground.

The woman immediately exited her car and hurried to Missy’s aid. She stooped down and lifted Missy’s shirt to check her side. “Don’t worry. I’m a nurse. That wound looks bad. You need medical attention as soon as possible. Are you okay with getting in my car, or do you want me to call 911 and wait for the ambulance?”

Missy shook her head. “I’d rather you take me. Can you please help me up?”

"Sure. Just lean on me." The stranger supported Missy as she got to her feet. She opened the car door and helped Missy scramble into the back. "There's a towel back there. Hold it on the wound lightly."

The woman closed the door and climbed into the front seat. "I'm not from around here, but I'll use my GPS to find the closest hospital." She glimpsed Missy in the rearview mirror and noticed that her eyes were already closed. Guessing that the other woman was unconscious, she used her Bluetooth to make a call. "It's Daphne. I got her."

Cole waited for the two officers to place Ted in the back of the squad car before she closed the door. She leaned against the wooden frame and breathed a sigh of relief. Cole was depleted, and she didn't think she could handle any more excitement.

She glanced at Blake, who was on the phone, explaining to Captain Kessler what had happened. His sandy-brown hair was wet, which gave him a boyish, sexy look. Cole's body trembled with awareness as she ogled his muscular physique through his cotton T-shirt. His smoldering presence awakened something latent inside of her. It tugged at her heart and drew her to him.

Blake sensed Cole's magnetic stare and yielded to the longing he saw in her eyes. He disconnected the call and placed his cell in his pocket. He rose to his feet with determination and moved purposefully toward her, never once breaking eye contact. Blake stopped directly in front of Cole, so close that he could feel the heat from her body against his. He extended his hand and delicately stroked her face. The electricity in the room pulsated wildly, leaving them both breathless.

Cole straightened, reflexively expecting his next move. "Blake, I don't think …"

She didn't finish her sentence. Blake crashed into her, his mouth devouring hers in an all-consuming kiss. The fire between them quickly grew into a four-alarm blaze, vibrant and uncontrollable. They both sanctioned the inferno to burn free and untamed, like their undeniable hunger. Their tongues greedily made love as their bodies demanded to get closer.

Blake feverishly ran his fingers through Cole's unruly tendrils. His hypnotic touch triggered chills that raced along her spine. Cole could feel him against her, and her body quivered in anticipation. Instinctively, she pressed against him, her desire uninhibited as she moaned with pleasure.

Blake severed the kiss and eagerly pulled at the bottom of her red blouse. Cole lifted her arms to accommodate him as he raised the garment over her head. His eyes never strayed from hers, and Cole was mesmerized by the yearning she saw there. She could see not only Blake's vulnerability but also his love for her.

Cole placed her hands on his brawny chest and relished the strength that radiated from him. Her fingers glided down his torso until they reached the edge of his shirt. She removed it and then grabbed his belt and unfastened it.

Blake exhibited supreme discipline as his hands closed lovingly around Cole's throat, and his thumb stroked her moist lips. Cole opened her mouth and captured his thumb. Blake groaned as she sucked on it.

He brushed his fingertips across the top curves of her breasts, teasing her, stroking one through the fabric of her bra. Blake's soft touch was a beguiling sensation, but it wasn't enough for Cole. She swayed forward, craving more.

Blake unhooked the rear clasp and watched the bra fall away. His gaze was riveted as he took in the full sight of her bare chest. "I want you," he whispered huskily as he kissed her again.

Blake's body melted with hers. His tongue pushed past her lips and swept her mouth like a searing torch. He played havoc with her senses, first plunging deep and then teasing with rapid, elusive darting. The sensual lingual stroking went on and on, depriving her of air yet bringing her to life.

His nibbling lips wandered along Cole's neck to her ear. He teased her earlobe and pulled on it tenderly. He probed inside with his tongue, which caused her to cry out, her body trembling against him.

Blake sank to his knees and, with Cole's assistance, removed her jeans. His hands molded to the curve of her hips. Then he flattened his palm over the mound visible underneath her white cotton panties. "You are so beautiful, Tinks," he murmured. "I've never seen anything as exquisite as you are." He removed her underwear and devotedly kissed Cole's stomach, hips, and thighs with his mouth.

He stood, picked her up, and ascended the stairs to the bedroom. Blake laid Cole down and removed the remainder of his clothing. He then joined her on the bed. They luxuriated in the feeling of skin against skin, heart against heart, soul against soul. Neither stirred for several seconds as their eyes met one last time before their passage into ecstasy began. They eavesdropped on each other's heartbeat, unveiling the mysteries of their long-awaited union. They both savored every nuance as the scents of their bodies fused together to create an intoxicating chemistry.

Cole flipped Blake on his back and mounted him. She shouted his name as she began moving. Cole increased the tempo, slowed it down, and then intensified it once more. She propelled Blake to the brink, and when she sensed he was about to go over, she skillfully reigned in his passion.

After a few minutes of teasing, Blake could no longer control himself and pitched Cole gently onto her rear. He kissed her ravenously and took over the tempo. Both were wrapped in the throes of an unfathomable passion, unlike anything they'd ever known. Together they moved up and down, around and around, until Cole screamed out in release. Her body convulsed and leaped off the sheets.

Seconds later, Blake united with her on that plateau, his gratification equal to hers. And as they tumbled back to earth, they held on to each other, cocooned in their bliss. Neither Blake nor Cole had the energy to speak, so they closed their eyes and fell asleep.

Blake propped himself up on a pillow and read the text message again: "If you don't follow the instructions I send you in the next few hours, I will tell my sister that you knew about my involvement with Cavanaugh. And that you and your superiors let Danielle stay undercover knowing that I'd out her."

Blake glanced at Cole, who was still napping, and lightly touched her face. The thought of losing her made his heart constrict in agony. His worst nightmare was becoming a reality and at the most inopportune time. If he allowed David to force him into doing something illegal, he'd lose his job. But if he told Cole the truth, he'd lose her. No matter what decision he made, Blake acknowledged that his life would never be the same. And that instilled in him a fear far greater than anything he'd ever faced on the streets.

Blake was about to leave the room to make a call when he noticed that Cole was tossing and turning in her sleep. He debated whether to wake her or let her struggle with her demons. The choice became unnecessary as Cole vaulted up and looked blindly around the room.

Blake laid his phone on the nightstand and wrapped his arms around her from behind. "Everything is okay, Tinks. I'm here," he uttered softly.

Cole wrestled to get her emotions under control. "Blake? What happened?"

"You were having a nightmare."

She sighed heavily. "I'd hoped to get a reprieve from them with you lying next to me."

He removed his arms and scooted beside her. "I'm sorry my presence wasn't enough to slay your monsters, Tinks, but maybe talking about it will help."

Cole's uncertainty was perceptible, even in the darkened room. "I don't know if I can do that. It's too painful."

Blake was hurt by her unwillingness to communicate, particularly after what had just happened between them. However, he realized that for Cole, change might not be feasible, at least not this soon. "I don't want to push you, but I'm here for you. Always."

Cole contemplated whether she should share the most intimate details of her childhood with him. She had suffered a dark series of experiences that even as an adult threatened her sanity. Cole was worried that once she revealed the unspeakable atrocities to Blake, he'd think less of her.

Blake turned on a nearby lamp. "Whatever you tell me will not alter my opinion of you, Tinks."

The sincerity of Blake's words was enough to open the portal into her troubled past. Cole hesitated at first but then began to speak in a tone devoid of feeling. "I've had countless days filled with suffering," she murmured, "moments bruised so harshly with affliction that they contaminated my physical and mental being like an infectious disease. His smell, his breath, the unforgettable footprint that he left on my soul have formed the beasts that now inhabit my nightmares."

"I'm afraid I don't understand," Blake whispered. "This doesn't sound like you."

"He stole things from me—did things that broke my spirit and shattered my youth."

"Tinks, you're speaking in riddles. Who are you talking about?"

"My father."

"What did he do? Please, just tell me what happened."

She nodded. "I was ten, and my brother David was eight. My father's cruelty had reached a new plateau, and it was becoming more and more difficult to avoid him. We didn't talk to him unless it was necessary and did everything exactly the way he wanted to avoid his wrath.

"After endless hours of practice, with my help, David had finally become a decent swimmer and marksman. He wasn't an expert, but at least he was competent enough to keep my dad from beating him every day. The problem was that David was a mama's boy, and David Sr. wanted him to be more of a man. I would often hear him yell at Mom about their relationship because he believed it was detrimental to David. My mother did baby him, but he was just a kid. She would sneak him dolls even though she knew my father didn't approve of David playing with them. One day my father found a Barbie in the den, which set off a series of events that forever changed my life." Tears streaked down Cole's face, but she quickly wiped them away with her hands.

Blake reached over and intertwined his fingers with hers. He'd never seen Cole cry in all the years he'd known her. She hadn't even shed a single tear during or after the Cavanaugh case, and he knew how much pain it had caused her. "If this is too hard, you can stop," he said gently.

"No. I want to finish." She inhaled deeply and then continued. "I tried to protect David by telling my father that the doll was mine. But he knew I was lying. He gripped me by my hair, dragged me to my room, and locked the door. He said that if I wanted to suddenly be a girl, he would show me firsthand what it entailed and would have some fun too."

Intuitively, Blake understood what was coming, at least part of it. A fury unlike anything he'd ever known enveloped him. He was torn between the desire to hold Cole and the desire to hunt her father down like an animal.

Cole's body shuddered, and her stomach roiled. Vomit came up in her throat. "He ..." She faltered a bit. "He threw me on the bed and climbed on top of me. He reeked of alcohol and cigarettes. I'll never forget that smell. The stench filled my nostrils as my father touched me and did unspeakable things." Cole could no longer constrain her sobs. "Once he was finished, he kissed me on the forehead and quietly left the room. I knew he would go after David even before I heard my brother's high-pitched screams a few minutes later. I was in pain, but like I'd done numerous times before, I went to save my brother.

"By the time I arrived, my father had mounted David on the living room floor and was punching him. I tried to pull him off of my brother's tiny frame, but he flung me to the ground. I jumped up to dial 911, but when I noticed my father's jacket lying on the recliner, I came up with a new plan. I grabbed the keys to the gun cabinet from his pocket and unlocked the glass door. I removed the Smith and Wesson and yelled for him to stop. My father saw the pistol aimed at him and said I didn't have the guts to fire. I warned him again, but he continued to hammer David. He left me no other choice but to pull the trigger. The bullet struck him in the chest, and he crashed to the floor."

"Thank God your brother wasn't shot too."

"I never miss my target, Blake, not even while under duress. My father taught me how to focus on nothing but the kill."

Blake shook his head. "So while other little girls were playing with toys and makeup, you were learning how to hunt."

"Yes."

"Where was your mother while all of this was happening?"

"She stayed hidden in the bedroom whenever anything bad happened in the house. That way, she could pretend that it didn't occur. She never tried to help us, nor would she go against my father."

Blake shook his head. "Unbelievable. Did you call 911 after you shot him?"

"Yes, but first I checked on David, who was thankfully alive. My father was lying beside him, clearly in pain, yet he still had enough energy to accuse me of trying to kill him. I reminded him that if I had truly wanted to end his life, he would be dead. I detected a smidgen of fear in his eyes, which meant he recognized the truth of my words. That's when he started shouting my mother's name over and over. He thought I might finish the job, so he needed her there to protect his sorry ass."

"So what happened, Tinks? You obviously didn't go to prison or juvie since you were able to become a cop."

"No, I didn't. My father claimed I had been a little overzealous during target practice and accidentally shot him. He told the officers that after I wounded him, he had hauled himself into the house."

Blake was skeptical. "And they believed him, even though there wasn't a trail of blood leading from the outside into the living room?"

"They didn't have a choice. My mother and I both corroborated his story. And there was no way my father was going to press charges against me. That would mean an investigation, and he didn't want people to discover that he was abusing his kids. Besides, he'd have to admit that a child—a girl at that—had gotten the best of him. In his mind, he had a pristine reputation to maintain, but everyone knew that he was a hateful, dishonest son of a bitch."

"What about David? How did your father account for his bruises?"

"He didn't. David hid in his room when the paramedics came."

"But didn't he need medical attention?"

"My mother was a nurse. She took care of David at home with medical supplies my father made her steal from the hospital."

"Was he violent toward her too?"

"Yes. David Sr. was an equal opportunity abuser. My mother was obedient, so it didn't happen often to her."

"I'm almost afraid to ask, but were things worse after that incident?"

"Of course, they were. When my father was released from the hospital, he came home but stopped talking to me. His only daughter was dead, except for when I tried to shield David from his bullying. Then I became his primary punching bag, which meant my brother was spared."

"Did he … I mean … what about the other thing?" Blake inquired awkwardly.

"My father wanted to, but I think he was scared because he saw the transformation in me. I no longer cried when he hit me. And although he'd bring the full force of his strength down on me, I wouldn't flinch. I somehow learned to separate myself from the pain. My father's power was rooted in my discomfort, so I took that away from him. And when I told him that if he ever touched me in that way again, I'd stab him to death in his sleep, I'm pretty sure he believed me."

"Probably a wise choice on his part," Blake commented.

Cole nodded. "Yes, it was. Eventually, the beatings stopped too." *But the fact that he never molested me again doesn't keep the nightmares at bay. It doesn't prevent me from remembering and reliving every second. It doesn't stop me from envisioning his cold, calloused hands when others try to touch me, cruelly reminding me of when I wasn't in control. I can't ever lose my power again. And I can't allow intimacy to weaken me, no matter how much I care about the person.*

"Where is your father now?"

"What? Why?"

"Just curious."

She detected the unevenness in his tone and lightly touched his shoulder. "I don't need you to be my hero, Blake. It was the past; it's over now."

"I know, but if I ever met your father, I'm not sure what I'd do." He cupped her cheek. "The idea of anyone hurting you ..."

Cole found Blake's valor endearing. She appreciated the fact that he had been able to create an environment relaxed enough for her to talk about her past, which was no easy feat. Cole recognized that she had a long road ahead, but for the first time, she felt a glimmer of hope.

"Thank you for caring about me, Blake," she said sincerely.

"There's no need to thank me, Tinks. It's my pleasure."

"Mine too," she beamed.

He smiled. "As much as I would like to stay in bed and discuss pleasures with you, we need to head back to relieve Thomas."

Cole nodded. "Sadly, I agree."

The sound of gunfire resonated in the room. The man on the floor gasped inaudibly before he took his final breath. His dead eyes stared eerily at the ceiling.

The man holding the gun reached into his pocket, retrieved his cell phone, and made a call. "You need to get here as soon as possible. There's been a problem."

CHAPTER 11

CAVANAUGH GLANCED AT ONE OF THE other prisoners and nodded, signaling that it was time. He placed the pill in his mouth and continued to load the laundry into the dryer. Within minutes, his organs started to churn, and his insides felt like they were about to explode. The throbbing in his chest brought him abruptly to his knees as he labored to breathe. He tumbled to the floor and began to convulse uncontrollably.

The prisoner hurried over to where Cavanaugh was lying and screamed for the guard. The correctional officer kneeled beside the man's body and checked for a pulse. He radioed for assistance once he realized that Cavanaugh was barely breathing and foaming at the mouth. A few minutes later, a guard appeared with a gurney to transport Cavanaugh to the infirmary. Upon his arrival, the prison doctor immediately examined him, but he couldn't determine what had caused Cavanaugh to collapse. So he elected to have the unconscious inmate transferred to the nearest hospital.

While the ambulance idled at a red light, the accompanying officer, Donald Sampson, watched as Cavanaugh went into cardiac arrest. The paramedic administered CPR to get the patient into a shockable rhythm then used defibrillation to try and restart his heart. When that failed, he announced that Cavanaugh was gone. The idea that his cuffs were on a dead man's wrists creeped Sampson out so he quickly removed them. He knew he wasn't following protocol, but Sampson felt that the prisoner no longer posed a threat.

The light changed to green, and the ambulance started moving again. Sampson retrieved his phone from his pocket to alert the precinct of Cavanaugh's death, but before he could place the call, an SUV rammed into the back of the van. Once the jolt from the impact was over, Sampson extracted his weapon and tried to calm the EMT. He heard a commotion on the left side of the vehicle and realized this was an ambush. The driver's screams and the subsequent gunshots signaled to Sampson that he was outnumbered.

The back of the ambulance rattled, which meant that someone was trying to enter the van. Sampson radioed for backup and then recklessly discharged his weapon through the back door. A loud groan suggested that a bullet had hit one of the perpetrators, but Sampson didn't have time to revel in that small triumph. The doors swung open, and two masked men appeared. The next series of shots left both Sampson and the paramedic dead.

One of the cloaked men removed his mask and crouched down beside Cavanaugh's lifeless body. He pulled the syringe from his pocket and inserted it into Cavanaugh's arm. After administering the antidote, he stood and grabbed Cavanaugh by the shoulders. The second man grasped his legs, and they carried Cavanaugh out of the ambulance. Together, they loaded him into the back of the SUV.

Sirens sounded in the distance. The men promptly leaped into the vehicle and slammed the doors. They pulled off, abandoning their injured partner, who lay bleeding on the asphalt.

"What about Sanchez? We shouldn't have left him there," the driver stated.

"There's nothing we can do for him now. If you want, you can get out and wait with him until the police arrive," the passenger said. "Of course, that means going to prison, but I guess Sanchez's life is worth more than your own."

He accepted the other man's silence as acquiescence. "Besides," he continued, "I checked. Sanchez is dead." David grinned subtly in the shadows. *No one will ever know that I was the one who shot him both times*, he thought. *Cavanaugh will need a new right-hand man, and I'm the perfect guy for the job.*

"I hope Missy is okay," Cole said anxiously.

"They put out an APB, so I'm sure she'll be found soon, Tinks."

"I can't believe my investigation has come full circle, and I wasn't there to connect the dots."

"Don't blame yourself. You can't be in two places at once," Blake said supportively.

"But I would have been there if I wasn't …" She stopped midsentence.

"Having sex with me?" His tone was biting.

"Please don't put words in my mouth. That's not what I was going to say."

"Really? Isn't that why you've completely ignored me since you got that phone call? Why we got dressed in silence? Why you won't let me touch you?"

Cole shook her head. "It's not like that."

"Then what is it like, Tinks? Do you regret what happened between us? Should we just forget about it and go on like nothing ever happened? You may be able to, but I certainly can't."

"I can't either," she said, her voice full of remorse.

"And that bothers you because you're afraid of us."

Cole wasn't sure how to respond. She didn't want to hurt Blake, but he was right. Her feelings for him were frightening, and she wasn't ready to discuss them "Blake, I—"

His phone rang, interrupting her. "Saved by the bell," Blake whispered. He pressed the answer button on the steering wheel in his car, enabling his Bluetooth. They both listened as Thomas explained that the local police wanted to remove the body and seal off the house.

"I would prefer that the crime scene remain intact until we get there," Blake said. "I know we're out of our jurisdiction, but maybe they can extend some professional courtesy to us."

"Thomas, please don't allow some backward-ass deputies, who've probably never even seen a real homicide, sully the evidence for our case," Cole interjected.

"I got it covered, Cole," Blake snapped. "Remember, I'm still the one in charge."

"Fuck you," she muttered under her breath.

"I believe you've already done that," Blake mouthed.

"Thomas, just tell them that your lieutenant doesn't want the crime scene to be touched since he seems to think that pulling rank works," Cole announced.

"What's going on between you two? You both sound strange," Thomas said.

"I think it's the acoustics in the car," said Blake. "I don't get great reception out here in the boonies. The closest cell tower is probably miles away." He waited for Cole to make another remark, but she remained silent. "Cole and I will be there in about thirty minutes, Thomas. Can you hold out that long, or do you need to go to the hospital now?"

"I'm fine. It's just a flesh wound. There's a paramedic here to keep an eye on me."

"Glad to hear that. We'll see you soon." Blake disconnected the call.

"You're wasting your time. Thomas will only infuriate Barney Fife, and we'll be completely fucked."

"Your attitude isn't helping, Tinks. Let's just call last night what it was: a mistake. It happened, we both enjoyed it, but now it's over, and we're back to business as usual," Blake said doggedly.

"Is that what you want?" Her voice trembled slightly.

"Well, I don't want a relationship with a coward. I need someone who's willing to give me 100 percent, and as of now, you're not that person. I'm not interested in quasi-love."

His words stung, and Cole struggled to hold back her looming tears. An unfamiliar yet strangely comforting ache settled in her heart. She had never imagined that it would hurt so much or that she would care so deeply. She wanted to tell Blake that she longed for the things he could offer, but instead, she let the silence speak for her.

"Are we going to the hospital?" Missy asked faintly from the rear of the car.

"Oh, you surprised me. I thought you were unconscious," said the woman who had picked her up. "I'm following the directions from my GPS. We're headed there now."

"Where are you from?"

"Excuse me?"

"You said you aren't from around here."

"Yes, I did say that. I'm from Hartford, but I accepted a gig in Bridgewater as a private nurse. I was supposed to be at the location hours ago, but an accident on the highway forced me to take another route, and I got lost even with the GPS."

"I think you're my nurse. Were you hired for Melissa Melendez?"

The woman pulled the car over and turned to face her. "How did you know that?"

"I'm Melissa Melendez."

"You're kidding, right?"

"No. Someone tried to kill me, but I escaped. I need to use your phone to call the detective who's protecting me."

"You're in no shape to call anyone. Give me the number, and I'll do it. I'll let her know that you're okay and that I'm taking you to the hospital."

Her raspy tone seemed familiar, which generated doubts in Missy about her identity. "Don't you have the number of the person who hired you?"

"Uh … actually, I think I have it saved in my phone." She grabbed her cell from the passenger seat and looked at it for several seconds. "I do have Detective Cole's number. I'll call her right now." She pushed a few buttons and pressed the phone to her ear. "Hi, my name is Patsy. I'm the nurse assigned to take care of Melissa Melendez. I found her on the side of the road and wanted to let you know that's she's all right. We're on our way to New Milford Hospital now." There were a few moments of quiet. "You're welcome. I'll text you once we get there."

"What did she say?" Missy inquired curiously after the nurse disconnected the call.

"She thanked me for taking care of you. She has to handle a situation at the house but promised to come see you after that. She's relieved that you're okay, and she said to stay put until she comes to get you."

Missy breathed a sigh of relief since Cole's portion of the conversation sounded realistic. The situation she had mentioned was, in all probability, Thomas and Adams. One or both were undoubtedly dead. But something still niggled at her. "I thought your name was Daphne, not Patsy," Missy murmured. "My head was a little fuzzy, but I could have sworn I heard you say Daphne earlier."

"You misunderstood me, probably from blood loss. That reminds me, I need to get you to the hospital ASAP."

Missy's mind was a bit hazy, but she gradually began to put things together. "Patsy, how did you know a woman was guarding me?"

The woman pulled the vehicle back on the road. "You must have mentioned it."

"I didn't," Missy declared adamantly.

"A woman hired me, so I just assumed it was the same person."

"Detective Cole's boss, who's a man, is the one who called you about the private nursing position."

"Shit," the woman muttered. "Why couldn't you just leave it alone, Mrs. Melendez? It's not my job to kill you, but you might make me do it."

Missy connected the final piece of the puzzle. *She's the woman in my vision who was chasing me.* "You're on the list, aren't you? Daphne, the only female."

"A real honor for me."

"There's no honor in being a criminal."

"For me, there was. I personally found it rewarding. Fortunately for you, I'm currently into saving lives, not taking them. But my friend has no problem with killing, and you're his bounty. Be prepared to die a slow, agonizing death because he's a sick bastard."

Daphne's pledge sent shivers of terror through Missy's body, and she started to violently shake. "Adams is most likely dead, so I'm sure the bounty expired with him," she said with false bravado.

Daphne laughed. "Even if that's true, the bounty doesn't die until you do. And I'm not talking about Adams. He was a religious freak but great at his profession."

"You speak about him like he was a doctor or something."

"He was, in a way. He knew how to operate, but instead of a scalpel, he used a gun."

Missy ignored the other woman's absurd interpretation and glanced around for something she could use to help her get away. She spotted Daphne's medical kit in the far-right corner of the back seat. Missy tried not to attract attention to herself as she slid closer to the bag. Her pain was growing increasingly worse, but she didn't make a sound. She unzipped the bag, reached inside, and blindly sorted through the contents. Missy located a pair of shears and grasped them tightly. She moved behind Daphne, lifted the scissors, and thrust them into the woman's shoulder.

The car swerved as Daphne's earsplitting scream ricocheted off the interior glass. She tried to regain control of the vehicle but veered dangerously on and off the two-lane highway. Horns blared as she came close to colliding with oncoming traffic. Daphne abruptly hit the brake and stopped, causing the car behind them to slam into the rear of her Toyota Camry.

Missy jerked forward from the crash, her head slamming against the back of the driver's seat. She quickly opened the door and scrambled out of the car. Adrenaline kicked in, and Missy ran, despite the dizziness and throbbing in her side.

Daphne grabbed her gun from the glove compartment and clumsily chased Missy down the freeway. "Stop!" she yelled. She discharged her weapon, but the bloody gash in her shoulder hurt her aim, and she missed her target.

Bullets whizzed past Missy's head in rapid succession. She continued to move, but the pain coursing through her body nearly brought Missy to her knees. She glanced back at her captor to gauge the distance between them. The road spun wildly in front of her, but Missy knew that if she paused to rest, she would die. *I don't know how much longer I can stay upright. Cole, where are you? I need you right now.*

Something is wrong with Missy. "I'm going to call the sheriff and see if there is any news. I have a bad feeling," Cole said nervously.

"I'm sure she's okay. Looks like there's some kind of commotion up ahead—undoubtedly an accident. There's a car on the wrong side of the road."

"Let's try to go around it or find an alternate route. We need to get to the house and find Missy."

Gunshots echoed in the distance. Blake immediately pulled over, and both he and Cole hopped out of the truck brandishing their guns. They both searched for the shooter, but what they saw was Missy running down the highway, near collapse.

"That's Missy!" Cole exclaimed. "I'm going to get her. Cover me, Blake."

"No, Tinks. Let me do it."

Cole disregarded Blake's directive and ran toward Missy. After she reached the other woman's location, Cole was forced to engage with the shooter while dodging bullets. She grabbed Missy's hand to escape but gasped in horror when she abruptly fell to the ground. *Oh my God, she's been hit.* Cole bent down and was relieved to discover that Missy hadn't been shot.

"I'm going to help you up," Cole said, "but we have to move quickly. We're sitting ducks out here in the open. Can you make it, Missy?"

"Yes," Missy whimpered.

Daphne recognized Missy's rescuer and decided to desert her hostage. She knew it was only a matter of time before the police arrived, and she didn't want to get caught. She let off several more rounds and ran from the scene.

Blake fired at the shooter as Cole and Missy slowly made their way to the vehicle. "Quick, get in," he urged. "I'm going after her." The minute they were inside, Blake took off running, but there was no sign of Daphne. He was about to give up when an elderly man approached him.

"Excuse me, but are you a police officer?"

"Yes, I am," Blake confirmed as he holstered his gun.

"Good, because some crazy woman just put a gun to my head and stole my car."

David parked the SUV in the rear of the warehouse. He walked to the entrance and pounded on the aluminum. The door slid open, and David stared down the barrel of a shotgun. He instinctively went for his weapon, but he hesitated once he heard the gun cock.

"I will put a hole in you the size of a bowling ball if you draw your weapon," the man said ruthlessly.

David raised his hands in surrender. "Hey, I don't want any trouble. I'm only here to drop off precious cargo."

"I recognize the password, but I don't recognize you. Where's Sanchez?"

"I'm David. Sanchez didn't make it."

He lowered his gun. "Carlos is dead?"

"Yes. He was shot multiple times by the officer riding in the ambulance."

"Was Cavanaugh harmed? Where is he?"

"He's in the back of the truck, but he's unconscious. I'm not sure the drug worked."

"If Cavanaugh is still alive, then the antiserum definitely works," the man stated proudly.

"Did you design the drugs?"

"Yes. Cavanaugh was my human guinea pig."

"It's incredible that you were able to create a drug that temporarily stops the heart and an antidote that shocks it into beating again. Are there any plans to distribute it?"

"Perhaps, but I'm not willing to share any details with you. I deal strictly with Sanchez, and until Cavanaugh tells me differently, I have no information for you."

"Understandable. I'm sure Cavanaugh will give you permission to disclose everything to me once he's awake."

"Fine. First, I need to check his vitals. I have to ensure that there are no complications or side effects from the doses."

"No problem. Tucker and I will bring him inside."

"Oh, I didn't realize Tucker was with you. You go get the cargo, and I'll tell my boss he's here. We need to get him prepped for surgery."

"I thought the operation wasn't going to happen for a few days."

"Cavanaugh demanded that it be done now. He must have some upcoming projects that he wants to take care of as soon as possible."

"How long will it take him to recover?"

"I'm not certain because each patient is different, but we could be looking at up to eight weeks, maybe longer." He anxiously looked around. "I think we've talked long enough. Let's get Cavanaugh inside before someone happens along and sees your vehicle."

"Right. We both know how dangerous this situation is, and we can't afford any mistakes."

The man nodded and walked away, leaving the door ajar for David. He entered the lab and watched as the doctor placed surgical tools on the table next to the hospital gurney. He sat down in the chair next to the entrance and laid his rifle on the floor. "He's here," he announced.

"I heard. Honestly, I'm a bit surprised. I didn't think Cavanaugh's plan would succeed. That's why I didn't prep earlier for his arrival. He took an enormous risk, trusting you with that new drug and believing that his men could get him out safely." He picked up a scalpel and gently rubbed the unsharpened side back and forth across his hand. "Now it's my turn to bring the dead back to life. But if Cavanaugh doesn't keep up his end of our deal, I'll cut out the very heart you so cleverly resuscitated."

Missy detected something volatile between Cole and Blake the moment Blake got into the truck. The tension between them was tangible like the frost on a cool winter's morning. Missy's curiosity was piqued, which induced unsolicited flashes of the former partners' earlier encounter. She was suddenly bombarded with primitive emotions and energy so potent that Missy had to resist the urge to crawl into a fetal position. She waited out the roller-coaster sensations, but the horrors she experienced in those few seconds nearly made Missy scream out in pain—not for herself, but for the nine-year-old who had perished in the firestorm of her father's carnal brutality.

"I guess she got away," said Cole.

Blake placed his phone in his pocket. "Yes, she stole a car at gunpoint. The sheriff is sending someone over, but I told him that we couldn't wait. We'll stop in later to give our statements." He slowly drove from the scene, snaking his way through the nosy onlookers. "Should we head to the hospital?"

"I've asked Missy that same question a hundred times. Her wound needs to be redressed, but she's applying pressure to slow the bleeding. We can have someone look at her while Thomas is at the hospital."

"I don't need to see a doctor," Missy stressed. "I just need to lie down and recuperate."

"I feel terrible for asking," Cole said, "but do you feel up to telling us what happened, specifically the part about how you came to be on this highway?"

"Maybe she should wait until Thomas is present. That way we can get the complete story."

"I'd rather hear Missy's version first. Of course, you can always decide to wait for Thomas, and I, as your subordinate, wouldn't argue or go against your orders." There was an unmistakable edge to Cole's voice.

"I would pay good money to see you compliant, Tinks, but we both know that performance will never hit the big screen," Blake said drolly.

"Yes, it's a private show that you will definitely never experience again," she uttered quietly.

"Works for me," he murmured. "Mrs. Melendez, please tell us what happened and start from the beginning."

Their subtle innuendo caused the image of them intertwined in Cole's bed to reemerge in Missy's mind. A sudden wave of loneliness flooded her senses, and she was swept away in a tsunami of hurt. Uncomfortable with her feelings, Missy eagerly recapped what had transpired at the house in an effort to lessen her pain.

"Thomas went out into the backyard to smoke a cigarette. While he was gone, Officer Adams knocked on the door. He was there to relieve Thomas, who had a date back in Hartford."

"Wait … what in the hell was Thomas thinking, bringing someone else into this situation for a fucking date? He basically handed you to Adams on a silver platter."

"Calm down, Cole," Blake said coolly. "Thomas didn't know Adams was our killer."

"I know. It's just so frustrating that it was a cop who was under our noses the entire time," Cole said curtly. "I'm sorry, Missy. Continue."

"Adams told me not to bother Thomas and to let him finish his cigarette. He took off his jacket, and I noticed the tattoo on his right arm. It was the American flag and the US Army star logo. I remembered hearing you talk about that tattoo on the way to the house, and I became nervous. I knew it couldn't be a coincidence. I pretended like my side was aching, and he volunteered to get my medicine. The minute he proceeded up the stairs, I went to look for Thomas, but Adams caught me. After I confronted him, he proudly admitted that he was the one who murdered Robert and Kayla." *I can't tell them about the visions I had and how I really knew everything about him*, Missy decided.

"He admitted that he was there to kill me and put a gun to my head. Adams was on the verge of pulling the trigger when Thomas came out of nowhere and knocked him to the floor. They wrestled for control of the weapon, and I could tell that Thomas was wounded. I didn't think he stood a chance against Adams, so I got the hell out of there. I started running and didn't stop until my body crumpled. A woman pulled up beside me in her vehicle and asked if I needed help. Turns out she was the woman hired to be my personal nurse. She told me her name was Patsy, but I heard her say her name was Daphne on the phone. She thought I was unconscious, so she didn't realize that I'd heard her conversation."

"Shit. It must be Daphne Todd. It seems like all the people on your husband's list are involved in this case. I guess she has a new face too."

"I'm not sure, but Daphne told me that there was a bounty out on me. She was supposed to take me to the person so that he or she could kill me, but she said it wasn't Adams," Missy explained.

"Damn," Blake said. "It looks like this thing is much bigger than we originally thought, with a lot of players."

"Yeah," Cole replied. "Missy, did Thomas say whether he was the one to specifically ask Adams to come?"

"What are you thinking, Tinks?"

"I'm just wondering if there is another leak in the department—someone who knew where we were and sent Adams."

"Thomas said something about your captain being involved, so I thought he was the one who sent Officer Adams, but I could be wrong."

"Wait! Thomas said the captain knew about Adams coming here?" Cole was visibly puzzled.

"Yes. He said the captain knows everything."

"Blake?"

"I will call Captain Kessler as soon as we get to the house."

"And we need to put an APB out for Daphne Todd too. Did you get a good look at her? If so, we can sit you down with a sketch artist to help identify her."

"I ... well ... it was dark, and I was in a lot of pain." *I did see her in my dreams, though.*

Cole couldn't mask her disappointment. "Okay ... that would be a no."

"I'm sorry."

"No need to apologize, Mrs. Melendez. We understand," said Blake.

"If it helps, I stabbed her in the shoulder with a pair of scissors."

"You did?" Cole asked incredulously.

"Yes. What choice did I have? She was trying to kill me."

"That's probably what saved your life," Blake said as he pulled up to the house. He parked behind the sheriff's car in the driveway. "We'll only be here for a few minutes, Mrs. Melendez. Then we'll head to the hospital to have your wound checked. Just stay in the car and close your eyes for a bit. We won't be long."

Cole glanced at Missy in the rearview mirror. “Please take it easy until we return.” She turned toward Blake. “Let’s pray that these country yahoos know how to preserve a crime scene, or we’re in trouble.”

Although the desire to contest was strong, Cole didn’t argue when Blake proposed that he go in unaccompanied to talk with the sheriff. Cole knew that getting the evidence needed for the case might involve more than a detective’s badge. It made sense that someone with equal or greater authority should try to persuade the rugged man with the permanent scowl on his face to relinquish evidence to strangers.

After his conversation with Sheriff Connell, Blake joined Cole in the foyer. “It didn’t go as well as expected. Unfortunately, Connell doesn’t want us anywhere near his crime scene. He did throw us a few bones, though. He agreed to give us a copy of the forensics report once it’s completed. Also, he’s going to let Stevens assist the medical examiner with the autopsy, so we’ll have that information sooner rather than later.”

Cole shook her head in frustration. “I guess that’s better than nothing. Hopefully, Thomas was able to get everything we need to move forward with the investigation. Where is he, by the way?”

“He’s at the hospital. Connell forced him to go because he nearly passed out.”

“That doesn’t sound good. I hope he’s okay.”

“We’ll head over there in a few minutes. First, I need to call the captain.”

“I want details, Blake. Maybe Captain Kessler can tell us who’s been sabotaging my case.”

“I think it’s safe to assume that Adams was the one responsible for the files disappearing, Tinks.”

“I’m not so sure of that. Something doesn’t feel right. If you were still a detective, you’d have the same doubts. I guess you’re just out of practice,” she said derisively.

“Well, once this investigation is over, I’ll ask for a transfer to another precinct. That way, you won’t have to worry about me or my instincts going forward.” The finality in his voice was unmistakable.

“Blake, I didn’t mean—”

"Forget it, Cole. Why don't you go check on Mrs. Melendez?"

Cole refused to look at him. She didn't want Blake to see how much his dismissal upset her. "Fine. I'll wait for you in the car."

"I did see the woman's face," Missy whispered as Cole climbed into the car.

"I'm sorry. Did I wake you? I was trying to be quiet."

"No, I wasn't asleep. I'm too upset to sleep."

"I know you've had a tough night. I apologize for not being there to protect you."

"I don't know if there was anything you could have done differently, Dani. And before you get upset or misconstrue what I mean, I'm not questioning your capabilities as a cop. I just think Adams would have shown up no matter what the circumstances were. He was resolute about killing me."

"More than likely, you're right. Whose face did you see?"

"Daphne's."

"Wait … you said it was too dark."

Missy hesitated. "It was, but I saw her in a vision."

Cole shook her head. "Please don't start this again, Missy. I thought I made it clear how I feel about your psychic crap."

"You don't have to believe me, but I know exactly what she looks like—take it or leave it."

"I'll leave it," Cole said. "I'm not going on a wild-goose chase based on your hallucinations."

"One day my abilities will save your life. Then you'll have no other choice but to believe me."

"I seriously doubt that, Missy," she scoffed. "Maybe while we're at the hospital, you can have a doctor examine your head too. You're clearly delusional."

Missy sighed heavily. "I guess I should just shut up since you think I'm crazy."

"Good idea, because nothing you say or do will ever convince me to believe in that supernatural bullshit."

"Or in me, right?"

The hush in the vehicle spoke volumes. Missy tried to quell her feelings of disappointment, but she couldn't suppress the sorrow that rocked her body.

She closed her eyes and felt indebted to the shadows for shrouding her tears and masking her expression of her hurt.

Cole and Blake pulled aside the curtain and walked over to Thomas's bed just as the ER nurse was about to leave. "Are you family? Because if not, he can't have any visitors."

Blake flashed his badge. "I'm his boss. And she's his partner."

"Okay, but don't stay too long," she said and then disappeared into the chaos of the reception area.

"I was so much prettier in my hospital gown than you are, Thomas," Cole said jokingly. "How are you feeling?"

"I'm fine. I lost a lot of blood, so they want to keep me overnight for observation. Luckily, the bullet exited my shoulder, and they were able to patch me up quickly."

"Good to hear," said Blake. "It seems as though everyone involved in the Melendez investigation has been injured in some way or another. It's like this case is cursed."

"Not the case, just Melissa Melendez," said Cole. *With all of her physic mumbo jumbo.* "I mean, think about it. Each time one of us is hurt, she's there. You should be careful, Blake, or you might be next."

Blake shook his head. "I was joking, Cole. I don't believe in black magic. The bad guys have just been two steps ahead of us on this assignment."

"That's because they had inside help," Cole said defensively.

"No one is denying that fact. We just need to be more diligent moving forward, and that may mean putting additional men on Mrs. Melendez."

"Yeah, but we don't know who we can trust. What if there are more like Adams in the precinct?"

"Wait! Are you saying Adams wasn't the only leak, Cole?" Thomas's tone was incredulous. "What proof do you have?"

"She doesn't have any proof, Thomas. Just her gut," Blake declared cynically.

"Well, Cole's instincts have gotten me out of trouble a few times, so I'm going to take her side on this one, Lieutenant."

Cole glanced at Blake smugly. "Thanks, Thomas."

"There's something different about you, Thomas, but I can't pinpoint what it is," Blake said.

Cole stared at Thomas for several seconds, making him visibly uncomfortable. "I know what it is. Your eyes are a different color," she announced.

Thomas nodded. "Doris loved men with green eyes, so I got in the habit of wearing colored contacts. After she left, I kept wearing them just in case ..." His unspoken words hung in the air. "Anyway, I lost one in the fight with Adams, so I took the other one out."

"Wow! Your wife was really fucked up, Thomas. I'm glad she's no longer a part of your life. For the record, you look better with brown eyes."

Thomas smiled. "Thanks, Cole. So where is Mrs. Melendez? Your text said that she was with you."

"She's next door, being examined by one of the ER doctors. We'll explain what happened to Missy after you tell us about Adams," Cole stated.

"There really isn't much to tell. It all went down so fast. I was in the backyard smoking a cigarette when I heard a noise. I pulled out my gun and headed toward the fence. Before I could figure out where the sound had come from, I was shot."

"Did Adams shoot you at close range and then enter the farmhouse?" asked Cole.

"No. The bullet came from a distance. Based on the trajectory, I'd say it came from that run-down four-story mill across the street."

"Does that mean there were two attackers?" asked Blake.

"I doubt it, Lieutenant. He probably thought he'd killed me with plenty of time to get to the house and kill Missy before anyone alerted the authorities. I'm not sure how long I was out, so I don't know if he checked to see if I was dead."

"If he had, he would have put a round in you," Blake announced gravely. "This guy doesn't leave behind loose ends."

"Blake's right," said Cole. "What happened after that? When did you wake up?"

"It could have been minutes or hours. I remember opening my eyes and struggling to get to my feet. I made my way to the front of the house and sneaked in quietly. Adams had a gun to Missy's head, and he was about to pull the trigger. I leaped on him from behind, and we ended up on the floor.

We wrestled for his gun, and it went off. Adams was hit. I checked his pulse, and once I realized that he was no longer a threat, I called you."

"I'm glad both you and Missy are safe," said Cole.

Blake nodded. "Ditto that. The captain was shocked when I told him about Adams. He agreed to let the rookie babysit because he thought Adams could use the extra money. He was the sole caretaker for his mother, who has Alzheimer's."

"Ulrich filled me in on Adam's mom," said Thomas. "That's why I recommended him for the gig. I thought he could use the overtime."

"You chose Adams?" Cole asked.

"I suggested him and a few other guys. I guess Adams won out because of his financial situation. Between the medications and doctor visits, Ulrich said it cost Adams thousands of dollars a month to care for his mother. Definitely more than a rookie can afford. It's probably why he decided to become a hit man."

Blake gave him a sideways look. "Sounds like you feel sorry for him, Thomas. Contract killing is never the way to make a living, no matter what the circumstances are. We all have a sob story."

"I'm not sympathetic. I just understand the desperation. I had to take care of my dad after my mom died. It took me years to pay off those hospital bills. The health care system in this country sucks."

"I didn't know that, Thomas. What happened to your mom?" Blake asked.

"She had cancer. Her death wasn't a surprise since she'd been sick for a while. Didn't make it any easier, though."

"Sorry to hear about your mom, Thomas."

"Thanks, Cole. It was a long time ago."

"I hate to change the subject," said Cole, "but were you able to get anything from the crime scene? Adam's gun? Phone? Anything?"

"I had both, but Sheriff Connell confiscated them."

Cole shook her head. "Shit. We really have nothing then."

"Nope. You said Missy was in the hospital. Was she hurt?"

"She reopened her wound, but she should be fine. She got into a car with a woman who said she would help her. Turns out, it was Daphne Todd posing as the nurse Blake hired."

"You're kidding me," Thomas exclaimed in disbelief. "Where is Todd now?"

"She fled the scene."

"That means she's still out there. Do you think it's wise that Mrs. Melendez is alone, especially if Todd knows her way around a hospital?"

"You're right. I should go check on her," Blake said, politely excusing himself.

Once Blake was gone, Thomas looked to Cole. "I'm not even going to ask what's going on between you two."

"Is it that obvious?"

"Has been since day one, but I know how private you are. You play everything close to the vest. But eventually, those feelings will break out of the bottle, and you won't be able to put that genie back."

Cole didn't respond, and Thomas interpreted her silence to mean that he should change the subject. "How did Melissa get away from Todd?"

"She stabbed her."

Thomas couldn't hide his shock. "Are you serious?"

"Yes. Since Todd is injured, it shouldn't be that difficult to find her. We have every cop in the region looking for her."

"What do you know about the real nurse?" asked Thomas. "Is it possible that Adams talked Daphne into pretending to be Patsy?"

"Either that, or Patsy and Daphne are one and the same."

"Damn, I never even considered that. No one is who they seem to be in this case. Just one surprise after another."

Their conversation was interrupted when Blake rushed in the room. "I just got a call," he announced. "Sanchez is dead, and Cavanaugh has escaped from prison."

CHAPTER 12

THE RIDE TO HARTFORD WAS A SOMBER affair, with the three occupants of the vehicle in deep thought. Each person was concerned about how Cavanaugh's freedom and their new strategy to catch the person who had hired Adams would affect their lives. Cole understood that she'd placed Missy in a precarious position with her suggestion to use her as bait. However, after Blake's revelation in the hospital, Cole felt they had no other choice. She couldn't concentrate on both Cavanaugh and the Melendez investigation. Therefore, drastic measures needed to be taken to draw out Adams's boss and solve the murder.

Initially, Blake had rejected Cole's idea, but Cole helped him to realize that it would be the best way to catch the killer. The moment they agreed on all the specifics, Cole had visited Missy in the adjacent room and shared the information with her. The plan was for Blake to hold another press conference, in which he would reveal that Missy was still alive. He would divulge that Adams was the primary suspect in the Melendez murder case and that he had been killed by Thomas when he tried to execute Missy.

Once the press conference was over, Cole would drop Missy at home. That would give the person in charge the impression that the ordeal was over and that a police escort was no longer present. Cole would find someplace close by to hide, and when the killer showed up, she would arrest him. She hoped that Adams's boss would be the one to emerge to finish the job, but if not, Cole would force his flunky to disclose his name.

Missy had quietly listened to Cole's proposal and consented, but only if she could visit her father beforehand. She wanted to explain to Ted in person what had happened and why she couldn't tell him. Missy didn't think it would be fair for him to discover that his only child was still alive by watching the news. Cole had reluctantly agreed to Missy's request. She had neglected to inform her that Ted was currently in jail for attempted murder.

At 5:40 pm, Blake pulled into Missy's driveway and shut off the engine. He knew that the house had been cleared as a crime scene, but he wasn't sure if Missy would be comfortable there since it was her first time back since the murder.

His phone beeped, and he glanced at his text message. "Oh shit," he muttered.

Cole paused with her right hand on the door handle. "Is everything okay?"

"Yes. Just some bad news in the case Ulrich is working on." Blake grabbed her left hand. "Are you going to be okay?"

"I'll be fine."

"I'm not comfortable with you and Missy being here alone, so if you need anything, please call me. I know how difficult this is going to be for you."

"This is hard for you too, Blake. He nearly destroyed both of our lives," she said glumly.

"We won't let that happen again."

"You know he's going to come after me, right? He's been sending me letters and calling my house."

"What? Why in the hell didn't you tell me?"

"He couldn't get to me, so it didn't matter."

"I can't let you stay here. It's not safe. He'll come for you, and that will put you and Melissa in danger. You can both stay with me."

"Blake, something has been bothering me about the person who shot Thomas."

"Cole, I was talking to you. Are you even listening to me?"

"No … uh … I mean yes. I just think it's strange that Thomas only had a flesh wound since Adams was a professional."

"Honestly, the thought did cross my mind. Maybe Adams miscalculated. He has missed his targets before. You and Missy are perfect examples of that."

Cole was quiet for a few seconds. "Then that would mean Adams wasn't an expert."

Blake looked closely at her. "I know you. What are you thinking?"

"Adams couldn't have been our only shooter. You mentioned the possibility in the hospital, but Thomas had a feasible explanation, so I dismissed it."

"I guess it's possible that Daphne helped Adams since we know she was there. She may have seen Melissa run and followed her."

"That makes sense since Daphne came from the direction of the house yet claimed to be lost," Missy asserted quietly. "She did mention that I was someone else's bounty—that's why she didn't kill me."

"I thought you were asleep," Cole said coolly.

"I heard your entire conversation. I think it's a good idea to stay at Lieutenant Blake's house. I don't think anyone will look for us there."

"It's settled then," Blake declared. "We'll bunk at my house for tonight. I have three bedrooms and two baths. There's plenty of room."

Missy yawned. "I'm okay with it if Cole is."

"I guess it's all right. Missy is exhausted, and I'm clearly outvoted."

"Good. We'll stop and get something to eat, then head over to my place."

"No Chinese food," Cole said.

"No problem. I doubt I'll ever be able to eat Chinese food again."

Wearing a ski mask and gloves, Merck went through every square inch of the Melendez house but still came up empty. Time was running out, and he needed to find those files. Not only did his life depend on it, but his family's lives did too.

His phone rang, and he answered it. "Merck."

"You need to get out of there. Missy Melendez is probably on her way there."

"That's impossible. She's dead."

"She's not. Blake is going to hold a press conference in a few hours announcing that she's alive. He's also going to tell reporters that Adams was the one who murdered Melendez."

"What? Adams killed Melendez? That's crazy."

"It's also true. Just get out of there, and we'll talk later. I shouldn't be on this line. It's unsecured." The caller disconnected.

Merck headed to the kitchen and rushed out the back door. Once he was in his unmarked police car, he paused to contemplate the new development in his quest for vengeance. He still had to atone for his sins, and now he needed to add another person to the list. There wasn't any other way to rid himself of the guilt except to slowly destroy his enemies.

Blake walked into his office the next morning and was surprised to see Merck seated in one of his chairs. Blake wanted to take a few minutes to call and confront David about the text he'd sent earlier. But Merck's presence postponed his plans. He closed the door and sat behind his desk.

"Did we have an appointment scheduled this morning, Merck?"

"No. I heard about the early press conference and figured you'd be in here prepping. There's something I need to talk to you about. It's important."

"Okay, but make it quick. They're waiting for me."

"I left out some details during our previous conversation about Cavanaugh's operation in New York because I didn't want you to think that I was too emotionally involved to do my job."

"I don't think I like the sound of this," Blake said warily.

"Just hear me out." After a pregnant pause, Merck continued. "For the four years before I came here, I was deep undercover in narcotics, investigating Cavanaugh's organization. My partner, Kevin Palmer, and I focused on the local guys operating in the five boroughs, Mitchell Conrad and Trevor Moore. I was their inside man who warned them about upcoming busts. I made evidence disappear, which helped their guys dodge lengthy prison terms. I was the quintessential dirty cop. Things started getting too hot, though, and their demands started to distort my morals. The line between right and wrong blurred, and I was as two-faced as the villain in Batman. I no longer recognized myself, so I resigned. But something happened that pulled me back into the case."

"I understand firsthand how difficult it is to maintain your integrity while undercover," Blake said sympathetically.

"Yes, I know you do. That's why I decided to share the whole story."

"Okay. What pulled you back into the Cavanaugh case?"

"Moore killed my partner ... my best friend," Merck said, choking back tears.

"I'm sorry to hear that. I know that must have been hard."

"Thank you. It still hurts every day."

"So the reason you're here in Hartford is personal."

"Yes. I asked for a transfer here because I knew Moore was somewhere in Connecticut. I assumed he was still working for Cavanaugh in some capacity, but it's been challenging to track him down with a different face and new name."

"I sympathize with your pain, but I can't have a maverick cop on my team."

"Maverick? Moore repeatedly raped and stabbed Kevin's wife, Cathy, in front of him. Then the bastard shot his five-year-old twin daughters, Amber and Ashley. After he was done with them, he tortured Kevin, before killing him execution-style."

"That's horrible, Merck," Blake said contritely. "I'm so sorry. Were there any survivors?"

"Cathy made it, but I wouldn't exactly call her alive. She's emotionally dead. She lost her entire family that day. At their funerals, I made a promise to myself and to her that I would find Moore and get justice. I owe them that."

"Are you disclosing your intention to kill Moore once you locate him?"

"Absolutely." His tone was resolute.

"I can't condone murder, no matter how justifiable it seems, Merck. I can't be a part of your professional suicide mission."

"I know that, Blake. I'm only here because I heard from a reliable source that Moore is posing as a cop. With a different face, he could be anyone."

Blake was taken aback. "You think one of my cops is Moore?"

"Yes."

"Wait … do you think it was Adams?"

"He's about the same height and weight. Hair and eye color match too. So yeah, I think there's a strong possibility. That's why I came to you."

Blake nodded. "I guess the easiest way to know for sure is to have his prints checked."

There was a knock at the door, and Blake told the visitor to come in. The receptionist entered and laid several sticky notes in front of him. "I apologize for interrupting, but Lieutenant Jamison from Philadelphia is on the phone for you. He's already left several messages, which I put on your desk."

Blake glanced at his watch. "Tell Jamison I'll give him a call in about an hour, Lynette. I have a press conference, and I'm running late."

"Yes, sir," she replied before she exited.

Merck stood. "I think that's my cue to go. I need to pick up my wife from the hospital, and I don't want to be late."

"I heard about that. I'm glad she's better. How's your daughter?"

"She's holding her own. Hopefully, I'll be bringing her home soon also."

"I'll pray for your little girl," Blake said sincerely.

"Thank you. Please keep me posted on those prints."

"Will do. Let me know if you discover anything else about Moore. And Merck …" Blake paused. "We never had this conversation."

Missy skulked back and forth in the precinct's holding area. She was angry with Cole and exhibited it through her body language and tone. "I find it hard to believe that my father threatened you, Dani. And even if he did, locking him up seems a bit extreme."

"I didn't have a choice. It was for his own protection."

"How is putting my father in jail protecting him?"

"He had a gun. He could have harmed me or himself."

"He was obviously upset about my 'death' and wasn't thinking straight."

"I know that, which is why I let him off easy. I was thinking about how much this would affect you."

Her admission caused Missy to soften a bit. "I appreciate your thoughtfulness, but I still don't like it."

"I understand. He's in interrogation room B, straight ahead and to the left."

"Where will you be?"

"I'll be right outside the door, but I wanted to give you some time alone."

"Okay, but don't leave," Missy said anxiously. "It's not safe."

"Missy …"

"Please, you have to believe me," she implored. "You're in danger." *And according to my vision last night, it's going to happen soon.*

"I'm not going anywhere, but not because I believe you. I just have some things to check in the police database. With all the craziness of the last few days, I haven't been able to access that information on my laptop."

Missy hesitantly walked down the hall. Her instincts screamed for her to stay with Cole, but her trepidation was forgotten the minute she entered the room and saw her father. She rushed over to where he sat and hugged him.

Shock registered on Ted's face when he saw Missy. He stood and returned her embrace. "Oh my God, I must be dreaming," he whispered.

"Daddy, I missed you so much."

"You're alive. How?"

"I only have a few minutes to tell you everything that happened. Let's sit down."

"I don't care about the reason. I'm just happy to have my baby girl back."

Missy closed her eyes and permitted the smell of his cologne and timbre of his voice to soothe her. It transported her to a happier place, a time before her mother's death, before the disturbing visions, before the murders. And before Cole …

I should have found a better way to convince her of my abilities because if she leaves this station, I may never see her again.

Cole's phone rang. "Cole."

"Hey, it's Stevens. I'm down here in Bridgewater and wanted to give you some preliminary results."

"I can't believe you're there this early."

"I was out of the house by 4:00 a.m. and arrived here a little after 6:00. The medical examiner is an older gentleman who is going to retire in a few months. He's grateful to have someone else doing the majority of the work."

"What do you have?"

"Preliminary toxicology appears clean. I'm putting the time of death at around 8:00 p.m., give or take an hour. I extracted a bullet. It was from a Glock 9-millimeter."

"That was probably from Adams's service revolver. Thomas said they struggled on the floor for the gun."

"Wait … what did you just say?"

"Thomas and Adams fought for the weapon, and it went off."

"That's not possible, Cole. From the bullet trajectory, the person who shot Adams in the chest was standing over him. And Adams didn't have any powder residue on his hands, which he would have if the gun discharged while he was holding it."

Cole was silent for several seconds. "But Adams shot Thomas."

"I'm telling you that there is no evidence that Adams fired a gun."

"Okay," she said slowly. "Anything else?"

"Not yet. I'll have those files on your desk later today."

"You're awesome, Stevens. I'll talk to you soon."

Cole hung up and dialed a number. She listened to Blake's voice mail greeting and sighed. "Blake, it's Cole. I can't make the press conference. I have a lead I need to check out. Missy is in room B with her father, so please come and escort her outside. Text or call me once you get this message. I'll explain everything later."

Cole hopped out of the cab, paid the driver, and glanced around at her surroundings. The house was rustic and sat on two acres of forested land. The thought of being alone in such an isolated area made Cole edgy. She fixed her hand on her gun and headed toward the rear of the cabin. The wicker furniture on the small deck was dirty and covered with dead bugs. The potted plants sitting in the corners had perished from obvious neglect. A moderate breeze caused the brown foliage to scatter across the stairs, making a rustling sound that reminded Cole of her parents' ranch.

Cole searched for a spare key but came up empty-handed. She tested the windows and was surprised to discover that one was unlocked. She disregarded the ache in her back and scaled the short distance into the house. Once inside, she looked for anything that seemed unusual. Surprisingly, the house was much like hers, utilitarian and practical, except hers didn't have a smell. Cole expected to see decor hinting at a woman's presence, but other than the planters, it was a typical bachelor pad.

Wanting to pinpoint the source of the odor that seemed to pervade the walls, Cole explored the upstairs first. Unable to unearth anything damning, she headed for the cellar. Before she opened the door, she inhaled deeply to calm her nerves. Cole was afraid that she'd encounter some of her furry friends, and the thought tormented her. Still, she moved forward, and the aroma of death struck her instantly. Her heart beat wildly with fear and anticipation as she descended the steps. Cole wasn't certain whom or what she'd discover, but she suspected that the missing pieces to the Melendez case were buried in the basement.

Blake knocked on the door and peeked his head in the room. "I'm sorry, Mrs. Melendez, but it's time for the press conference. One of the officers will take your dad back to his holding cell, and I'll escort you outside."

"Where's Cole?" Missy asked, panic in her voice.

"She went to check on a lead."

"But I told her not to leave. She's in danger!" Missy squealed.

"What are you talking about? Did your dad say something to you?" Blake glanced at Ted.

"I can assure you, Lieutenant Blake, that I have nothing to do with this," Ted said rigidly.

"No, this isn't about him. It's about Dani. You have to find her."

"Cole can take care of herself, Mrs. Melendez. I'm positive that she's fine because she left me a voice mail."

"You don't really believe that, Blake. I can tell. Please check on her."

Something in Missy's demeanor instigated Blake's concern. "I'll call her."

"And you'll make sure she's okay, right?" Missy asked tensely.

"I promise. Now let's get this over with so we can catch a killer."

After the press conference, Blake headed to his office and dialed Cole's number. She didn't answer, so he left a quick message asking her to phone him as soon as possible. He then made another call. "Hi, Captain Jamison. It's Lieutenant Blake. I'm returning your phone call."

"Hi, Lieutenant. I won't keep you long, but I'm concerned about Thomas. He was supposed to attend a retirement party yesterday for his former partner and never showed up."

"That's because Thomas was working a big case, and unfortunately, he got himself shot. He's fine, though. He should be released from the hospital tomorrow."

"That's a relief. No one has spoken with him or Doris for months, and we were all getting worried. It's unusual for him not to keep in touch."

"Well, I can assure you that he's all right. I can't speak for Doris, though, since she left Thomas months ago."

"What?" Jamison's tone conveyed his shock.

"You didn't know? She left him right after he transferred here. I never even got the opportunity to meet her."

"No, I wasn't aware that Doris left him. She didn't talk to many people and doesn't have much family. From what I was told, she just has a half-sister in California, and they only talk about once or twice a year during the holidays."

"What about friends?"

"Mostly cop wives, but none close enough to notice her absence."

"She's not missing, Jamison. She ran off with her boss."

"Doris? I find that hard to believe, Blake," he said incredulously.

"I don't remember the guy's name, but he was the reason she came to Connecticut in the first place. Thomas followed her here."

"I knew Doris was transferred because that's what Thomas told me, but he never mentioned that she was having an affair."

"He was probably embarrassed."

"Makes sense. Can you tell him to give me a call once he recuperates? The guys miss him."

"Will do. But before you go, Jamison, can you please resend me Thomas's paperwork?"

"I mailed that file months ago, Blake."

"It must have gotten lost in the mail. I need another copy. Hopefully, it wasn't damaged in the fire."

"What fire?" Jamison asked curiously.

"The fire at your precinct."

"There has never been a fire here. Who told you that?"

An uneasiness settled in Blake's stomach. "Can you scan and email me the file right now?"

"Yes, I'll do it the moment we hang up. Do you want to tell me what's going on?"

"I'm not sure yet, Jamison. I'll update you once I receive the documents."

"Great, because you're making me nervous."

"I'm nervous too, but with any luck, your email will prove me wrong."

Cole wandered around the dark, damp space until she noticed a black trunk partially hidden underneath the stairs. She worked to drag it out into the open, but its weight, along with the throbbing in her back, impeded her progress. Eventually, she was able to move the trunk far enough to undo the clasp. She lifted the lid and immediately vomited her breakfast.

When Cole's stomach settled, she glanced at the bodies again. The corpses appeared to be a man and woman, judging by their clothing. Cole reached into her pocket and retrieved her phone. She tried to dial Blake's number but couldn't get a signal. She closed the trunk and headed upstairs to the kitchen. Once there, she held her cell in the air in search of a signal. After a few minutes, Cole located a spot with enough bars to call Blake. She phoned him again, but before he could pick up, someone struck Cole over the head.

Blake was fixated on his computer while he waited for Jamison's email. The moment it came through, he opened the PDF and judiciously perused all the information about Detective Charles Thomas. Despite Blake's suspicions, nothing appeared to be out of the ordinary, except for a few write-ups that Thomas had never disclosed to him. Blake was about to close the file when he noticed something on the final page. He enlarged Thomas's graduation photo from the police academy and gasped aloud. The disparities in appearance were minuscule. However, the eye color told Blake that the Thomas he'd worked with for the past nine months was an imposter.

Blake picked up his desk phone and made a call, but it went straight to voice mail. "Tinks, I don't know where you are, but you need to get in contact with me immediately. It's urgent." The knot in his chest tightened as he dialed 411, requested the number to Bridgewater Hospital, and quickly made the call.

"This is Lieutenant Joshua Blake from the Hartford Police Department. Can I have Charles Thomas's room, please?"

"Hold on." There was a long pause. "Mr. Thomas was discharged this morning."

"Are you sure?" He listened to the receptionist explain that he had been released several hours ago. "Thank you."

An inescapable fear clamped down on Blake like manacles, and he shivered with dread. He suddenly remembered Missy's warning and hopped up from his desk. He raced out the door and silently prayed that Missy could help him find Cole before it was too late.

Despite the excruciating pain in her head, Cole opened her eyes. She was disoriented but concluded that her view of the ceiling meant she was lying on a bed. She slowly sat up and realized that her arms were bound together by duct tape as well as her legs. Cool air tickled her skin, and she gasped when she realized he'd stripped her down to her underwear.

"I see you're finally awake. I was afraid that I hit you too hard." Thomas sat on the edge of the bed. "I'm curious as to how you found this place since it's not listed in my files."

"I went to your house first, but when you weren't there, I remembered that you owned a cabin."

"I never once mentioned this property to you," he stated irritably.

"No, you didn't. I heard you talking on the phone a few months ago about selling this place. You said it was on almost two acres of land in Middlesex County so I looked up all the properties for sale here. There was only one, which made my decision to come here very easy."

"I guess I should have waited and taken that phone call in private."

"Probably."

"So where's your SUV, Cole? When I pulled up, I didn't see it. Did you hide it someplace?"

"I took a cab. I didn't want to draw attention to myself by showing up in an unmarked police car. Plus, I'm not supposed to be driving."

He shook his head. "Since when did you start following doctor's orders?"

Cole turned her head to face him. "Today, apparently. So who are the dead people in the basement, Thomas?"

"You really know how to go straight for the jugular, don't you, Cole?" He paused. "They're just some people who got in the way."

"So I guess this is the part in the program where you boast about your crimes, and I acknowledge how smart you were to fool us all."

Thomas chuckled. "I do like you, Cole. You're a beautiful, strong woman. At first, I was disappointed that the arsenic Adams put in your pills didn't kill you. But now I'm glad. You and I are going to have a lot of fun together before you die." Thomas extended his hand to stroke Cole's cheek, and she twisted her head to avoid his caress.

Memories of her father's touch flashed through Cole's mind. "I wish you wouldn't do that."

He gripped Cole's face and forced her to look at him. "I plan on doing much worse. Don't worry, I haven't gotten any complaints yet."

"That's because none of the women were alive to complain," she asserted caustically.

"You have me confused with Adams. That sick bastard liked his woman deceased. I prefer them hot-blooded."

"And tied up," she said.

"Good point," he said blithely.

"Are you going to tell me who the people are in the trunk or not? I'm getting bored."

"I promise you that you won't be bored for long. Because you asked nicely, I'm going to tell you." He rubbed her arm. "Sort of like an appetizer before the main course."

Cole shuddered with revulsion. "Just spill it and stop with this seduction game. It's as disgusting as you are."

"Your mouth is saying no, but your body is definitely saying yes."

"Don't flatter yourself," she spat distastefully. "I'm just cold."

"I'm going to have fun breaking you. It'll be like taming a wild horse."

"I'm not a fucking animal. And rape is for cowards."

"Well, I'll be a happy coward." He grabbed the blanket from the end of the bed and covered Cole with it. "Now stop complaining so I can have my five minutes of fame," he snickered. "This is the moment in the movie where everyone holds their breath … the revelation of truth." He took a dramatic pause. "The real Thomas is the one in the trunk—him and his lovely wife,

Doris. I needed a cover, and poor, pathetic Thomas was the ideal choice. He and I had similar features; he was perfect. I searched for someone whose existence wouldn't be missed, and I was right. I've been living Thomas's life for almost a year now, and not one person has come to check on him—not even his former partner. He was nothing but a lonely, bitter cop, which made it easy to become him."

"But how did you do it?" Cole asked quietly.

"I followed Thomas for months and learned enough about him to put my plan in motion. I discovered through observation that Doris was his Achilles' heel, and I used that information to my advantage. Like most cops, the job came first for Thomas, which meant Doris was desperate for attention. I hired a personal escort, and his job was to make the middle-aged woman fall in love with him. It was an easy task because she was neglected at home. My guy wined and dined her right under the real Thomas's nose. A few orders of flowers, some well-rehearsed sentiments about her beauty, and she was a goner. Doris liked to read romance novels, so she longed to be carried off into the sunset by a handsome prince. Well, I gave her exactly what she wanted. I carefully chose all the players in my little charade, and it worked out perfectly. After a few weeks of passion, Doris's lover pleaded with her to move to Connecticut to be with him, and naturally, she said yes. He even told her that he had a job for her at the bank where he worked as the VP of Operations. Of course, it was all a lie, so when she arrived in Hartford, he just disappeared. I knew she'd call Thomas, and he'd come running. The poor sap was so lovesick that he followed his cheating wife here even though she'd left him for another man."

"Such an elaborate plan. Why Connecticut?"

"Isn't it obvious? Cavanaugh is here."

"I should have known that you were somehow connected to Cavanaugh. But I don't understand how you learned to be a cop. Is there a school somewhere for felons that you and your buddies attended?"

"Very funny, Cole. For your information, I went to the police academy right after high school. Unfortunately, I couldn't finish training because of a back injury."

"If that's true, then you obviously used to believe in justice. Why the change?"

"Life. I had to compromise my beliefs, grow up, and leave that starry-eyed teenager behind. The world was cruel, and I had to learn to be cruel with it."

"I don't believe that. I've known you for almost a year, and I honestly think that deep down you're a good person."

"Please stop with the psychological bullshit. It won't work. All I care about is maintaining Thomas's persona. And I will destroy anyone who gets in my way."

"Is that why you hired Adams to kill Melendez? Because he was about to blow your cover?"

"Yes. No one in Hartford knew that I wasn't Thomas except the surgeons at HPS. I signed a contract that guaranteed full anonymity, but that asshole Melendez broke the agreement. He tried to blackmail me by threatening to expose my true identity. When I refused, he revealed that he had a file on me with all the details of my identity, including before and after surgery photos. With that type of information and the files Melendez kept on other people, the police could not only track me down, but could also find my associates. I couldn't let those documents become public knowledge, so I broke into Melendez's office and went through his records. I wasn't able to locate any documents on his 'special' clients. So it was decided to eliminate the problem."

"Who made that decision? You, Daphne Todd, and Adams? Who else is involved? How do Roman and McCain fit into this?"

"I guess it won't hurt to share specifics since you'll be dead soon," Thomas sneered. "Roman wasn't involved in the blackmail. In fact, he was pissed when he discovered what Melendez was doing behind his back. All he cared about was protecting the HPS name and exterminating the man who was stealing his clients. That's why Roman gave us the intimate details about Melendez's life. We used that info to get rid of him."

"What about McCain?"

"He was collateral damage. His shooting was just a warning to keep his mouth shut. McCain was helping Melendez with the bribes, but only because he was being blackmailed by Melendez too. I don't know what Melendez had on him, though."

"So who has the extortion files? Because I doubt it's Missy."

"I agree. And if she does have them, she doesn't know it." He squeezed

Cole's knee. "Now are there any other questions before I get this party started?"

"Why did you kill Adams if you two were working together?"

"He wanted the $150,000 bounty on Missy's head so he decided to kill me to get it. He was sloppy because he never checked my body after he shot me. He just assumed I was dead. What he didn't know was that I had on my Kevlar. And, of course, after he double-crossed me, I couldn't allow him to live."

"But you were actually shot. I saw the bandages on your shoulder when we were at the hospital. How did that happen if you were wearing a bullet-proof vest?"

"Before I called you, I went outside and shot myself using Adams gun. I had to make sure my story was plausible."

"You really are a sick son-of-a-bitch." Cole paused as a thought suddenly came to her. "Wait. If you didn't put the bounty out on Missy, then who did?"

"Beats me. There are a lot of people that wanted Missy dead because of her husband so it could have been anyone that he blackmailed."

"And what about your link to Cavanaugh?"

"For years, I was one of his top guys. I even had plans to commandeer half of his operations. Sadly, that idea got shot to hell when they got suspicious of you. Cavanaugh had Sanchez start watching his employees because they assumed someone was helping you. That's when Sanchez uncovered my plot for a hostile takeover of Cavanaugh's largest territories. A hit was put out on me, and I was forced to disappear. I came to Connecticut for a new face and identity—right under Cavanaugh's nose. I didn't realize that you two had such an interesting past, though. I'd heard that he'd fallen for a cop, but I didn't have access to the confidential details until I became Thomas."

"If you worked for Cavanaugh, then I must know who you are or at least have heard of you. I know you've been dying to tell me. What's your real name?"

Thomas violently yanked the blanket from her body. "No more talking," he bellowed. "I've waited a long time for this moment. I get to have what Blake was never man enough to take." His eyes brimmed with lust as he stood. He quickly disrobed and then grabbed his knife from the nightstand. He climbed onto the bed and laid on top of Cole. He kissed her hard and bit her lower lip. Cole yelped in pain, which made him smile.

"I'm Trevor Moore. Pleased to meet you, Detective Cole," he whispered in her ear.

Blake breathed a sigh of relief when he caught sight of Ulrich and Missy heading to the interrogation rooms. He sprinted the short distance to catch up with them and tapped Ulrich's shoulder. "I've been looking all over for you, Detective," he announced. "Where have you been?"

"I took Mrs. Melendez across the street to get a new burner phone. Then we went to the cafeteria to grab something to eat. Why? Is something wrong?"

"Nothing. I just need to talk to Mrs. Melendez alone. Can you wait out here while we use one of the rooms?"

Missy couldn't mask her fear. "Is Dani okay?"

"Yes. Why don't you go in and have a seat, Melissa? I'll join you in a few minutes."

Blake closed the door behind her. "Ulrich, I need you to see if you can locate another address for Detective Thomas other than the one we have on file. I went there, but no one was home. Also, see if you can trace Cole's phone. I want to know where her last cell tower ping was. Hopefully, that will help me pinpoint a location."

"I'll get right on it. What's going on? Is Cole in danger? And why are you searching for Cole at Thomas's house? Isn't he still in Bridgewater?"

"I don't have time to answer your questions, Ulrich. I need that information ASAP. Cole's life may depend on it."

"Okay, I'll be back soon."

Blake waited until Ulrich left and then entered the room. "Melissa, do you have any idea where Cole is?"

"Oh my God. He does have her," she whispered miserably.

Blake moved within inches of her. "Who has her? Where? I need to find her."

"I don't know who he is. I can never see his face. But they're in an isolated cabin, and Dani is half-naked and terrified," Missy said, choking back her tears.

"How do you know this?" he asked anxiously. "I don't understand."

"You won't believe me," she muttered.

"I wouldn't be here if I didn't think you were telling the truth about Cole being in trouble."

"I ... uh ..." She hesitated. "I see things. I've had several visions of Dani being tied up and tortured by someone wielding a knife. At first, I thought it was Adams because the person quoted Bible verses. But last night I had a dream, and it was different. The man's voice was familiar, and it wasn't Adams's. It seemed real, like I was right there with Dani. I could see what she saw—the house, the room, the bed."

"What else did you see? I need something that will lead me to her."

"I'm trying to remember, but it's been harder for me to focus lately."

"Give me anything, Missy, no matter how small you think it is."

"Wait ... I kept seeing a yellow cab and the number 1172. Maybe she took a taxi to the house."

Blake seized Missy by the shoulders and hugged her. "Thank you so much! You may have just saved Cole's life. I can have the cab company tell me where they dropped her off." He released her and headed to the door. "If you don't mind being in this room a little longer, I'll get Ulrich. I should be back soon."

"With Dani, right?"

Blake smiled. "Yes. With Dani."

"I shouldn't be here, David. The police are looking for me," Daphne murmured.

"I don't think anyone has seen you. Just keep a low profile until they show up."

"What if the police come before they do?"

"I doubt that'll happen," he said irritably. "They haven't arrested you, so it's possible that my sister hasn't pieced it all together yet. Maybe they think you were just pretending to be Patsy. If that's the case, then your cover remains secure, Daphne. Besides, I'm sure Trevor has taken care of everything for you."

"Please stop calling me that. In public, I'm Patsy." She nervously surveyed the area. "By the way, jealousy doesn't become you."

"I'm not jealous," he grunted.

The tension between them was tangible. "I don't have time to argue with you, David. I need to get as far away from Hartford as possible."

He nodded. "I know. How's your shoulder?"

"Hurts like hell. I can't believe that bitch stabbed me."

"I can't believe you let her overpower you. Clearly, you're rusty."

"I am, but I don't need you or anyone else to point that out." She dropped her tone to a whisper. "How's Cavanaugh?"

"He's fine, but things would have gone a lot smoother if you'd been there as planned. Maybe Sanchez would still be alive."

"I had something important to take care of, David."

"I get that, but it'll make Cavanaugh question your loyalty, especially since you almost got caught."

"He has no right to question anything. I don't owe him my life."

"If it weren't for Cavanaugh, you wouldn't have a life."

"I know," she said impatiently. "You don't need to remind me."

"Obviously, I do."

"What about the files? Any luck?"

"Not yet. Keep working on McCain, though. Hopefully, he'll give us an idea of where to find them."

"If not, are you going to take care of him?"

"Yes."

"What about Roman?"

"Bill is fine for now. He and Cavanaugh are friends."

"There is no such thing as friends in this business. I'll work on McCain, but I think he's harmless. Now please leave before someone sees me talking to you."

"No problem. I need to check on Cavanaugh anyway. The surgery was a success, but he'll be out of commission for a while."

"I'll drop off the medication this evening as scheduled. You know how to get in contact with me if necessary."

He stroked her hand. "Yes, I do."

She hastily pulled away. "I told you it is over, David. Go be with your wife and kids."

"You don't mean that. I know you still want me, Daphne. Forget Trevor."

"He'll kill you if he finds out," she warned.

"No, he won't." David smiled at her.

"Just leave. I need to handle a few things so I can disappear."

"We need to take care of the problem we discussed over the phone first. After that, I'll go."

"Okay, let's get it done quickly."

Thomas flipped the blade to the unsharpened end and leisurely dragged it down Cole's stomach to her belly button. Cole thought she heard screaming and realized that it was the nine-year-old child inside of her, pleading with her adult self to keep her safe. Again trapped by a man's cruelty, Cole saw no way out of her nightmarish situation. *I'm sorry, but I can't save you this time either.*

"This can be satisfying for both of us if you relax and let it happen, Cole. Think of it as one last pleasure before you die," Thomas asserted.

She spat in his face. "Being forced to have sex is not pleasing under any circumstances, Thomas."

He slapped her. "You want it rough. Fine. Have it your way."

Tears glistened in Cole's eyes. "I'd rather die than give you the satisfaction of my acquiescence."

Thomas turned the knife over and inched it along her body, leaving a small trail of blood in its wake. He strategically positioned the long, sharp blade underneath the fabric between her breasts and cut her bra. He then brutally ravaged each tiny globe with his mouth and then his teeth.

Tears of pain and humiliation trickled down Cole's cheeks. She closed her eyes and tried to remember the charges in Moore's file—rape, torture, sodomy, murder, robbery, assault. *A knife is his weapon of choice*, she remembered. *He carves his initials on his victims' bodies while they are still alive, then discards their remains somewhere out in the open.* Cole silently pleaded for mercy as her body shook in fear. She grasped what Moore was capable of and realized that she was about to suffer a fate worse than death.

Thomas's breathing became erratic as he situated himself between Cole's legs. He sliced her panties and moved the knife down her bare thigh. He then repeated the motion on her other leg. "I can tell from the terror in your eyes that you know just how talented I am with a knife. I can smell your fear. It reeks from your pores," he said ardently. "I want to hear you say it. I want you to plead for your life." He branded her bare skin with cuts, stinging and raw.

"No! I'm not going to engage in your sick fantasies," Cole cried.

He placed the tip of the blade in her most intimate area and pressed. "If you don't, I'll use this in ways that would make an S and M porn star blush."

"I'd rather die."

"Well, it won't be as much fun for me, but you'll get your wish … soon." Thomas laid the knife aside and positioned himself to penetrate her.

Cole squeezed her eyes shut in preparation for his brutal intrusion.

"Freeze, Thomas!" someone yelled.

Cole opened her eyes to see Blake in the doorway with his gun trained on Thomas.

Thomas swiftly picked up his knife and lodged it against Cole's neck. "Drop your weapon, Blake, or I'll slit her throat."

Blake edged closer. "By the time you do that, I'll already have a bullet in your head. Now drop it."

Thomas gradually lowered the knife and set it on the bed. "This isn't over, Blake."

"Move away from her slowly," Blake advised.

Thomas shifted suddenly and extracted a gun from underneath the pillow. He fired before Blake could get off a clear shot and hit the lieutenant in the torso.

Blake clutched his chest and fell face-first to the floor.

"No!" Cole screamed.

Thomas waited to see if Blake would stir. When he didn't, he breathed in Cole's ear, "Now where were we?"

"Please … don't let him die, Thomas. I'll do whatever you want," Cole begged.

"The name is Trevor, and you're too late, sweetheart. The time for bargaining is over. I'm going to get what I want. After that, you and Blake can die together in this house like the real Thomas and his wife. Two star-crossed, dead couples. How Shakespearean."

Panting heavily, he kissed her and then with his tongue eagerly followed the crimson path of blood he had left on her body.

"You're crazy," she cried in anguish.

Thomas rose to a sitting position. Just when he was about to force himself into her, a hail of bullets streamed through the window, striking him in the back and head. Blood splattered on the sheets and walls as he crumpled on top of Cole.

"Help! Please help!" Cole shrieked.

The killer paused outside and dialed 911. He lingered out of sight in the woods until the police and paramedics arrived and then faded deeper into the trees.

George entered his office and was shocked when the chair spun around. He immediately recognized the occupant and dropped his coffee. The hot liquid splashed on his expensive suit and Prada shoes. "Damn it!" he shouted.

"Didn't mean to frighten you."

"How—" George stopped short as the man raised a gun and aimed it at his chest.

"I'm afraid I need your help, George. You need to come with me."

Cole's heart beat erratically as she stood in a robe provided by the paramedics, watching the swarm of people in the room. She quivered with loathing as images of Thomas molesting her played over and over in her head. Hysteria threatened to overwhelm her, but she couldn't break down, not at the moment and certainly not in front of her male colleagues.

She watched the EMTs lift Blake and place him on a stretcher. He wasn't breathing when they arrived, but the duo had been able to resuscitate him. They had worked on Thomas also, but he hadn't survived. She glanced over at his dead body lying on the floor. The temptation to find her gun and shoot him herself was potent, but she resisted.

"You sure you didn't see who shot Thomas?" Captain Kessler asked keenly.

"I didn't, Captain. The person shot him from outside, and I wasn't in a position to see anything. But we agree that no one else should know that the shooter was outside, right?"

"Yes. I put a gag order on everyone here, Cole. You should ride in the ambulance with Blake and get those cuts checked out," he suggested. "One of the guys found your clothes in the other bedroom."

She walked over to the paramedics and stared at Blake's lifeless body. "Is he going to be all right?"

"I don't know. We're trying to control the bleeding, but I'm not going to lie—it looks bad. We need to get him out of here before he goes into shock."

Her vision blurred with tears. "I'm riding with you."

Marie glimpsed at her watch as Merck rushed through the hospital's double doors. "You're late," she said.

Merck kissed her. "Sorry, babe, but I had some police business to take care of first."

"I figured that's what was keeping you, but I refuse to let anything spoil my good mood. We're taking our little girl home today. I still can't believe it. I thought it would be weeks before she was strong enough."

"That's because she's resilient like her mother." He clasped her hand. "Now let's go get our tiny Miracle."

Merck and Marie walked to the maternity ward and stopped at the nurses' station. The woman seated there seemed vaguely familiar to Merck, but he couldn't place her. She was talking on her phone, so he tried to eavesdrop on her conversation, but she turned away, and Merck heard only fragments.

Daphne spoke in a hushed whisper. "They're finally here. I'm going to leave the minute I'm done with them. The cop looked at me suspiciously, so I think he may recognize me." She listened for a few seconds and then disconnected the call.

The nurse set down her phone and looked up at Merck. "Can I help you?" she asked courteously.

"Is Doctor Lehman around? We're here to pick up our baby."

"Doctor Lehman is in the delivery room performing an emergency C-section. But I can help you if he already signed the release papers. What's your baby's name?"

"We're Jay and Marie Merck." He studied her face to gauge her reaction to their names. "Our baby's name is Miracle."

The nurse appeared impassive as she typed the name into the computer.

"Looks like the doctor signed the paperwork. I just need to see some identification." She glanced at their driver's licenses and then waved over a nurse. "Lorie, can you take Mr. and Mrs. Merck to the nursery?" She handed them back their IDs and passed a clipboard to Lorie. "Please make sure they sign off on the paperwork."

"Will do," Lorie said, taking the clipboard. "Just follow me."

Daphne observed them walk away and took that minute to make her escape.

Merck and Marie watched Lorie through the glass as she entered the nursery.

"Do you see her, Jay?" Marie asked. "Because I don't."

Merck gazed around the room but didn't see Miracle among the other babies. "No, I don't, but I'm sure there's a reasonable explanation. Maybe they still have her in the NICU."

Marie took a deep breath. "That makes sense. It's just a miscommunication."

They watched anxiously as the nurse ambled back toward them with an envelope. Merck knew something was wrong from her body language. She handed the envelope to him and said, "I'm sorry. I need to go report this."

Merck waited for her to leave and then opened the letter. The words that leaped off the page brought devastation and pain unlike anything he'd ever felt before. His body shook, and he got down on his knees to keep from falling.

Marie stooped down in front of him. "Jay, what is it? Where's Miracle?" she shrieked.

He knew he couldn't hide the truth and simply handed her the note.

We have your daughter. If you don't bring us what we want in 48 hours, you'll never see her again.

Marie's tears soaked the paper, causing the ink to run. She gazed at her husband in despair. Merck swiftly pulled her to him and held her firmly as she sobbed uncontrollably.

CHAPTER 13

MISSY MELENDEZ'S EYES WERE CLOSED when Detective Ulrich entered the interrogation room with her father. He was hesitant to disturb her since she seemed to be in the throes of a nightmare. Ulrich moved closer and gently touched her arm. Startled, Missy leaped out of her chair.

"I'm sorry, Mrs. Melendez. I didn't mean to scare you, but you and your father are free to go," Ulrich announced.

"What?" Missy asked, visibly confused. "Is Dani … I mean Detective Cole all right?"

"Cole is fine. The investigation is over."

Missy shook her head. "But I don't understand. What happened?"

"You're no longer in any danger, Mrs. Melendez. There were never any formal charges filed against you, Mr. Delaney. You both can go home."

Father and daughter exchanged glances. "I know Robert's killer is dead, but you're saying they caught the person who put the hit out on my daughter too?" Ted's tone communicated cautious relief.

"I'm not authorized to give you details, but yes."

"Where's Cole?" asked Missy. "Why didn't she come and tell us this herself?"

"Cole is at the hospital."

"I thought you said she was okay!" Missy exclaimed.

"She is. She just has a few cuts and bruises. It's Lieutenant Blake who's hurt."

"What happened? Is he …"

"No. He's in surgery, but they're not sure he'll make it."

"Cole must be worried sick, and she's all alone. I should go to her."

"Missy, you've been through a lot," said her father. "I think it's best you go home now that this ordeal is over."

"I will, but I'm going to check on Detective Cole first."

"How many times do I have to tell you that she's not your friend, sweetheart? You were nothing more than a suspect to her."

"You're wrong, Daddy. Dani will appreciate having me there." *Especially after the vision I just had and if my suspicions about Thomas are true.*

"Although I disagree, I'm not going to argue. But I am coming with you."

"Okay, let's get out of here. I've had enough of police stations to last me a lifetime."

Ulrich waited until they departed to make a call. "She's on her way to the hospital. Don't worry, I put the tracking device in her phone."

The sound of a baby crying echoed throughout the house. David took the stairs two at a time and burst into the room. He wrapped his hands around Susan's neck and squeezed. "I told you to keep that baby quiet," he said through clenched teeth.

"I'm trying," Susan said, choking. "She's so tiny and won't drink from the bottle. She's probably used to breast milk."

"Well, you need to figure out a way to make it work without the milk. I can't have her constantly crying and risk someone finding out that she's here."

Susan gasped for air. "I can't do anything with you strangling me, David."

He gradually released her. "Where are the boys?"

Susan reached into the crib and picked up the infant. "They're with your mother."

"What?" His tone was livid. "Did she see the baby?"

"No. Miracle was sleeping. I thought it would be easier if they weren't here."

"You should have asked me before calling her, Susan. I warned you not to make decisions without me."

"When are you giving the baby back?"

"Who said I was?"

"You did when you brought her here. You said it was temporary."

"Plans change. If her father does what's expected, I'll return her. If not, she'll be sold on the black market."

Susan gazed affectionately at the baby in her arms. "That's horrible. I can only imagine what kind of pain the parents are in right now. Who are they?"

"I don't care about their pain. Look, just because we had that little therapy session a few days ago doesn't mean we're partners. You already know too much and almost got me killed because of it. You're my wife and nothing more."

"How did I almost get you killed?" she asked.

"Sanchez didn't feel he could trust you and was going to kill us both. After I paid Tucker two grand, he told me everything. Fortunately for us, I was able to finish off Sanchez before he made it official."

Susan rocked Miracle in her arms, and the baby slowly closed her eyes. "I didn't ask to be involved in any of this."

"Well, Sanchez is dead, so it no longer matters."

"I guess it doesn't." She laid the baby in the crib. "I need to go to the drugstore. Maybe the pharmacist can suggest a formula that she'll actually drink."

"You can't take her out of the house, and you can't discuss her with anyone. Google formulas. I'm sure something will come up."

"Fine, David. But I still need to get it. You can watch her while I'm gone."

"I'll give you an hour. If you're not back by then, I will come looking for you," he said ominously.

"It won't take long, I promise. Hopefully, I can do something to make Miracle's life a little better."

The doctor had informed Cole that Blake was in critical condition, with a single gunshot wound to the chest. The bullet had pierced his lung and lodged near his heart. That news, along with the announcement that he had only a 40 percent chance of survival, had caused Cole to disintegrate. She couldn't fathom living her life without her best friend—her lover.

Cole had never been a religious person, but she kneeled at the altar in the hospital's chapel and prayed. For the first time in her life, Cole didn't think. She just allowed herself to feel as the tears flowed unabashedly down her cheeks.

A soft whisper came from behind her. "Dani?"

Cole turned her head, and when she spotted Missy, something inside her snapped. She stood and wordlessly strode toward the other woman. They stared at each other for several seconds until the anguish in Cole's eyes beckoned to Missy. She gently grabbed Cole and embraced her tightly. Cole dissolved in Missy's arms as grief overpowered her.

Missy stroked her head and murmured, "He's going to make it, Cole. Blake is strong."

Embarrassed, Cole took several deep breaths and then gradually pulled away. "Sorry. I didn't mean to fall apart like that."

"Don't apologize. Showing emotion is perfectly normal under these circumstances."

Cole wiped her tears with the back of her hand and sat on the bench. "I'm surprised to see you here. I thought you'd be at home, enjoying your newfound freedom."

Missy took a seat beside her. "I heard about Blake, and I thought you could use a friend."

"Thank you."

"How did Blake get hurt?"

"It's a long story. But Blake tried to save me, and Thomas shot him."

"That's awful, Dani. Was it an accident?"

"No. Thomas was one of the criminals who acquired a new face from your husband. His real name was Trevor Moore."

"What? So Thomas is Trevor Moore?" She shook her head in disbelief. "I remember seeing Moore's name on Robert's list, but not his alias. Maybe if I had, none of this would have happened, and Blake wouldn't be fighting for his life."

"Don't feel guilty, Missy. Thomas … Trevor is dead. You couldn't have done anything to change what happened."

"Ulrich said you were injured. Are you okay?"

"I'm fine. Apparently, Trevor had a thing with knives and bondage."

"I'm so sorry, Dani. I wish …" She vacillated. *I wish I could have done more to protect you.* "I'm just relieved this ordeal is over."

"Me too. Don't worry, I really am fine. You don't need to stay."

"Who's the mind reader now?" Missy said with a laugh.

"I guess you're rubbing off on me," Cole declared jokingly.

Missy extended her hand and grasped Cole's. "I want to be here for you, the way you've been there for me."

Cole glanced at their intertwined fingers and then at Missy. "I don't know."

"Allow yourself to lean on someone else for a change. I promise that I won't let you fall. Trust me," Missy said.

Cole's vulnerability fleetingly gleamed in her eyes. "All right. I guess it's about time that I had a friend."

Missy grinned and rubbed her thumb across Cole's hand in a comforting gesture. "I'd say you're long past due. You don't have to be alone, not anymore."

The atmosphere unexpectedly shifted as Cole peered into Missy's eyes. She recognized the sincerity in them but also detected something else, something unknown. Cole reflexively moved closer to the other woman, suddenly craving her warmth.

Missy swallowed deeply, unsure of what to do with the foreign feelings she was experiencing. Without thinking, she leaned in until she was inches away from Cole. She could feel the other woman's breath on her skin. Missy instinctively closed her eyes, and their lips lightly touched.

"Detective Cole?"

Cole quickly rose and turned to see the doctor. "Is Blake okay?" she inquired anxiously as she walked to the chapel door.

"He made it through surgery, and he's stable for now."

Cole exhaled. "Thank God. Is he going to recover?"

"Only time will tell. But he has a long road ahead of him."

"When can I see him?"

"You can go in for a few minutes, but I'd advise you to go home and get some rest. You've been through quite a lot today."

Missy stood and waited for the doctor to leave before she spoke. "Dani, about what almost happened ..."

Cole interjected. "I think I'm going to take the doctor's advice and head home after I check on Blake. My back is sore, and I need my medication."

"So we're not going to talk about this?" Missy asked softly.

Cole avoided looking at her. "There's nothing to discuss. We're both just emotionally stressed."

Missy was disheartened by her indifference. "You're blaming that kiss on stress?"

"What else could it be?"

"From the moment we met, there has been a connection between us. Don't tell me you haven't felt it."

"Again with the psychic stuff? Listen, I can't have this conversation with you."

"Right, you're going to simply ignore it like you do everything else."

"I'm sorry, but I honestly think it's the best solution for both of us."

Missy opened her mouth to speak, but Cole rushed out of the chapel before she could utter another word.

Cole reclined in Blake's chair and attempted to fill out the paperwork for the Melendez case. She had hoped that his office would provide her with privacy—away from all the prying eyes and questions regarding what had happened to Thomas. But even with the solitude, Cole couldn't concentrate. Her mind reeled with terrifying memories of Thomas's torture, which unexpectedly intermingled with memories of her father's abuse.

Cole tried to quiet her thoughts, but her attention switched to her kiss with Missy. Cole didn't want to admit it, but she'd lied to Missy about their bond. Initially, it had caught her off guard, but then Cole had welcomed it. She craved her friendship. But Cole was confused about her other feelings for Missy. And until she figured it out, she planned to keep her distance.

The knock on the door interrupted Cole's musings, and she was stunned when she recognized her guest. Cole rose and strolled around the desk. "Oh my God. I can't believe you're here." She gave her sister-in-law an enormous hug.

"I hope it is okay. Detective Ulrich said you were in here hiding."

Cole released her and stepped back. "Of course, it's fine. Come in and have a seat. How are the boys?"

"They're getting so big," Susan said enthusiastically as she sat down.

"I'll have to visit them soon." Cole sat in the chair next to her. "What are you doing here? Does it have anything to do with David's shooting?"

"No. David dropped the charges."

"Well, that's good news. But honestly, I'm surprised. That doesn't sound like my brother."

"It's not. I had to do something for him first. Believe me, he didn't give me much of a choice."

Cole shook her head. "I don't like the way this sounds, Susan."

"It's bad, Dani. But I only have about fifteen minutes to explain everything. If I'm gone too long, David will get suspicious and come looking for me."

"Okay. Tell me what's going on."

Cole practiced extreme self-control as Susan revealed David's involvement with Sanchez and Cavanaugh. She tried not to let her hatred fester, but when she learned it was her own brother who had blown her cover, that hatred spread like cancer.

After Susan finished speaking, Cole sighed heavily. "I'm sorry that David got you mixed up in all this."

"Me too. There's more. David brought home an infant today. He's blackmailing someone and using their baby as a bargaining tool. There's no way I couldn't try to do something as a mother. I can't even imagine the kind of pain that baby's parents must be going through."

Cole recalled the gossip she had heard when she entered the station that morning. Ulrich said that Merck's daughter had disappeared from the hospital. Her name was Faith or Charity or something like that.

"Do you know the baby's name?"

"Yes. It's Miracle."

"Shit," Cole muttered. "That's Merck's kid. Where's the baby now?"

"At the house."

"I need to get a team over there and get her back."

Susan panicked. "But he'll know I told you. He'll hurt me," she said.

"Don't worry, I'll be there to protect you. Just go home and try to act natural. We don't want to alert him that something is amiss. I'll take care of the rest."

"David's shrewd. He'll figure it out."

"I'll keep you safe, Susan. I promise." Cole picked up the phone and made a call. "Merck, this is Cole. I have a line on your daughter. Meet me in Blake's office."

Despite Cole's reassurances, Susan couldn't shake an unsettling feeling. She laid the plastic bags from the drugstore on the table and walked up the stairs. She entered Miracle's room and peered inside the crib. She was relieved to see that the little girl was still there, but that didn't ease her tension.

"Mommy!"

The tiny voice startled Susan. She glanced at the doorway and saw her six-year-old running toward her. She smiled and bent down to embrace him. "Hi, Brady. I thought you were with Grandma. How did you get here?"

"Daddy brought us."

David entered the room with Hayden in his arms. His anger was palpable, which only heightened Susan's angst.

"I thought we agreed to let the boys stay with your mother," she said.

"I changed my mind." He paused. "How's my sister?"

Susan floundered, unsure of how to respond. "I … I don't … know," she stammered. "I haven't seen or talked to her in months."

"Cut the crap, Susan. I know you went to see her. I'm guessing I only have a few minutes before she shows up here with the cavalry."

"What are you going to do?"

"I warned you about what would happen if you betrayed me."

Tears welled up in her eyes. "No, David. Please don't take the boys away from me."

"I didn't do this. You did. You chose Danielle over your own children." He gazed at his son. "Brady, give Mommy another hug." He set Hayden on the floor. "Hayden, go hug Mommy."

Susan squeezed them tightly and kissed them both on the cheek. "David, please," she cried.

"Boys, go play in your room until Daddy comes to get you. Brady, keep an eye on your brother."

After the boys departed, Susan curled into a ball and wailed, "Don't do this, David."

"It's already done." He kicked her hard in the back and smirked as she screamed out in pain. "That's for your disloyalty."

"I promise that I'll do better. Just take me with you," she pleaded.

"It's too late. You've proven that you can't be trusted." He reached into the crib and grabbed the baby. "And please give my sister a message from me. Tell her that I win again."

When Cole arrived ten minutes later, she found Susan in the same position on the floor. She kneeled beside her and squeezed her hand. "Susan, are you okay?"

"No!" she shrieked. "David took my babies, and I'll probably never see them again."

"I'm sorry. This is all my fault. We should have gotten here sooner, but there was an accident on I-84. We had a hard time getting through."

Merck stepped forward. "Excuse me, Mrs. Cole. I hate to bother you at a time like this, but did your husband mention anything about my daughter?" he asked apprehensively.

"Who are you?"

"This is Detective Merck, Susan. He's Miracle's father," Cole said softly.

Susan was ashamed to reveal the truth and lowered her head. "I'm sorry. David plans to sell her on the black market. She's gone."

Missy drifted through the house in a cloud of ambiguity. It had been weeks since she'd been home, and her surroundings seemed surreal. Tears blurred her vision as she stared at the wedding photos of her and Robert on the wall. Missy no longer recognized the blissful woman in those images. Instead, she'd again become the broken vessel illustrated in the thirty-two-inch portrait that Robert had commissioned for her thirtieth birthday.

Leading up to that portrait, Missy had been the happiest she'd ever been in her life. She was expecting, and Robert had planned to immortalize her pregnancy on canvas as a birthday gift. He had hired a local artist to paint her, but at the sitting, Missy had started to cramp severely. She was rushed to the hospital, where misfortune intervened again. Missy lost her second child. The doctor informed her that she had APS—antiphospholipid syndrome, which was a disorder that elevated her levels of antibodies and clotted her arteries. It was what had caused her miscarriages, and Missy discovered later that her mother had suffered from the same disease.

Despite what had happened, Robert had the portrait completed. The grief that emanated from the painting served as a reminder to Missy that she might never have children. Robert had wanted to continue trying, but Missy wouldn't risk it. Her visions had warned that she would die in childbirth, and Missy couldn't bear the thought of her baby being raised without her. So she had begun to take birth control pills behind Robert's back. When he discovered the truth, he hit her. Robert apologized profusely afterward and tried to pacify Missy by showering her with expensive gifts. But Missy never truly forgave him. *Maybe that's why he cheated on me.*

Missy headed to her darkroom and flipped on the light. *This space always comforts me and makes me feel safe*, she thought. She gazed at the twenty cameras lined up on the shelves and smiled. Each one represented a specific period in her marriage. For Missy, seeing the world through a lens had given her a sense of purpose and liberation. In an environment filled with domination by others, her photography was the one thing she could control.

Missy climbed the stepladder and pulled down her Canon S100. She temporarily lost her footing, and it slipped from her hands to the floor. *Please don't let it be damaged*, she thought as she climbed down. When she bent to retrieve the camera, she noticed that a portion of the floorboard was uneven. She tried to press the wood back into its rightful place but then noticed that several other sections were loose. Missy detached the loose pieces and discovered that there were files underneath. *So this is where Robert hid his records.*

Missy pulled out a file and read it. *This is much worse than I thought. I should call Dani and tell her.* She removed the handful of folders and stood. Missy headed for the door and was shocked to see a man hovering in the corner. She let out a high-pitched scream as he rushed toward her and grabbed her.

Marie greeted Merck at the door of their condo. "Please tell me you found her."

"Miracle wasn't there, but I know who took her. We issued an APB, and we're trying to trace his cell."

"You promised that you'd protect her, Jay," Marie cried hopelessly.

"I know." He lightly touched her arm.

"This is your fault. You and your job did this." Marie pulled away from him. "I can't do this anymore, Jay. You said that things would be different here, but clearly, they aren't."

"Please, just give me some time, Marie. I'll find her. After this case, I'll quit. I swear on my mother's grave."

She allowed the tears to flow. "Let's hope that grave doesn't include our daughter too."

Merck extended his arms out to her, and she reluctantly accepted his gesture of comfort. "Don't think like that, Marie," he said, hugging her tightly. "We'll have our baby girl back soon."

Marie nodded but believed deep down that Miracle was lost forever. Despite his assertions, she knew that Merck suspected it too.

"I see you're still hiding out in Blake's office. How is he?" Stevens asked with concern in his voice.

Cole glanced up from her paperwork. "He's getting stronger but still not out of the woods."

"I'm surprised to find you here. I thought you'd be at the hospital."

"I call every hour. I'm sure they're tired of me by now. I just have too much to do with what happened with Adams and fake Thomas to sit idly in a hospital lobby. Plus, there's the matter of my brother kidnapping Merck's baby."

"I still can't believe he's involved. I was shocked when you called to tell me. Have you had any luck finding him?"

"No. We have all our free manpower searching for him and Cavanaugh."

"Are you concerned that Cavanaugh will come after you now that he's escaped?"

"Yes, but I don't have the time to worry about it. I need to finish reading these forensics reports too."

"Well, at least you have the files now. That's a positive."

"True. I'm grateful that you got them to me so quickly. I was just reviewing Robert's autopsy and going through your notes."

Stevens nodded. "I suppose you have questions."

"Definitely. According to the report, there were several sets of prints in the Melendez house. I recognized everyone associated with the prints except a man named Edward Cortez. I looked him up in our database, and he has a full jacket, including murder and armed robbery. I thought I had all the players in this case figured out, but I have no idea where Cortez fits in. I know Thomas hired Adams to kill Melendez, but I'm thinking Thomas has a boss too."

"Edward Cortez?"

"Yes. But who is Edward Cortez? He could have had his face changed too and be anyone at this point. I can't just go around randomly checking people's fingerprints."

"You're right," he chuckled. "Is it possible that Cavanaugh's behind everything? Trevor Moore, Dale Mecham, Samuel Nixon, and Carlos Sanchez were all involved with his organization. It can't be a coincidence that all these criminals who are associated with him are suddenly dying."

"I see your cop instincts are still sharp," Cole said warily. "But how do you know about Nixon?"

"Put your suspicions away. We've been friends too long for that. I know almost as much as you do about this investigation because Blake talks to me. We go out for beers twice a week at Louie's. He asks me forensic questions, and I answer in exchange for details on some of your juicier cases. Robert Melendez has been the topic for weeks."

"I didn't know that."

"Well, you've been a bit preoccupied."

"Yes, with this assignment," Cole said brusquely.

"Uh … what's that tone for? I didn't say anything about what you were preoccupied with."

"There was no tone," she asserted adamantly.

"I know better than to argue with you. But honestly, I think you should consider Cavanaugh. It all points back to him. Edward Cortez is probably just another one of his men."

"If that's true, then Missy may still in danger. Whoever Edward Cortez is, he's out there somewhere. He could be posing as a cop too." Cole picked up the phone and dialed Missy's number, but there was no answer. "I'm going to head to her house. She's not picking up, and I have a bad feeling."

"Good idea. If you have any other questions, I'll be in my office working on faux Thomas and finalizing the paperwork on Adams."

"I guess this case is keeping both of us busy."

He winked at her. "Just the way we both like it."

Cole smiled and grabbed her jacket. "True. I'll walk out with you."

Before Cole could leave the station, a man approached her. "Excuse me, but are you Detective Cole?"

"Depends on who's asking," Cole replied.

"I'm Alan Christie. I was told you were looking for me."

George clasped Missy's arms behind her back and secured her wrists with duct tape.

"You don't have to do this, George," Missy pleaded as she squirmed in the dining room chair.

"I'm not being given a choice, Melissa. This would be much easier if you'd stop moving."

"Sorry, but I'm not going to make killing me easy."

George stooped in front of her and wrapped tape around her ankles. "If you cooperate, then maybe we'll both get out of this alive."

"Who's making you do this, George?"

"I can't tell you that." He stood and pulled a syringe from his jacket pocket. "My instructions are to get the files and administer the contents of this needle."

"What's inside? Poison?" Her voice was panicked.

"I have no idea."

"You have what you came here for. Please let me go."

"Sorry, but it's not my decision."

George inserted the needle into her arm and watched as her eyes closed.

"Have a seat, Mr. Christie. I'm glad you could come in. I've been eager to speak with you."

He sat down in one of the empty chairs in Blake's office. "My secretary told me that you'd called several times. What is this about?"

"Robert Melendez."

"Who?"

"You may know him as Robert Costa."

Alan was taken aback. "What about him?"

"I can see from your expression that you know exactly who he is. What can you tell me about him?"

"Robert was one of my foster children. He was an intelligent kid. He did his work, obtained good grades, and was respectful most of the time. It was his brother who was the problem."

"Wait, Robert had a brother?"

"Yes, EJ. He was two years younger than Robert and a real troublemaker. He lied, stole from my wife and me, and had a problem with truancy. We overlooked a lot of it because we thought Robert had a bright future, and we didn't want to split the brothers up."

"Did his brother leave you at the same time Robert did?"

"Leave? No, Detective Cole. They both got kicked out."

"Why?" Cole asked curiously. "What happened?"

"My wife Tracy came home early from work one day because she wasn't feeling well. She was three months pregnant and was having horrible morning sickness. There was a small group of teenage boys in the house watching television and smoking pot, when they should have been at school. Tracy told EJ's friends to go home, and once they left, he got very angry. EJ shoved Tracy, and she fell and hit her head against the table. Instead of helping her, that bastard ran away. Luckily, Tracy and the baby were okay. We sent the police after EJ, but we refused to allow him back into our home. We gave Robert the option to stay but warned him that he couldn't have contact with his brother, at least not on our property. Robert remained with us, but it wasn't long before he broke the agreement. EJ would come to the house while we were all asleep and spend the night in Robert's room. Robert would sneak him food and even started stealing money from us. Once we discovered the truth, we asked Robert to leave as well."

"Did you keep in contact with Robert?"

"No. Occasionally, I would hear rumors about both brothers, but I never saw either one of them again. I was told that EJ went to prison, which didn't surprise me. Robert became some kind of doctor."

"What does EJ look like? I would like to find him, if possible."

"It's been years, so I have no idea what he looks like now. But people used to comment all the time on how much he and Robert looked alike. They could have been twins."

A seed was planted in Cole's mind, and it began to take root and grow. "What was EJ's full name, Mr. Christie?"

"Edward Costa Cortez Jr."

Missy was groggy when she finally opened her eyes. She gazed around the dining room and saw George lying on the floor in a pool of blood. She wanted to scream but couldn't muster the energy.

"That was a short nap," a man behind her declared.

"Why did you murder George?" she mumbled.

"He was supposed to kill you. But since he disobeyed my orders, he died first. He'll be the one to take the rap for all of this when I vanish."

The voice was familiar, but Missy was too light-headed to focus on the person's identity. "So you were going to kill him anyway."

"Of course," the man said arrogantly.

"What did George give me?"

"Just a mild sedative."

"Who are you? Why won't you let me see your face?"

"You mean you don't recognize me?" He walked around the chair and stood in front of her.

Missy glanced up at him and was flabbergasted. She was grateful to be tied down because it kept her from falling out of the chair.

"Hello, Melissa. Did you miss me?"

"Robert," she whispered.

Cole made an urgent call on her way to Missy's house. "Stevens, it's Cole. When you performed Robert's autopsy, were there any signs that he'd had plastic surgery done?" Her voice was thick with tension.

"Didn't you read my notes? Melendez had rhinoplasty, chin and cheek augmentation, and lip enhancement. Nothing unusual given his profession."

"Actually, it might be the most important piece in this case."

"Why do I get the feeling that you're not going to explain?"

"I can't. There isn't enough time. I'll explain later."

"Cole, with your back injury, you shouldn't be driving."

"I know, but it's an emergency."

"Please be careful."

"I always am." She disconnected the call.

"You can't be Robert. He's dead," Missy whispered. "I saw the body myself."

"That was my younger brother, Edward. He's the person you were sleeping with before my untimely death."

"What the hell are you talking about? What brother?"

"I needed a decoy, someone who could die in my place and wouldn't be missed. Edward was perfect."

"I don't understand."

Robert grabbed another dining room chair and positioned it across from Missy. "Okay. Then I'll start from the beginning." He sat down. "A few months before I was supposedly killed, one of my patients informed me that a professional hit had been put on my life. I formulated a plan to disappear, but fortunately for me, fate devised a better scheme. My brother Edward called me to beg for money. I hadn't talked to him in years, not since his last prison stint, but I decided to meet him. Sitting across from Edward at the table, I realized how much he resembled me, and a plot began to form. I offered Edward $10,000 to become me for a few months. He was in dire need of cash, so he readily agreed."

"I performed the necessary surgery to make Edward my twin and spent weeks training him. He became an expert on you, this house, and my practice. I promised him that once everything was over, I'd give him back his original face."

"I guess you forgot to mention to Edward that he would die."

Robert chuckled. "He knew there were risks involved. I had every detail worked out to the letter. Once you were pronounced dead, I would conveniently show up as Robert's long-lost brother, Edward, his sole living relative. That meant I would get all his money—well, technically, my money back—including the millions from the insurance policies. I included Edward on all the policies as a beneficiary."

"It's all starting to make sense now—why he wouldn't touch me or let me touch him, his silence and refusal to perform surgery, his mood swings and underlying anger, the change in his eating habits. I can't believe I didn't see it."

"If you had seen it, then my duplicity wouldn't have worked."

"I can't believe how simple it was for you to sacrifice me. I loved you and thought you loved me."

"I do love you, Melissa. But I couldn't ruin my plan. It was either my life or yours."

"That's not love. What I felt for you was real. I would have given up everything for you."

"Sadly, Melissa, you're about to do just that." He leaned in and kissed her on the forehead. "I have to admit, it was difficult thinking about my brother being here with you. He wanted you, and he had a difficult time saying no to such a beautiful woman. But there was no way in hell I was going to let him have sex with my wife. I would have killed him with my bare hands first. I understood that he had needs, though, so I gave him Connie instead."

"Am I supposed to be flattered that you allowed your brother to sleep with your mistress but not your wife? Because I'm not." Her tone was scathing.

"I see you've changed, Melissa. I imagine that's from spending so much time with the cop. Ted must be proud," he said caustically.

"Don't talk about my father."

"Why not? His hands are just as dirty as mine. He was the one who got the criminal charges dropped against my clients. And he assisted me in getting them new identities."

"He already told me his role in all of this." *That's not true*, she thought, *but Robert doesn't need to know that.*

"You forgave him, but you won't forgive me."

"You're kidding, right? My father didn't try to have me killed, Robert."

"True. I guess I'm wasting my time with you then," he stated coolly.

"Yes, you are. I'm not going to relieve your guilty conscience. You can go straight to hell!"

"I was there for the last two years, living with you, Melissa. After you lost the baby, you changed. The woman I knew and loved was gone. I had no idea how to get her back."

Robert's sincerity touched something deep within Missy, and a single tear trickled down her cheek. "You're right. I was devastated and shut you out. I simply had no idea where to put all that pain."

"You should have let me help, but—" Robert's phone buzzed, interrupting him. He glanced at his text message and abruptly switched gears. "I need to leave, Melissa. My patient just woke up, and I need to check on him. I believe you know Roy Cavanaugh—although once the bandages come off, he'll be a different person."

"You changed his face too?"

"Yes. He wanted the best, and that's me. I suspect that Detective Cole told you all about Cavanaugh since they have such an intriguing history together."

"I know who he is, Robert, but I don't get how he's connected to all of this."

Robert grabbed the syringe from the table. "Well, I would love to explain that to you also, but I don't have the time. I'm sure the police will be here soon."

"Why don't you just shoot me like you did George?"

"Because that would be too risky. I can't afford to have a forensics team discover that this was staged. I need them to think that George injected you with poison, then took his own life. I even had him write a suicide note confessing to everything to make it more believable."

"Sounds like you thought of everything," Missy replied miserably.

Robert moved behind Missy. "I did. Don't worry, the potassium chloride will kill you quickly. You won't suffer … much." He stooped down and positioned the tip of the needle in her arm. Missy felt the slight pinch and silently prayed for intervention.

"Freeze, Melendez!"

Robert straightened and glanced at Cole. "I don't believe we've had the pleasure, Detective."

"This is not my idea of pleasure, Mr. Melendez. Now drop the needle and put your hands where I can see them."

Missy spied someone sneaking up behind Cole and yelled, "Dani, watch out!"

Before Cole could react, David had his gun in the small of her back. "Lay your gun on the floor and kick it to the right," he instructed.

Cole did as she was told and then spun around to face the aggressor. "What the hell are you doing here, David?"

David aimed his weapon at Cole. "Hey, sis. Nothing much. Just keeping an eye on Melendez. Can't let anything happen to Cavanaugh's new friend."

"What? Cavanaugh really is involved in all of this?" Her tone was incredulous.

"Yup. I would have thought you'd have that figured out by now, Super Cop," David said mockingly.

"We don't have time for a family reunion, David," Robert interjected. "I'm sure there are more police on the way, so we need to get out of here."

"You're right. Give Missy the poison, and I'll take care of my sister."

David reached for Cole, and she kneed him in the groin. While he was hunched over in pain, Cole grabbed his gun. She thrust David in front of her and pointed the weapon at both him and Robert.

"Nice display of heroics, Detective Cole, but do you really think you can save Melissa?" Robert punctured Missy's shoulder with the syringe, and she shrieked in pain. "All I have to do is press the top of this needle, and she'll be dead within minutes."

Cole suddenly spotted a police officer coming up behind Robert from the other side of the dining room. "Drop it, Melendez!" he demanded as he inched closer to Robert from the rear.

"Do as Officer Curtis says, Melendez. It's two against one, and we'll put ten bullets in you before you have the chance to administer that poison."

Robert wavered but after a few seconds extracted the needle. He let it fall to the floor and put his hands in the air. Curtis rushed toward Melendez and picked up the syringe.

Cole sighed in relief. "Thank God you came when you did, Curtis. How did you know I was here?"

"I didn't. Lieutenant Blake asked me and two other officers to keep an eye on the Melendez residence during our patrols. Several of the neighbors called and complained about strange cars circling the block and watching the house. I saw the lights on, which I thought was suspicious, so I came to check it out."

"Well thank God you arrived when you did."

"I'm glad I could be of help, Detective Cole. Now why don't I take David to the station and book him, while you get things wrapped up here," Curtis offered.

Cole kept her gun trained on Melendez. "That's fine, but I need you to radio this in."

"No problem."

As they talked, Missy sensed Robert's nervous energy and realized that he still had the gun he had used to shoot George. Missy tried to get Cole's attention to warn her, but she was too busy facilitating David's arrest.

Missy closed her eyes and tried to send Cole a telepathic message. *Dani, Robert has a gun. You have to be careful.*

Once Robert was certain that the officer and David were gone, he reached for the weapon in his jacket and directed it at Cole. He was about to pull the trigger when Cole shot him. Robert crumpled to the floor, and Cole hurried over and checked his pulse. He was still alive, so she cuffed him and read him his rights.

"Are you okay?" Cole asked as she cut the tape from Missy's wrists and ankles.

Missy threw herself into Cole's arms, which took them both by surprise. "Thank you so much, Dani."

Cole awkwardly stepped back. "You're welcome. Excuse me while I make a call. I need to get an ambulance over here for Melendez."

When Cole was done with the call, Missy once again thanked her. "I owe you my life," she said.

"No need to keep thanking me. I'm just glad that you told me about Robert's gun, or this situation could have gone very differently."

"You heard me? I wasn't sure if it would work."

"Of course, I heard you. I'm sure Robert did too." She glanced at the man who was now unconscious on the floor.

Missy was visibly confused. "He didn't. I never said the words out loud. I said them in my mind."

Cole shook her head. "That's impossible. I heard everything you said clearly."

"Yes, you did. But that's because we're connected and—"

Cole cut her off. "Just stop it, Missy. I've already told you how I feel about this."

"Fine. Deny it all you want. But when Blake wakes up, he'll verify my abilities. Then you'll have no choice but to believe me."

Cole promptly changed the subject. "Did your husband happen to mention where he hid his files? I assume he wasn't just here to kill you. They must be somewhere in the house."

"Yes, they were under the floorboards in my darkroom."

"Literally right under your nose," Cole said gingerly. "Robert probably assumed the patrols had stopped now that you're back home and felt it was safe to retrieve them. Good thing you have such nosy neighbors, or he would have taken them already and been long gone."

"So you think Robert had someone watching the house?"

"Yes, him and whoever else was trying to get their hands on those files. Are they still under the floorboard?"

"I don't know. They should be there, unless he gave them to your brother."

"Well, if he did, then the files are perhaps in David's car. I'll check it later."

Suddenly, there was a loud thump at the front door. Cole immediately pulled out her gun and forced Missy behind her. A bloody Curtis burst into the house and exclaimed, "Someone hit me over the head and helped David escape."

Missy set the flowers on the table and then moved over to Blake's hospital bed. He was asleep, so Missy studied his face to try to gauge why she no longer trusted him. She reached out to touch his hand in hopes that it would trigger a vision, but she was interrupted by Cole's sudden appearance.

"Looks like Blake is pretty popular," Cole whispered as she placed her vase of flowers beside Missy's. "How did you get in here, Missy? Only family is allowed."

"I told the cop at the door that I was his sister."

"And he let you in without checking?"

"Yes. But it's not his fault, Dani. I can be rather charming," she said teasingly.

"Don't I know it," Cole muttered under her breath.

The tension in the room became palpable as they gazed at each other. Spirits intermingled until silent words became audible and doubts transformed into certainties. Both wanted what their hearts so eloquently communicated, but neither was willing to sacrifice her normalcy.

Cole was first to break the spell. "So … uh … did you sleep okay last night at Blake's?"

"Not really, but thank you for letting me stay there. I don't think I can ever go back to my house again. Too many bad memories."

"Well, I'm sure Blake is fine with you staying there as long as you need to. He'll be in here for a while, recuperating."

"I'm going to check out apartments later this week. I should be out in a few days, hopefully."

"If you need help with anything, let me know."

"Any news on Cavanaugh or David?"

"No. It's like they just disappeared. Merck is searching frantically for his baby. I feel horrible that my brother is responsible for his daughter's disappearance along with my nephews. I won't be able to rest until I find all the children."

"If anyone can find that little girl, you can. Don't blame yourself. You're not your brother's keeper."

"I know, but that doesn't alleviate my guilt."

Missy glanced at Blake. "Has he spoken yet?"

"No. The doctor said he's stable, but he's still in and out of consciousness."

"I'm sure he'll be fully awake soon. He's …"

Sounds from the bed caught their attention, and they hurried to Blake's side.

"Blake, it's Tinks."

Blake's eyes slowly opened. "Tinks," he mumbled.

She clasped his hand. "Yes, I'm here."

"What happened?"

"You were shot."

His voice was weak. "I vaguely recall Thomas shooting me. But did someone kill him, or was that my imagination?"

"Yes. But the shooter was outside, so I didn't see him or her."

"I think I may know," he muttered.

"Who?"

"Merck."

Cole was taken aback. "Seriously? I need to speak with him then."

"Just leave it alone for now, Tinks." He turned his head toward Missy. "Thank you."

"For what?" Missy asked.

"You saved Cole's life. If you hadn't been so urgent about finding her, or you hadn't given me the details about the cab she took to Thomas's house, I never would have gotten to her in time. All the clues fell into place right after I talked to you. It was like you were leading me to Thomas."

"We both know that's impossible, Blake," Cole said guardedly.

He looked at Cole. "I'm not a superstitious man, but I'm telling you it was her."

"She won't believe you, Blake," Missy said. "I've already tried."

"Enough of this paranormal idiocy. What about Merck?"

"The Merck situation is a long story, Tinks. We'll discuss it over dinner. You do recall the promise you made me, right?"

"Yes, and I do intend to honor my promise. I must admit, I'm curious as to why you want me to hold off on questioning him."

"He's a complicated guy with a complicated history."

"Hell, that only makes me more curious." She warily glanced at Missy but continued to speak. "So I found out that David is working with Cavanaugh."

Blake was noticeably agitated by her words. His heartbeat accelerated, and his monitor started to beep wildly. After her unsuccessful attempts to mollify Blake, Cole rushed out of the room in search of a doctor.

Missy walked over to the bed. She clasped Blake's hand and spoke calmly to him. "I know you're concerned that David is going to tell Dani that you knew about his involvement in the Cavanaugh case the entire time. And if David tells, you'll lose Dani. Don't worry—you're safe for now. If that changes, I'll let you know. Take a few deep breaths, and please relax."

Blake slowly began to breathe normally again. "How did … how do you? I don't understand."

"All I ask is that you make Dani happy. As long as you do, I won't tell her."

Cole hurried back into the room, followed by a doctor. Both women stepped aside while the doctor checked Blake's vitals. He advised Blake to take it easy and said he'd return in thirty minutes.

"God, I was so worried about you, Blake. Don't ever scare me like that again," Cole said anxiously.

Blake smiled. "I won't. Does this mean you're willing to give me—us—a chance?"

Cole furtively glanced at Missy. The dejection Cole perceived in her eyes tore her apart. She realized that if Missy untangled the mysteries of Cole's heart, she'd find the same emotions. The thought terrified Cole. She couldn't allow her feelings for a woman to flourish and become recognizable, to Missy or to the rest of the world. Cole didn't want to invite any more confusion into her life. And she believed that any type of intimacy with Missy would cause discord and give the gossips at work another reason to ridicule her. Therefore, Dani decided to put distance between herself and Missy by fully embracing her relationship with Blake. He was uncomplicated and familiar, and Cole believed he could help her eradicate her monsters.

Unbeknownst to Cole, her seamless connection to Missy had already comforted her in some of her darkest hours and prevented her scariest demons from emerging from the shadows. Their bond was innate and beautiful, alive with the wonders of passion and amity. Cole knew this would be difficult to ignore, but she was determined to try. She was just sorry that it would hurt Missy. *And it will hurt me too, if I'm honest*, she realized. *But I need to somehow forget the yearnings of my heart.*

"Yes," she said, looking back at Blake. "I would like to try."

"You just gave me the best medicine that any man could ask for," Blake declared.

Missy observed the exchange and realized that it was time to go. She felt like an intruder, an outsider. She quietly exited the room as misery devoured her insides, leaving her shattered and hollow. She sat in one of the lobby chairs and gave in to her broken spirit. The dam burst, and relentless tears poured down her face.

"Are you okay, lady?"

Missy glanced up and was surprised to see a man wrapped in bandages like a mummy. She couldn't help but gawk at him. "Yes, I'm fine," she uttered.

"Sorry. I didn't mean to startle you. I was in a car accident, and my face was badly burned."

"No, I'm the one who's sorry. I didn't mean to stare."

"It's been a dreadful ordeal, but I'm grateful for my family and friends who've supported me despite what I look like." He took the seat beside her. "You can talk to me if you want. Sometimes strangers make the best listeners."

"You shouldn't worry about me. I should be the one asking about you."

"There's nothing I can do about my situation. But once these bandages come off, I'll be a brand-new person. I'm excited about the possibilities."

"Your bravery is admirable."

"Thank you. Now tell me about you."

"There's not much to tell. But it's funny where life takes you sometimes. You think you know everything and have your life planned. Then you're thrown a couple of curveballs, and your whole outlook changes."

"I have no idea what you're talking about," the man said, his tone bemused.

She laughed. "I'm sorry. I know I'm talking in riddles. It's just ... well ... I recently accepted that I have feelings for someone, but I can never be with that person."

The man's gaze drifted to Blake's room. "I know how you feel. There's nothing more important than love and being with the person you care about above all else. Maybe one day, we'll both get what we want."

"This person *is* in love, just not with me," Missy declared glumly.

Cavanaugh watched Missy grapple with her emotions and wondered if what he suspected was true. If so, he knew exactly how he'd use this situation to win back Cole. Missy's feelings for the other woman would make her the perfect pawn in his cat-and-mouse game.

"I'm sorry that your love is unrequited. You never know what fate has in store for you. Please never give up, miss." He nodded at her and then walked away.

Missy's eyes glistened with tears. She shook her head in denial, but she needed to admit the truth to herself. She was hopelessly, undeniably in love with Danielle Cole.

Cavanaugh climbed into the car and fastened his seat belt.

"Did you see her?" David asked.

"No. She was in the room with Blake. But I did find out some other useful information."

David shook his head. "I'll never understand your fascination with my sister."

"It's not for you to understand. Now that you've replaced Sanchez, I have a job I want taken care of immediately."

"What's the job? Maybe we can have the new guy take care of it. Sort of like an initiation." He turned to the person in the back seat. "How about it, Ulrich?"

Ulrich nodded. "Sure. It'll be my pleasure. What do you need done?"

"I want you to kidnap Melissa Melendez and kill Joshua Blake."

"I can do that. But we need to be careful because Missy has psychic powers. I was secretly listening to her and Blake while they were in the interrogation room. I heard Missy tell him exactly what was going on with Moore and Cole, and she wasn't even there. She knew what the rooms looked like and the number of the cab Cole used to get to the house. Spooky stuff."

"Well, I guess that means you need to be extra careful then, Ulrich," David said flippantly. "You wouldn't want your wife to use her abilities to discover that you're her long-lost husband, Shawn."

ABOUT THE AUTHOR

I LISTEN TO THE VOICES IN MY HEAD. Those vibrant personalities that struggle to permeate empty spaces. They're nameless, yet familiar faces, that constantly speak to me and beg to be liberated. Until I acknowledge them, there is no inner peace as they endeavor to unearth the impetus that inspires me to create. Once they've succeeded, those impulses are ignited, and I have no choice but to tell their stories of suspense, romance, mystery, and heartache. These characters are my family. They are a part of me. And they are the reason I write.

Welcome inside the mind of Robin Michele Carroll, a writer who currently resides in Englewood, Colorado. Robin began writing short stories at the age of nine, but her artistic journey didn't truly begin until eleven. That's when she created her own soap opera in junior high and became known as the little girl with the big imagination. Her formation of "The Search for Love" made her popular amongst her peers as the pages of Robin's drama circulated throughout the halls of the middle school she attended. Eventually, the teachers learned about the content, and Robin was called to the principal's office with her mother. She was told that the subject matter was too mature, and that she was no longer allowed to share it with her classmates. However, the school didn't want to squelch her talent, so they placed her in an English class with a teacher who helped Robin hone her skills. There, the seeds were planted, and Robin realized that she was born to be a storyteller.

Made in the USA
Middletown, DE
05 February 2024